Praise for

JUNIPER & THORN

"Utterly astonishing. This masterful, complex retelling conjures the pure horror of powerlessness as modernity crashes into tradition, and bodies are transformed and consumed. *Juniper & Thorn* is the dark fairy tale brought to perfection: terrible, and true, and full of teeth."

—**Shelley Parker-Chan, bestselling author of**
She Who Became the Sun

"In this baroque Grimm retelling, Reid proves again that theirs is a powerful and essential voice. Through Marlinchen—a layered and unforgettable heroine, brought to life with immense compassion—she tells a tale of fear and survival, hope and yearning and defiance, in timelessly elegant prose. It will enchant you, break your heart, and chill you to the very marrow."

—**Samantha Shannon, bestselling author of**
The Priory of the Orange Tree

"This is a dark and bloody tale, full of magic both otherworldly and familiar, and despite its monsters, it reads like comfort. After you read it, you'll start saving space on your shelf for Ava Reid." —**Kendare Blake, #1** *New York Times* **bestselling author of** *Three Dark Crowns*

"This riveting, atmospheric dark fantasy unflinchingly explores the disturbing roots of classic fairy tales." —**BuzzFeed**

"Haunting and great." —*Paste* magazine

"*Juniper & Thorn* is one of my favorite books of the year and I know I'm not alone in that sentiment. Reader after reader has found something in this book that rings true to their heart, resonates with their experience."

—Tor.com

"A gothic masterpiece. Reid weaves threads of unsettling horror and abuse with astonishing empathy." —**Kat Dunn, author of** *Dangerous Remedy*

"I was thoroughly enchanted by *Juniper & Thorn*, because it felt like the kind of timeless classic that gets at the core issues of being human in a way that seems fantastical, but upon introspection is all too real."

—*Lightspeed* magazine

"*Juniper & Thorn* is a Gothic wonder of a novel."

—*The Magazine of Fantasy & Science Fiction*

"Reid expertly weaves a dark and delightful tale that packs a sting. Love, betrayal, and a heroine for our time. I absolutely loved this novel."

—**T. L. Huchu, author of *The Library of the Dead***

"Ava Reid's spellbinding prose will draw you deep into this dark fantasy about three gifted sisters who are trapped by the magic of their wizard father. Thrumming with feminist power, and riveting in its worldbuilding, *Juniper & Thorn* is an unforgettable tale."

—**Ausma Zehanat Khan, author of *The Bladebone***

"It's haunting and sad, but it makes its way towards hopefulness and love. Ava Reid has a talent for telling these woeful tales in a way that encourages you to look beneath the horror to pull out the messages within."

—**FanFiAddict**

JUNIPER & THORN

ALSO BY AVA REID

The Wolf and the Woodsman

JUNIPER & THORN

A NOVEL

AVA REID

HARPER Voyager
An Imprint of HarperCollins*Publishers*

A hardcover edition of this book was published in 2022 by Harper Voyager, an imprint of HarperCollins Publishers.

FIRST HARPER VOYAGER PAPERBACK EDITION PUBLISHED 2023.

Designed by Paula Russell Szafranski
Interior art © GB_Art/Shutterstock.com
Map design by Nick Springer / Springer Cartographics LLC

Library of Congress Cataloging-in-Publication Data has been applied for.

ISBN 978-0-06-297317-7

23 24 25 26 27 LBC 6 5 4 3 2

For Dorit

Yes, I live. I can cross the streets asking, "What year is it?"
I can dance in my sleep and laugh
in front of the mirror.

—"AUTHOR'S PRAYER," ILYA KAMINSKY

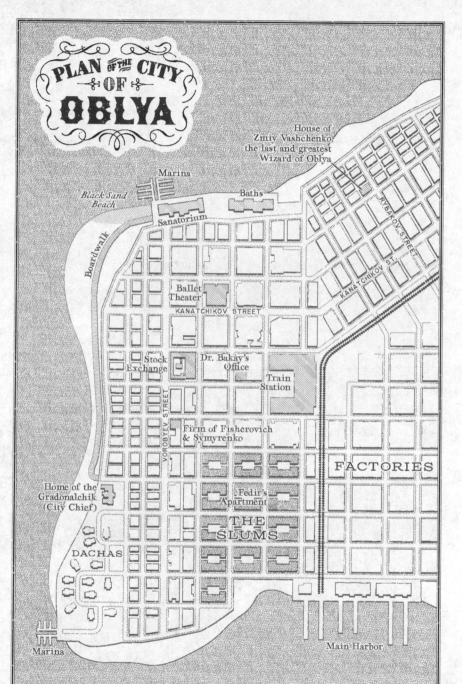

PLAN OF THE CITY OF OBLYA

House of Zmiy Vashchenko, the last and greatest Wizard of Oblya

Marina

Black Sand Beach

Baths

Sanatorium

Boardwalk

RYBAKOV STREET

KANATCHIKOV ST.

Ballet Theater

KANATCHIKOV STREET

Stock Exchange

Dr. Bakay's Office

Train Station

VOROBYEV STREET

Firm of Fisherovich & Symyrenko

FACTORIES

Home of the Gradonalchik (City Chief)

Fedir's Apartment

THE SLUMS

DACHAS

Marina

Main Harbor

Map Copyright SPRINGER CARTOGRAPHICS. New Jersey, USA. MMXXII

CHAPTER ONE

I checked under my bed, but the monster was gone. It had been gone since morning, when the pink fingers of dawn flushed it back to its favorite hiding place in Rose's garden, spiny tail banded around the trunk of the juniper tree. It would lie there, belly-flat and hissing, until I or one of my sisters went to feed it our leftover chicken bones or give it a rub behind the ears. Of all the creatures that lived in our house, it was the most easily sated.

By evening, the garden was lucent with the speckle of fireflies, rustling with the susurration of wind through the willow branches, but otherwise quiet and still. From my bedroom I could see the whole brindled sweep of it, the stout, swollen hedges and the ivy that trawled over the rust-checkered gate. If anyone in Oblya walked down the road past our house, they might feel green tendrils curl around their ankles, or hear the whisper of ferns through the fence. The pedestrians whispered back: rumors about Zmiy Vashchenko and his three strange daughters.

When I was younger, their mean words made me cry. At twenty-three, I learned to close my ears to them, or even to relish them with a resigned, perverse bitterness, closing my fist around the old hurt. After all, the meaner their words, the better their business. The rumors deposited clients at our doorstep like a cat leaving its mangled prey at the feet of its master. The more jagged and gruesome the rumor's shape, the more our clients gawked at my sisters, as if their beauty were a velvet carpet laid over a hole in the floor, something that might fall out from under them.

My sisters were beautiful without ruse or artifice, which was my curse, really, not my father's. My father's curse was never to be satisfied with anything, so to him my sisters were beautiful, but not beautiful enough. He had been cursed by Titka Whiskers, the last true witch in Oblya. My father had done all he could to run her out of business, to make himself the last true wizard in the city, so she'd repaid him the only way a witch knew how. Of course, then he *was* the last true wizard in the city, and he wasn't satisfied with that either.

The clock gonged nine. I had heaped old throw pillows and a sack of scrolled autumn leaves under my quilt, molding them to a shape that approximated my sleeping body. Rose had cut a sheaf of dried wheat stalks for my hair, the color slightly too pale, and with none of my real hair's untended frizz. But if, *when*, our father rose from his bed and stumbled half-dreaming past my room, I hoped he would not look closely enough to know the difference. The curse, too, meant he could sleep for hours and hours and still wake with the faint itch of exhaustion under his skin.

Outside, the sky darkened in increments, like an obsidian blade lowering over Oblya's pale throat. The sound of footsteps, quick and light, on the wooden threshold. I turned around. My sister, Undine, stood in the doorway.

"Dear Marlinchen, no one will believe we're anything but witches if you don't put a comb through your hair."

A flush crawled over my cheeks. I left my bed and sat down at my boudoir, scrutinizing my face in the mirror. My sallow cheeks now bore two splotches of red. My hair was a mess of coils that fell as heavy as a quilt over my shoulders.

"I don't know what to do," I said. "It's too long."

All of our hair was too long, and far too long for the current fashion, those slim curls like rolled tobacco that the other women in Oblya sported. Our father would not let us cut even an inch. The clients, he said, liked that there was something charmingly rustic about us, our untrimmed hair the relic of an older, simpler time. To them we might be sweet singing milkmaids, torn right out of some wealthy man's pale pastoral wallpaper. I did not have a dulcet singing voice, but I smiled at our clients as sweetly as I could.

"Rose," Undine called softly. "Come here and help. Quickly."

My second sister swept through the threshold in a crinoline gown, her bared shoulders as sharp as kitchen knives. She took in my hair, and Undine's angrily flared nostrils, and sighed. Our mother's ivory-handled comb lay on our bureau, a bit of my dark-blond hair snarled in its teeth.

But Rose, being the second sister, was gentler. She began to work through my curls with the comb. The last time anyone had done so was my mother, and that was years ago.

Rose managed to tie up my hair with a ribbon, in some butchered emulation of the Oblyan women's hair. The pink silk ribbon matched my dress, a crinkled cranberry with a neckline low enough to make me blush. Not that it mattered very much. Pinned between my beautiful sisters, I was little more than a piece of furniture, a particularly elaborate candle stand.

The clock gonged ten, and then we were off.

Through the garden, the damp soil sucking at our shoes. Arm in arm, we picked our way past the scrying pool, as bright as a tossed coin, through the thistles with their purple buds, careful to bypass Rose's delicate meshwork of baby's breath and feverfew. The flowering pear tree coughed white petals at us, but all the monsters were cowed or slumbering.

Still, we were quiet. We could not risk waking them, or worse, waking our father. We had risked tiny rebellions before—or at least, Rose and Undine had—but never something so large and illicit and wrong. This rebellion was like a book with all its pages torn out. I did not know its beginning, middle, or end.

The thought of Papa seeing us made me woozy with dread, and our very own garden began to feel terrible and strange.

To outsiders, it was always terrible and strange, even in the daylight; they were not accustomed to it the way we were. There were the glass apples, which tasted sweet and made you wine-flushed if you could bear to put those hard, sharp bits in your mouth. There were the black amber plums, fat as bruises, which were suffused with a fatal poison. Our father had nurtured an immunity in his daughters by feeding us slivers of the fruit from the time we were infants, and now we could bite into the plums and taste only the tang of their rotted bitterness, not the poison underneath.

But even we were warned never to touch the juniper tree, which bore berries of the most dangerous variety: both poisonous and sweet. Whatever sick thing was in them, we could not be inured to it.

In my twenty-three years, I had seen the garden come to be occupied by a number of other things, and I had come to consider these things *ours*. Our fiery serpent, which looked like a regular snake until it caught the sunlight, and then its black scales glimmered with a flame-bright sheen. It spoke in a human voice, without moving its mouth; the voice seemed to enter your head as if you were the one conjuring its words. It would promise you silken handkerchiefs or ceramic beads, and if you accepted, its gifts would materialize in your hand, spun out of nothing—for a price: the milk from your breast. But even if you paid, in the morning all the gifts would turn to straw and manure. I didn't know what would happen if you asked it for something more than trinkets, or why it would be so terrible to give suck to a serpent. I watched it wind through our garden now like a slick of oil, leaving pale coils of shed skin in its wake.

There was also our goblin, the poor thing, who had lost its home when the Rodinyan land surveyors drained the marshes outside of Oblya. Its single eye shone like a lantern in the dark, its beard as long and white as lichen grown over a log. In its gratitude for our hospitality the goblin had become excessively protective of my sisters and me, and had taken to trying to bite our clients in the ankle when they crossed through the garden into the house. After the goblin cost us a hundred rubles and nearly brought the city's Grand Inspector to our door, my father made sure it was always shut up in the garden shed whenever we had visitors. Last time when I'd gone to let it out, it had already chewed a hole through the wood and was sulking in Rose's bed of tarragon.

We had patched the hole painstakingly, each taking turns keeping an eye out for Papa, and then shut the goblin in again. Undine had wanted to gag it, to make sure its tears didn't wake him, but such a thing felt unspeakably cruel and I managed to convince her out of it. As we passed the shed I heard its cowed whimpering.

My least favorite of all our creatures was Indrik, a bare-chested man with the legs of a faun or a goat. He was forever bemoaning his fate as a refugee, as he had fled the mountain where he'd lived when Rodinyan miners had begun to plumb it for silver. He languished by Undine's scrying pool, mournfully examining his reflection, claiming he'd once been a god and everyone in Oblya had worshipped him. They'd left him offerings of slain geese or painted eggs and their prettiest, bleating ewes—I shuddered to think what he had done with those ewes, given the lustful way he'd eyed our milking cow before she'd died. I didn't know if he'd ever been a god at all, but it was no use trying to argue with him; he would only weep.

To make sure Indrik did not catch us as we left, Rose had fed him a sleeping draught. I saw the blurry shape of him beneath one of the pear trees, the coiled muscles of his back as huge as boulders. His snoring was a soft whistle, like the train that I could sometimes hear very distantly from my bedroom window.

There were other creatures that I could not name, ones that I could only refer to as monsters. Badger-looking things that snuffled the earth for roots and truffles; spiny-tailed weasels with beady red stares, such as the one that liked to hide under my bed; eyeless ravens that winged blindly through our rhododendrons. They ate the rabbits and squirrels that came to masticate Rose's herbs, so we let them stay, and besides, we didn't know what would happen if we chased them out. There were no stories about these types of monsters, or maybe the stories had been lost. Either way, my sisters and I were all afraid we might wake up cursed just like our father if we did them any harm.

But all precautions had been taken, and none of those creatures were roused tonight. When we reached the gate, Undine swung it open, and we brushed all the dirt from our shoes and the hems of our gowns. Like we were serpents shedding our skin, we swept the mustiness and sorcery of the house off of us.

While I stared down the cobblestone road that unspooled before us, my stomach knotted with fear.

"Come on, Marlinchen," Undine said, looping our elbows and giving me a vicious tug. "We only have a quarter hour."

We sprinted down the street, as quick as our crinolines and corsets would allow. I could feel the cobblestones through the soles of my slippers, all of their hard ridges that seemed to lurch up at me with every step. We passed the day laborers, dull-eyed men slouching toward the brothels and taverns, or back to their apartments above the shops. Whenever their gazes spun toward us, I felt another thread of panic loose in me, but Rose and Undine only pulled me along.

Kanatchikov Street bore us into the city plaza, a glorious facade of buildings that ringed the massive fountain. Dolphins leapt from the stone basin in arrested motion, water shooting from their spouts. A marble sea god sat in his chariot, thick brows drawn over his eyes, frozen and immortal. He was not a god that I recognized from my father's codex; he had vague and hurried features, as if the man who had carved him was trying to remember something that he had seen only once, many years ago.

Oblyans were gathering in the square, women in their puff-sleeved gowns and men in their top hats, all herding toward the ballet theater like sheep trussed in satin and lace. Their mingling voices had the low tenor of rolling thunder. Pipe smoke rose in greasy clouds. All the smells and sounds pressed in on me, and a gasp came out of my throat.

My sisters had made such trysts before, but I'd never had the courage to join them. Tonight I had been yoked into their rebellion like an ox, intoxicated by the promise of something newer and brighter and better than any of us had ever seen. But now that I was here, everything was too new, too much.

"I don't want to go," I whispered, leaning closer to Rose than to Undine. "I think I've changed my mind."

"Well, it's too late now, isn't it?" Rose gestured vaguely toward the theater, but her voice was not unkind. "There's no one to walk back with you. You'll have to stay." She must have read the horror on my face, so she went on more gently, "Listen, it will be all right. Once we're in our seats—"

"Oh, she's being a baby, as usual," Undine snapped. "She doesn't want to come, but she doesn't want to be left behind."

I bit my lip on a reply; Undine was right. The last time they'd left at night without me, I'd gone paralytic with fear. Although my body had been at home in bed, my mind raced down a thousand dark alleys, wondering what awful fate my sisters were meeting, or worse, wondering what my father would do if he woke to find them gone. I would have been the only one there to answer to him, to swallow his fury like gulps of seawater and pray I didn't spit them back up again until he had stormed out of my room and slammed the door shut behind him.

Rose had found me asleep under my bed that night, face streaked with salt, our spiny-tailed monster nibbling anxiously at my garter belt.

It was only because of Undine that they'd started leaving at all. A year ago, it had been unthinkable. Our father had barred us from setting foot outside the garden, not with his spells, but with his words and threats. Oblya was as dangerous as a viper pit, he said, and something or someone would snap you up in an instant. I believed him. The men who came to see me, my clients, were frightening even in the safety of our own sitting room.

But all of Undine's clients were half in love with her and went weak-kneed with her every word. And one day one of them had, in lieu of rubles, offered her tickets to see an orchestra play downtown. She had refused at first—or so she said—but the man had insisted. And once the thought of leaving was in her mind, it grew and grew like reaching vines and could not be hacked down.

That first night had planted the same flowering seed in Rose's mind. Their seats, she told me, were in the very back row, so they had to strain to see the stage over a topiary of feathered hats, and the heat of so many bodies had made them both return soaked with sweat, but there was a magic to it all; I could sense that even from a distance. A sly, coaxing magic had drawn my sisters out of their beds at night, reveling in the recklessness of it all, the thousands of possibilities that flitted around them like moths.

For my sisters, it was revelry, or even just the petulant thrill of knowing they had disregarded our father's orders. For me, it was fear. I did not want to be left behind, not after that one awful night.

So I let Rose and Undine drag me through the crowd, chest heaving beneath my corset. The scents of strangers, sweat and violet perfume, soaked my skin like rainwater. Words poured into my ears.

". . . found his heart torn out, like someone had plunged a fist into his chest . . ."

". . . liver gone, too, just empty . . ."

Stomach tensing, I leaned toward Rose again. "What are they talking about?"

"Some nonsense from the penny presses, I'm sure," she said, eyes trained forward. "The Grand Inspector found two men dead at the boardwalk, and someone started the tale that they'd been killed by a *monster*. More likely they beat each other down in a drunken brawl, or just drank themselves to death, which would explain the comments about the liver. But that doesn't make as lurid of a story, and it doesn't sell very many papers."

I nodded, my belly uncurling just a little bit. Rose seemed to be able to understand things about the world that I could not, even though we were all trapped in the same house, under the same aegis.

She also must have done a good enough job wrangling my hair, because I did not receive any lingering stares. Women's eyes passed over me and angled toward my sisters with suspicious jealousy. Men's stares swept past me as well, landing on the cleft of Undine's breasts or Rose's bare shoulders. I could see the hunger, but also the guilt running under their gazes, the quiet fettering of desire. They knew anyone who desired a Vashchenko girl was doomed.

More voices swam toward me.

". . . paid double the price to see him, but I don't regret it . . ."

". . . said it was the best show she'd ever seen—brought tears to her eyes . . ."

This time, I did not have to ask Rose what they meant. We were here for the same reason as the rest of them. As Undine maneuvered us toward the ticket booth, I drew in a steeling breath. My corset felt strangling-tight. She produced our three tickets and then smiled at the attendant, batting her lashes. I did not know how much they were worth—I hardly knew how many kopeks made a ruble—but judging by the size and eagerness of the crowd, I suspected it was quite a lot. Perhaps this particular client was even more in love with my sister than most.

Two attendants in black velvet bowed to us and pushed open the oaken double doors. Undine and Rose let go of my arms, knowing I had no choice but to follow. I trailed after them, gaze on the ground, my brow shining with sweat, and the ballet theater snatched us up and shut its jaws behind us. Another thread of fear loosed in me. When I raised my head at last, I was dizzy with the lurid brightness.

Volutes of gold clambered up to the domed ceiling like vines wreathing the trunk of a tree. Between each gilded column were a dozen seats, upholstered in crimson velvet. The chandelier whirled gently with candlelight, each flame glinting like a knifepoint. The ceiling was one sprawling fresco, painted the pale blue of the sky in earliest spring. Satyrs—which remarkably resembled Indrik—chased bare-chested nymphs across it, and burly men lounged on riverbanks, wearing nothing but laurel crowns. A flush prickled my face.

In the time I'd spent staring at the ceiling, I'd nearly lost Rose and Undine. I followed the bright pearl of Undine's blond head and caught up with them as they were sliding into their seats. My throat was dry with anxious embarrassment.

"I think they recognized you," I told Undine in a whisper. "The ticket attendant, the men in line—"

"Well, of course they would recognize me," Undine said briskly. "But they won't tell Papa. They know they'd never get to see me again if they did."

On my other side, Rose let out a low, laughing breath. She was my ally in exasperation at Undine's vanity, and she showed her chagrin more openly than I ever dared. Luckily, Undine was usually too preoccupied with herself to notice.

More whispers started. The voice of a silver-haired woman in the row behind lisped past my ear.

"They say his rib cage was crumpled like a sunken roof. They say his eyes had been plucked out and replaced with plum stones."

I whipped my head around, and immediately Undine slapped my arm. The effect was so instant that I thought my body had punished itself; who else but me could be so in tune with my own aberrations? Undine's blue eyes were thin.

"Don't," she snarled. "It's rude to eavesdrop, especially *here*. You really don't know anything about the world, do you, Marlinchen?"

I couldn't tell if by *here* she meant the ballet theater, or if she meant Oblya as a whole, the huge, gray sprawl of the city outside our garden walls. In the theater we were hemmed in by the men and women of the upper curia, as colorful as candied fruits in their silks and satins; outside in the streets we were surrounded by drunken day laborers, with their fox-lean faces and their loose, fat lips. I did not know which was worse. I raised my shoulders and sunk down in my seat. Rose was thumbing through a pamphlet, each page embossed in gold.

"They're doing *Bogatyr Ivan*," Rose said. "They must do it every night. If Papa knew that, he'd have one of his fits."

I cringed at the thought. *Bogatyr Ivan* was Oblya's most famous ballet, and it was a corrupted version of one of the stories in our father's codex, transfigured by Rodinyan influence and otherwise eroded by time. The titular Ivan had gone from steppe warrior to saint, and his bride had gone from chieftain's daughter to tsarevna, and any number of other small changes had turned the story into something else, something that was scarcely recognizable to me.

But it pleased the Oblyans, and, more important, the Rodinyans. These newcomers arrived waving the tsar's banners, talking of things like *land development* and *city planning*, or else under the emblems of private companies who squeezed every drop from Oblya's day laborers and then vanished, only to be replaced by other men, under different emblems but with the same goal of bleeding the city dry. They were the reason Oblya's port bustled with trade from the east, and the reason why our streets were laid out as neatly as wheel spokes. I did not think much of them, except that when they came to our gate, our father instructed us to ignore them until they left.

But now the theater was packed elbow to elbow to see one Rodinyan incomer grace the stage. I peered over Rose's shoulder at the pamphlet, searching for his name, like I might glean something important from the particular arrangement of the letters. Her finger went up and down the page, skimming his biography.

"They say he's the youngest principal dancer in any Rodinyan ballet company, *ever*," she said. "Only twenty-one. That's so sad, isn't it?"

"Why is it sad?"

"Because," she said, "what do you do when you're twenty-one and you've already achieved everything that most people can only dream of? You have the rest of your life in front of you, but nowhere else to go."

I felt sorry, somehow, that I had asked.

Before I could say another word, the orchestra warbled out its opening notes and the velvet curtains parted and the whispers around me went silent, all eyes drawn toward the single light onstage, round like a rime of ice. Cellos sang languidly under the trilling of flutes and oboes.

I had never seen *Bogatyr Ivan* with my sisters before, so I could not anticipate the crescendos and decrescendos and when the snare drum would kick in or when the harp would add its sultry voice. With every unfamiliar beat I felt something plucking at me like a string, my bones rattling, my blood singing. I knew the vague shape of the story, but the music added something new to it, something that made it almost too big for my eyes to hold. The first ballerinas flurried across the stage, like snow drifts in their white tulle. Male dancers in red bounded after them; they were the Dragon-Tsar's animate flames.

The ballerinas swooned dramatically. I knew from the story in Papa's codex that they were the spirits of ice, of pure virginal frost, of Oblya's land before the conquerors came to burn and spoil it. Black-clad, the Dragon-Tsar mimed laughing as the cellos droned gravely. I knew, too, that eventually Ivan would enter, clumsy and swordless, just a farmer's son and a peasant until he became a warrior—and, in this version, as the pamphlet's synopsis had told me, a saint. There were no saints in Papa's version of the story, but there was always Ivan.

Though I had spent so many years conjuring an image of Ivan in my mind, I was not prepared to see him now: black hair streaming, chest bare where his shabby jacket parted. As soon as he was there under the lights, it was impossible to look anywhere else. It was impossible not to follow his path across the stage. In his presence, the flame-men wilted like cut roses. The snow-women stirred, silver faces brightening with nascent hope. He stumbled past them to the Dragon-Tsar; even his floundering was graceful.

The Dragon-Tsar reared, as if to strike him down, and then the pretty tsarevna danced between them, pleading with her father while Ivan retreated and the snow-women simpered. The Dragon-Tsar swept offstage with his flame-men, leaving Ivan and the tsarevna to circle each other like hesitant wolves.

Ivan's threadbare shirt tumbled off his shoulders, and in that moment I felt as if all the audience was holding the same long breath. Sevastyan Rezkin was so lovely under the livid candlelight that I had to force myself to exhale.

My eyes traced the delicately corded muscles down his abdomen and along his thighs. He took the tsarevna's hand and kissed it. Her movements seemed somehow clumsy next to his, as if she were counting the steps in her head. Sevastyan's steps were as fluid as a spill of water, as though he could not imagine moving in any other manner. He lifted the tsarevna's leg. Her fingers stroked along his face.

I felt like a voyeur, like some uncouth intruder witnessing a tender miracle not meant for my eyes. I felt the same way I did when I watched the gulls and cormorants arc from the pier over our rooftop, embarrassed of my own heavy, flightless body.

His knee parted the tsarevna's thighs, and I blushed so profusely I knew Undine would mock me for it, if she had been looking at all. But every face in the theater was turned toward Sevastyan. He was the beacon of a hundred unblinking stares.

Whatever my sister's suitor had paid for the tickets, I would have paid double. Triple. For the first time I began to understand Undine's and Rose's reckless desire, the thrill of possibility that drew them out of their beds at night, shucking our father's dire warnings.

My fingers curled into a fist in my skirts, and I did not unclench them until the final act, when Ivan emerged as a saint. Sevastyan was bare-chested again, wearing only thin nude stockings that he looked like he had been poured into, for all the modesty they afforded him. His chest was leafed in gold, whorls of gilded paint that crawled up his throat and spiraled onto his cheeks. Even his lashes were daggered with false pearls. Over his shoulders he wore a winged mantle, white feathers ruffling with his twirls and leaps.

I could not fathom how he spread his legs so wide, or how he jumped so high, or how he didn't crumple with the shudder of inertia when he landed again. As the music quavered to its end and Sevastyan and the tsarevna bowed, half the theater lurched to its feet at once, thunderous with applause. Several of the women around me were weeping, kohl tracked down their pink faces.

"I *told* you," Undine said as she hauled me out of my seat. Even her voice was breathy, her blinks too quick. "It was worth it, wasn't it?"

But the curtains had closed, erasing Sevastyan from view, and I felt as though I had been left unanchored, adrift in the sea of voices. The noise was pressing into me and the heat of all the warm bodies was making my head swim. The air tasted sour with so many tittered words. And once again I could scarcely breathe, like some hot, invisible hand was closing around my throat.

Faces pinwheeled past me. I could not tell the wolves from the sheep.

"I have to go," I managed, jerking my hand from Undine's grasp. My voice sounded like it had been wrung from wet cloth. "I have to get out of here."

Rose made a garbled protest as I pushed past her, but I did not stop. My steps fell clumsily on the red carpet. I could hear the rustling of silk as the audience members shuffled from their seats, though a haze had fallen over my eyes, and everything looked as bleary as the grass covered in morning dew. By some gift of mad, manic instinct, I found a side door by the left of the stage and barreled through it, gasping as I tumbled out into the cold blue night.

Relief felt like the snapping of a thread. I leaned back against the side of the building, my forehead damp with a cool sweat. My hair had come loose from Rose's pink ribbon and fell in coils all over my face. I brushed it back as best I could, fingertips buzzing.

The alley stretched out to either side of me, boundless and black.

Overhead, the stars were smog-veiled, and the only light was leaking through the windows of the ballet theater, a pale yellow film. It had only just occurred to me to be afraid when the door swung open, and someone else staggered out.

The man was doubled over, one arm bent across his abdomen. With the other hand, he braced himself against the wall, turned away from me, coughing and spluttering.

"Are you all right?" It was all I could think to say. Reeling, my mind still addled with its ebbing panic, I picked my way toward him and leaned down to examine his face. "Sir, are you ill?"

He retched, sick splattering the cobblestones and the hem of my skirt. I was so well accustomed to the sight and sound and smell of vomit that I didn't flinch. Instead I leaned closer, squinting at the man's face in the dark.

"Sir, please," I said. "You're ill. I'm no healer, but I can fetch my sister—"

He wiped his mouth on the back of his hand and looked up at me. The curve of his cheek caught the light, and I froze like a rabbit mid-leap. I was staring into the misty blue eyes of Sevastyan Rezkin.

A white silk blouse had been pulled haphazardly over his shoulders, but it was sagging open at the chest. I could see the gold paint flaking off his skin, off his cheeks, smeared where he'd rubbed at his mouth. A single white feather drifted from his black hair.

I mumbled something that was unintelligible, even to my own ears. Sevastyan held my gaze, eyes wavering. The whites of them were cracked through with red. I remembered his soft and graceful landings, the way his thighs tensed beneath his tights, the way his hips had pressed taut to the tsarevna's, and my face went torridly hot.

His lashes fluttered with their false pearls, a fringed shadow over his sharp cheekbones. His skin was as pale and unblemished as the ivory handle of my mother's comb, smoothed by so much time spent in my or my sisters' hands. Thinking of it only made me blush further.

Even now, sweat-dewed and smelling of sick, he was so beautiful I couldn't look away.

Before either of us could speak, the door swung open again. Another dancer, sandy-haired, still wearing his flame-red blouse and tights, burst through and sighed. His breath was a white cloud in the cold. He looked between Sevastyan and me and folded his arms across his chest.

"Come on, Sevas," he said wearily. "Derkach is looking for you."

Sevastyan stood up, wincing and holding his side. "Lyoshka," he mumbled. "My hero."

Sighing again, the other dancer took him by the arm and began to lead him toward the door. Sevastyan's gait was unsteady; all his steps lurched sharply toward the left.

"Wait," I said. My voice sounded too loud, as discordant as a gull's cry. "You can't—he's very ill."

The other dancer—Aleksei—paused and turned. The corners of his mouth quivered, and I could not tell if he meant to smile or to frown.

"He's not sick," he said. "Well, I suppose he *is*, but there's nothing you or I can do for him, miss. In an hour, he'll vomit up another half a liter of vodka and then fall asleep, and his body will punish him in the morning."

With that, he took Sevastyan through the door, and they both vanished as it swung shut. Several moments passed before I could bring myself to move again, my own belly churning like laundry in a washtub.

Undine scowled and slapped my arm when I found them; Rose sighed and smoothed back the curls from my face. I did not tell either of them about my encounter with Sevastyan—I could still hardly convince myself that it was real.

As we hurried down Kanatchikov Street, I trained my gaze on

the stained hem of my dress, the splattered toe of my slipper. My mind kept circling back to Sevastyan's damp, shining face and his bright, quivering blue eyes. The whites of them were split like hairline fractures in Papa's good porcelain. I could not fathom how he had managed to dance like that after half a liter of vodka; perhaps Aleksei had exaggerated. I'd never had a sip of vodka myself. Maybe a liter was hardly anything at all, just a little blurring at the corners of your vision.

I told myself that, but I didn't really believe it. When we came to the gate, it unlatched for us so easily, without a sound, that I was astonished. It was like a wanting mouth, eager to swallow us back down. The goblin had ceased his whimpering. Indrik still slept. The eyeless ravens had not stirred from their perch.

My mind should have been spinning out like a compass point, fear turning me manic and unmoored. Yet the walk back through the garden passed me by almost obliviously. I was focused only on Sevastyan. All other thoughts had been momentarily evicted. It was as though I had forgotten how to even feel afraid.

Was this the magic that kept pulling my sisters out of the house? In that moment it seemed almost as strong as Papa's spellwork. The city was a song that crooned unceasingly in my ear, and if my mind was a compass, Sevastyan's face was true north.

Back in my room, I removed my dress and unlaced my corset, fingers trembling. I extracted all the dead leaves and wheat stalks from my sheets and tucked them under my bed, where the monster was snoring softly. When it was sleeping like that, I could not see the red ovals of its eyes.

They say his eyes had been plucked out and replaced with plum stones.

My teeth came together with an audible click. Lurid tales from the penny presses, nothing more. That I could let myself believe; Rose's assurances were as easy to swallow as cool stream water. The only monsters left in Oblya lived here, under my bed or in our garden, and none of them had any lust for human flesh. All *those* sorts of monsters had died out long ago.

I climbed into bed and pulled the quilt up to my chin. I had expected my limbs to feel heavy with exhaustion after our nightly sojourn, solid, weighty relief lowering my eyelids. Yet my legs felt light and delightfully cold with the memory of the frigid outside air.

I could not sleep. I could only think of Sevastyan, his naked chest daubed in gold. My mind wandered back through the garden, down the dark streets, and into the alleyway again, to where I had stared at his sweat-slick face in the pallid light.

I thought of him, and my fingers slipped between my thighs. As I stroked myself, I bit down hard on my pillow, so that I would not risk making a sound.

CHAPTER TWO

Pieces of light fell on my face like dead leaves. I bolted upright just in time to hear the tapping of the monster's claws against the floorboards as it scurried out from under my bed. I caught sight of the end of its spiny tail before it vanished into the corridor.

The clock gonged seven. I stripped off my covers. A stalk of wheat fell out of my hair. Dust motes drifted through beams of latticed sunlight, illuminating the fine gray film that covered my mirror and my dressing table, and the bone-white handle of my mother's comb. My pink shoes were peering like blind kittens through the crack in my wardrobe door, the heels clotted with dirt. Above them, a flash of cranberry silk, the drooping, unfastened laces of my corset. A thrill of something loosed in me, a memory shaken free: Sevastyan's gold-daubed chest. Flushing, I closed the wardrobe door tightly, sealing my dress and shoes and evidence of our night of revelry inside.

I had half an hour to bring my father his breakfast—less time than usual. I had slept too indulgently, dreaming of Ivan and the tsarevna. I hadn't even dared put myself in her body; I had only watched as they spun and spun, like the figures in a music box, like Ivan and the princess from my favorite of Papa's fairy tales.

I pulled on my housecoat and hurried barefooted down the stairs, my steps echoing dimly. My eyes followed the monster's path, the furrow its tail had traced through the thick carpet. I guessed it had already found its place beneath the juniper tree. It rose early, as did our eyeless ravens. I didn't know if the fiery serpent slept at all—you could see it only out of the corner of your eye, and whenever you turned to look at it head-on, it would vanish. Half the time you would mistake it for a black ribbon someone had dropped in the grass. Even without Rose's elixir Indrik slept most of the day, his snores rustling sprigs of lavender. The goblin was still shut up in the shed.

Undine herself would sleep for another three hours at least; we saw no clients on Sundays. Rose would wake with the sound of our father's discontented clamor but wouldn't always come down. Until then, the house was mine, all twenty rooms branching out around me like the canopy of an enormous oak. I could have paced my way through it with my eyes shut, feeling along the polished mahogany banister, fingers running through the fringed lampshades.

Where Rose and Undine owned the garden, the kitchen and adjacent sitting room were my domain. The hanging copper pots jangled like wind chimes above my head. Since I had already rolled out the dough for varenyky last night, I floured my hands and cut it into neat diamonds. A tray of ground meat, congealing and pale, was chilling in the icebox. I didn't remember making the filling, but I must have—no one else entered the kitchen except for me and our spiny-tailed monster, snuffling for crumbs on the counter or licking grease off the pan with its long barbed tongue.

While the varenyky boiled, I sliced two fat hunks of black bread and smeared them with butter. I cut two onions, eyes stinging, and browned them with the varenyky. There were three heavy jars of pickled cabbage, so I took a scoop from one and added it to the plate, staining the edge of my sleeve purple. I heaped sour cream beside the varenyky and poured a glass of milk.

When I was finished, I stuck the spoon in my mouth. I could taste the smooth richness of the cream and the sour bite of cabbage, and underneath the lingering smokiness of onion and browned butter. I licked and licked until all I could taste was rust-tinged metal.

I brought the tray to the sitting room and placed it on the walnut-inlaid table. Its four iron legs ended in hooves; it always reminded me of Indrik when he crouched in the grass, nibbling indignantly at Rose's sage grass. I wiped the dampness from my brow and let out a breath.

Overhead, the chandelier quivered like willow fronds in the breeze, and the wood groaned with my father's footsteps.

He lurched down the stairs, still in his dressing gown. His feet were ensconced in velvet slippers. Papa's hands made me think of white spiders, his skinny fingers clenching down hard on the banister. The belt of his dressing gown was wrapped twice around the wisp of him, like how the sailors at the port would tie their sails to the mast with a length of rope, so their ships wouldn't be wrenched this way and that by the wind.

Papa brushed a dry-mouthed kiss to my forehead and sat on the couch. He surveyed the tray with his usual resigned misery. The bags under his eyes were as blue and fat as a rich woman's purse.

"Thank you, Marlinchen," he said.

"Of course, Papa."

He always thanked me, so how could I begrudge him anything? For the hours he took from me while I washed plates in the kitchen and poured vinegar into jars of cabbage. Unlike my sisters, who took after our mother, I could see foggy mirrors of my features in his. The length of our noses, certainly, with their low bridges and dramatic slopes, the distinctly sallow tone to our skin, and the slight upward slant to our pale brown eyes.

They said my father had been handsome, once, but his curse had whittled away at him like a lubok carving. Now there was something distinctly inhuman about him, a wooden falsity to his rare smiles.

"Next time, you should put cheese in the varenyky," Papa said. "And plums. Do we have plums?"

I stiffened. *They say his eyes had been plucked out and replaced with plum stones.* "Do you mean the black amber plums?"

"No, of course not; don't be stupid. You aren't stupid, Marlinchen. I don't want to eat poisoned plums, even though they wouldn't kill me. We have a purple plum tree too."

"Right." I blinked. "I can make plum preserves."

"I'll eat them with mlyntsi."

My father licked the blade of his knife. I sat across from him, fists curled in my lap, watching the food vanish. Flecks of it were caught in his beard. It was a relic of earlier days, before the Wizards' Council had been disbanded. Once you were approved for your license from the council you got a new title and some arbitrarily deigned feature that meant you could never hide your status. Titka Whiskers had a cat's yellow eyes, and lids that closed vertically, like pulling a long drape over a window. My father had a beard of deep indigo. He kept it long because it hid the paunch of his cheeks, which were sagging and distended from the early days of his curse: when he'd cram his face full of cheese wheels and stale bread loaves, thinking he could sate that depthless hunger.

Now it fell to me to keep my father fed. But no matter how much he ate, his belly still ached at the end of it. And nothing could stave off his gauntness either—his wrist bones pushed up against his skin like air bubbles in cake batter. Thinking of it made me feel so terribly sad that my own belly growled in sympathy. I would eat the rest of the black bread and cabbage when my father was done.

While my father ate, green-hued light trickled in from the garden, sieved through the meshwork of leaves and branches. Sundays were my favorite days, when the house was quiet and empty, only my sisters and me doing our work in silence, and no clients at the door. Not that they had been much of a nuisance recently. Our stream of visitors had been dwindling as of late, so much that even I had noticed, and Rose and Undine whispered about it, but none of us dared to broach the subject with our father. After what he had done to earn our monopoly on witchcraft in Oblya, it seemed cruel to suggest that his sacrifice was perhaps beginning to wear thin.

I told myself not to worry about it. My sisters were cleverer and more beautiful than me, and Papa was a canny businessman. They would come up with a way to restore our clients to us.

If the Wizards' Council still existed, Undine would have been officially called a water witch, though she was not a very good one. She could see the future by staring into her scrying pool, or into the polished backs of our silver dishes. (Of course, Rose and I liked to joke, Undine's divination involved gazing endlessly at her own reflection). Her predictions were as muddled as stagnant pond water, but she had more clients than Rose and me put together, even now. While Undine stared and stared into her scrying pool, her clients stared and stared at her.

They never touched her, though. She was like a winter's first snow, and no one wanted to be responsible for spoiling her ivory perfection.

I couldn't blame Undine too much. In all the stories the eldest sisters were wicked, and Undine was still less wicked than most. It was only her birthright to cruelly lord her beauty over me.

Rose would have been called an herbalist, and *her* magic was good. She made healing poultices that worked better for wounds than leeches or bloodletting, and she could even cobble together mixtures of herbs that made you dizzy with joy for an hour, or, if slipped into an enemy's soup, would make him mad enough to tear his hair out until the poison abated.

She charged fat handfuls of rubles for those, and only gave them to customers she could trust, usually fretful women with pinch-faced husbands. Rose was beautiful, too, with her long black hair that turned iridescent in the sunlight, and her deep violet eyes. But she was usually covered in dirt and smelling of wormwood or catmint, and always carried with her a pair of gardening shears, their blades flashing at her hip. So the men didn't dare to touch her either.

There was a scuffling in the garden, and bare branches tapped the window like something asking to be let in. I rose to my feet and peered through the white petals of our flowering pear tree. There was one of our eyeless ravens pecking at an unripe pear, roughly the shape of a fallen tear. There was the goblin scratching at the shed door. And there were two men rattling the gate.

"Papa," I said as my face blanched with fear, "there's someone outside."

"More Rodinyan land surveyors, probably." My father tore off a chunk of buttered bread, chewed it, and swallowed. "Or missionaries. Ignore them, and they will go away."

From such a distance, I could not make out the men's faces, but they did not wear the brown robes of the devout Sons and Daughters, or the red badges of the tsar's envoys. One of the men saw me looking, and from his pocket he withdrew a satchel, bunched tight with a drawstring. He held it up and shook it. I could see the vague shapes of coins jostling inside.

"They have money," I said.

Instantly my father lurched from his seat. I wondered if they might be Undine's clients, so determined to see her that they would offer twice what she usually charged. I knew they weren't Rose's—only women came to Rose with such untimely desperation. My father shouldered past me and stared out the window, eyes narrowing.

After a moment, he said, "We'll let them in."

"Papa," I said, panic rising in my throat, "I'm not dressed—"

But he was already walking toward the door, leaving his plate half-eaten. All I could think as I followed him was that a year ago he would have never let a client through our gate on Sunday, no matter how much they begged and pleaded, and would have even shouted at them from our front stoop that if they kept on rattling he'd turn them into spiders.

From the window, I watched my father speak to the men through the locked gate. I hugged my housecoat around myself, excruciatingly aware that my hair was as tangled as a briar patch, curls falling over my face, and that I reeked of cooking oil and onion. To my father's credit, he did not care what my clients thought of how I looked. If they wanted to see someone beautiful, they would patronize my sisters.

One of the men passed the bag of rubles through the bars. The other one skulked back, hands in his jacket pockets, head down. He had black hair and looked very pale.

The gate unlatched, and the two men followed my father down the garden path. The goblin's scratching grew furious. I hurried to the door, heart beating as soundly as footsteps on a marble floor. I told myself that whoever it was, at least it was not Dr. Bakay. I would have known his hunched silhouette and his silver hair anywhere.

As the door swung open, my breathing had steadied. My father stood in the threshold with the two men. The older one was blond, with hair that was gelled thickly, as if to compensate for its encroaching thinness, and he had the jaunty look of a carriage horse, eagerness in the flashing of his gray eyes.

The other man was a dour, unsmiling Sevastyan Rezkin. I choked on air.

"Hello," the jaunty man said. "I'm Ihor Derkach."

I waited for words to come, but they only gathered brittle and unspoken on my tongue like burnt sugar. My father gave a rattling cough of annoyance, the loose skin of his cheeks flapping, and stepped over the threshold.

"This is my daughter Marlinchen," Papa said. "As you can see, she is quiet—and discreet. If you value a secret kept, she is the witch for you."

"Excellent," said Derkach. "We'd like to get started right away."

Sevastyan was staring at the ground, but at Derkach's prodding he looked up. Our eyes met for the briefest moment, but in that time I saw the flicker of recognition, and under it something odder and unexpected: fear. It was gone again before I could puzzle over it.

Perhaps he was afraid of witches. Rodinyans were superstitious. As I watched him walk toward the living room, I almost burst into tears at the terrible absurdity of it all: Sevastyan Rezkin pacing my floorboards, perched on my chaise longue, scarcely four long steps from the kitchen where I hummed wordless songs to myself while I beat eggs for mlyntsi. Had my furtive nighttime desire somehow summoned him here? I dismissed the thought at once. I didn't have that sort of magic.

No, this was just a confluence of awful luck, and now everything might be ruined.

Papa sat back on the couch and directed Sevastyan toward the armchair. His voice sounded distant and deadened, the way it did when I held my head underwater in the bath.

Derkach was chattering animatedly. Papa had gone back to his food. I stood there stupidly, trying to will the tears from welling up in my eyes, and then Papa said loudly, roughly, "Marlinchen, don't be rude. Offer our guest a refreshment."

I gave myself a brisk shake, as if I were a dog with fleas. I tried not to look at Sevastyan. As I spoke, even the familiar words felt like ash on my tongue.

"Would you like anything to drink, Mr. Derkach? We have blackberry kvass."

"No thank you, my dear." He gave me a tight-lipped, bracing smile. "Tell me, what sort of witchery do you practice? Are you a soothsayer? A hedge-witch? A phrenologist?"

I stiffened. My gorge rose. I might have retched right there on the carpet, but Papa's swift and cutting gaze forced me to mumble out, "No, sir."

"I took Sevas to a phrenologist here in Oblya, but he didn't give me much help. He told me that the Yehuli's brains were adapted to capitalism—well, you only need to look down *their* streets to surmise as much. Their businesses are thriving! Anyway, I am hoping you can succeed where other doctors have failed, and diagnose Sevas's affliction."

I was scarcely able to hear him over the spring-water rush of blood in my ears. Painfully, I turned toward Sevastyan. He was slouched in the armchair, a petulantly indignant expression on his face. There were shadows under his eyes, but he did not seem otherwise particularly ill. I remembered how he had looked last night in the alley, sick dripping off his chin. Aleksei had assured me that he would be fine in the morning. I wondered if it was possible that Derkach didn't know he'd downed half a liter of vodka.

"And what has been ailing him?" I asked Derkach, unable to bring myself to address Sevastyan directly.

Derkach leaned across the table, and patted Sevastyan's knee. Sevastyan tensed instantly, and there was a beat of silence as his shoulders rose beneath his black jacket. Time jerked forward again, and Sevastyan looked up at me, strands of dark hair feathering across his forehead.

"There isn't much to tell, Ms. Vashchenko," he said. His voice was low, level, and he held my gaze. "I've been, ah, falling ill after my recent performances. It happened sometimes in Askoldir, but it has been more frequent since I've come to Oblya."

Hearing my name on his lips made me flush profusely. I couldn't help it. Could he somehow sense, when he looked at me, that I had pleasured myself last night while holding his face in my mind? It was unbearable to contemplate. Even more unbearable to realize that he knew me, recognized me, and at any moment he might reveal me. I prayed to every god that I could remember from Papa's codex for something that would stop him, for the ceiling to crumble and bury me, for Indrik to wake and start his deafening lamentations, for one of the eyeless ravens to fly into the window and shatter it.

Nothing happened. My prayers were always awkward and stammering, and besides, our gods had no power in capitalist Oblya.

With great difficulty, I cleared my throat. "And how long has it been since you came from Askoldir?"

"Six months," said Sevastyan. His gaze flickered to Derkach. The other man's hand was still on his knee.

"Yes, that's right," Derkach said. "Give or take a few weeks."

There was something overbright and false about Derkach's smile. It reminded me of Undine's porcelain figurines, with their relentlessly cherubic grins. They had all been repatriated to my bedroom ever since she'd proclaimed herself too old to play with dolls.

"What is your relation?" The words flooded past my lips before I could stop them. "To Sevastyan, I mean."

"I'm his handler," Derkach replied, chest puffing with pride. "I have been ever since Sevas was twelve years old. I was the one who secured his position as principal dancer in Oblya's ballet theater."

Abruptly the room went silent. My father took his fork from his mouth mid-bite, and a darkness came over his face. The familiar furrow between his brow and the sharp breath that whistled through his teeth made me freeze with fear. I stood as still as the rabbits in our garden did right before our spiny-tailed monster pounced at their throats.

"You're a dancer," Papa said. The syllables ticked out of him like blood dripping onto the floor.

"Why, of course," Derkach said. "The youngest principal dancer Oblya's ballet has ever seen."

I made a strangled noise that no one seemed to hear. Of all the things Papa loathed about capitalist Oblya, he loathed none more than the ballet theater. He railed against it more than he did the Ionik merchant sailors, who he said brought with them the fish-stink of the east, and more than he did the Yehuli, who he claimed were out to drain the city of its wealth the way an upyr sucked the blood of virgin women. He hated the cotton mills and the day laborers, and the factories that chuffed black smoke into the sealskin sky. But he hated the ballet theater most.

Fodder for wealthy hags whose husbands won't touch them, and wealthy men who are too shy for the brothels, he often said. I flushed even more deeply now, remembering his words, and thinking of my own hand slipping between my thighs.

"Right," said Papa coolly. His gaze swept over Derkach, over Sevastyan, and then over me. "Marlinchen, go on."

How many rubles had they offered him to swallow his revulsion? I was certain that a year ago no price would have bought Papa's silence, but I would never know. Papa always took money from the clients on my behalf. I wasn't smart enough to make sure they didn't stiff me, he said.

Miserably, I looked at Sevastyan. Derkach had lifted his hand from his knee, and I gave my own unconscious twitch of relief.

"I will do my very best to name your affliction," I said, which was what I told all my clients, usually with a demure smile. I couldn't manage one now. "Where would you prefer to be touched?"

Sevastyan's gaze snapped up. "What?"

"Marlinchen is a flesh diviner," my father said impatiently. He was gripping his grease-marbled knife in his hand, blade turned up. "Her readings require skin-to-skin contact."

There was that odd fear in Sevastyan's eyes again, and I couldn't make sense of it. All my clients were men, and none had ever been anything less than enthusiastic when I told them how my readings worked. If my father was not in the room, they would smile their languid smiles and try to guide my hand over their gleaming belt buckles. I would laugh weakly and rebuff them the best I could without causing offense, without making them rescind their rubles.

They all relented eventually, grinding their teeth, all except Dr. Bakay. And my father had been in the room then.

For years I had prayed every night for the absent gods to grant me a witchcraft like Rose's or Undine's, something that I could perform from a careful distance. As much as I envied their beauty, it was mostly because it rendered them impregnable. Untouchable.

"Yes," I said shakily. "I'll do it however you find most comfortable."

Sevastyan stared up at me, shoulders rising and falling with his heavy breaths. I thought of how he had struck down the Dragon-Tsar, the muscles in his arms quivering like the plucked string of a balalaika, and the way he had run his hands so fluidly over the tsarevna's hips.

Desire tensed inside me, shameful and aching. Whoever desired a Vashchenko girl was doomed, but the opposite was also true. Wanting anything ended only in misery. And even as I waited for him to speak, for this to be over, I dreaded the thought of watching him leave.

Slowly, Sevastyan reached up and began to unbutton his blouse. The collar fell open, exposing the pale column of his throat.

"Here," he said, tilting his head. "Do it here."

Derkach clapped his hands together, eyes sparkling. "Oh, I've always wanted to watch a real witch do her work."

I almost told him that I wasn't a real witch; the Wizards' Council had disbanded before I could earn my official title. The last true witch in Oblya was Titka Whiskers, whose real name was Marina Bondar. She'd adopted the moniker Titka Whiskers for a bit of calculated flair, the Old World charm that our clients sought. I had realized when I was quite young that most of them did not want to be helped, not really. They came to us for the same reason they came to the ballet theater: spectacle. Distraction.

I was not nearly as enthralling to watch as Sevastyan, done up in his feathers and painted lambent gold, but my clients came to me, rather than my beautiful sisters, because I offered what Undine and Rose could not—or rather, what they did not have to. Proximity. Intimacy. Palms spanning bare chests, fingers pressed against throats. I found jawbones and earlobes particularly fruitful, of all the places I allowed myself to touch.

Face unbearably hot, I considered what sorts of secrets I could leach from the cleft of Sevastyan's chin.

With a steely breath, I approached him. Last night he had appeared as lovely as an oil painting of an angel, or one of the Patrifaith's many saints. Now, in the butter-yellow morning, I found he had a bit of a craggy look to him. If he'd been carved from marble, I could see the places where the sculptor's chisel had slipped. The dip of his nose canted sharply to the right, and his chin thrust out at an angle that made him look always on the verge of smirking. His eyes were deep-set, but in daylight they seemed an even more brilliant hue of blue, jeweled and nearly translucent.

My heart raced at those thoughts even as Sevastyan inched forward in his chair, until he was perched on the very edge of it. His legs opened, leaving room for me to stand between his spread knees.

"Go on," Sevastyan said. His throat bobbed in the green-washed sunlight.

Where his shirt had slid open I saw a flash of his collarbone, the beginnings of a bare shoulder. Dark ink was scrawled into his skin—a tattoo? It must have been covered up by gold paint or brushed over with powder last night.

Behind me, my father cleared his throat. Once again I was painfully aware that my skin was misted with the grease of the kitchen, with the odor of burnt butter and sour pickled cabbage, and that my hair was tumbling over my shoulders in disheveled ringlets. One of my curls skimmed Sevastyan's cheek.

Perhaps what I'd seen earlier hadn't been fear but disgust; maybe he would have preferred my beautiful sisters. But they were both asleep, and the truth was, if anyone in this house was something close to a real witch, it was me.

I was still standing above him hesitantly when, with a sudden feckless impatience, Sevastyan took my right hand and pressed it against his throat.

The vision blistered over me, like oil splashed in a pan.

Sevastyan stood in a velvet-curtained dressing room, wearing peasant-Ivan's shabby clothes. There was a bottle of clear liquid on his boudoir, mostly empty. I could taste the acrid sting of it on my own tongue and feel my vision tilt and blur. Undine once told me that she watched her visions unfold from afar the way she watched storm clouds roll across the sky, and after hearing it I'd been sour with envy for weeks. My visions poured into my eyes and ears and nose like warm bathwater.

Through the dewy brightness of Sevastyan's gaze, I saw the velvet curtains part. One of the snow-maidens slipped inside, her blond hair pulled into a tight chignon, her cheeks dusted with silver. She flurried toward Sevastyan, their lips meeting, and he stumbled back against the boudoir. Her fingers knotted in his hair. My stomach lurched, but I could not tease apart whether it was my own discomfort or Sevastyan's, until the snow-maiden's hand slid between his thighs.

All at once, everything turned bitter and dark, as if I'd bitten into a fruit curdling with rot. Oddly, Derkach's face rose in my mind, shimmering like heat above the stovetop. It vanished in an instant, and Sevastyan thrust the snow-maiden away from him, both of our twinned bellies roiling.

He reached for the bottle again and then the vision winnowed away, leaving me shaking and sweat-chilled back in the sitting room, hand still pressed to Sevastyan's throat.

His blue eyes were narrowed, his bottom lip chewed nearly to bleeding. I tore my hand away and stepped back. I could hear Derkach murmuring behind me, and my father shifting on the couch. Sevastyan met my gaze, and in it I saw the same bridled fear, more comprehensible now. It was never me he had been afraid of.

Very slowly, I turned toward my father and Derkach. My skin felt damp, cold.

"He's having trouble adjusting to Oblya's sea air," I said. "It's not an uncommon affliction for newcomers to the city, especially ones who have never spent much time by the ocean." I was fairly certain Askoldir was landlocked, but I hoped my gamble didn't doom us both. "My sister Rosenrot has a draught that will help ease the symptoms until Sevastyan begins to feel more at home."

Derkach rose from his seat and shook my hand vigorously. "Oh, that's excellent work, my dear, thank you. The whole of Oblya's ballet theater is in your debt."

From over Derkach's shoulder, I watched dark smoke clouds bloom over Papa's face. I wondered who would pay for this later, and how. There was always someone who had to answer for my father's rage.

"Fine, then," Papa said briskly. "Marlinchen, take him to your sister's storeroom. Mr. Derkach and I must discuss compensation."

Still reeling, I gestured vaguely to Sevastyan. He stood, buttoning up the collar of his shirt, and followed me into the foyer. My hands were still trembling; I didn't dare look back. I breached the threshold of Rose's storeroom, musty-smelling and cobweb-wreathed, and didn't pause until I heard Sevastyan say, "That was one of the most practiced lies I've ever heard leave a witch's lips."

I paused while perusing a drawer of dried motherwort and turned slowly to face him. A heat had spread over my cheeks. "How many other witches have you known?"

"I suppose that depends," he said, "on what you would call a witch."

I stared at him in silence, breath held. Rose's storeroom was small and windowless, with scarcely enough space for us to stand without touching. The walls were lined with homemade cabinetry, white paint peeling in long strips. Filmy candlelight clung to Sevastyan's profile, to the dusty workbench, and when I inhaled again I tasted basil and thyme in the air.

I could still hardly believe he was here, in our dragon's hoard of nefarious sorcery. It was impossible, improbable, dangerous.

"I didn't want to lie to my father," I said at last. "Or to Mr. Derkach, but . . ."

Sevastyan stiffened again at Derkach's name. "I think you have already lied to your father, Ms. Vashchenko."

He rolled up his left sleeve. I saw another black tattoo scrawled across the back of his hand. Looped around his wrist, discolored with filth, was Rose's pink ribbon. My heart shot into my throat.

"Please," I said. "Don't say a word—I'll give you a draught for sea-sickness; Derkach will never know the difference."

Sevastyan only stared at me, incredulous. "I don't have any plans to reveal you, Ms. Vashchenko. I just wanted to give this back to you. And to thank you. I don't think many people would have stopped to help a man being sick on himself in an alley."

"Oh." I must have been the shade of a ripe beet by now, with how much I had been flushing since he'd walked through the door. "It only seemed like a decent thing to do."

"You are likely the only person in Oblya who thinks so." He laughed, but there was something hollow in it. "Did you enjoy the show?"

Could he possibly have guessed how I was thinking of him? Could he smell my desire like some scent on the air? Sometimes I worried that when I was reading my clients, they were reading me back. As if my touch leached secrets into their skin too.

But Sevastyan just arched a brow at me, looking expectant. Not smug.

"Of course," I said softly. "You—it was beautiful."

If he noticed my near slip, he didn't comment on it. He ran a hand through his hair, mussing it to a state of perfect dishevelment, then began to pull at the ribbon on his wrist. When he struggled to get it loose with one hand, I cleared my throat and said, "Let me."

Obediently, he held out his arm and I unlaced the ribbon, fingers quivering when they brushed the inside of his wrist. His skin was so pale that it had a marbled look to it, blue veins webbing beneath it like a river with many tributaries. I got the ribbon off him and closed it in my fist, feeling the heat that his body had left on it.

It occurred to me, suddenly, that he hadn't taken the ribbon when Aleksei had guided him into the theater again. "Did you . . . go back for it?"

"Not for the ribbon." Now I saw the faintest beginnings of a flush spread over his face. "I went to look for the kind girl who'd tried to help me, even though I'd been sick on her shoe. But you were gone by the time I was sober enough to walk straight."

"You really shouldn't drink so much," I found myself saying, as if I were some chiding nursemaid, but really my heart was pounding like hoofbeats. He had come back for me. "I don't know how you managed to dance at all, in that state. I felt how drunk you were when I was doing my reading—I could hardly see, and I couldn't think."

"I don't need to think when I'm dancing," he said. I could hear his Rodinyan accent now, the harder edge to his consonants. "I've been performing *Bogatyr Ivan* since I was twelve years old. It's natural to me, like breathing."

"It doesn't seem nearly so effortless for the other performers." I was thinking of the tsarevna. He'd made her look clumsy by comparison.

"That's why they are not the principal dancers," Sevastyan replied, lips thinning with a smirk.

I remembered what Rose had said—that he had his whole life ahead of him, and nowhere else to go. I imagined a long hallway unspooling before him, black and endless, like one of the unlit corridors on the third floor of our house. "I suppose so."

Sevastyan's smirk lost a bit of its brazenness. "What else did you see in your reading, Ms. Vashchenko?"

"Marlinchen," I said quickly, automatically. "That's—just call me Marlinchen."

"Marlinchen," he said. "What else did you see?"

My name in his mouth made my knees go weak. I remembered the snow-maiden and felt a kick of jealousy in my belly. I had to swallow hard before answering. "I only tell my clients what they need to know."

"And do you enjoy peering into your clients' heads, seeing all their tawdry secrets?"

"No," I said, surprising myself with my vehemence. "I don't enjoy it at all. Most of the things I wish I'd never seen, and most of my clients are people I'd never had to touch."

I thought, horribly, of Dr. Bakay, and my stomach folded over on itself. Sevastyan's face shifted at once, his eyes taking on a limpid softness. It reminded me of the way he'd looked at the tsarevna, when she'd first leapt between him and her dragon father.

"Right," he said. "I can imagine that."

Papa's words listed through my mind. *Fodder for wealthy hags whose husbands won't touch them.* I remembered the way the women in the audience had stared at Sevastyan, lips wet and red like glazed cherries, and the way Derkach's hand had closed over his knee. We looked at each other for a long moment, and then I couldn't stand it anymore, both the proximity and the space between us driving me different degrees of mad. I whirled around a plucked a sachet of chamomile and borage from the shelf, heart stammering, and held it out to him.

I couldn't remember if it was a cure for seasickness. I couldn't remember if it was a cure for anything at all.

"Here," I said in a trembling voice. "Take this. Sevastyan."

His name leapt off my tongue like a spark vaulting over the grates of a hearth, just before someone snuffed it out. Quick and bright. Sevastyan took the herbs from me, his lovely brow furrowing, and said, "You might as well call me Sevas."

Sevas. I tried out the diminutive in my mind, and even thinking it made me feel hot. Then I spoke it, quietly: "Sevas."

The corner of his lips lifted in a smile.

"You know," he said, "if watching the same story play out over and over again doesn't bore you as much as it bores me, perhaps you can come back to the theater. I think it would make me very happy to see your face in the crowd, Marlinchen."

When Derkach had settled his account and Papa was holding his rubles, when Sevas had tucked his poultice into his pocket, when both of our guests had left through the garden gate, white petals falling over them like rice thrown at a bride and her bridegroom, when I had looped the ribbon around my own wrist and hidden it under the sleeve of my housecoat, when Rose and Undine began traipsing sleepily down the stairs, Papa turned to me.

"Marlinchen," he said, "tell me why we live in Oblya?"

This was one of Papa's questions that was not a question at all but a trap laid at your feet. You had to speak carefully, considering every syllable, every intonation, to keep yourself from tumbling into it.

"We have lived in Oblya before it was even Oblya," I said, chewing my lip. "When there was only the long, flat steppe that fell into the sea with nothing to stop it. Since the days of the bogatyrs and their gods, when you couldn't pass by a stream without a rusalka calling to you sweetly, when you left your third-born sons in the woods for the leshy, and when you prayed in four directions to please the domovoi that lived in the cupboard."

Rose and Undine had stopped halfway down the steps, sensing the danger. You could hear the beginnings of Papa's rage from anywhere in the house, like boiled water squealing inside its pot.

Papa gave a brittle nod, which was the best I could have hoped for. My answer had not pleased him, but it had not riled him further. He turned to my sisters on the stairs.

"And you, lazy girls, thankless girls, wretched girls, what were you doing sleeping away the morning while your sister worked?" He shook his bag of rubles; it sounded like the gnashing of iron teeth. "Do you think it brings me joy, to take this tainted gold from the coffers of Oblya's ballet theater? You must think me no better than a Yehuli moneylender, swallowing up rubles without a care for where they came from, when they might as well be coated in poison and filth? Shall I go crawl on my hands and knees on the cobblestones in search of dropped kopeks? Shall I polish the tsar's boots with my tongue? Is this what my own daughters would ask of me?"

"Papa, please—" Undine started, fisting the pearl necklace at her throat. It was one of our mother's.

"Silence." Papa held up a hand. "Have I not done enough for you, my vain, ungrateful daughters, to keep you in fine silks with your bellies full? I took Titka Whiskers's curse for you, that ugly, jealous witch. Have I raised my daughters to be no better? Shall I write a spell to give you cat eyes and hooked noses and chicken feet? Perhaps I shall. Perhaps I shall turn you all into hags."

Undine made a choked sound. Rose was silent, her face pale. None of us were certain exactly how strong Papa's magic was, only that it was stronger than all of ours put together. That was precisely what he'd been known for, when he had sat on the Wizards' Council, and it was what had earned him his license: transformations.

"And you," Papa said, wheeling toward me. "I saw the way you went weak in the knees for that dancer. He's Yehuli, you know. I should have spied it right away, and then I wouldn't have let him in for anything. He has an unscrupulous set to his jaw, and the brow bone of a man with capitalist schemes in his mind. You are not a stupid girl, Marlinchen. But you are a girl. Wipe away the dewiness in your eyes and scrub the flush from your cheeks. Do you think he desires sallow-faced witches with the stink of the kitchen on them? Do you think I would ever let his serpent's jaws close around you, even if he did? You are far too dear to me for that."

Papa did not raise a hand to me now; he never had before. He only let his fury unfold from him like a mist, until it dampened our brows and snuck into our veins and made us freeze there, as still as graveyard statues.

It was good magic. I couldn't move and scarcely breathed as he paced the foyer, the loose skin of his cheeks flapping under his beard like our eyeless ravens beating their wings.

"Enough now," he said to himself, then looked up at my sisters and me. "I have two spells to cast. I will tell you what they are. The first is that no one from Oblya's infernal ballet theater will ever pass through our gate again, or else they will turn into a pile of vipers. And the second is that no one will leave this place without a bowl of black sand."

Before any of us could react, he slammed through the door and vanished, taking his magic with him. Undine fell to her knees on the stairs, letting out a broken howl.

"This is your fault," she snarled, looking up at me from between the curtains of her blond hair. "We let you come *one* time, and *this* is what happens? I don't know what you did, but you drove him here—"

"Undine," Rose said, voice sharp. "Enough."

But Undine just stared at me, seething, shoulders rising and falling with her labored and furious breaths. Tears made my vision blur like wet glass.

"You ruin everything," she bit out.

Rose came down the steps and paused before me, reaching up to smooth the curls from my face. I was vaguely aware of Undine letting out another wrenching howl before fleeing to her room, pale hair streaming out behind her.

"Come on now, Marlinchen," Rose said. "Don't cry."

But there was something hard in her voice. She hadn't seen what had happened, but she blamed me too. It was my fault that there would be no more midnight sojourns, no more orchestras, no more ballet theater. No more Sevas. One night was all it had taken for me to spoil what my sisters had so carefully and furtively built, like a clumsy child knocking over a stack of dishes. No one would leave the house without a bowl of black sand, and the only black sand was far away on Oblya's beaches, where the smog from the dredging ships dyed the shores the color of ink.

"I'm not crying," I said, blinking back the tears that had gathered hotly in the corners of my eyes. "I'm just hungry."

Rose let out a breath through her nose, a breath of wordless anger. I brushed away from her and she let me. I went through the sitting room, snatching up Papa's empty plate, and into the kitchen. I put his dish in the sink and opened the icebox.

There was the rest of the filling for the varenyky, cool and hard. There was the blackberry kvass, and a round lump of butter. There was the rolled dough that I hadn't used yet. I took it all into my arms. I cut the dough into diamonds and filled them. I let the varenyky sizzle in the pan.

As I waited, I saw a full glass of dark juice resting on the counter. I couldn't remember pouring it for myself, but I must have. It had the color but not the consistency of blackberry kvass. I snatched it up and downed it in one long gulp. It tasted of nothing, the way food always did in these moments.

I dropped sour cream onto a plate, and a heap of pickled cabbage beside it. I cut the rest of the bread into five fat slices and buttered them all. I spooned out my twelve varenyky, still steaming hot.

And then I ate everything, the black bread slick with butter, the pickled cabbage that made my eyes water, the sour cream that turned to a white film on my gums. I ate the varenyky even though they burned my tongue. I only tasted it in quick, hot bursts, the way you could still see the bright-orange splotches of lamplight after you closed your eyes. When I was finished, my heart was pounding and my chest heaving, and my stomach felt like a wineskin filled to its cork.

I did not want to risk seeing my father, so I took the back exit into the garden, through the disused maid's quarters. The doorframe was cobweb-crusted, wood swollen in the late summer heat. I pushed through it with a thrust of my shoulder and stumbled into a bed of dandelion weeds and thistle grass. Nettles seized the hem of my nightgown, and my bare feet sank into the soft dirt.

Out of the corner of my eye, I saw something brown and furry. Indrik was standing up tall on his hind legs, nibbling at one of our apricots. When he noticed me, he paused and trotted over, muscles bulging in his bare chest.

"You look distressed, young maiden," he said. "Would you like to call upon the might and magic of a god? I can shoot a star out of the sky and whittle it into a sword of immense power, or I can summon a bolt of lightning and strike down the lover who spurned you. Have you been spurned by a lover? Perhaps ravished by a group of drunken men? I have had many centuries to think of all the ways to punish those who wrong me and my devoted worshippers."

"No," I mumbled. "No, thank you. Please, Indrik, I'd like to be alone."

Indrik snorted through his nose, affronted, and then trotted away again. I heard the poor goblin scratching at the shed door, and Papa pacing the line of the fence. He was already muttering the magic that would keep us here. As many times as he had warned us with his words, he had never erected a proper spell before.

Undine was right; I *had* driven him here, with my pathetic flushing and trembling knees and the baldness of my wanting.

When Indrik's tail had disappeared behind an exuberantly green rhubarb plant, I leaned over, stuck two fingers down my throat, and vomited.

It didn't take long for everything to come back up, lubricated by the black juice. My throat was burning and raw. I wiped bile from my chin. As I did, Sevas's face hovered in my mind, his words caressing the shell of my ear.

I think it would make me very happy to see your face in the crowd, Marlinchen.

There was no use thinking of him. I would never see him again.

I knelt in the grass and buried my puddle of sick, dirt caulking under my nails. My stomach churned emptily now, and my mouth tasted greasy with acid. When I looked down, I noticed that vomit was streaked across my nightgown, the black color of the juice I'd swallowed. I cleaned my hands on a soft gray bushel of lamb's ear and stood.

Even as the memory drove knives into my heart, my mind turned over the name he had given me. *Sevas*, he had said, wrapped up like a china dish or an ostrich egg hollowed out and painted blue. A gift, and I had nothing to offer in return. Diminutives were a mystery to me; my sisters and I had names that eschewed diminutives. Rose's sweet, pretty nickname was one we only whispered to each other in secret, never in Papa's presence.

Papa had given us our confounding names on purpose. Undine, Rosenrot, and Marlinchen were not names for people in the city of Oblya, in the empire of Rodinya, in the smog-choked mortal world. They were characters in Papa's codex, monsters, maidens, minor gods. Marlinchens did not lose their fingers in the machinery of cotton mills; Rosenrots did not gag on tobacco smoke in the back rooms of cafés; Undines did not marry lecherous sailors from Ionika. Our names were the best spell that Papa had ever cast, better than rabbit's feet or burning sage. They were a veil of protection, a caul that never came off. I imagined my father murmuring a prayer for each of his daughters as he pulled us from between our mother's legs.

Let her eat black plums and never taste the poison. Let her bathe naked in a stream without ever drawing a hunter's wanton eye. Let all the bears she meets be friendly and pliant, and never men in disguise. Let her never fall prey to the banality of the world.

Let her never fall in love.

CHAPTER THREE

H ere is what happened to our mother.

You should know, of course, that there are only two kinds of mothers in stories, and if you are a mother, you are either wicked or you are dead. I told myself so many times I was lucky to have the dead kind. Further, when your mother is a witch, it is almost impossible for her not to be wicked, so our father married a pretty blushing woman who was not a witch at all. Most of the wizards in Oblya took mortal women as their brides, due to the fact that witches have a tendency to become wickeder when they become wives. Some, I had heard, even grew a second set of sharp teeth and ate their husbands.

I could hardly imagine having a witch as a mother. It would have been so dangerous! I pictured my sisters and myself cradled above boiling cauldrons, or reaching with our fat infant fingers toward capped vials of precious firebird feathers and bottled sirens' screams.

But our mother wasn't a witch. Before she was dead, she was pretty and quick to flush, with skin that reminded me of the inside of a conch shell, it was that smooth and pale. She had Undine's golden hair, bright as an egg yolk, and Rose's shining violet eyes. I got nothing from my mother except our identical half-moon nail beds, and maybe the little leap of our brows when we were surprised. I also inherited my mother's love for the fairy tales in Papa's codex, which was why she had wed him in the first place. She fell in love with the story more than she fell in love with the man. She told me so when she took me on her knee and used her comb to smooth the knotted coils of my hair, whispering her secrets into my ear.

She wed our father in the early days of gridiron Oblya, municipally planned Oblya, right before the tsar freed the serfs with the slash of his pen. The tsar's edict hacked up the land of the feudal lords like it was a big dead sow. My father wrapped his land in blood-soaked butcher paper and sold each parcel of it to the highest bidder—mostly Yehuli men, but some Ionik merchants as well. Meanwhile our mother worried in the foyer, her measured footsteps matching the ticks of our grandfather clock. She held me on her hip; Undine and Rose hid in her skirts.

The Yehuli man in the sitting room had a horned devil's silhouette, Undine said when she peered out. The Ionik man was soaking wet and had silverfish crawling all over his suit, Rose said. They left with Papa's land in their teeth, or so our mother said, and then she blew her nose into a lace doily. There was a water stain on the chaise longue that never came off.

Then Papa had only the house, and the garden, and half the number of servants that we used to because he had to pay them all the tsar's wage instead of mortgaging their work in exchange for tilling his squares of land. That was the time when our goblin came to us, weeping out of his one big eye, when the marshes were drained and made into the foundation of a beet refinery.

Our mother's tears splattered the mahogany floor. She wiped them onto the cheeks of our marble busts.

"My mother warned me not to marry a wizard," she sobbed. "What will we do now, Zmiy? There is no market for sorcery in Oblya, not anymore. The poor want to smoke narghiles in Merzani coffeehouses and play dominoes in gambling dens, and the rich want to build dachas along the shore and take mud baths at the sanatorium. No one wants to see their cat turned into a cat-vase, or their carriage turned into a gourd. There is already magic lining every road— electric streetlamps!—and inside every newspaper print shop—rotary presses!—and at every booth on the boardwalk where you can get a daguerreotype of your children for two rubles. They only charge two rubles for a photograph, Zmiy. How much do you charge to turn their parasol into a preening swan?"

"Quiet, woman," Papa said. "If you didn't want us to starve, you would have given me a son instead of three useless daughters." He didn't know, yet, that we were witches.

But he went anyway to one of the copy shops and asked them to print up a hundred notices that all said the same thing: Titka Whiskers asks for the gouged eye of a second-born son as payment for her work. Titka Whiskers has Yehuli blood. Titka Whiskers fornicated with a leshy and gives birth to stick and moss babies, and then they go out and brawl with the day laborers at night.

Soon all her clients fled from her doorstep in fear. Soon the Grand Inspector came and boarded up her shopfront and gave it to a Yehuli couple who opened a pharmacy. Soon Titka Whiskers was outside, pale-faced and dressed in dark rags, rattling our gate. I remembered her yellow eyes opening and closing sideways from behind the bars of the fence, her fingers so thin and white they looked already dead.

"Hear me, Zmiy Vashchenko," she called in her warbling crow's voice. "Never again will you feel sated after a fat meal. Never again will you wake refreshed after a long sleep. Never again will you look upon a sunset and marvel at its beauty. Never again will you look upon your daughters and feel your heart swell with vast and mighty affection. From now on your belly will always ache as if it is empty, and your eyelids will always droop as if you have not slept since your cradle days, and every sunset will look drained of its color, and your daughters will always appear to you like nettlesome strangers."

And then she closed her eyes and fell over and died. Her body turned into a mass of writhing black vipers, which leached into our garden like dark tree roots. It was another year before we finally trapped and killed the last one; our maid fried it in a pan and served it to my father with boiled potatoes.

He was already whittled as thin as a wishbone by then, and our mother had moved up to the third floor of the house, where she combed her hair for hours in front of the mirror that never lies and drank only sour-cherry kvass. I climbed the steps every day to see her, so that she could comb my hair, but I was too big to sit in her lap by then, and I was too afraid to look into the mirror that never lies.

"Don't marry a wizard, Marlinchen," she always said. "Your father is a dragon of a man. Even before the curse, he ate up everything his hands could reach. When he was young, he was as handsome as Tsar Koschei, and I was a fool. Wait for your Ivan, dear Marlinchen. He won't care that you are plain of face."

Papa guarded his codex on the very top shelf of his study, but by then both my mother and I knew the story by heart. I swallowed her words and let them harden in my belly like a seed.

Indrik came to us soon after, his chest stippled with hack marks from the miners' pickaxes. Eyeless ravens landed on our mulberry branches and sang in dead languages. Undine discovered her magic, and our father dug her a scrying pool. Rose discovered her magic, and our father planted her a garden. I was nine and still chewed on my knuckles at night.

All around us, Oblya gasped and panted like a woman in a too-small corset. Artisan schools and almshouses burst from between its ivory boning. An eye clinic and an electric station flowered up in two quick exhales. And then, at last, the ballet theater, with a breath that ripped the corset's seams and exposed Oblya's pale, heaving chest. Tourists walked from one of her bared nipples to the other, from the

Yehuli temple to the onion dome of the oldest church. They gathered at the ballet theater in the valley of her breasts, right above her beating heart.

The tourists were good for our business, too, but it made Papa so angry to listen to them chatter in their foreign tongues, to see the gold-lettered signs that said WELCOME! thrice-over in Ionik and Yehuli and Rodinyan. Travel brochures called Oblya the city with no infancy. They said it rose up like a mushroom after a rainstorm. I was ten and just starting to shiver when anyone touched me.

It happened in the middle of the night, the moon outside my window as slim as a lemon rind. There was a clattering over my head, and dirt shook from the ceiling. Voices dripped through the floorboards like water: my father's, low and rasping, and my mother's, low and wheedling. Something thumped the ground hard. And then there was only the sound of distant wings beating.

The next morning, our father sat us down at the long ebony table. "There has been an accident," he said.

"An accident?" Undine echoed.

"What kind of accident?" Rose asked.

I gnawed on my knuckle.

Papa took us upstairs to the third floor. The mirror that never lies was covered over with pale cloth. Our mother's comb gleamed like melted moonlight. Her gold charm bracelet had the bleary luminance of sunken treasure. And in the center of her room was a great gilded cage, and inside it a white bird.

"One of my transformations went wrong," Papa said. "This is your mother now."

"I hate you!" Undine shouted, and beat our father's chest with her fists. Rose began to cry quietly, one hand over her mouth. I approached the cage and stared at my mother, her body cut into white planks by the golden bars.

Later, I stole Papa's heavy codex from his shelf, but this time I did not read about Ivan and the tsarevna and the kingdom of winter.

I read all the stories about women who became birds, thinking there might be a spell to fix what my father had done. There was, of course, in our mother's and my favorite story: the tale of the tsarevna who became a bird and who was kissed back into her human skin by the handsome bogatyr who loved her.

Mama had told me to wait for my Ivan, but all the bogatyrs were gone.

In the stories there were helpful finches and hopeful doves, and ravens that cawed bad omens. There were grateful sparrows who thanked you for rescuing them from briar patches, and ruby-breasted robins who offered you their chirped wisdom. There were starlings and blue tits with human voices, and a woman-headed hawk that hatched eggs with thunderstorms inside them. There were, of course, firebirds with magic feathers that could tell the wicked and the good.

But there were no stories about wives whose wizard husbands had turned them into birds by accident; I could not even tell what kind of bird my mother was. I squinted at her as she plucked sunflower seeds from my cupped hand. She had violet eyes and a pure ivory plumage, and feet as yellow as egg yolks.

I was eleven, and I had discovered my magic at last, an uncommon talent that would have made me a darling of the Wizards' Council, if the Wizards' Council still existed. It was the closest to happy that I had seen Papa since his curse. He drew up posters advertising my services, and as he did he sang to himself, familiar words, turning the stories I loved into songs. For some reason my ears ached to hear them, like someone had rung a bell too loud and too close. Even for days after, in the silence, my body felt shuddery and weak, the echo of the music living on in my bones.

Men started to come for me. They were freed serfs and the sons of freed serfs, day laborers whose backs were hunched under the weight of their ugly work. They canned beets or washed wool or turned stinking tallow into soap beneath jaundiced factory lights; the happier ones drove trams and carriages or loaded cargo ships in the harbor.

When they came, I hid under my bed or in my wardrobe. I covered myself in the sheet that Papa had thrown over the mirror that never lies. He always found me eventually, and dragged me back down into the sitting room, and held me by the collar of my dress while the men laughed their vodka breath across my face.

Later, in the dark, I blew my shameful secrets through the bars of my mother's cage as if they were smoke rings, and stroked her soft white feathers. I wondered if she could still think like my mother, or if her mind, too, was a plum that my father's spell had left out to parch and wrinkle in the sun. I wondered whether her bird-heart still loved me, even if her bird-mind could not. I filled her water dish and cleaned her droppings long after my sisters had lost interest in her, like she was a darling kitten that had grown into an ordinary and ill-tempered cat. I was twelve, and it had been two years since anyone had taken a comb to my hair.

By then, we had no maids or servants left at all. I went up to visit my mother one morning and found her cage empty, the floor of it covered in droppings like banked coals and a layer of white down like new-fallen snow. The door was hanging open.

Despair sank its black teeth into my heart. I cried and cried, so loudly that I woke both my sisters and finally my father, who came lurching up the stairs and told me that my mother had gotten out of her cage and flown away.

"That's not true," I said, my nose running. "She wouldn't have left her mirror or her comb or her bracelet or her daughters."

"What do you need a bird-mother for? Come downstairs, Marlinchen," Papa said.

And I did, but first I took the charm bracelet off the boudoir and held it against my chest, cold metal seeping into the valley of my just-budding breasts. A dark red drop on the floor caught my eye; at first I thought it was a button that had come loose from Papa's coat. But I could see my reflection in it, warped and tiny, a minnow trapped in a dirty gather of rainwater. I felt as if my whole childhood was caught in that drop: my long, matted hair like dust gathering on a bald china doll, my father's hand around my wrist, my sisters' beautiful faces, my mother's shed tail feathers and the seed that her stories had planted in my belly, invisible to everyone but me.

I went downstairs and cooked my father varenyky with a filling that I could not remember making. I was thirteen.

In the days following Sevastyan's visit, I saw only three clients. Every time I heard someone rattle the gate, my head snapped up to see if Sevas might be standing there, and both despair and relief curled in my belly when he was not. In my mind, I stretched out the short conversation we'd had in Rose's storeroom into hours, like the last small bit of dough under a rolling pin, until it was so thin that it was translucent when you held it up to the light. I'd committed every single detail to memory: the shadow of his lashes on his cheekbone, his smirk and the arch of his brow, and of course the way he'd said *I think it would make me very happy to see your face in the crowd, Marlinchen.*

It didn't matter, of course. I could not leave the house without a bowl of black sand, and Sevas could not enter without being turned into black snakes, like Titka Whiskers. I ate very little those days, and tried to avoid the reaching vines of Papa's rage.

Three was a lucky number in all the fairy tales, but it was a very bad number in capitalist Oblya when it marked the sum total of the clients I saw in a week. The first was an Ionik dockhand who had an odd rash; Papa feared typhus and sent him on his way without even taking his pestilent rubles, then cast a cleansing spell over the whole house. It was just twenty years since the last pandemic, and if Papa had read the weather omens properly, it meant we were due soon for the next.

The second was a Yehuli skupshchik, a petty buyer, who wanted to know if he would find a wife soon. I did not like to make predictions about matters of the heart; they were too fickle and easily skewed, but he was asking about a wife, not about love. So I told him that his future bride was an enormously tall woman who wore a hat of quail feathers, and he would first be taken by her beauty and her height when he saw her drinking kumys on the boardwalk. I checked his shadow on the wall, but I didn't see any horns. The Yehuli man left with a spring in his step.

The third was one of my regulars, Fedir Holovaty, a carpenter who survived through odd jobs and a bit of grifting. His palms were always hard and bubbled with yellow calluses, and he was always short a kopek or two, but I liked Fedir so I saw him anyway, and cajoled my father into charging him less than the rest.

In truth, nothing was ever wrong with Fedir, not really. If he had a cough that lingered, he was convinced he had come down with the plague, even though we had not seen a case of it in Oblya or its environs in more than a hundred years; if a gash on his ankle resisted scabbing, he confessed to me in a tight, fearful voice that he thought he might have poisoning of the blood, and that a doctor would have to amputate his leg at the knee. So I did feel a bit guilty about taking any money from Fedir at all, but knowing how much we needed it, I kept letting him come back.

"Thank you very much, Ms. Vashchenko," said Fedir. This was after I had pinched both of his earlobes and fabricated a vision wherein the pounding of his head was only the result of his flatmate dropping a tankard on him while he slept, and not in fact the portent of a deadly fever, and also wherein he won the next three games of dominoes at his favorite Ionik coffeehouse. "All the other doctors in Oblya charge so much for their work, and most have stopped answering the door when they glimpse me through the letterbox. Dr. Bakay on Nikolayev Street measured my head and told me I had the skull circumference of someone who was a bit simple."

I did not entirely doubt Dr. Bakay's diagnosis, but my stomach clenched nevertheless. "You can come see me whenever you like, but perhaps next time, to save your money, you should try and wait to see if something is truly wrong."

"But what if I come too late?" Fedir asked. His brow furrowed miserably as I lifted my hands from his shoulders. "What if, by the time I come, there's nothing that can be done?"

"Then I will come to you," I said, ignoring the shape of my father in the threshold, tall and narrow as the first letter of a sentence. "Just call for me, and I will come."

When Fedir was gone, Papa swept through the room, mumbling another cleansing spell. I felt the weight of his magic and his anger settle over me, a cold mantle, and pulled at the ribbon around my wrist. It was hidden under the sleeve of my dress but still I feared that a keen-nosed spell might sniff it out.

There was a certain kind of newt that lived in gently trickling streams with particular configurations of river stones. The newts spent their whole lives in the same water, growing thick with moss and mold, and if a single stone was shaken out of place, they would die. Papa was like that. He could sense the smallest of disturbances, a hairline fracture in a marble bust, a debt gone unpaid, and he repaired and resettled it at once. Even a secret could shift the stones in Papa's stream bed.

"You should wash, Marlinchen," he said shortly. He had still not forgiven me for Sevastyan and Derkach, despite the exorbitant sum of money they had paid. Every hour since their visit had been wrapped in his frigid, silent fury like twine around sausage links. "The filth of our clients is on you, and I don't trust that Ionik man only had an allergy to prawns. Run yourself a bath upstairs. And then come back down, and I will check you and your sisters.

A bad feeling simmered in me, like the last bit of grease in a pan. "Papa . . ."

"Go, Marlinchen."

And so I did, picking my way up the stairs. I had only reached the second-floor landing when I ran into Undine leaving her room. I stumbled backward, uttering a noise of shock. I had last seen her out in the garden, sat beside her scrying pool, with a client whose face was turned away. Her legs were stretched out like bare birch branches and her blue dress was pulled up over her knee. The client's hat bill had been angled downward, tracing a line over the curve of her calf. Several yards away, Indrik had looked on unhappily and gummed a mouthful of chicory. There was an odd sullenness in his black eyes that had vexed me.

Now Undine drew herself up with a sharp breath, her blue eyes cold fire.

"Get out of my way," she spat.

I ducked my head and mumbled, "Sorry," but my eldest sister didn't move.

"This is all your fault," she bit out. "My last client tried to give me tickets to the ballet—*expensive* ones, orchestra seats. I told him that I couldn't. Because of *you*."

The icy rage in her voice reminded me of Papa. "I didn't mean to do anything."

"I should have known you couldn't be trusted. You're twenty-three and still quivering with lust over the first handsome face you see? Rose and I never should have brought you along. You've ruined everything for us."

And then she pushed past me, her shoulder clacking mine with such force that I stumbled backward, grasping at the banister to keep from tumbling down the steps.

I listened to my sister traipse down the stairs, gulping my breaths. Guilt pricked me all over like thorns. She was right; I had done this, and now none of us would ever see *Bogatyr Ivan* again. That story would be like all the others that sat heavy in my belly like a handful of seeds, spoiling, unable to bloom.

Biting my lip against the sting of tears, I went into the bathroom and locked the door. There was the porcelain tub, like a halved oyster, and the mirror that gleamed as brassily as a wet kopek. Slowly I unbuttoned my gown and let it puddle to the floor. The mirror seemed to look at me narrow-eyed, and my reflection rippled like water near to boiling.

As the tub filled, I watched myself bending over to twist the knobs, to scoop my fallen dress up off the ground, my belly folding, my breasts swaying. The first time I had seen my sisters dressing for the ballet I hadn't been able to keep from staring at the neat lines of their bodies and the unblemished whiteness of their skin. Their breasts seemed polite somehow, unobtrusive; certainly they would never be rude enough to split the seam on a bodice. Their shoulders were slim, their bellies soft and flat. I always imagined they could be easily stowed away in a wardrobe like a starched white dress, slipped in among a dozen identical others. Your gaze would skim right across their bodies; there were no crags to cling to, no crevices to fall in.

I had always thought of my body as something that needed to be tackled and brawled, pelted and pinned down and bruised into submission, then trussed up like a chicken and laced into a whalebone corset. In my childhood I'd wished for well-mannered breasts and an obliging belly, for golden hair and violet eyes. I'd searched for spells that would breathe magic into my wanting. My eyes were the color of weak tea and so was my hair, wavering unenthusiastically between blonde and brown. Taken with my skin, which had a sickly yellowish tint, I looked as if I were trapped in a tintype photograph, sepia-toned and unsmiling.

But I'd only found spells that could drain beauty from their targets like blood from a belly-slit animal, and they all promised some sort of gruesome reckoning for their jealous caster, hideous boils or being turned into a toad.

Magic was always like that: it had ugly undersides. Wanting anything was a trap.

Most days I could not even stand to sate my own hunger. The fullness of my belly was unbearable, but with two fingers jabbed down my throat I could make it all vanish, turning back my indulgence like a scratched record, undoing it and making myself clean and empty and new again.

I tugged at the ribbon on my wrist, filthy knot still holding fast.

On my other wrist was my mother's charm bracelet. I unclasped it as I stepped into the tub, holding it up above the frothing water. The charms rattled like a sack of lots to be cast. Once I was submerged to the throat, I twisted off the knobs and let my body drift, half-suspended. My hair floated around me in clumps of sand-colored flotsam.

I could feel the grime sloughing off me, the glaze of onion and cooking oil, Fedir Holovaty's fearful mists. Still holding my mother's charm bracelet with one hand, I scrubbed between my legs until my skin hurt, wishing I could wash Sevastyan's memory from me too. All my doomed and foolish desire. My body turned the bathwater a filmy gray.

I fondled my mother's bracelet, the chain leaving indents on my damp fingers. There were eight charms and I knew them all by touch alone: the tiny hourglass filled with real pink sand, the miniature bicycle with wheels that actually spun, the thimble-sized whale with a mouth that opened on a hinge, the bell that really rang. There was a golden box inside which a paper note was folded over a hundred times, fit so snug that I could not pry it out, even if I'd ever dared enough to try. I didn't know what the note said, if it said anything at all. There was a whistle that sang faintly when you blew into it, and an owl with little pearls for eyes. There was a book that opened up and had the names of my sisters and me etched onto its gilded pages, along with the years of our birth. I laid the bracelet over my face, the chain stretching from my brow over the slope of my nose, past the bow of my lips, the last charm dangling into my mouth.

I pried the little latch open with my tongue. I tasted all three of our names, tangy and sharp as a bite of bloody meat. That was the flavor of wet gold.

Soon I was clean and my thumb pads were pruning. I stepped out of the tub and dried myself and watched it drain, cloudy water spiraling downward. Halfway through, the pipes gave a choked protest, and the water ceased its circling.

I stopped toweling my hair. I knelt down next to the tub and dipped my hand into the gurgling water. When I pulled it out again, there was a small mound of black sand in my cupped palm.

A ragged breath tore out of me. I couldn't fathom how the pipes had spewed the sand out at me. Could it have been chafed off my skin, rinsed out of my hair? I hadn't been to the boardwalk in years, long before our mother had died. I could sometimes hear the tugboat horns from the garden, or smell the briny air seeping through my window at night, or see the gulls circling our house's wood-rotted turret.

And then panic struck me like a match. What would Papa think if he found it? He would know we had been gone, and he would be right, even if my sisters and I had never dared wander as far as the shoreline on our clandestine outings. He would concoct some punishment even worse than what he'd already done, and I couldn't even imagine what it would be, and that—the unknowing—terrified me to my marrow.

Hurriedly I scooped up all of the sand and shut it inside the clamshell compact lying on the edge of the sink. Inside it would mingle with our mother's white face powder and scratch away at the small, rust-flecked mirror, but at least it was hidden. I closed my finger around the compact, feeling its ridges. It was unmistakably heavy now, like the hunk of polished obsidian that Papa used as a paperweight.

Fear was a winged pulse in my belly. There were river stones shifting under me.

As if summoned, Papa's footsteps echoed up through the floor. I knew he was pacing the foyer, following his perfunctory route from the grandfather clock to the threshold of the sitting room, then back again. I put on my clothes and my mother's charm bracelet and hurried to my room. My thoughts were scattered like leaves. I flung open my wardrobe and tucked the compact inside one of my satin slippers.

A pair of red eyes blinked at me from under the bed. I combed frantically through my wet hair as I clambered down the stairs again.

Undine was already perched on the chaise longue, her face pale and drawn. When she saw me, her gaze narrowed like a knife blade. Papa's head swiveled, eyes pinning me to the wall.

"Go fetch your other sister," Papa said. "And do it quickly. The draught is already cooling."

I nodded and wordlessly went to the storeroom, my heart pounding in my throat. The smell of basil was leaking through a crack in the door. The weight of this new secret was like a sodden dress; I felt it clinging to me with every step.

Rose was bent over the table, butcher knife in hand, cutting the stems off sprigs of meadow rue. When she heard me, she turned around without dropping the knife and said, "Papa wants us, doesn't he?"

"Yes," I managed, not trusting myself with more words. The secret was stinging my tongue like a pinch of paprika.

"What's wrong, Marlinchen?" Rose came to me, frowning. "You don't have anything to fret over with the draught . . . do you?"

"No!" I said, heat rising in my cheeks. "No, of course not."

My objection was too vehement. Rose's brow furrowed. "You would tell me first, wouldn't you? Before Papa, of course, but also before Undine."

"I would never tell Undine anything I wasn't proud to speak aloud," I said, and Rose smiled at last, our mother's violet eyes filling with affection. She put the knife down on the table, patted both of my cheeks, and followed me out into the corridor.

Papa was leaning over Undine now, holding the capped vial in his fist. As a child, my oldest sister had been the one who wailed the loudest and the longest, the one who tearfully protested every perceived injustice. The years had bled most of that petulance out of her, but there was still a clear outrage even to her silences. Her fury lifted off her in vapors, like steam rising from boiled water. My shoulder still ached where she'd shoved me.

"Open your mouth, Undine," Papa said.

Her pink lips parted, eyes wavering with anger. He poured a bit of the red-black liquid onto her tongue, and she shut her mouth and swallowed.

Seconds trickled past us, the grandfather clock keeping their time. When the minute hand had gone a full circle, Papa gave a curt nod, and Undine let out a breath and stood and stalked out of the room at once. As she brushed past me wordlessly, I saw that her lips and tongue were dyed a garish red.

"Now you, Rosenrot." Papa beckoned her toward him.

I watched him pour a swallow of the potion into her mouth, feeling my damp hair drip down my neck and onto the carpet. The dark spot of water grew and grew. Rose licked her red lips.

After another moment, our father nodded. "Good. You can go."

She went, and it was only Papa and me. The flaps of his cheeks quivered under his beard. When I did step toward him, I could smell the breakfast I'd cooked for him on his breath: mlyntsi with cottage cheese and six boiled eggs, kasha with butter, and the last of our blackberry kvass. My own empty stomach began to roil.

He held my chin and tilted my head back and said, "I trust you, Marlinchen. You most of all."

The draught tasted as it did every time, like sulfur and ash, like the end of a tobacco pipe if you licked it. Tears gathered in my eyes as I swallowed, but Papa didn't notice and I was so glad, because this time I was more afraid than I had ever been.

Papa's potion was a test to see if we had kept our thighs unbloodied, our maidenheads unspoiled. I was always careful when I touched myself never to let my fingers slip too far inside, never to break what Papa wanted intact. He told us, too, what would happen if we drank the potion when we were ruined: we would vomit it back up along with our livers, and then he would hold up our own naked organs to us as proof of our deception, proof that we were thankless and debauched daughters who would sully the Vashchenko name.

Papa measured his own virtue by our virtues; our patronymic, he said, could not be noble and clean if there were any blackened, putrid parts. I knew that a single rotten branch would kill an entire tree, so he was right about that.

But I did not know the scope of his spell, how many lies the potion could dredge out of me. It had never made me spit up my other secrets before, but none had ever bloomed so quick and bright in my mind, like flowering marigolds.

The clock ticked its remorselessly steady rhythm.

Finally, Papa let me go. I put my hand to my mouth and wiped; my fingers came away smudged, as if with blood. My cheek stung where his nails had dug their small divots. My ribbon was still on my wrist, my compact was still tucked inside my slipper, and Sevastyan was still safe in the vault of my mind. My stomach lurched, but nothing threatened to come back up, least of all organs. I nearly shuddered to the floor in relief.

"You know why I have to do this, Marlinchen, don't you?" Papa asked, returning the empty vial to his pocket.

Another trap laid at my feet. "Yes, Papa."

"The city has taken so much from me. The tsar forced me to auction off my land to foreign tradesmen and scheming merchants, and watch them build apartments and factories and municipal banks upon it. I had to watch the tsaritsa coax foreigners to Oblya like a shepherd calling down his flock. I had to watch them tear up the beautiful steppe—do you know what they used to say about Oblya? That it was the place where two oceans met: there was the sea itself, and then the steppe, and the covered wagons that navigated it were like ships with white sails. They killed an entire ocean, Marlinchen. And there are so many little deaths as well. When the cotton-spinning factories ripped up the grasslands, they took with them the last steppe foxes. We on the Wizards' Council used to do so many spells with the fur or eyes or teeth of a steppe fox. I even used its tail once for a cleansing ritual— when I spoke over it, the tail flew up and swept the grime from the mantels and lampshades!"

We had all seen Papa's fox tail. I still used it every Sunday to dust the sitting room. But I didn't dare remind him of that. I was still dangling over his pit of spikes.

"But worst of all is how much they love it." Papa's hand was on my face again, thumb stroking my cheekbone. "You would think this town was forever on holiday, with how the night air is always filled with music and laughing and the tobacco smoke floating from cafés. The day laborers stumble drunkenly from flophouses to gambling dens with giddy smiles on their faces. I have to hear their joy in five languages. And the ballet theater, the wretched ballet theater. How many rubles did they spend to raise up that monstrosity, to lure performers from all over Rodinya, to costume them in feathers and gold? I have lost so much, Marlinchen—you understand that. The least they could do is not dance on the ashes of it all."

"Yes, Papa," I whispered.

He grabbed my face again, holding it tighter than before, and then kissed my forehead gently. "You have always been a sweet and dutiful daughter, better than your sisters. Sometimes I think your mother made you just to look after me when she was gone. So you understand that I have to keep you safe, and keep the rats from the door. They can wriggle in through the very cracks—Yehuli men, ballet dancers, the worst of this whole debased city. But the spell I've cast is a good one. If anyone from the theater tries to cross the threshold, they will turn to a mass of vipers, just like that infernal witch Titka Whiskers. I wouldn't even eat them, Marlinchen." He leaned close. "It would make me sick to my stomach."

At last he lowered his hand. I waited and waited, without breathing, to make sure all the daggers at my back had been sheathed, to make sure there was no steel in his smile. I knew I had been released when Papa turned and stalked toward the foyer, but I didn't sprint up to my room until I could no longer hear his footsteps on the floor.

Upstairs I knelt before my wardrobe and took the compact out of my shoe. In that brief, suspended instant when even the labored breathing of the monster under my bed had gone silent, I wondered if perhaps I had dreamed it. The black sand.

I lifted the lid of the compact. The mirror was flecked with tiny scratches, and the once-ivory powder was now an ashen gray. Salt-smell curled into my nose. I snapped the compact shut again.

Now the desire in my belly began to unfurl, like the smallest shoots of green. I could leave again, if I chose. And there would even be a good reason for it: I could imagine Sevas finishing his performance and running outside to retch again, Derkach finding him in the alley by a puddle of his own sick. He would rail against the guileful witch who had swindled him out of his rubles. He would march in an indignant fury back to our doorstep with Sevastyan in tow, and they would both turn into a spew of black vipers as soon as their boots crossed the threshold.

I remembered how Derkach's hand had closed over Sevastyan's knee. Perhaps the other outcome was worse—that Derkach visited his anger upon Sevas instead of me.

Either way I needed to warn him, and now I had the means to do it. But the thought of leaving alone made me grow dizzy and weak. Legs quaking, I stood. The heels of my slippers were still clumped with dirt. I shut the wardrobe door, my mother's compact clutched in my fist. The taste of Papa's draught on my lips was like bad mussels, like burnt rubber.

Downstairs there was a half-gutted chicken in the icebox. When evening came on and the sky turned a bruised violet I would cook its liver with onions and parsley. Papa would lick all the grease from the plate, and his magic would swell over our garden like varenyky stuffed to bursting, and I would not sleep for wondering if the next black snake I saw was Sevastyan.

I did not doubt Papa's spellwork. I had fed our mother from my hand for years.

I was halfway to Rose's room before I had even made up my mind. My hair was damp against the back of my neck and my heart was rioting in my rib cage. I knocked once and, hearing her voice on the other side of the door, pushed my way inside. My sister lay belly-flat on the bed, paging through her tattered herbalist's compendium.

"You look like you've seen Mama's ghost," Rose said with an

arched brow, propping herself up on her elbows. "What's wrong, Marlinchen?"

Suddenly all my words abandoned me. How could I explain the knot of fear and wanting that had coiled in my belly and was now curling up my rib cage? I had never bothered to tell either of my sisters Mama's and my favorite story. I knew they would just scoff and sneer at it, even Rose. Whatever my sisters' desires, they were not so bald or so childish or so damning.

I could confess neither my stupid hope nor my stupid terror, so in the end, all I managed to do was hold out Mama's compact. I flipped it open with my thumb and let the black sand trickle out onto Rose's carpet, and my sister's eyes grew wide as plums.

CHAPTER FOUR

Rose leapt off her bed and knelt on the floor and scooped up
as much of the sand as she could. She snatched the compact from my hand and poured it back inside, and all the
while I could hear her breathing in quick little gasps, and
her panic leached into me and soon I was on the floor beside her,
picking grains of black sand from the bristles of the carpet. Behind
me the closed door seemed to ripple and shudder, like a tin roof in
the rain. There was still a brine scent rising from the rug in a fine
mist.

"You must be mad, Marlinchen," Rose whispered, shoving the
compact inside the folds of her dress. "Where did you get this?"

I didn't know how to answer her. I could not even explain it to
myself. Black sand had somehow peeled off me in the bathtub and
then the pipes had coughed it back up. So I only told her that, because
it was all I knew, and then I told her how afraid I was that Sevastyan

would come back and it would be all my fault when he turned into a mass of vipers at our door.

I did not tell her about the way my hand had slipped between my thighs, or the way that I had spread that small bit of hope so thin that it wore out like an old stringy rag.

But my second sister was canny, and her eyes grew narrower and narrower until they were knives that cut right to the core of me.

"Why did you give him that herb mix?" Rose snapped, when I was done, and for a moment she sounded as angry and mean as Undine. "You could have woken me. I have draughts for men who can't keep their lips from the liquor bottle. Papa was right. You were stirred by that dancer. You *wanted* him to come back."

I had never learned how to lie to anyone, I realized, or perhaps I had never had anything worth lying about, any secret worth keeping. But upon opening my mouth to confess it, all that came out was a choked laugh. Of course my wanting would doom its object. Of course anything I desired would become a black snake in my hand.

"I can't let him end up like Titka Whiskers," I whispered, and even saying her name made my tongue burn like I'd sipped at scalding tea. That was how good her magic was—the curse hadn't even been directed at me, and yet it had its roots in me even after she was gone. "I couldn't bear it, especially knowing it was because of me."

Rose regarded me, her stare still perfectly cold. "Undine will try and take it from you, if she ever finds out."

"No," I said, shaking my head and shutting my eyes, as though I could armor myself against the truth of her words. "No, she wouldn't risk Papa's anger like that. She wouldn't risk breaking his spell . . ."

Yet I knew my sister was right. Undine wasn't clever like Rose, who knew exactly how much to fear Papa the same way she knew how much motherwort to add to a poultice, and she wasn't weak like me, who cowered at every clenched fist or sharp breath. She was vain, and cruel, and somehow had learned not to apologize for her wanting.

But what about my second sister? Rose only looked at me with calm, bridled anger. She had always been less enthusiastic than Undine about their midnight sojourns, and never tried to organize the outings on her own. Whatever desire she held closest to her heart, it was not orchestras or ballets or laughing and dancing in the street.

"What would you have me do, Marlinchen?" Rose asked at last. "The dancer will either return, or he won't. And now you've made it worse for all of us, with this black sand. Undine will tear out your hair and slap you pink until you hand it over to her, if she finds out. And if Papa finds out it will be worse."

"I know," I said miserably. "I'll get rid of it." The words spilled from my mouth before they had even flickered like a light in my mind. "I'll use it to leave once, to warn Sevas, and then we'll never see it again."

Rose's eyes shifted, suspicious as a cat's. "Just once?"

"Just once," I promised, and hoped she would believe me even though my voice trembled.

She exhaled, and a bit of the meanness leaked out with her breath. "I'm sorry for what's happened," she said finally. "If only Papa let us have anything of our own, you wouldn't pounce on the first pretty thing that caught your eye. It isn't your fault. And your witchcraft is just for showing; it isn't for doing or changing or making. That's not very fair either. I can help you a little bit, but you must promise me three things first."

I wanted to cry now, at her acquiescence. My nose grew hot as tears gathered in the corners of my eyes. A little hope started to gleam in me like a pearl. "Anything."

"First, you must take the black sand, and destroy it." Rose's gaze rested on me as heavily as steel, as if I were a bogatyr from the old stories who had just won the favor of a king. "I don't care what you do, but don't bring it back here. Use it to leave once, and then never again."

I nodded fervently, fisting the fabric of my dress.

"Second, you must return by the clock's strike of three, before the dawn lifts Papa's eyelids."

I nodded again. "Of course."

"And third, you must bring nothing more back with you. Your hands and pockets must be as empty as when you left."

It was only then that I realized what I had truly asked for, what she was giving me permit to do. "You want me to go out into Oblya alone?"

"Well, I'm not coming with you," Rose said. "It would be more dangerous if I did. Every gaze in the room turns to a Vashchenko girl when she walks in, and if there are fewer of us, perhaps it will draw fewer eyes. We can't have any word of this getting back to Papa."

That was why Rose was kinder than Undine. Even vexed like this, she tried to protect my feelings. We both knew I would draw no gazes, lascivious or otherwise. I was ugly in the most forgettable sense, like the unmatched silverware in a drawer, the dull knife that your hand passed over without your brain supplying a reason why.

Rose stood up and went to her boudoir and brought back Mama's ivory-handled comb. Lips pressed thin, she started to brush through the tangle of curls, and I felt myself go weak a little in the knees; although her strokes were rougher than Mama's, it was so rare an occasion that anyone tended to me.

But when she reached for her box of ribbons, I said, "Papa will see me when I bring him his supper and he will think something is wrong if there's a ribbon in my hair." So she left my hair down.

I did not mention that I still had her filthy pink ribbon knotted around my wrist, hidden under the sleeve of my dress.

And so with my hair loose around my shoulders I went and cooked Papa's dinner: the chicken liver with browned onions and parsley and a splash of spiced wine, because I thought it might make him fall asleep faster, or stay asleep longer. Pouring it over the chicken made the pan hiss with steam and droplets of grease leap up at me and it felt like the most dangerous thing I had ever done.

The whole time I was breathing shallowly, wondering if I was pouring my secret in with the wine. What if Papa could taste my deceit like a growth of rot when he put the food on his tongue? I served up the liver with kvass, my fingers quivering. When I lifted the tray, it was almost unbearably heavy, and my legs were burning by the time I made it to Papa in the sitting room.

"Thank you, Marlinchen," he said, like he always did, and picked up his fork. I shut my eyes as he took his first bite.

In the silence, I heard him chew and wet his lips. I heard him sip the kvass and then put the glass back down on the cloven-footed table. I didn't open my eyes again until he asked, "Is there any more bread?"

Blinking, I stared down at his plate. My lie was there, like bits of eggshell, or a stray hair, but he had eaten without noticing it.

"Yes," I managed, and then went into the kitchen to cut more black bread with butter.

Finally, supper was done and Papa had gone to sleep. The sky was the color of blood welling under a nail. I ate two slices of the black bread myself and every bite hurt to swallow.

Upstairs, Rose was waiting in my bedroom. She tussled with my hair for nearly half an hour before managing to pin up half of it in a precarious meshwork of braids that looked like a heap of fishbones all piled on one plate. The rest curled down my back, heavy as a tablecloth. I got out my pink dress again, and my dirty slippers, and clasped my gold charm bracelet. On the other wrist I wore my pink ribbon, the one that Sevas had returned to me.

Rose helped me lace my corset, and inside my bodice, right between my breasts, she placed Mama's clamshell compact.

"Destroy it, Marlinchen," she said, holding my chin in her hand. "Don't be selfish."

I nodded, unable to speak. The metal was already beginning to warm against my skin.

"You'll have to take this, too, or else you won't be able to find your way home." Rose thrust toward me a sachet the size of a closed fist, the drawstring pulled tight. "Drop one of them every few paces, and then follow the trail back. Juniper berries leave the blackest stains." She tied the sachet around my wrist with a red ribbon. "And this too." She produced a small vial and tied this one with a second ribbon around my throat. "It's a tincture for bravery. All you need to do is smell it."

Her kindness struck me with such a dizzying lurch that I couldn't help but lean forward and hug her, the sachet pressed between our collarbones. I breathed in the smell of lemon balm and rosemary, and a whiff of spearmint that came on as if it were an afterthought. When I let her go, I could already taste its burn at the back of my throat, like a swallow of hot air, and then when it reached my belly it quelled all the nervous roiling. I felt like I did after I vomited: everything clean and empty, and my mind sharp and clear as glass.

"Thank you," I whispered.

Rose kissed both my cheeks. "Come back by the strike of three, Marlinchen, and remember—nothing in your hands or pockets."

I nodded.

"One night," she said, her voice grave now. "One night to indulge this foolish desire, and then no more."

I understood that she did not mean it cruelly, but all I could think of was how I had fed our milking cow her favorite sugared plums before we slaughtered her for Papa's supper and hoped that at least she could still taste the sweet on her tongue when we slit her throat.

Without my sister's tincture I might have been more afraid of crossing the threshold, of the door creaking shut behind me, of Papa's spellwork filling the air. I was afraid, too, that Undine might see me leave, though it was not so much the fear of her mean words or her stinging slaps. It was that she might take the black sand from me and use it for herself. The black sand was the only secret I'd ever had. The only thing that belonged to me and me alone.

The crickets' chirped lullabies guided my sprint through the garden, through the clutching roots and the tangling vines. I pushed open the rusted gate and hurled myself into the street, and when it closed after me, I could hear the metal latch sing.

I had done it. I had left, and now Oblya's black roads stretched out in front of me like bolts of silk unfurled. I drew a breath of lemon balm and pried open the sachet around my wrist, letting the first of Rose's berries tumble out onto the cobblestones. It landed right in the gridded shadow of our fence.

My first and second steps were so light I scarcely felt the ground under me. And then before I had realized it, I was all the way at the end of our street and turning onto the main concourse that led to the theater.

Puddles of lamplight littered the street like dropped rubles. Shining storefronts and cafés with green awnings scrolled past me, spewing tobacco smoke and laughter. Men in groups of four or five loped down the road, their faces bright and damp, their eyes gleaming with the eagerness of a boy-knight, of a not-yet-bogatyr, on his first jaunt.

I veered carefully away from them, but they didn't even seem to notice me. Music piped from open doors and cracked second-floor windows. Just on Kanatchikov Street, I counted four languages. If it weren't for Rose's tincture, I might have frozen there, foreign words dribbling into my ears, trying to determine which consonants and vowel sounds spelled danger.

But I had her magic, and more, I had a goal set out in front of me, and only one night to taste the sweet thing that my tongue wanted, to fill the aching hunger in my belly. So I kept a brisk pace down the concourse, loosing a juniper berry every third step.

At last there was the theater, which ringed the plaza like a fine bracelet, its white facade as bright as a boiled chicken bone. The fountain was bubbling cheerily for no one; I had come too late and the crowd was gone, the doors closed. Even breathing in the tincture I felt a bit of panic turn loose in me and go skittering up the notches of my spine.

Briskly I paced through the courtyard, past the fountain, right up to the theater, and then turned down the alley to the left. The cobblestones were slick and pooling with oily light, just enough for me to see the door on the side of the building. My memory painted silhouettes on the wall: there was Sevastyan, bent over and retching, and me crouched beside him, both of our faces black and featureless. I blinked and our shadow puppets vanished, and I was staring only at the shut door that Sevas and Aleksei had gone through.

I had made up my mind to wait outside and I was practicing what I would say, even though I knew there was a good chance my words would dissolve in my mouth like a sugar cube. Then, not thinking at all that it would work, I tried the handle.

The door swung open easily. I gave a little gasp of shock and leapt back, and through the crack there leaked a staggering golden light and the swell of orchestral music. Very carefully I stepped through the threshold, bathing just the toe of my shoe and then the rest of me in that amber warmth.

The crimson velvet curtains rippled. I was half-cloaked in the shadow of the state box, where Oblya's gradonalchik, the city chief, watched over the brim of his profuse mustache. After a beat I ducked farther behind one of the marble pillars. From this vantage point I could see only a sliver of the stage, just the honey-bright wood and the white slippers of the snow-maidens.

Then came the oboes and the snarling drums and there was Ivan, sauntering up to the Dragon-Tsar. Even though I knew how it all would end, that the Dragon-Tsar would die, I held my breath and my heart rattled like kopeks in a can. I peered out from behind the pillar, straining onto the tips of my toes.

Sevastyan's bare chest was gleaming, his shoulders coiled and ready. Never had I felt so flushed with the lustful violence of it all, not when I was sitting fists clenched between my two sisters or later that evening. Never before had such a heat risen in my cheeks while I watched Ivan's blade lash out quick as a tongue and the Dragon-Tsar crumple like a black pine lightning-struck.

Biting down on my knuckle, I wished for more gore than just the ruby cloth strewn over the tsar's false wound. I wanted to see Ivan's sword thick with real blood, the viscosity and the sheen of boiled cherries. I wanted to smell the wet copper smell of it in the air. That feverish yearning pulled me through time, as if I were a puppet on a string. The rest of the show whorled obliviously past me: Ivan and the tsarevna's mimed kissing and the Celebration of the Snow-Maidens and the erection of Oblya proper, the painted skyline rolling up behind them and all the flutes trilling happily. Finally I took my chewed knuckle out of my mouth.

When the curtains drew shut, my cheeks were still burning and I could hear nothing but the manic pulse of my own blood. But seeing the audience rise to their feet woke me; I would be trampled if I didn't move, and suddenly I remembered the heavy metal between my breasts. I turned toward the door, but already the crowd was pressing in.

Panic rattled my teeth. I couldn't smell Rose's tincture at all. *Oh,* I thought as a woman's sharp elbow caught me in the ribs. *I've made a bad mistake.*

And then the sound of my name arced above the heat and the noise. I turned and saw Sevastyan trotting down the steps that led off the stage, and I thought I had imagined him saying *Marlinchen* until the crowd parted for him and he was standing right in front of me.

He was still painted in gold and wearing his feathered mantle, and his chest was still heaving but there was no muddle of vodka in his gaze, nothing between his eyes and mine. I felt oddly naked then, even though he was the one bare-breasted. I felt stared to my marrow, looked at in a way people only ever looked at my sisters. It was like someone were fishing for coins in a fountain and had finally closed their fingers around the one that was me.

Pink-cheeked, I dredged up the words from the very bottom of my belly. "I need to tell you something."

"I can't hear anything when we're standing out here," said Sevastyan. Already three women had stopped to gawk at him, their mouths unlatched and falling open. "Come with me."

He turned, and I was so numb with shock that I could do nothing but follow him through the ebbing crowd. Perfume and tobacco smoke turned the air hazy, and the scent of Rose's lemon balm grew fainter and fainter. I started to seize up like a rabbit hearing a branch snap, and with a twitch of panicked instinct I reached out and grasped at Sevastyan's feathered cape.

He looked back at me, blinking in surprise, and I let go again with a vicious flush. But he read the fear on my face as calmly as a broker read the price of wheat on the weekly stock report, and then he took my hand in his.

I hoped he could not hear the choked noise I made as he led me up the steps, and behind the drawn curtain, to a narrow corridor lined with small doors. He stopped in front of the one that said his name and opened it, then pulled me inside after him.

By the time I could get my hand away my palms were slick. A bit of him was seeping into me, like little shoots of green. I saw behind my eyelids the smear of a memory, gauzy and brief: someone's belt buckle glinting. A film of sweat chilled my brow. If I was touched long enough, held tight enough, my magic stirred and showed me things, no matter how much I ground my teeth against it.

It was an awful feeling, to draw secrets like blood, without the person even knowing that the needle was in them.

"I've never had a girl make me feel so loathsome before," Sevastyan said.

We were standing in the same dressing room that I'd seen in my first vision, the boudoir mirror hurling our reflections back at us. "What?"

"You let go of me so quickly I thought I might have been bruising your hand, but now I wonder if you just find me repugnant."

"No, I—"

"And you were so eager to get me out of your house that day, you and your father both. I can't help but conclude that your stomach turns at the very sight of me. I know I didn't make the finest of first impressions, retching on your shoe in a half-lit alley, but—"

"*No*," I managed, nearly stumbling upon just the one word, cheeks furiously warm. "I don't find you repugnant. I didn't want you to go, but my father was furious. You don't know what his rages are like. And this time, it was my magic that pulled me away. I don't want to drain your secrets from you."

Sevas only stared at me, a bright cheer in his blue eyes. He loosened the feathered cloak and let it pool at his feet. "Well, I'm happy to know I don't repulse you."

If he'd known what was really running through my mind when I'd stood with him in Rose's storeroom, he'd have me thrown out of the theater for obscenity. The thought only deepened my flush.

Sevas began picking at the gold paint on his shoulders and chest, the lacquer flaking off him like rust. Where a bit of it peeled away I could see the beginnings of black ink, symbols scrawled along the line of his collarbone, down his forearm, over the back of his hand. I squinted at them, for a moment all my flustered panic vanishing, and asked, "What are they?"

"Blessings," he said, and drew his thumb across the one on his shoulder blade. "Some of them, at least. My mother wanted me to take a copy of the holy book with me when I left for Oblya, so I told her I would compromise and get her favorite prayers inked on me, instead. When I came home from the tattoo shop she threw the book at my head."

I could recognize the letters from the storefronts in the Yehuli quarter. "Why?"

"Because the tattoo artist was a Rodinyan man who misspelled our word for heaven?" A smile pulled up one corner of his mouth. "No, I'm only joking. More likely because my people have prohibitions against inking your skin. But there's hardly anything in life worth doing that doesn't make *somebody* angry. They say they won't bury you in one of our cemeteries, but why should I care what happens to my body after I die? Cook up my heart and liver if you have a particular craving for the flesh of Yehuli men, though I think I'd be a bit gamy with all my years of dancing."

As he spoke, he drew a white blouse over his head and buttoned it to his throat. I couldn't help my mouth falling open a little bit, trying to square the humor in his voice and the glimmer of jest in his gaze while he spoke of such gory things. I saw Ivan's wooden sword lying across the boudoir; from this close it looked even more obviously like a prop, the silver paint offering none of the luminance of real steel. Sevastyan ran his fingers through his hair, disheveling it with careful intention.

Then he began to strip off his stockings.

"Wait," I choked out. "I can go—"

He glanced up, brows quirked. "I don't have much of my modesty left to preserve, Ms. Vashchenko, so don't leave on my account. But if it's your propriety you're worried about, feel free to turn around."

I did, my face as hot as a stovetop. With my back to him, I whispered, "Marlinchen."

"Marlinchen," he said. His voice sounded odd when I couldn't see his face, quieter somehow, more like a boy's than a man's. "I didn't forget. But since I'd started wondering if you despised me, I thought you might prefer me to address you with some formality."

"No," I said, still staring with utmost concentration at the wall. "There are three Ms. Vashchenkos, and only one of them is me. Whenever I hear it I always think someone is asking after my sisters."

I heard Sevas draw a breath. "You can turn around now, if you'd like."

Cheeks still burning, I did. Sevas was now wearing black trousers, his flesh-colored tights balled up and abandoned on his boudoir. Looking at him, the beautiful line of his mouth, the bright, clear blue of his eyes—all rational thought flooded out of me.

"I really am glad to see your face again, Marlinchen," he said. "I wasn't sure that I would."

The softness and uncertainty in his voice drew forth a memory: Derkach's hand closing over his knee. It reminded me that I had come to the theater with a purpose. I drew a breath, tasting the lemon balm from Rose's tincture and letting the courage leak into my stomach, and said, "I really do have something to tell you."

Sevas assumed a solemn look. "Go on."

All at once my words curdled like bad cream. He would think I was a fool, maybe a madwoman, a witch with her Old World ways, a slave to the moth-eaten lunacy of her father. That's what the other Oblyans thought of us, when they weren't staring down my sisters' dresses, and even sometimes when they were. Their debasing curiosity drew them to our doorstep, a magic that seemed sometimes even more powerful than the fear my father tried to instill in them.

To the women we were party stories, yarns spun between close faces. To the men we were imagined conquests, a dreamscape wherein they acted out their wickedest fantasies, the ones they would never inflict upon their sweet, blushing mortal wives. They asked my sisters and me if we fornicated with our father, or with each other, and the thought seemed to make them perversely aroused. I had watched so many mustaches grow sweat-damp as the men picked apart my answer with their teeth, biting down on the lusty bits. If I flushed, it was as good as a confession, and more fodder for their vulgar dreams.

Sometimes I thought of telling them what they wanted to hear, reciting all the tawdry details that I could already see playing behind their eyes. Sometimes I thought of telling them what really happened after I crawled into bed at night: how I imagined clipping off my nipples with Rose's gardening shears, two neat cuts so that they fell like flower petals, bloodless and pink. I imagined pulling back the band of white flesh around my nail, peeling it in spirals like potato skin, until my whole hand was gloved in red. I visited upon myself one small violence after another, inside the safe bunker of my mind. I concluded that it would probably arouse them too; sometimes I even felt myself go slick under the sheets.

But Sevas was not looking away from me, though it certainly had been too long since he'd said a word, and my face must have looked flushed and miserable. I thought of the way he'd spoken about such horrific things without flinching, and I found within me a courage to speak too.

"My father is a great wizard," I said at last. "He can fill the air with a mist so cold that it makes you freeze and tremble while your mind goes black with terror. He can pry open your lips and see the lies pooling on your tongue before you've even said them aloud. He can build glass walls that you can't see but that never shatter, and holes in the floor that you don't notice until you've fallen into them. But he likes transformations best of all. When Oblya was older, or newer, his clients would pay him whole sacks of rubles to turn their pocket watches into water clocks or their music boxes into songbirds. He even turned my mother into a bird, by accident. But because the Rodinyans came and started transforming gas lamps to electric and changing fields into factories, my father doesn't see clients anymore, just my sisters and me. He says that now Oblya has no appetite for his brand of magic, and so he hates all the Rodinyans, and the ballet theater most. He was so angry when you came that he put a spell over the whole house, so that no one from the theater could cross the threshold again or else they'd be turned into a mass of black snakes. Last time a witch turned into vipers at our door my father ate them. And since I'd given you the wrong elixir I was afraid you would come back, not knowing about the curse, and maybe I wouldn't even realize it until I was sitting in the garden and a black snake slithered over my shoe."

I was so breathless by the time I finished that I had to put a hand up against the wall to steady myself. Sevas blinked once, lips parting, and I thought he was preparing to laugh me out of his dressing room. After another moment passed, he said, "Thank you."

"What for?"

"For warning me," he said. "For treating me at all. If your father is as powerful and cruel as you say, it was kind of you not to turn me away." His gaze drew up and down me, and then I saw the tips of his ears go pink as dawn. "He must not know that you're here now, in the loathsome ballet theater with its most loathsome principal dancer."

Fear noosed me like a yoke, and not even Rose's tincture was enough to stop it. "No, he doesn't. But he's not cruel; he only cares for his daughters so much that it terrifies him, the thought of anything happening to us."

I was too afraid to say more, like speaking it aloud might imbue the words with a magic that would make them real. Sometimes I did wonder if my father would kill my sisters and me, rather than lose us to the world. I considered, not infrequently, that we would be safest in ashes and in urns.

"So now I've told you," I went on, my voice wavering, "and now you know not to ever come back. I can give you the right elixir so that Derkach won't be angry. My sister has draughts to keep men's lips from liquor—"

"I'm not a completely hopeless sot, you know," Sevas said, and he nodded toward the glass bottle under the boudoir, still a few fingertips full of clear liquid. "You'll be pleased to learn I haven't touched any vodka since I came to see you, and not just because Derkach has been more hawkeyed than usual. I can't say I have too much experience with sorcery, but I didn't think breathing the smell of borage would keep half a liter of vodka from coming back up. And I didn't want to bring Derkach fuming to your door and rile your father even more."

Several more moments ticked by before I realized he'd done me a kindness. Just as I hadn't wished to visit Derkach's anger upon him, he hadn't wished to visit my father's anger upon me.

We stared at each other from across the warm and narrow dressing room, him nearly a head taller than me, both of our brows dewy with sweat, my baby hairs curling out of Rose's careful braids. Everything looked golden and bright, like sunlight through a jar of kvass, and my father's house felt so tremendously far away. Even the air tasted sweet and my desire curled its long tendrils out of my belly, blooming in the light and the heat.

Sevastyan opened his mouth, and my breath caught as I waited for him to speak. And then there was a scuffling noise followed by the door clattering open.

It was the other dancer, Aleksei, his right cheek smeared with fiery orange paint. When he saw me he gave a low chuckle and said, "Taisia is going to strangle you with her stockings."

"It isn't like that," Sevas said, but his ear tips were still discernibly pink. "Though she did watch me undress."

"I turned around!" I protested. Sevastyan was grinning now, and Aleksei was laughing, some joke happening in the space around me, and even though it went vaporous between my fingers I didn't sense any sharp edges to their smiles. No lidded meanness in their eyes. I felt welcomed in the laughter. I could not remember the last time I'd been part of something so warm.

"We should get out of here before Taisia starts shrieking and Derkach starts scolding," Aleksei said. His gaze drifted vaguely toward my half of the dressing room; if he recognized me as a Vashchenko girl, a witch, he made no mention of it. "Is your, ah, friend coming with us?"

My heart leapt, and yet I found I could not speak. It would be foolish to go, selfish, to tempt the hours that Papa slept, to test Rose's patience. She had to be pacing the floorboards now, waiting for me to come home. I felt I had to make a perfunctory protest, even if it made my stomach shrivel like a wilting violet.

"I can't," I said quietly. "My father . . ."

Aleksei turned to Sevastyan with a look of great dismay. "Please tell me you haven't chosen another girl whose father can sharpshoot."

"He was a half-deaf veteran of the Rodinyan Imperial Army and he owned a rusted flintlock. Always the dramatics with you, Lyosha. And no, even better. Her father is a wizard who wishes to turn me into a mass of black snakes."

"I thought wizards in Oblya went the way of spinning wheels," Aleksei said, though he didn't seem particularly bothered by the existence of a wizard, or by the prospect of his friend becoming an abundance of vipers. His accent, I noticed, was Rodinyan too. All the wizards in Rodinya had been gone even longer.

"It *would* be just my luck, to draw the ire of the very last wizard in Oblya," said Sevas, as he buttoned his jacket. He turned to me. "But if your wizard father doesn't know you're gone, what could be the harm in staying out a little longer?"

At that, Rose's words drifted through my mind. *You must return by the clock's strike of three, before the dawn lifts Papa's eyelids.* It could be no later than eleven now, and so many hours stretched out between me and Papa's waking. But there were a thousand dangers that waited along the way, in the streets of Oblya or the hallways of our house, where Papa might rouse early, hunger-ridden, and pass by my empty bedroom.

Yet none of that seemed to matter now, all my imagined protests vanishing like smoke. Rose had given me one night to indulge my headiest, most foolish desire—when else would I have such a chance spread out before me like a table full of treats? I smelled the lemon balm and the rosemary and the sharp note of spearmint and it went down my throat and hardened in my belly, giving me the courage my sister had promised. With it was the pull of want between my thighs, and when I stared at Sevastyan he stared at me back.

The whole room went wonderfully hazy, like it was all a waking dream. If it was really a dream, it was the sweetest I'd ever had, and I didn't yet want it to end.

I found myself following the curve of Sevas's sharp, bright smile, my own lips parting in turn as I asked, "Where are we going?"

CHAPTER FIVE

Oblya at night was so full of color and noise that I didn't know how I had ever been afraid of it.

Happy couples held hands in the puddled glow of streetlamps. The storefront awnings were turned upward at the corners, like smiles. Trams and carriages clattered by, and the horses pulling them were cheerfully huge, like circus bears in ruffled collars. We passed the cafés and restaurants on Kanatchikov Street and I no longer worried that the foreign words would snare me like fishhooks. So many eyes passed over me, but none lingered with suspicion or malice. I figured it must help that I was flush between Sevas and Aleksei, who were pulling me along through the street, laughing in wisps of pale smoke, though I could scarcely feel the cold.

Was Oblya like this every night? I wondered. While I pressed my face into my pillow and a flock of gory things came to roost in my mind, was the city awake and bright outside my window, heaving with a life that was unknowable to me?

Once I had picked up a large stone from our garden and saw what looked like hundreds of small creatures moving and writhing underneath, tiny snakes with red bellies and long insects with a thousand scything legs, woodlice and pill bugs and beetles with iridescent shells. I'd gotten so frightened that I'd run inside and hid upstairs in my bedroom, and I hadn't gone into the garden for nearly a year after.

It wasn't that I was so scared of red-bellied snakes and centipedes; they were harmless, I knew that much. I was more afraid that every time I walked through the garden, I was trampling hundreds of living things without even realizing it.

And now, seeing all the joy and merriment before me, I became similarly afraid to impinge upon it. Oblya was no danger to me, but I felt, for one stretching moment, that *my* touch was ugly and ruinous. What did this city care for a plain-faced witch with too-long hair and only carnage behind her eyes?

But somehow the thoughts sloughed off me. I didn't know if it was Rose's tincture or simply that Sevas was standing so close, the heat of our bodies mingling in the knife-slit of space between my arm and his. He led me to a tavern with dark and narrow windows and two gas lamps guttering on either side of the door, which was cracked open and leaking black smoke.

For a moment I shrank back, chest constricting with imprecise dread, and Sevas said, "The most dangerous thing inside is the vodka. I hear it once made a man go blind."

Aleksei snickered and slipped through the door, vanishing into the crowd of people. I hesitated in the threshold still, thinking of Papa's stories about taverns full of foreign men who turned to blood-drinking upyry after sunset. But he'd not been quite right about Ye-huli men—not quite right about a few other things too—so I steeled myself with a breath of lemon balm and followed Sevas inside.

The tavern was brighter than I had expected, with a whole space set out in the very center for dancing. Under my feet the floor was sticky. The left wall was gleaming from floor to ceiling with liquor bottles, green and brown and white, some of them clear and jewel-hued and the others frosted like sea glass. There were women inside, too, which took me by surprise. I stared at their rolled tobacco curls and their painted lips, the overbright rouge on their cheeks, the way they fingered their slender pipes and brought them to their crimson mouths. Looking at them I felt more and more like an underfoot child. These women laughed daintily, coquettishly, like they were spilling swarms of tiny butterflies from their mouths.

Sevas took me up to the bar, the wood slick-looking in the amber light. Before I could stop him, he ordered two glasses of vodka. He must have seen my face blanch.

"You don't have to drink it," he said. "But it's rude to let a lady sit empty-handed at a tavern. All the other patrons would think so poorly of me if I didn't buy you something my reputation would never recover from it."

I could not tell if it was another jest. I looked around to see if there were any other women without drinks in their hands, but our glasses arrived soon after and Sevas lifted his into the air and told me, "It's also rude not to cheers," so I picked mine up, too, and our glasses clinked together with a sound like silvery bells.

He drank, and I held the glass up to my face and took a dubious sniff. It smelled worse than any of Papa's potions. It smelled like what I used to scrub the rings of soap from our bathtub. Maybe it had the same kind of magic as the apples in our garden, or one of Rose's bubbling elixirs: maybe it tasted as sweet as peach kompot if you could pinch your nose shut against the awful stench. I tried the smallest of sips, and it scalded my throat so badly that I began to cough and splutter.

Sevas leaned forward with grave concern. "Please tell me I haven't killed you. There are some stories I've heard where witches burn up at the taste of vodka."

"I'm not that kind of witch," I said. My tongue felt fuzzy and thick, but my mind remembered the stories he was talking about.

Those kinds of witches were long-extinct forest hags who gave shelter to young girls with cruel stepmothers, on the condition that they perform all sorts of tedious, miserable chores. "How can you stand to drink so much of it?"

"It gets easier with every swallow," he said. "Like anything, really. If you do it for long enough it stops hurting. Then other things stop hurting. I thought I would die the first time I did a grand jeté. That's the great leap where your legs are stretched out as far to either side as they will go. I thought the insides of my thighs would never cease their aching; I thought I would never manage to get high enough, or stay in the air long enough. But ballet is a sport of attrition. The best instructors are war generals. You have to beat your body until it obeys you. And this," he said, holding up his glass, "helps."

I had to keep myself from telling him that I often thought of my body the same way: uncouth, deserving of debasement. "To the audience, you know, you look as graceful and free as a seabird. It looks like the easiest thing in the world."

"Of course it does. That's the mark of a good dancer. Just like the mark of a good drinker is one who swallows vodka without wincing, with a smile on his face." Sevas drained the rest of his glass and grinned at me over the brim. "Have you never tried any before?"

"No," I said. "My father wouldn't let us. He says that liquor is the refuge of weak-minded men with something they want to forget."

Sevas put a hand to his chest. "I've never been so thoroughly eviscerated by a man I've only once met. Is that his sorcery, to make such cutting assessments of character?"

"He's wrong about that." Even so far away from our house, it gave me a little thrill of fright, to say such a thing. "No one with a weak mind could dance the way you do, and drunk besides."

"Do you mind if I tell Derkach as much?" Sevas's mouth was smiling, but there was an odd quiver in his eyes, brisk as the wind through dead leaves. "He shares your father's concerns. He thinks I'm incorrigible, and since arriving in Oblya it's been even worse. But I can't help that there are twice as many taverns here as in Askoldir."

I thought of what Rose said: that he had his whole life ahead of him, and nowhere left to go. "Were you happy to leave Askoldir?"

Sevas shrugged. "I left my family there, my mother. But I hadn't seen much of them since I was young anyway. When you show some promise as a dancer, the ballet companies pluck you up and place you with a handler and make you spend long hours at the studio and take you on tours across the country. As Derkach said, I've been in his care since I was twelve years old."

His voice dropped off, like something being kicked down a great flight of stairs. Silence stretched between us; Sevas ordered another drink. I remembered the look of Derkach's hand on his knee and wanted to say something about it, but Sevas was already smiling again, and asking me, "But do you know one of the greatest benefits of vodka?"

I shook my head.

"Well," he said, pausing to drain the vodka in my glass and then setting it down on the counter again, "it gives one the courage—or insouciance—to do things like dance in taverns."

He had already taken my hand and begun to lead me out onto the floor before I realized what he meant. "Oh no," I said. "Please. I don't know how—"

"Marlinchen," said Sevas, with a bit of impatience, "you are with the Oblyan ballet company's principal dancer. No one will notice your missteps."

"Or perhaps they'll only be thrown in harsh relief by your grace and assuredness." My face was burning.

Sevas considered that. "A compromise," he said.

And then he put an arm around my waist and pulled me forward, so that my feet were on top of his. Our bodies were nearly flush, our right hands joined. My heart clattered; there was nowhere else for me to put my left arm except to rest it on his shoulder.

We began to rock, a bit unsteadily, and my nails dug into the fabric of his jacket. Where our fingers were interlaced I felt my palm grow slick, my skin buzzing with burgeoning magic. His thoughts and memories began to seep into me like the slow trickle of water, just flashes of color behind my eyelids, and quickly I blurted out, "If we keep touching bare-skinned I'm going to know all your secrets."

"I don't have any secrets," Sevas said. "At least, none that I would mind you knowing."

My flush only deepened. The music skipped and twanged, too upbeat for our awkward swaying, but how could I care about such a thing now? Our hands were knitted; our bodies close. I smelled him, catching the faint note of liquor on his breath, and the lingering scents of the ballet theater: acrylic paint and cold sweat and nylon, all the things that he'd been trussed up in to turn him into Ivan.

Sevas moved faster and I tripped a little bit, stumbling backward. He caught me before I fell.

"I'm sorry," I said. "I'm a terrible partner."

"Don't be sorry for anything," he said, with such firm conviction that I wasn't sure if he was actually telling *me* such things, and not some other girl over my shoulder. "This is the most enjoyable dance I've had in years."

I frowned in bewilderment. "Surely you must enjoy the applause and the adoration and the pretty tsarevna."

"Oh, Taisia loathes me to my marrow," Sevas said with a laugh. "She says she hates kissing someone who stinks of booze and has a dozen other girls' perfumes lingering on him, even if it's just pretend."

Jealousy knotted in my belly, but I bit my lip and stayed quiet.

"And besides," Sevas went on, "this is the first time in a long while I've gotten to dance in a place that I chose, with a partner of my liking, without playing the same role in the same insipid story."

"You don't like *Bogatyr Ivan*?"

"What's there to like? It's a fairy story for children and a doctrine for zealously patriotic men. Besides, how can anyone be entertained when the ending is so obvious? Of *course* the Dragon-Tsar will fall. Of *course* Ivan will win the tsarevna's hand."

"I like it," I ventured, surprised at my own boldness. "It reminds me of a story my mother used to tell me, before she died."

"Before she became a bird."

"Yes. There was an Ivan and a tsarevna in that story too."

"And did it have a happy end?"

"It did," I said, and my chest tightened suddenly, as if my body had become aware of all the strings that bound it. The clamshell compact between my breasts, the juniper berries and the charm bracelet circling my wrists, the memory of Rose's words wrapping around my brain like endless lengths of twine: *Come back by the strike of three, before the dawn lifts Papa's eyelids. Nothing in your hands or pockets. Don't be selfish.* I was so tangled in all of them that I felt like an insect trapped in a spider's twisting, snarling web.

"Well," said Sevas, "you'll have to tell it to me someday."

Another lurch in my belly, strings tightening further. "Maybe."

Sevas gave a soft laugh. "You're so inscrutable, Marlinchen. I think you like bewitching me."

And that drew a laugh from me, too, unexpected and genuine. "No one else has ever said such a thing. I've never been able to keep a secret or to tell a lie."

"But you escaped your wizard father's house to come here." Sevas arched a brow. "Surely that involved some subterfuge."

My cheeks pinked. "Well, you're my first secret then, my first lie. Does that please you?"

"Only if it pleases you."

I was blushing so furiously then I could no longer meet his eyes, and the closeness of his body was so intoxicating that I was certain I'd do some manic, lascivious, animal thing if I couldn't get away from him. My gaze caught on something white on the floor.

In a heartbeat I managed to remove myself from Sevas's grasp, bend down, and pick it up. It was a white feather, smooth and glistening with a faint brush of gold paint.

"Here," I managed. "This must be yours. From your cape."

Sevas's mouth fell open. I could tell that my odd behavior was perplexing him, but I wasn't doing it by design. I was only trying to keep him safe from the strange and garish thoughts in my mind, from the desires that would doom us both, even if they were only mine.

"Why don't you keep it?" he said. "You can use it in one of your witch's brews."

"I told you, I'm not that kind of witch."

"Keep it anyway," Sevas said. "If you ever find yourself in dire financial straits, I'm sure there are women in Oblya who would pay a baffling amount of rubles for a feather that once touched Sevastyan Rezkin's skin."

He said it all without a trace of smugness or pride. The feather felt warm to the touch, as though his flesh had leached some heat into it, as if it still held the memory of being under those sweltering stage lights. With a heedless rush of wanting, I tucked the feather into the pocket of my dress.

"I know a story about a beautiful bird who was the envy of all the other fowl," I said. "They all loathed him for his beauty, but he just wanted their love. So he gave away one of his beautiful feathers to each of them, until he was plucked completely bald."

"I think I like that story better than *Bogatyr Ivan*."

My brow furrowed. "But why?"

"Because at least it's closer to the truth. People are resentful and cruel and desirous." Sevas shook his head slightly, as if he wanted to rid himself of the thoughts. I saw a small metamorphosis in him then: a shift from the brute, unpleasant reality to the smiling, indulgent dream-world. From Sevas to Ivan, a glimmer of mischief in his eye. "Have you ever taken a stroll down the boardwalk?"

"No. Not since my mother was alive. My father—"

"Let me guess, he finds fault with the sea itself. But your father isn't here. So let me show you."

There was another spell of silence, a long moment like a held breath. Behind me, a woman's laughter rippled the air like the susurration of tiny wings.

"You can't," I said at last, even as the lemon balm wafted into my nose and the spearmint parched my throat. I was thinking of the salt air and the black sand, all the things that would reveal me without Papa even needing a potion. "It's so far from here, and I need to be getting back home . . ."

"It's not even midnight, Marlinchen." He leaned closer, and suddenly I felt the metal between my breasts burn like a bullet, all its shrapnel fissuring outward. I felt half-dying, and there was lead in my veins; how could he stand to be so near to me? Wasn't he scared that whatever I was would catch?

I drew my hand over my chest, as if to cover the wound, but Sevas didn't pull away, and said, "What use is there sneaking out from under your father's nose if only to run back again before you've even gotten to see your own city?"

"It's not really my city. The Vashchenko family has lived here since before it was Oblya, when there was just the steppe that ran right into the sea without anything to stop it. Before the land was lashed to bits and each scar was given a name like Kanatchikov Street. Oblya is a rude intruder to the place we've always known."

"And I am an intruder upon the intrusion?" Sevas arched a brow. "You don't need to drag around your family history like an old dead dog."

"That's easy enough for you to say—your family is hundreds of miles away." My breath caught at my own meanness.

"It's not easy at all," Sevas said quietly, and finally drew away from me, raising himself to his full height and rubbing some of the sweat-dampened gold paint that remained on his cheek. "Do you think I left everything in the slums of Askoldir? Dr. Bakay tells me that history lives in the planes of my skull and the thrust of my brow. I don't know of any surgery that can excise a century. That's how long my family has lived in Rodinya, give or take a few years. But I know that, if I could, I *would* shave off those years like slivers of bone."

He kept his voice low, but even so I felt I was a wave that had come upon a seawall, his words solid and immovable. What did I know of any history besides my own, and even that hazy, half-remembered? There was a whole world spreading its roots outside my father's house, and oaks just as old as the ones in our garden. I grew up with his words and the stories in the codex, but did I really know anything at all?

And then there was Dr. Bakay's name in his mouth, which might have made me retch if not for the waft of Rose's tincture.

"I'm sorry," I said embarrassedly. "We don't have any history books in our house. No books at all, aside from my father's codex."

Sevas gave a short laugh, and his eyes were bright again, as if it were all forgotten. "Those were the least cruel words I've ever heard spoken on the subject; trust me, there's nothing to be sorry for. But have you really never read a book, an actual book?"

"I don't know what you mean," I said, still feeling mortified. "Papa—my father's codex has lots of stories and spells, and recipes for potions." It had the smell of damp moss and was as ancient as Indrik claimed to be. "I like the stories where swans turn back into maidens so they can marry princes."

"Now I see why you love *Bogatyr Ivan*," he said with only the barest of smirks. "Heroes triumphant, evil banished, crowns won and wedding vows sung. There are so many books like that you could spend your whole life reading, just like I'll play Ivan every night until I'm too old and ugly for it—likely around age thirty."

The idea of him ever turning ugly was as unthinkable as a spell to turn iron into gold, the most impossible of all impossible alchemies. Yet Rose's prediction lingered. "And what will you do after?"

"I don't give much thought to it. I may very well be dead before that day comes. I try to live each night like death is riding for me at the very first hour of dawn, so I'll have very few regrets when it does finally appear in the tavern door." He glanced toward the threshold, as if he really did think he might see a black-clad figure there. In Papa's codex, Death was a man with willow fronds for hands and drooping ears so huge you could fold yourself into them and fall soundly asleep.

"I think I would regret it deeply, if I died at dawn knowing it's been so long since you've seen the ocean. Won't you let a rude intruder show you your own sea?"

And selfishly, like a feather-veiled maiden, I did.

Overhead the moon was as pale as a woman's face on a cameo pin, its reflection so bright and solid it seemed a dredge boat could scoop it right up out of the water. The black shoreline bunched and flattened, like the sash of a dress. Running alongside it, the boardwalk was still busy even this late at night, studded with flat-roofed pavilions piping organ music and stalls that sold tall, frothing glasses of kumys. A little ways down the boardwalk was the white coronet of the carousel, and as far as I could squint my eyes to see, the electric lamps burned like live embers.

Couples ambled past us: women in dresses with huge sleeves and even more enormous bustles, and men in top hats that seemed each to grow taller than the last, as if they were in private competition, trying to outdo one another in height. Even in my dated dress and with my wind-snarled hair, nearly all of it now come loose from Rose's braids, it filled me with a very pleasant warmth to know that these strangers looked at Sevas and me as if we were another couple, with ordinary lives before us and behind.

I tried not to think of the snow-maiden that had kissed him, of the other perfumed women that he'd spoken of, or of Derkach's hand on his knee. Deep down I knew, even in the haze of this waking dream, that Sevas would never imagine me the way I imagined him, with such futile desire. But still I grew hot all over when he laughed, blushing down to the hollow of my throat.

The black tide lipped the blacker shore, with a sound like hundreds of riled serpents, and suddenly I remembered something.

"Do you ever read the penny presses?" I asked him, training my eyes on the vanishing tongues of foam.

"Of course," he said. "They're always good for a laugh. Just yesterday I read a lascivious story about the gradonalchik's wife and her unseemly consorting with a postman. Why do you ask?"

"I heard a story," I said, slowing my pace, "that there were two men found on the boardwalk, dead. I think it was in the penny presses. They said that the men were missing their hearts and livers, and that they had plum stones where their eyes had been."

Sevas cast his gaze out toward the sea, and then turned back to me. "There were two men found dead here not long ago, and of course the penny presses were astir, printing stories about a monster. They only thought so because the bodies were so thoroughly butchered it couldn't have been a man who did it. I did read that their hearts and livers were gone. The city police scoured the whole coastline and found a pack of stray dogs living under the boardwalk with blood on their muzzles. They were all put down, but the penny presses will never print a story about *that*. It's funny, isn't it, how much the city is salivating to imagine a monster in its midst? I suppose with all but one of its wizards extinct, and with its only witches sweet and gentle, they need something else to sate their desire for violence."

I felt my heart stutter crookedly. "Sometimes I do think my clients wished I were more wicked."

"Perhaps you ought to consider it—as a business opportunity, of course. Feed them draughts of newt's eye and cackle over your cauldron. Turn your spurned lovers into pigs."

The notion that I had any lovers, spurned or otherwise, was so absurd that I choked out a laugh, even as Sevas raised his brow. "Papa is the one who does transformations, not me. And there would not be any pigs."

Sevas gave a quick nod, and I thought I could see his ear tips pinking again, though perhaps I had wishfully imagined it. We stopped at one of the stalls and bought two glasses of kumys, cold and sweet. It occurred to me that I had never had anything to eat or drink outside my father's house. Inside, when I did eat, I was usually wracked with panic, wondering when and where I would throw it up afterward. The kumys went down as easily as water. Organ music swooped like a gull through the air.

In the distance, the carousel scythed with blades of orange light, casting them out over the water, as bold as lighthouse beacons. I wondered how deep it was, and how many strange things were adrift in its waves. I wondered what was on the other side.

Sevas had stopped walking and placed one hand on the iron railing, staring out over the sea as though he were a weather-eyed captain at his ship's helm. In that moment I could imagine him a sailor as easily as I could a bogatyr, both dashing and brave.

"Is it how you remember it?" he asked me, very softly.

Was it? I could remember the wind in my hair and the salt smell in my nose. I could even remember the sand under my bare feet, the way that it yielded beneath me. But such a thing would have been impossible—even before my mother was gone, I never would have been allowed to play barefooted on the sand.

A strange memory inhabited me; it possessed me like a ghost. I was standing on the shore beneath a blade of silver moonlight. Even the gas lamps had been extinguished. There was a copper taste on my tongue. There was someone else's labored breathing, loud and close enough that it drowned out even the ceaseless roll of the tide.

"Marlinchen?" Sevas's voice prodded me from my stupor. The memory drifted away, a balloon with a cut string.

"I—I don't know," I confessed. I wiped my hands on my skirt. They had felt stained and damp, though with something heavier than sweat. "As a child I was afraid of everything. Last time I was here, I think I hid in my mother's skirts or wept into her shoulder. At least, that's the way my sister tells it."

"Which sister?"

"The eldest," I said. "Undine. She's very mean. All eldest sisters are."

His mouth quirked up at the corner. "Who says so?"

I blinked at him. "Do you have any brothers or sisters?"

"No," he said. "I'm my mother's only son. But in my absence she's started feeding seven stray cats and every bird that lands on her balcony."

I smiled a little, imagining it. He asked me about Undine, and why she was so mean. I told him how she took my ribbons and my pearls and then pretended they had always been hers. I told him how she smacked me for being stupid, for being scared, for being canny, for being rude, for not talking, for talking too much. He asked me about my other sister and I told him that she was kind, and even better to have than a mother, because mothers were either wicked or they were dead. He frowned and told me that his mother was neither. I said that I had never read about the mothers of Yehuli boys, and he laughed and told me that most were quite willful, but they always loved their sons very much. Ships floated in the harbor like horses at their hitching posts, sails lashing gently.

"Tell me that story from your father's codex," Sevas said. "About the swan-woman and the bogatyr. Maybe there's something I can incorporate into my performance."

"It starts a long time ago, at least two thousand years." The boardwalk was nearing its end, wooden planks eroding into black sand. "Almost all stories begin with a happy couple: a rich man and his beautiful, pious wife. If they have daughters, it is generally a sign that something will go wrong. Daughters usually have a bad time in stories, especially if there are three or more. I think this is my favorite story because everything goes right, when it's all said and done. And it's not such a bad thing to be a bird, if you can find someone to kiss you back into a girl. My mother's problem was that all the bogatyrs are gone."

I was breathless by the end of my telling, and it occurred to me that I could not remember the last time I had spoken so much, the last time anyone had allowed me to speak so much. A flush crept over my face. I had revealed so much of myself, toeing the abyss of my darkest and deepest wants.

"Not true," Sevas protested, a smile dimpling only his left cheek. "I play a bogatyr every night, rude intruder that I am."

"With a wooden sword. And a Dragon-Tsar who breathes paper flames." Smog-wreathed, the moon now looked like one of my mother's lace doilies, stained with old spills of tea. "I fed her from my hand for so many years, after my sisters forgot she was still there in her cage and no one ventured up to the third floor of our house but me." I looked out again, past the black sand to the sea, and after a moment something seized my chest.

"Sevas, what time is it?"

"I don't know." He frowned. I wasn't sure what I expected him to say; he wasn't the type to fastidiously carry a pocket watch. We both turned, several paces from where the boardwalk ended, and began walking up the other way. Sevas paused before the nearest couple, a tall, thin man with an enormous mustache and his ruddy-haired companion, and asked, "Sir, do you have the time?"

The man opened the flap of his jacket and removed the watch, dangling from its gold chain like the pendulum of our grandfather clock. "A quarter to three, sir. Aren't you—"

I didn't wait to hear if it was me he recognized, or Sevas. Already I was sprinting down the boardwalk, wind catching its fingers in my hair. I scarcely noticed the glass of kumys slipping out of my grasp and shattering, a cosmos of cold milk streaking over the wooden slats.

I hadn't gone very far at all when I realized that I'd utterly forgotten Rose's juniper berries, forgotten to leave a trail that would help me find my way back home. But then again, I'd forgotten so much these last few hours, hadn't I? My hand went to the sachet tied at my wrist, full and useless, leaking black juice onto the pleats of my dress.

In the distance, the carousel whirled and whirled, and the gas lamps were so bright that they cooked my eyes like eggs. Through the damp fretwork of lashes, I saw couples pass by, giving me a wide berth; I was panting and bent at the waist, bile rising in my throat.

I wished Undine were there to strike me across the face. I wished

Rose were there to smooth the curls from my forehead and tell me that I would be safe, that all would be well, and that she would forgive me. The lemon balm smell had leaked out from her tincture, and now I could only taste the spearmint, like swallowing a fistful of nettles. I shut my eyes.

When I opened them again, Sevas's face was rippling in front of me. "Marlinchen, what's wrong?"

"I have to go home," I managed, the words squeezing out of me like air through chimney bellows. "I told my sister I would be back by the clock's strike of three, before the dawn lifts Papa's eyelids. I was supposed to leave a trail, but I didn't, and now I can't find my way—"

I held up my stained fingers, as if they were proof of anything. Sevastyan's lips pressed into a pale line, and he said, "I'll bring you back. Don't worry. Don't be afraid. It isn't as far as you think."

The tip of my nose was burning. "I don't know any of the street names."

"I do," he said. "I've walked them all, four times as drunk as I am now. Everything will be fine. Come with me."

There was something in my throat the size of a millstone, but I drew my arms around myself and followed Sevas down the board-walk. The street that threaded alongside it was mostly empty, lined with black-windowed beer shops and inns that advertised a bed for two rubles. In one of the doorways a woman stood only half-dressed, baring one of her breasts to the cold starlight. I looked away, stomach roiling.

At the corner of the street was a carriage drawn by two huge horses, white smoke curling from their nostrils. The man in the driver's seat leaned down, gave a gap-toothed smile, and said, "Half a ruble for an hour, one ruble for three." I could tell he was Ionik from the sound of his consonants, like pistols cocking.

"A quarter hour is all we need," Sevas said, though he pressed a gold coin into the man's open palm.

The man leapt down from his seat and swung the carriage door open, and I looked into the black mouth of it and felt the same nebulous dread I had felt staring through the threshold of the tavern. Papa warned us that carriages had their own magic about them: once you accepted a ride, you could not leave until the driver let you. You ceded the power of your legs to carry you as soon as you clambered inside.

That was a powerful magic indeed. I would have been less afraid to climb on the back of a seven-headed dragon. But Sevas didn't hesitate. He pushed himself onto the first step and held out his hand.

Only a witch wouldn't have taken it. A real witch, like Titka Whiskers, or the various extinct forest hags who ministered to motherless girls. It was not yet three, and I was still a feather-haired maiden under the peeled-apple moon, so I threaded our fingers and let him pull me up into the carriage after him.

The door shut, and our bodies were close on the bench, and then I heard the driver climb up and spur his horses and we went rattling down the streets of Oblya, window glass fogging with our breath.

"Why have you been so kind to me?" I managed. I couldn't help how miserable I sounded, like a lashed dog, my dream slipping away from me like snow melting in the sunlight. "You could have let me leave right from the theater, after I'd told you all that you needed to know."

"And you could have let me turn into a mass of black snakes at your door," he said. "I don't need a life debt to compel me to take a girl to a tavern, or walk with her down by the shore. Can't I enjoy those things without a wizard's curse hanging over me? I told you I wanted to see your face in the crowd. I'm happy that I did." He hesitated. "I want to see it again."

All the air in the carriage seemed to stiffen like tree roots in the cold. I could see the red flush traveling down my throat, over the cleft of my breasts, all the way to the gold clamshell pressed between them. The reminder of it hurt, like a pour of boiling water over ice, and it made my whole body hiss and steam. I wanted to press the heels of my hands to my eyes and weep.

The window was so thoroughly fogged that I had to rub a bleary circle on the glass to see through it as the carriage bore us down what I recognized as Kanatchikov Street. I could see the horses trotting, panting their pale smoke. Farther in the distance I could see my father's house, our wood-rotted turret wearing a gray shawl of clouds. I could not bring myself to look at Sevas.

When the carriage finally drew to a halt outside of our gate, I was thinking that not even Papa could have managed a transformation like this: to turn a plain-faced witch into a blushing mortal girl, and then back again by the clock's strike of three. All of Papa's magic had a singular direction—you couldn't make a flower unbloom. I watched my own face in the window wither and bloom and wither again in the span of seconds, a shuddering metamorphosis: *Witch, swan, girl. Witch-swan-girl.*

The carriage door opened and all three vanished.

I climbed out of the carriage, unsteady on my own legs, and Sevas followed close behind. In the shadow of our fence was my first dropped juniper berry, fat and taut with juice. Rose's words needled through my mind: *don't be selfish.*

"I think it might be a minute or two past three," Sevas said. "Will everything be all right?"

My voice dried up in my throat. When I did manage to speak, it was only in a whisper. "I never finished telling you—only sons are always heroes. Things always end well for them. They must end well for you."

Now it was his breath that spread white in the cold. "Who says so?"

With difficulty, I swallowed. "I have to go."

And then I turned and unlatched the gate and ran through it into the garden without looking back.

The night opened its black wings and took flight. I stood in a bed of purple hyacinths, as still as if my own feet had grown roots, as if I had only ever stood in this place, nothing before me or behind. From across the garden our goblin gave a muffled wail, nails dragging against the shed door where it was trapped—where it had been trapped for hours in the darkness, not even knowing that day had bled into night and was about to bleed into day again.

You must return by the clock's strike of three, before the dawn lifts Papa's eyelids. Sevas was right. I could not hear the gonging of our grandfather clock, which meant the hour of three had already passed. So that was one promise to my sister, broken.

You must bring nothing more back with you. Your hands and pockets must be as empty as when you left. I let my fingers card through the folds of my skirt until I found Sevas's feather, gossamer and still warm. Another promise broken.

You must take the black sand and destroy it. Use it to leave once, and then never again.

In the safety of the velvet dark, I removed the compact from my breasts. It was marbled and damp with sweat, hot as a bullet just fired.

I picked myself free of the hyacinths, careful not to crinkle their petals, and flung open the door of the shed. The goblin went tearing out into the garden, single eye blinking wildly as it adjusted to the ghostly starlight, open-shut-open-shut, and nearly tripping over its own great beard. It trudged through the wheat grass and vanished.

There was magic in the number three, maybe bad magic, but I didn't care. What was one more promise broken? I drew up my skirts and got on my hands and knees in the dirt and buried the compact right at the base of the juniper tree.

CHAPTER SIX

Here is the story I did not tell Sevas.

True enough, it starts with a happy couple: a rich man and his beautiful, pious wife. In this case, the rich man was a king (a tsar) and his wife was a queen (tsaritsa). They ruled over a domain of both wide plains and tall mountains. The people loved them, and the land was fertile, and many things could grow, except for in the tsaritsa's womb. No matter how many times her husband spilled his seed in her, nothing would take root. Her body was as barren as a salt flat.

And because she didn't know what a bad thing it is to be a mother in a story (and did not know she was in a story at all), the tsaritsa went out into the garden, into the snow, and peeled an apple. While she was peeling it, she cut her finger and a drop of blood fell into the snow.

At once her blood vanished, and then the snow said, "I've been hungry for so long. If you feed me, I can give you the one thing your heart desires."

"I want a child," the tsaritsa said.

"Feed me," said the snow.

So the tsaritsa cut all four of her fingers and her thumb and let her blood fall and the snow ate it up greedily. That night, her husband took her inside and kissed her cut fingers and put his seed in her again, and she went to sleep smiling.

The next morning when she woke, the tsaritsa looked out into the snow-blanched courtyard and saw that a white tree had flowered up in the place where she'd bled, tall and full as any of the other ancient oaks. She ran outside.

The tree was blooming with bright-red berries, so sweet-looking that the tsaritsa couldn't help herself: she put one in her mouth. It burst on her tongue and she swallowed all its juice, and then her thighs went slick with a bolt of pleasure and she felt something stir at last in her womb.

The snow melted, and the tsaritsa's belly grew. In nine months she gave birth to a baby girl, with berry-bright lips and hair the color of frost. And, because this is a story, the tsaritsa took one look at her daughter, smiled, and then died.

Between her legs was a spewing of ruby-hued blood. The tsar wiped it clean and took his daughter and held her close. The snow came again and blanketed the fertile land. Birds landed on the branches of the white tree and ate all the berries. The daughter blossomed into a beautiful tsarevna, the most beautiful girl in all her father's domain, and she was as kind and pious as her dead mother besides (if a mother is dead, she is allowed to be kind).

When she turned sixteen, the tsar decided it was time for his daughter to marry. Rumors of her beauty had already spread far and wide, beyond even his land of wide plains and tall mountains, to other kingdoms where the sun shines for only one hour a day. Men came from all over to seek the tsarevna's hand, and when they met her they were even more charmed by her lovely white hair and her lovely red lips and her lovely black eyes.

The tsar let each suitor spend one evening with his daughter, where they talked and made merry, and by the end it was not a rich man she fell in love with, or even the prince of the kingdom where the sun shines for only an hour a day. It was a warrior named Ivan, a bogatyr who was a simple farmer's son. The tsar set out to have them married right away.

On the day of their wedding, a fierce snow came and blanketed all the land in white. Ivan and the tsarevna were married happily, and went off to their chambers for the night. But as Ivan began peeling off his bride's wedding gown, he found underneath that the tsarevna was not a woman at all but a swan, with white feathers and black eyes and a blood-red beak. There was a great howling of snow and the swan flapped her wings and flew out the window and vanished.

Ivan ran to the window after her, and heard the snow speak.

"Your once-bride is my daughter, and the tsarevna of the Kingdom of Winter," it said. "Now that you have wed her, you are my son too, and a father has the right to kill his sons and eat them, if he so desires."

And then there was another great howling and the snow blew in through the window and nearly buried him. Ivan shook himself free and went to the tsar and told him what had happened.

"Your wife must have lain with Ded Moroz, Grandfather Frost, the tsar of the Kingdom of Winter. She took his seed and gave birth to a daughter of ice and bitter magic. If I am to be reunited with my love, I must journey to the Kingdom of Winter and defeat Ded Moroz in battle."

The tsar wept at the news, but he still loved the girl he had raised as his own. He dried his tears and said to Ivan, "I will give you a sword."

And so Ivan rode off to find the Kingdom of Winter, but the snow was falling thickly and his horse died right under him, still in its saddle. Ivan stopped for the night and built a fire and cooked and ate his horse.

He was taking shelter under a tall white tree when he saw a white bird fly down from the sky and land before him. Ivan blinked, and the swan changed back to the tsarevna, his bride. Her bare skin was the color of pure frost and her eyes were as black as juniper berries and her nipples were pink and knotted with cold.

"My love," he said. "Come home with me."

"I'm so hungry," she said.

"I have no food," said Ivan.

"Feed me," she whispered through her pale lips.

So Ivan took his sword and cut his own throat. His blood landed in the snow. The tsarevna crouched over him and ate his muscle and crunched his bones and swallowed his skin whole. When there was nothing left of Ivan, she turned back into a swan and flew to the tall mountains.

There she found the head of Ded Moroz, broad as a cliffside, his beard vast and pale and made of snow. His knuckles were the frost-capped hills and his long, long legs spread open right under the palace of the tsar, and where his seed spilled, white trees with red berries grew.

"Papa," she said, "let us feast to my marriage. My heart is full and my husband is in my belly."

And so Ded Moroz sprouted an ebony tree with huge, fat berries as black as bruises. "Here is my heart, daughter," said Ded Moroz, "and it is full."

And then the swan who was the tsarevna coughed up all the pieces of Ivan that she had eaten: his hunks of muscle and shards of bone and the skin that she'd swallowed whole. She breathed on him her own bitter magic—the magic of the tsarevna of winter—and his body stitched itself back together and he became a man again.

He raised his bloody sword and cut down the heart of Ded Moroz, and all through the tsar's land there was a great howling of wind, and then the snow melted and the plains were green underneath it. All the white trees died and the red berries fell, soft with rot. The black fruit landed in the snow, the last of Ded Moroz's vanishing beard.

"My love," said Ivan. "Come back to me."

And then he kissed the swan on her blood-red beak and she became a woman again. The tsarevna said she was sorry, so sorry, for what she had done, and that she had only been under Ded Moroz's spell. Ivan forgave her, and he picked her up and they embraced.

Both were eager to return to the palace of the tsar, to celebrate and to consummate their vows, but both had also grown very hungry, so first they sat down in the melting snow and ate.

All was well in the story, and in Papa's house.

I arranged my hours like holubtsi on a plate, each wrapped up neatly in its own cabbage leaf. From three to four I had buried the compact and stilled my racing heart. From four to five I had hidden away my clothes and crawled on my hands and knees, making sure no grains of black sand had gotten into my carpet. From five to six I had inspected every inch of my skin for sand and secrets.

I had stripped off my dress and removed my shoes and tucked them both in the very back of my wardrobe where you couldn't smell the ocean air that had seeped into the silk. My hair had eaten up all the salt-laced wind, too, so before Papa woke I turned on the faucet in the bathtub and let the water run and run.

The black sand had washed out of my hair, the color of soot from the chimney. I bit my lip on a cry and stumbled back, watching it circle the drain. I waited and waited, as if balancing on a blade's edge, but the tub sucked it down and did not spit it up again.

All at once, the same memory inhabited me: my feet against the soft, sucking sand, the close, labored breathing, the heavy, slick moisture on my hand. The hands both felt like my own hands and not. There was an unfamiliar strength to them, a dexterity, and when I closed my eyes some red haze fell over me. It all felt like a strange dark dream. Something else, like the black sand, that I could not explain.

When I opened my eyes again, all was gone, but I felt a deep, stomach-hollowing dread, like meat being carved off of bone.

I did not have time for dread. On the white tile floor, a rosy band of light fell like a dropped knife. I braided my damp hair and hurried downstairs in my housecoat, the spiny-tailed monster scuffling at my heels. I went into the kitchen and put the kettle on. In the foyer, the grandfather clock gonged seven.

The water squealed inside the kettle, and I poured it into two tea-cups. My hands, though shaking, looked as they always did: the old burn mark scored across my palm and my knuckles stippled with tiny scratches where my teeth cut into the skin when I jammed my fingers down my throat.

The most impossible of all impossible things had happened last night: I had gone out of the house alone and come back the same. My lie had not transformed me. Oblya had not sullied me. Foreign men had not ravished me, carriages had not trampled me, street music had not made me bleed from my ears. I had sneaked past Undine and not been caught. I had disobeyed Rose and I had not felt my stomach gnaw and clench in protest.

Perhaps, it occurred to me, I had undergone the most terrifying transformation of all. Perhaps I had become a girl who did not care about lying to her father or betraying her sisters. I thought of the compact I had buried under the tree, but the thought was evicted from my mind in an instant. I could hear Papa's footsteps on the stairs.

Breathing all too steadily, I went to the icebox. My scarred hands lifted the lid. It was empty.

No, this couldn't be. I closed the lid and opened it again, as if it were a music box and I could reset the song, start it over from the be-ginning. But still there was nothing inside.

I could not understand. I had cooked a chicken liver with browned onions for Papa last night, and it was well before Sunday, which was shopping day, when my father went out into the city and came back with all the meat and vegetables we needed for the week. The icebox had been full of varenyky filling and the jars stuffed to the brim with pickled cabbage and whitefish.

I let the lid slide shut and stood up and perused the shelves. There were only vials of herbs, mostly empty, and onion skins that lined the cabinet floor like autumn foliage. A roach skittered inches from my reaching fingers. I closed the cabinet door.

And then fear spread deep and cold in me, like a pond in winter. Papa had gone into the sitting room; I heard the floorboards groaning under his weight and the silk of his housecoat rasping against the couch's velvet cushions. The kettle on the stove had gone silent, and the water I'd poured into the teacups was only lukewarm.

My bare feet were numb against the tile as I crossed the threshold of the kitchen, to where Papa sat, without anything but my own trembling, empty hands.

"Marlinchen," he said. The bags under his eyes were exceptionally purple and fat. "Where is my breakfast?"

"There's nothing," I managed, the words squeezed through the small gap in my closing throat. "The icebox and the cabinets are empty. All the food is gone."

I watched the fury rise in Papa, fettered behind his eyes and bound in the white knuckles of his clenched fists. His whole body shook like a spirit trapped in an oil lamp. He stood up and came close to me, so close that I could smell the sourness of sleep still on his breath and see each bristling hair of his beard, straws of indigo that held none of the buttery morning sunlight, that swallowed all of it up into a matte and pitiless blue.

I shut my eyes and readied myself for the blister of air that his screams would visit across my face. But all that came was a whisper.

"I'm so hungry, Marlinchen," he said, his voice dreadfully soft. "I feel like there's a snake in my belly that eats the food that falls down my throat. I feel like it's been a hundred years since I last put a bite of anything on my tongue. I can hardly remember the taste of pork varenyky or sour cream or blackberry kvass. The curse has its teeth in my mind, not just in my stomach. It's chewed up all the parts of me that remember what it's like to be full. What it's like to be sated. It hurts, Marlinchen. It hurts."

I opened my eyes. There were tears beading on Papa's stubbly lashes, which were as blue as his beard but finer, limned with sunlight that made his tears look like morning dew on wheat grass. It took another moment, the grandfather clock ticking out each unbearable second, before I understood.

"Did you eat it all?" I squeaked out. "Everything in the icebox and the cabinets—"

Before I could finish, and in one swift, uninterrupted movement, Papa's hand was on my chin, fingernails digging into my cheeks. I gasped as his thumb pushed down hard against my throat, hearing my own pulse thumping under his skin.

"Would my own daughter be so cruel to me?" he rasped. "Must I tell you how I stood over the sink and ate the cold filling of the varenyky in my bare fists? Must I paint such an image in your mind? Must I tell you how I shattered the glasses of cabbage and whitefish and licked them clean down to their shards? It would be another curse, to have to confess such things so baldly in the morning light. Surely you do not wish to curse me so. You are not that sort of witch."

That's what he had done, then, as I had danced with Sevas in the tavern, as we had strolled down the boardwalk. As I had laughed and pretended to be an ordinary girl, or a swan-maiden with feathers in her hair, oblivious to the strings that bound me, my father had been here, devouring everything within his reach.

"I'm sorry, Papa," I whispered. "I didn't know."

Yet how could I have known? For years I had cooked him the same three meals, and they had sated him well enough, and he had not needed to raid my stores in a desperate midnight panic. I was lucky that he had not passed by my bedroom in his feverish craving. But I felt somehow that my jaunt had caused this. I had a secret now, and though Papa not uncovered it himself, it had shifted the stones in his stream bed.

I had always been told my magic did not have that sort of power: the power to do or change or make. And yet in some sneaky, winding way, I had done this to Papa; I had made him hurt.

"The curse has grown with me, Marlinchen," Papa said, his voice still low. "With every wrinkle that forms on my face or every silver hair I find in my beard, there is another pang of hunger in my belly. Titka Whiskers was truly a serpent of a woman. Her venom is still hot in my veins."

His hands were still on my face, but my heart gave a horrible wrenching of guilt, of pity. Whatever Papa had done, whatever way he made us live, this was a fate he did not deserve. Such agony, and all I had to do to ease some of it was a bit of labor in the kitchen. It would have been extraordinarily cruel of me to refuse. I would have been the meanest of all the daughters, in all the stories, written and real. Undine had already chosen cruelty, and Rose had chosen cleverness. What else was left for me but kindness? Third daughters always got the last pick of everything.

"I'll go to the market," I told Papa. "Just give me some rubles, and I will go. I'll fetch you the fattiest cuts of meat, the biggest chickens, the ripest fruits—"

But before I could finish Papa was already drawing a breath, air whistling through his nose in a way that my body remembered as danger.

"You aren't a fool, Marlinchen," he said, "but sometimes you so persevere in behaving like one. We have no rubles; that's the problem of it all. You and your sisters don't work hard enough, and take more than your share. I know what you do, dear daughter, in the garden when you think no one is watching. Eat the food and spit it up again. While your father starves, you bury your wasted food under Rose's mulberry tree? Is it to insult me? To mock my curse? Do you hate me so much?"

My whole body went slick with a cold sweat. How had he known? What keen-eyed spell had he cast to watch me when his real eyes could not? I started to say something, to apologize, but my lips would not move and my throat was impossibly tight and I could still feel my pulse butterflying under his fingers.

"Never again, Marlinchen, do you hear me?" he breathed against my throat. "Whatever you eat, you keep it down."

"Yes, Papa," I whimpered, barely able to talk past his steel grip. "I'm so sorry. I'll never do it again."

At last he let me go, but I stayed still, afraid to move, afraid that I would fall into a pit I couldn't see. Papa reached up again and I flinched, though it was only for him to pinch the bridge of his nose between his finger and thumb. The purple bags under his eyes pulsed.

"Go fetch your sisters," he said.

And so I did, rousing first Undine, who walloped me hard with her pillow, and then Rose, who woke with such a start it was as if I'd poured frigid water down her back. All three of us came downstairs in our nightgowns and housecoats, hugging our arms around ourselves, trying to breathe as quietly as we could. Papa paced the length of the sitting room. The grandfather clock ticked in time with his footsteps.

"Greedy daughters, selfish daughters, thankless daughters," he said, staring at the ground. "It's not enough that I waste away from this infernal curse, not enough that I built this house over your heads and planted the garden that surrounds it and the fence that keeps you safe. Now I cannot even eat. Tell me, daughters, will you rejoice when you find me, dead of starvation, in my bed? Will you make merry over my pile of bones and skin, laugh as you tip my body into its early grave?" He made a derisive sound in the back of his throat. "What would your mother think of the girls that she reared at her breast?"

He did not often invoke Mama's name, but it was always powerful magic when he did. A pall of dreadful cold settled over the three of us, my sisters and me, and I could not move or speak for how quickly and bitterly it crawled through my veins. Tears gathered wet and fat at the corners of my eyes, like a drawing of blood.

"So we have no rubles now." It was Rose who finally dared to speak, Rose the cleverest and most unflappable of us all. Papa gave a silent nod, sharp and furious, and I startled at that—hadn't Derkach just given us a large bag of coins? Rose had not been there, but did that mean it was already gone? "There is still much that we can do," she went on. "We can go to the printing shop and have flyers drawn up to advertise our services, then hang them around the city. We can charge all our clients a few kopeks more; most of them will not mind. And in the meantime, we can sell some of our things to pay for food and the printing fees."

Papa's head jerked up. "You want me to pawn our belongings like some pitiful barfly who needs his next fix?"

"Only the things we don't need, the ones we have little use for," said Rose. Her voice was firm, her face placid even as spittle flew from Papa's mouth and stretched like cobwebs across the carpet. "Some of our jewelry, perhaps. A lamp or two. We only need a bit to keep us going until our clients come back."

I heard Undine make a little noise of protest, but she did not speak. Papa stopped his pacing. In the foyer, the grandfather clock gonged nine times.

"Fine," he said. "Fine, then. I will bring the most viperous of Oblya's merchants to our door."

First he needed to recant his curses, dismantle his own complex architecture of spellwork like cutting down a dead oak before it falls. These were the spells of so many accumulated years, every whim or moment of fury that Papa had ("I cannot stand to see another proselytizing fanatic knocking at the door," he had said, and then cast a spell so that our house would look empty and uninhabited to any missionary who passed us by on the street). Papa went along the line of the fence, mumbling to himself, shaking out drops of liquid from various capped bottles. Plumes of violet smoke lifted from the earth and green miasmas trailed after him like leashed comets. I could not tell which by sight or smell or sound, but that last spell warding against Sevas and any members of the ballet theater—it was gone now too.

The eyeless ravens squawked from the tangle of birch branches, feathers ruffled. Indrik looked on from a patch of wormwood, chest swelling with silent indignation. He perhaps liked our rude, ungracious Oblya intruders even less than Papa did. The goblin sat down in the very center of the garden and wept, muddying the beds of at least three different herb plants. My sisters and I watched from the doorway and the spiny-tailed monster gnawed at the edge of my nightgown.

"This is mad," Undine said in an angry whisper. "If only Papa had done this ages ago—if only he stopped warding against every type of person that piques his anger on a particular day, we'd have twice as many clients and no money troubles at all. If he allowed us to make house calls, we'd have even more. I'm not going to sell my things."

"Yes, you are. Better than listening to him rage for hours on end," said Rose. "Besides, we don't need to sell very much. Only a couple of pieces of jewelry each—less if Papa will part with one of his lamps or cat-vases."

Undine scoffed and stalked away, slamming against my shoulder on her way. I watched Papa, a sick feeling boiling in my belly. He was getting very close to the juniper tree, its green fronds dripping with berries fat and black. I had been careful not to leave even the smallest mound of dirt where I'd buried the compact, no evidence that the soil had been disturbed and something planted within it. Still I wondered if Papa's most quotidian, instinctual magic might uncover it, like a hound suddenly catching the scent of a fox on the wind, ears pricking even as it lay slack by the fire. Papa was bred to sniff out secrets, and he always anticipated deceit.

I swallowed noisily, and with a start Rose gripped my hand.

"You got rid of it, didn't you?" Her eyes were as thin as knife slits.

I nodded. "Of course."

She released me again, her breath going out with relief. My lie felt heavy, like a bone in broth, leaching its essence into all my thoughts. But all I had to think of was Sevas's shining blue eyes and the feel of his arm circling my waist to remember why I had told the lie at all, and why I would do anything to keep it buried.

Papa swept past the tree and didn't look to the ground at all.

His magic came down like the dome of an old church, caving in on itself splendidly. I could not see it, not quite—it was just a shimmer of pale light in the air. But I knew how dead magic smelled: like grease and oil, like asphalt newly poured.

Finally Papa turned away from the fence and trudged back toward the house.

"It's done," he said. "I won't hear any more recriminations from either of you, or your wicked-tempered sister. None of us can eat gold."

As if they could feel the magic recede—as if its absence was an invitation—in another hour, our house was filled with men of all stripes. There were merchants who peered at us over the half-moon glasses that they balanced precariously on their noses, or squinted through their monocles as if they were portholes on a ship; skupshchiks who fingered our fringed lampshades and turned my father's cat-vases upside down to check if there was an artist's watermark.

Those were the ones who seemed to take a keen and genuine interest in our wares, but most of the others were only there for the same reason that most of our clients came to us—spectacle. We had already shut up the goblin and warned Indrik away from any of the guests, but still the visitors tried to sneak glimpses up the stairs or into the kitchen, glancing over our shoulders as they spoke to us, only pretending to swallow our words. They looked down long hallways as if they were staring down my sisters' bodices, eyes unblinking and mouths opened stupidly, like gutted fish.

I hated it so much that it made my skin itch. I imagined a horde of spiders had been spilled inside my dress. Papa stood at the top of the second-floor landing, arms folded over his chest and doing some good magic of his own to look like the Great Wizard Zmiy Vashchenko. The visitors deftly avoided his probing stare, and if they spent too long talking to my sisters or me, or if they stood a little too close, my father would look them down until they flushed and spluttered and slunk away.

I watched Rose hand off one of her peridot earrings to a petty buyer who rubbed it between his finger and thumb like he was trying to get some of the gold to slough off onto his skin. After a moment he slid the earring into his pocket, and then deposited a handful of rubles into Rose's open palm.

"Excuse me," said a voice, and I turned with a stutter of alarm. There was a thin man standing behind me whose face was shaven so clean I could see the rash where the barber's blade had been. "I'm so sorry. I didn't mean to startle you, Ms. Vashchenko. I'm a broker with the firm of Fisherovich & Symyrenko. I'm not sure if you've heard of us."

He drew a square of thick paper from his pocket and held it out to me. I could hear Papa's breathing hard from all the way at the top of the stairs, so I clenched my fingers in my skirts and didn't take it.

The man cleared his throat and put the card away again. "Normally we deal in much larger quantities of goods, but we have a specific foreign buyer in mind who might be interested in certain very particular wares. Are you in possession of any cursed objects? Any stones imbued with spectral magic? Dolls that stand up and move of their own accord. Any bottled spirits or haunted amulets? Please, do let me know if you are willing to sell."

My throat felt so dry and tight I almost could not speak. "Who is the buyer?"

"I'm not at liberty to disclose names, but the objects would be gathered for a gallery collection in one of Ellidon's new museums."

Ellidon, the tiny gray island that lipped the edge of Papa's ancient atlas. She birthed whole fleets of warships like white-muzzled wolves that ran voracious circles around the world in order to spread this wonderful thing called "democracy." Ellidon seemed farther than anything I could imagine, a kingdom where the sun shone only an hour a day through the veil of clouds and factory smog.

"We don't have any of those things," I said. "We have poultices and tonics, but you need an herbalist like my sister to make them do what they ought, and we have a scrying pool in the garden but only my sister

Undine can see anything in it. And you could take my hands for their flesh divining, but I don't think they would work if my brain wasn't still attached to them."

The broker looked at me as if I were some fascinating thing he'd just peeled off the bottom of his boot. "Well, then, I'm sorry to trouble you, Ms. Vashchenko." His gaze went up and down me, and finally caught on the charm bracelet around my wrist. "That looks like quite a unique piece of jewelry. Is it for sale?"

Papa was watching me intently from the top of the stairs and his eyes were hard and small like fruit seeds. Very slowly, with shaking fingers, I lifted my hand and unclasped the bracelet from my wrist. I held it in the flat of my palm, the charms jangling quietly and then falling still against my skin.

"There are eight charms," I said, in a voice so small it embarrassed me just to hear it. "There's an hourglass with real pink sand and a miniature bicycle with wheels that actually spin; a thimble-sized whale with a mouth that opens on a hinge and a bell that really rings. There's a golden box with a paper note folded up so small and tight you can't pry it out. I don't know what the note says, if it says anything at all. There's a book that opens up and has mine and my sisters' names etched onto its gilded pages, along with the years of our births. If you take it into the bath with you and press your tongue to our names, the wet gold tastes like bloody meat."

The broker studied the bracelet splayed in my palm. There were three lines between his brows that looked as if they'd been carved there with a hand rake. His horn-rimmed glasses gave him the appearance of a beetle with spiny pincers, like his eyes were made for snatching things up.

"Fascinating," he murmured. "And is it a family heirloom? A talisman of ancestral sorcery?"

I did not really understand what he meant. "Sort of. It was my mother's. But she was not a witch. She was only a woman, and then a bird, and then she was dead."

"I'll take it," he said, standing up straight again. "How much?"

I only looked back at him, blinking mutely, but in another moment Rose came marching over. She asked the man how much he would pay and then haggled with him and got him to give her almost double. I didn't know how she managed to do it, what special kind of magic she had that could ply and twist the broker whichever way she wanted, as if she were braiding dough for kalach. Before I knew it she was taking his rubles and putting them in her sack, which was so full I could see each coin's shape, its load pulling the drawstring shut, and didn't notice that my eyes were wet until after the broker had walked away.

"Oh, Marlinchen," she said. "Don't weep."

"That was Mama's bracelet," I said. "I wore it every day."

Rose let out a breath. "Would you rather have Mama's bracelet and Papa's rage or no bracelet and Papa sated?"

It was a question just like Papa's one that did not require an answer and, in fact, dared you to try and speak one at all. I wiped my eyes.

Undine was sulking by the grandfather clock because she'd sold her favorite pearls, which were also Mama's favorite pearls. I could hear the goblin wailing plaintively all the way from the garden shed. At last most of the visitors had gone, and Papa came stomping down the stairs to usher the rest out.

But the broker who'd bought my bracelet was still there, examining one of our marble busts with tremendous interest. When he saw Papa he went over to him and said, "Do you have any more of your wife's belongings to sell? Incidentally, I'm very sorry for your loss. Perhaps earning a pretty sum will ease a bit of your grief. I have some buyers who would, I think, be quite interested in baubles previously owned by a mother of witches."

I could hear Mama's charm bracelet jangling softly in his pocket. Papa looked hawkishly between the broker and me. His cheek paunch was rippling the way it did when he chewed the inside of his mouth.

"Your mother did have some other things, didn't she? Women's things, mostly. I remember a gold compact in the shape of a clamshell."

My blood went cold so quickly that I thought for a moment Papa was using more of his magic on me. But there was no shimmer of spell-work in the air; it was just my own lie turning over in my belly like a corpse in a river, churned this way and that by the current, bloated and foul. I opened my mouth but all that came out was choked air.

The seconds bruised past me, the grandfather clock keeping their time. And then at last something surfaced in me, a hasty idea that I hoped would distract him from the broker's question.

"Papa, I only just remembered," I said. "There's food here already. I can cook a monster for you."

It wouldn't have worked if my father was not already anxious to see the broker go. Papa told the man no, thank you, and pressed him toward the door and then slammed it shut as soon as he'd gone through. He was the last of our visitors, and the house was silent again, vacant of magic, and picked clean like a chicken for roasting.

I stood there in the foyer, trying to see all the places where Papa had laid holes in the floor or set out wires to trip on, trying to breathe shallowly so as not to tighten the noose around my throat. I held my-self still and kept my lips taut, Rose and even Undine just as motion-less, all of us doing our own silent arithmetic.

Had we sold enough to make Papa happy? Had we spoken too freely with the visitors and made him angry? I was sure there was a protractor, or some devious spell, that could measure the particular curve of a smile. There was certainly a concrete answer that could ab-solve us as merely polite, or damn us as brazenly promiscuous.

Papa loudly cleared his throat.

"Well, Marlinchen," he said. "I'm hungry."

The bitterest relief sluiced down my spine. I nodded and pushed through the door, only letting out my breath once it had closed again behind me. The day had grown quite late, afternoon seeping into dusk, wind blowing up white petals and dandelion fluff. Angry clouds were scrawled across the sky. I surveyed the garden with watering eyes, trying to swallow past the hard stone in my throat. Beneath the juniper tree, the dirt was still undisturbed, flat and innocuous as it had been the night before I buried my black sand there.

I stood there for as long as I dared—Papa's anger was an ugly wound that bled with very little prodding—considering my options. Indrik was out of the question, of course, and I didn't think I had time to seek out the fiery serpent, even though Papa had a good appetite for snakes. The eyeless ravens would also be too difficult to catch; they would squawk and flap away from me as I crawled up the trunk of the birch tree. And I didn't think I could bear to kill the sweet blubbering goblin.

My other option was not an option at all: to reveal Sevas, to reveal me. Anything to distract Papa. But I would sooner have died than done that, had my liver torn out and watched it bleed between Papa's fingers.

From the corner of my eye I saw the spiny-tailed monster pacing along the windowsill, its eyes narrowed to red gashes. I held out my hand and beckoned to it as if it were an alley cat, and it padded toward me and gave my palm a vigorous lick.

Its barbed tongue left a swath of tiny cuts across my skin, but before it could scamper away, I lurched forward and snatched it up by the scruff of its neck.

I hurried down the steps and around the exterior of the house and lugged it toward the disused maid's quarters while the monster hissed and spat and clawed at my skirts. Shreds of pink silk got caught in the burrs of its tail as I wrestled it onto the butcher block.

Now there was only the question of how to kill it. I had wrung the necks of live chickens many times, but the spiny-tailed monster had odd scales lining its throat and a plate of tough armor along its back. I held it down flat and squirming on the wood with one hand while I contemplated my options, and then with the other I reached for our biggest and sharpest knife.

Its claws raked the inside of my wrist and I gave a little huff of pain, tears squeezing to the corners of my eyes. Then I took the knife and cut a long slit down its soft belly, blood following my blade in a neat ribbon until it spilled over, unfolding and unfolding like a skein of red silk. It teemed over my knife and soaked into the butcher block and dripped onto the floor, rhythmic splatters that kept the time as well as the second hand of our grandfather clock.

I'd made a mistake, not getting something to catch all the blood—later I knew I would spend hours scrubbing it out of the floors, and days still finding it caulked black under my nails. The spiny-tailed monster only whined as it died, tails lashing, claws sinking into the wood with a muted finality. I'd given it a slow and bad death.

Undine would have mocked me for weeping over a monster, but I did anyway. My tears fell into the slit of its belly. It wasn't really a belly anymore, just a still-clenching wound. When finally the monster went still I removed its claws gently from the butcher block and turned it over to start skinning it.

It was hard going with only my kitchen knife; it seemed to turn blunt and dull within the monster's tough hide. I scissored two blades into its throat and peeled back the skin there. Its eyes plunked out of its skull, red and round as chokecherries. Most of the blood had drained by now, and the hem of my dress was drenched with it. The dense slickness of it on my palms was somehow familiar, but I shrugged off the twinging memory and I focused on the monster lying before me. It had two hearts, winging behind its sternum like a pinned butterfly. I cut the sinew from the cathedral of its rib cage and carved out its stomach.

Skin off and organs removed, at last I had pared away all the meat that I could, pink and wet-looking hunks that appeared somehow already chewed. It was not much, but I hoped it would be enough to sate Papa, for now. I threw it all into a pan with oil and dashed on what herbs I could find in the half-empty jars.

The whole time I thought of nothing but Mama's clamshell compact buried under the juniper tree. I wanted to curl up around it like a cat around its litter. I wanted to tuck it back into the cleft of my breasts and let it grow warm again with the heat of my body. If I could have forced it down my throat, I would have. There was nowhere safer for it than inside my stomach like a swallowed peach pit. It occurred to me very abruptly that I was hungry.

I served up Papa's food for him on a platter and poured him water from the sink. My left wrist felt so dismally buoyant without Mama's charm bracelet. I already missed its companionable heaviness, and thinking about it jangling and jangling in the broker's pocket made me want to weep all over again.

Papa was sitting on the chaise longue, leaning forward, elbows resting on his knees with the look of an animal about to lurch.

"Oh, Marlinchen," he said when I placed the tray in front of him. "You're the best and kindest of all my daughters. I'm sorry about your mother's things. You know I didn't want to sell them, but we hardly had a choice. I'll go to the market tomorrow and buy the fattest chicken I can find, still feathered and pecking. The ripest fruits and the freshest fish. Here, have a sip of this kvass."

There was a glass of something as black as pitch on the cloven-footed table. "What is that? I thought we didn't have anything to eat."

"I found it in the cellar. You must have made it. Don't you remember?"

I had made a great many things over the years, including kvass, which kept forever. I did not remember this one in particular, though I thought I would have: it was so dark and thick-looking. Yet I was hungry enough that my knees were trembling and my vision had gone blurry around the edges, so I simply nodded.

I perched beside Papa on the very edge of the chaise longue, our arms touching. He gave me a kiss on the top of my head and put the cup in my hand.

It was cold and smelled like nothing, but perhaps that was my own mind, my own fear and exhaustion rippling out into a spell that made everything seem ashen and empty. Perhaps my body knew that I would not be able to throw it up later, and it was doing me a kindness by making it appear sylphlike and void, nothing that would sit in my belly with too much unbearable weight.

I now counted out my hours like varenyky on a plate, each one wrapped neatly in dough. From seven to eight I had listened to Papa's yelling. From eight to nine I had roused my sisters from their beds. From nine to ten I had tidied the house in preparation for the visitors. From ten to eleven I had spoken to a skupshchik. From eleven to twelve I had spoken to another. From twelve to one I had spoken to no one and watched my sisters and tried not to weep. From one to two I had sold all of Undine's old china dolls. From two to three I had sold Mama's charm bracelet. From three to four I had killed and butchered the monster.

Outside the sky was black and close with storm clouds, the red gash of sunset bleeding thinly through. The gate groaned in the wind, metal latch opening with a clink. The juniper tree looked as stolid as a grave marker, unruffled. Under the dirt was the compact and inside the compact was the black sand and in every grain of that sand was Sevas, my first secret, my first lie, safe as death. I brought the glass to my mouth and drank.

CHAPTER SEVEN

I woke to the sound of rainwater dripping from the eaves. The storm had come and gone as I slept, and it had uprooted our saplings like needles drawn from a pincushion and blown ferns across my window. I rubbed at the marbled condensation on the glass and peered through, eyes scanning the ravaged garden until I found the juniper tree. It stood as straight and tall as a ship's mast, unperturbed, black berries gleaming as if there were a thousand-eyed animal ensconced in its scrubby foliage.

I exhaled my relief, fogging up the glass again. That was when I realized there was a water stain on my pillow. I touched the back of my neck. It felt oddly damp, my hair sodden. Perhaps something had leaked through the roof; I did not know how else I might have gotten wet. I stood up on my bed, unsteadily, and checked the ceiling for cracks. No hairline fracture, nothing.

I climbed down again, feeling both foolish and perturbed. I

wanted to ask my sisters if they had woken up damp, too, but Undine was still angry at me and still mourning the loss of Mama's pearls, and I knew Rose would just sigh and chide me for my fear and strangeness.

Sitting on my bed, another odd memory inhabited me. It was wispy and vague this time, like the vestiges of a dream. In the dream I was drenched in water; above me, the black sky was forked with lightning, and there were hard cobblestones under my feet. Perhaps my dream-self had carried me out of my bed and into Oblya's streets again. Yet how could my dreaming desires leave any mark upon my waking-self?

As I watched out the window again, the door of the garden shed flapped open and Indrik came staggering out, the goblin at his heels. He looked almost as despondent as the morning he'd first come to us; for days afterward the sky rumbled with artificial thunder. I felt sorry for him as he picked burrs from his coat, and sorrier for the goblin as it wiped its big eye on a loose rhubarb leaf.

I heard Papa lurching from his bed, so I put on my housecoat and hurried downstairs.

It had been a long time since I had seen the icebox so full, stuffed nearly to bursting with paper packages of hard, white fatback; jars of sour cream that tumbled over each other when I opened the lid; whole carp with their heads and eyes still intact. There was the chicken he'd promised, though it was already plucked and pimpled, and red, round apples with no bruises. I dug through the packets of butcher paper and the loose fruit until I found, strangely, a glass container with filling for varenyky I could not remember making.

I was pleased, though, that I could make Papa a proper breakfast at last. Surely he could not be angry at me or my sisters when there was a heaping plate in front of him and he was sitting on a whole heavy bag of rubles. I made the dough and rolled it thin, then fried up that filling with onions and oil. I put his varenyky on the plate with great care, dropping a spoonful of that fresh sour cream beside them, and another spoonful of pickled purple cabbage with it. I would serve it to him and he would smile and thank me and kiss my cheeks, and then we would print up the flyers and more clients would come and nothing else of Mama's would need to be sold.

I could not find the blackberry kvass Papa and I had drunk last night, so I poured him a glass of water instead. While I was arranging everything on the tray I saw a mangle of fur and skin and dried blood on the butcher block, what was left of the monster I'd killed.

A sick feeling jostled my belly, like someone prodding an overripe fruit on a sagging branch.

In the safe aftermath of the storm and in the quiet, gutted carcass of our house, I allowed myself to think of Sevas again. He would play Ivan tonight, feather-clad and gold-daubed, following the same steps over and over, trying to make every smile look new and every stumble seem dire.

An idea was pricking at my mind with the relentless rhythm of needlework: *I could go out again.*

The black sand was safely buried under the juniper tree, and I had already proven that there would be no gruesome midnight transformation, no furtive spellwork in the garden or any insurmountable dangers in Oblya's streets. I had lied to Papa and he had not tasted it in his liver or kvass; would it be so terrible to test my luck a second time?

The stories tended to give you three chances for these sorts of things. Three nights of revelry before your carriage turned into a gourd. Three questions to ask the wolf before he showed his teeth. Three bites of an apple before you ate the poison in it. I could mete out my three chances carefully, savoring them like caramels; I could suck on them and spit them out again into my hand. Even the imagining of it felt thrilling and tasted sweet.

I brought Papa's tray into the sitting room and placed it on the cloven-footed table in front of him.

"Thank you, Marlinchen," he said. The bags under his eyes looked smaller than they had in some time, and they were a washed shade of lavender. He must have slept well knowing that the icebox was full at last.

His praise and easy acquiescence made me soften. "Thank you for going to the market. There was so much food in the kitchen."

"Yes, but we will have to be careful. You and your sisters can't eat too much. Women need less to sate themselves than men, and none of you are cursed. If you're hungry between lunch and supper, eat some fruit from the garden." He glanced out the window but did not seem to notice the swath of damage that the storm had drawn across his property, vine tendrils still lashing limply in the scant breeze like the tail of a very old dog.

I was not very hungry, which came as a surprise. Ordinarily I watched Papa eat with miserable, guilt-ridden envy, wishing I could allow myself such rich foods, and then chastising myself for my own ugly, indecent desires. Now I felt very little as I listened to the sounds of Papa eating, and when I looked out at the garden, my mind filled like a tavern's coffers with thoughts of Sevas and vodka and the boardwalk at night.

I had the compact. I had the feather. I had, perhaps most important of all, the memory that assured me that it was possible to escape and return without consequence. Three secrets, three lies. Threes and threes and threes, like the stories said. Surely I could not be doing anything so terribly wrong if I was following the edicts of the tales in the codex so closely.

My vision glazed over and I almost didn't notice the man coming down the street toward our house until he stopped right at the gate and started rattling it with desperate vigor. For a moment I thought it might be Derkach again, but this man was young and had the lean, hungry look of so many of Oblya's day laborers. I didn't recognize him as any of my clients, or Rose's, or Undine's. I had never seen him before.

After a few more moments of futile rattling at the locked gate, the man began to yell.

Papa lurched up from his seat and joined me at the window. A dangerous breath feathered against my cheek. "Marlinchen, who is that?"

"I don't know," I said, stomach knotting. "He isn't one of mine."

"It looks like he might be mad. So many of Oblya's young men are these days, driven to lunacy by the wheeling carousel of pleasure houses and gambling dens and two-ruble taverns. If he doesn't leave soon, I'll have to cast a spell."

As far as I knew, Papa had not erected a new skeleton of magic over the house; we were as exposed as a crab without its conch, which only made Papa meaner and angrier.

But I did not see any sheen of madness in the man's eyes, only a fervent distress that squeezed out a drop of pity from me. A hasty, reckless lie rose in my throat, and before I could stop it, I said, "I think I do recognize him after all. He is one of my clients. He'll have money for me."

Papa's gaze shifted in a way that was almost magic, in a way that almost made me spit out my lie like a sip of bad milk. But he only said, "Let us go out and see this client of yours."

Together, and leaving his plate half-finished, we opened the door and stepped out into the ravaged garden. The goblin ran up to me crying and Papa made a noise of such scathing reproach that I felt sorrier for it than ever, and I just barely resisted the urge to scoop up the goblin into my arms. What had it ever done wrong?

My bare feet sank into the wet dirt, and crushed flower petals pasted themselves to my ankles. When he saw us coming, the man stopped rattling and only stared, eyes wet and shining.

I knew now without a lick of doubt that I had never seen him before, and I tasted the awful bile of my deception.

"The young men in this city have no sense of courtesy," Papa spat. "It's hardly past dawn, boy. Why are you rattling our gate like some dog in its kennel?"

"Please, sir," he said. "My name is Nikolos Ioannou. Niko. I'm a flatmate of Fedir, Fedir Holovaty. He told me he's one of your regular clients. Ms. Vashchenko's, I mean."

He was Ionik—I almost wished I had realized before I'd gone out to meet him. It would rile Papa even more.

Papa's anger blew off him like tobacco smoke, oily and hot. "And what need do you have of her services?"

Niko's face blanched. "Not me, sir. It's Fedir. He's terribly ill, and no doctors in the city will see him. He said that they don't believe him, that he's really sick. But he is, Ms. Vashchenko, I swear it. He's been vomiting for hours now, and our whole flat smells of death. He told me you're the only one who would see him—he said you promised him you would come if he called."

I drew in a breath, feeling only bewildered and scared. Papa spoke before I could.

"My daughters don't work for free. And they don't leave the house. If your friend is in such dire need of Marlinchen's help, tell him to come here himself, and with a sack of rubles in his hand."

"But he's too sick to come. He can't even walk." Strands of wheat-colored hair peeked out from under Niko's cap, sweat plastering them to his forehead. There was a faint gray hue to his skin, a marbled look like old milk, and from the way his body was trembling I wondered if he hadn't already caught whatever Fedir had. "Please, Mr. Vash-chenko. Sir. I can give you the money that I have now, and more when your daughter gets to our flat. I don't—Fedir is my friend. I can't watch him die."

Such a terrible swell of guilt came over me that I started to shake too, inhaling hot and fast. I *had* promised Fedir I would treat him, no matter the ailment. I had promised I would go to him. I said, "Papa, we need the money. We do."

Papa looked between Niko and me, head snapping back and forth so hard that his cheeks flapped and the wind bristled through his beard and he looked as mean as a bloodhound, trying to decide where first to close his teeth.

I had survived this quick-jawed fury before by staying quiet until it ebbed, and somehow Niko seemed to sense, too, that only silence and stillness would save us. He curled his white-knuckled hands around the bars of the gate and both of us held our breaths until the angry flush drained from Papa's face and at last he said, in a rough voice like black water breaking over rocks, "There better be rubles waiting for us when we get there, boy."

In another hour I had dressed and done what I could to tame my hair and taken a sample of every herb I managed to find in Rose's storeroom. I also swiped the compendium off her desk. Even though I was not an herbalist myself, I was still a witch and I hoped that maybe I could imbue the tonics and elixirs with a bit of my own magic to make them work.

It was only that—a hope. My magic was just for showing; it wasn't for doing or changing or making. But I had promised to go to Fedir and I knew I would not be able to bear it if he died without me trying everything I could to save him.

I had not been out into the city with Papa since before my mother had died, when he had taken my sisters and me with him to the market, or to the specialty shops, or to see Titka Whiskers and some of the other witches and wizards in Oblya. Mostly he was judging his competition, but Titka Whiskers always gave us squares of honey cake to eat and let me pull on her huge black lashes, which were as thick as crow's feathers, forcing her cat-eyes open and shut and open and shut, over and over again until I got tired and fell asleep curled in her lap.

My mother did not like Titka Whiskers. She said she wanted her daughters to be doctors' wives, not witches. She wanted to train us to host picnics and luncheons, not to make poultices for ringworm or see fortunes in the bottoms of our teacups. But no respectable man in Oblya would wed a witch, even a beautiful one. My sisters and I were only their furtive nighttime fantasy; we lived inside their heads, not beside them in their marriage beds.

The idea of his daughters marrying doctors was palatable enough to my father, and when he discovered that we were witches, initially he despaired of our prospects. Then he realized that he could use our magic and then Mama died and then none of us left the house so there were no men to meet anyway.

Now Niko led us down Kanatchikov Street, in the opposite direction of the ballet theater. The storm had made everything damp and muggy; I felt like I was being squeezed by a fist of air. My hair was already curling out of its tenuous updo. In the daylight the streets were busier even than at night, with trams and carriages skittering over the cobblestones like beetles and kumys sellers pushing their carts and brokers in snug black suits pacing furiously toward the stock exchange.

I had not been down any of these streets in the daytime before, at least not in a very long time, yet there was something immensely familiar about the way that cobblestones rolled beneath my feet. As if my body remembered something that my mind did not.

As we went on, we came across the beggars and the drunkards, propped up against the sides of buildings or clumped along alleyways like growths of mold, faces ashen and sweat-slick. I saw Papa curl his lip as we passed one of them, dark bottle still held limply between the man's finger and thumb. Magic rose from Papa like hair on a dog's hackles, and it was only because Niko sped up then that my father didn't loose his spell. The drunkard rolled over and pressed his cheek against the cobblestones.

In this part of Oblya, where I had never been, the buildings were like card houses half-toppled. Awnings were wind-thrashed and yellow with time. The windows were clotted with dead black flies and smudged with handprints that lingered like grease on a pie pan. Slack clotheslines crisscrossed above our heads, cutting up the gray sky into slivers. Greasy smoke chuffed from second-floor balconies and stray dogs limped down the road, nosing heaps of garbage.

And all around us were young men, the day laborers, though it shocked me more than anything how they seemed not to be doing any labor at all. They were sitting on the stoops and some of them were smoking and some had weathered sets of dominoes or half-empty vodka bottles, but most were only sitting there and staring, their teeth tobacco-black. I quickened my pace and caught up to Niko, even as Papa scowled and scowled, and asked in a whisper, "Why are they just sitting here?"

"There's no work for them today," Niko said. "Most of us don't have regular jobs, you see. We can go around to the factories and the shops and ask the foremen and owners if they need anything, but a lot of the time they don't, or someone else has gotten there first. And no jobs means no money and of course nothing to eat."

One man's eyes latched onto me, sharp and bright as the ends of kitchen knives. He leaned over and whispered something to another man beside him, and they both smirked like sated cats. A bit of sweat chilled on the back of my neck, and then Papa grasped me by the wrist and ushered me along.

Niko led us to a small grocery with Ionik lettering in gold along its glass windows and a green awning that drooped and sagged like one of Papa's cheeks. Inside, hunched behind the counter, was an acorn of a man with three precise tufts of black hair: one over each of his ears and one feathering across the top of his round head. He craned his neck slowly toward Niko, like a very fat dog rolling over, and the moment he saw him he began a muffled tirade, words inaudible behind the grease-smeared glass.

Niko's face went pale, and he hurried up to the building's side door, took out his key and twisted it, then beckoned Papa and me inside.

The hallway was dark and warm and had the wet, musty smell of laundry left too long in the wash basin. Papa stiffened up, his shoulders around his ears, and barked, "I'm losing my patience, boy. For a trip through the festering slums you'll owe us five rubles, and that's before my daughter even sees your patient."

"We're almost there," Niko mumbled, his face still bloodless. He led us up the narrow staircase, my knees starting to go weak beneath me and Papa's breath growing heavier and hotter against my neck. Perhaps I had made a bad mistake.

We reached another small door, and Niko began to take out his key again, but before he could manage to get it in the lock the door swung open before him. In the threshold was a black-haired man with blue eyes and such a craggy, handsome look that I recognized him at once, even squinting through the half-light.

Sevas.

He saw me over Niko's shoulder and his mouth opened once, wordless, then closed again. Papa's face was inches from mine but I didn't even glance back at him; I could tell from the hitch in his breathing that he recognized Sevas too. Silence fell over the darkened stairwell.

"Move, Sevas," Niko said. "I brought the witch and her father."

Still looking at me blankly, Sevas stepped aside and let Niko shuffle past. I followed him more slowly, each step groaning under my weight, all the while feeling the press of a hundred daggers at my back.

When I reached the landing I stopped, my stomach turning over on itself, and even though I knew Papa was there with his knives I whispered to Sevas, "I didn't know—how could I know—"

"Marlinchen." Papa's voice was like a pour of cold bathwater. "If you leave me standing on these stairs another moment I will turn you into a bluefish and gut you myself."

Very quickly I stepped farther into the apartment, a feverish red rising in my cheeks. The whole flat was only one room with three cots and a single dingy window. Right away I could smell bile and blood, both so strong that my eyes went fierce with water and I had to put a hand over my mouth.

Fedir was lying on one of the cots, bare-chested and still, sick crusted in the corners of his lips. There was a pail of it on the floor beside him and even more splattered on the wood. A heap of filthy rags had been used to clean it, and him, and now they were littered around the flat like a strewing of beached carp. My fingers curled around the spine of the herbalist's compendium, the whole room tilting and heaving.

It began to crystalize in me that I had indeed made a bad mistake.

Papa saved me from speaking. He shouldered right past Sevas and up to Niko. "Before my daughter does a lick of work I want to see that you have the rubles. Ten for coming all the way to the slums, and twenty more for your friend's healing."

"Outside you said five!"

"I'd be happy to take my leave again if the price doesn't suit you. But as you said, no other doctors in the city will see you, and your friend doesn't look like he has time to spare for your haggling."

Niko's face pinked. He went to one of the small cabinets and took out a sack of coins. Mutinously, he counted out ten rubles. I thought of the men I'd seen outside on the stoop, the gray, blank hopelessness on their faces, and I could feel something tightening around my heart like a length of copper wire.

Papa took the coins and stuffed them into his pocket, distending it badly, the way I sometimes saw his cheeks swell when he ate too much too fast. Sevas was standing so close to me that I could feel the air stiffening between us, and while my father argued with Niko over the rest, finally I turned to look at him.

I had not seen him in such a state since that first night in the alley, and this was perhaps even more disarming. Sevas's eyes were exceptionally bloodshot and his hair was falling over his forehead with none of its usual deliberate dishevelment. Above his sharp cheekbones were two sleepless bruises, like daubs of violet paint. And I could tell by the coiled tension in his shoulders and how quickly his chest rose and fell that he had been kept awake these nights by panic, by terror. A swallow ticked down his throat.

"Marlinchen," he said, and even now hearing my name on his lips made me quiver. "Please. I don't know if there's much you can do for him, with your magic or otherwise, but you must try. Fedir is my friend. He's a good man. He doesn't deserve to die—as if death has any care for who deserves it."

He laughed, but it was a raw, scraped-out sound.

"Of course I'll try." My eyes were bleary with the smell of Fedir's vomit. "Papa will kill me if I don't."

"I wouldn't let that happen."

"You would not be able to stop him," I said, though I bit back a smile at the thought that he would try. "Do you really live here? I assumed you would live with Mr. Derkach . . ."

I trailed off as Sevas's face shuttered. "No, I don't live with Derkach. Not anymore."

"Marlinchen," Papa barked. "Stop talking to that boy and come here before this man drowns in his own sick."

He must have settled on a deal with Niko. Trying not to inhale through my nose, I crossed the flat and knelt beside Fedir's cot. His eyes were shut and he was as still as death, but when I leaned over his mouth I could feel the barest whisper of air against my cheek.

My relief came and then went as quick as a snuffed match. I had never seen a man this sick before, and even if I could discern what was ailing him, I didn't know if I could cure it. My magic wasn't any good for that. But Papa was staring at me with blades behind his eyes and Niko had his head in his hands and Sevas's bottom lip was chewed up so terribly that I saw little black spots of dried blood in it, and so I looked up at them and asked, "When did he first start showing symptoms?"

"He came home last night and we thought he'd been drinking." Niko peered at me through the gaps in his fingers, voice low. "He kept going down the hall to the bathroom, once an hour and then twice an hour, and then eventually he couldn't move from his cot. We brought him a pail so he wouldn't have to leave, and he kept us up the whole night with his retching. By morning he could scarcely speak, except to tell us not to call any of the doctors in Oblya. Only you."

I let out a trembling breath, almost a laugh if I had dared. I was nothing close to a doctor and all I had was a satchel of herbs and my sister's compendium. Still, I swallowed the rising fear in my throat and said, "And have either of you started to come down with anything?"

"No," said Niko, and Sevas shook his head. "Whatever he's sick with, I don't think it's catching."

That, at least, was some good fortune. I let my fingers unclench and prepared to take Fedir's face in my hands, but before I could he began to cough and splutter, sick bubbling between his lips.

Panic slid down my spine and I tried to prop him into a sitting position so he wouldn't choke, but his skin was so damp and clammy that I couldn't find purchase and his body was so limp and heavy that I couldn't have lifted him either way, and as the stream of panic turned to ice in my belly, Sevas knelt beside me and helped me to push Fedir up.

Together we held Fedir by the shoulders as he leaned over the bucket and was loudly, violently ill.

"I've got him," Sevas said quietly as he began to rub a slow circle against the small of his friend's back. "You can let go, Marlinchen."

So I did, fingers trembling horribly. Papa's breaths had gotten loud and dangerous and I knew it was because Sevas had been too friendly with me by saying my name and, by his estimation, I was more than friendly in return.

I could no longer afford so much as to smile at him, not with Papa in the room. I waited until Fedir had finished retching and then said in a sharp voice, "You aren't getting paid anything to help."

Sevas's eyes darted between my father and me, then he gave a quick nod and stood up again. He knew my meanness was only for Papa's sake, and a shudder of both yearning and fear went up my spine at that silent understanding between us.

Once Fedir was lying down again, lashes fluttering weakly, I could pinch his earlobe between my finger and thumb and hold my other hand along the line of his jaw.

The vision seeped into me like someone had cracked a soft-boiled egg and let the yolk run past my eyes. The flat winnowed away, and I was standing in Oblya's streets at night, everything slick-looking in the dark. My hands were rough with yellow calluses and I could tell right away that they were Fedir's hands now. There was a tremendous ache running from the back of my knees all the way up between my shoulder blades—the ache, I assumed, of a long day's labor and longer days without enough to eat. The road that stretched out in front of me was studded with bright, smiling faces, the faces of other young men who looked like adolescent borzoi as they loped down the street, all elbows and gangly legs.

I went after them, unsteady on my own legs, and there was a haze that made everything seem as dewy as the morning after a storm. All of us went laughing down an alleyway and then through a door into a tavern, which I could tell right away was a poorer establishment than the one I had been to with Sevas, because there were only blackened oil lamps inside and no women laughing daintily.

At the bar, we ordered vodka in dirty glasses and drank it all without stopping for breath. And then, as my sight—as Fedir's sight—got blearier and closer, I stumbled into the bathroom and leaned over the sink and turned on the faucet. Water poured into my mouth and I swallowed. After the vodka it tasted like nothing at all.

Darkness closed around me, and when I managed to open my eyes again I was back in the flat, still kneeling over Fedir's body. Gooseflesh rose on my arms as the vision ebbed, and I took my hand off his jaw and let go of his earlobe. It was bright pink and swollen where my fingers had pressed so hard into it.

Sevas was watching me with a sort of bridled concern, though Papa's glare kept him from speaking. When I had managed to calm my jaggedly pounding heart, I said, "He went to a tavern last night, and drank water from the sink. Have any of you ever—"

Before I could even finish, Niko let out a groan. "Oh, Fedir, you damn idiot. Everyone knows that tavern bathrooms are about as clean as the end of a street sweeper's broom. You might as well lick the cob-blestones. There's something in the water that got him sick."

I had heard floated rumors about illnesses you could catch from drinking dirty water, and a few years before I was born there had been a spate of deaths that Papa recounted happily, because the slums were purged of nearly a third of their residents. Now I felt my own stomach churn and roil.

As I brushed back tendrils of sweat-damp hair from my forehead, there was a knock on the door.

All of us went quiet, and I could hear only the sound of Fedir softly moaning. There was another rap on the door, more urgent this time. I began to speak, but Niko put a finger to his lips, eyes glassy with panic.

After the knocking had ceased again, he whispered, "It's the land-lord. We're two weeks behind on our rent."

Papa gave a huff of anger. "Boy, he knows you're inside. It reeks like death in here and I'm losing my patience with this whole en-deavor. My daughter's work is already costing more rubles than you can spare."

As Niko opened his mouth to reply, a voice came from the other side of the door. "Sevastyan, if you don't open up I'll bring the Grand Inspector and his men to break your lock." It wasn't the landlord.

It was Derkach.

What little color there had been drained from Sevas's face. With-out speaking, he paced slowly across the apartment and paused with his hand on the knob. I could see his chest swell with a held breath. After a moment, he opened the door just enough to peer out, knuck-les whitening around the knob, but before Sevas could say a word Derkach stuck his foot into the knife-thin crack and barreled into the apartment.

He scarcely paused to take in the scene before wheeling on Se-vas. "Are you absolutely mad? Practice began an hour ago and none of the other dancers can start without their Ivan. It would be one thing if this was the first practice you've missed, or even the second or the third, but since coming to Oblya you're gone more than you're there, and that's not even considering how many times you run out into the alley after a show to retch. I found the vodka in your dressing room; don't think you can lie to me about *sea air* any longer."

As Derkach stopped to inhale, at last his gaze ran over the small flat. He saw Fedir sprawled on his cot and me kneeling beside him and my father standing above us both and Niko slumped against the wall, face in his hands. Sevas was staring at the ground. Derkach turned back to him and said, "What the hell is going on here?"

"Fedir has been sick," Sevas mumbled. "My flatmate. I had to stay here and help."

Derkach's lips went thin and white. His voice was very low when he said, "And what did I warn you would happen, Sevas, if you moved out from under my roof? I told you the only lodging you could afford would be in the slums, shared among workingmen without more than a ruble to their names on any given day. What if you come down with your poor flatmate's illness? What will the company do without its Ivan, and what will your mother think when I tell her I had to bury her only son in Oblya?"

"It isn't catching." I was so surprised to hear myself speak that I flushed at once, all the way from forehead to chin. "Fedir's illness, I mean. Sevastyan will be fine."

"Ms. Vashchenko," Derkach said, and when he looked at me his eyes narrowed like I was something imperceptibly small, "I appreciate your concern, but *I* am the one who is paid to fret over Sevas. Please return to your work and leave me to my charge."

My cheeks were burning. Sevas still had not looked up from the floor.

Fedir coughed again, and with shaking fingers I opened the herbalist's compendium. The parchment was as thin as onion skin, and Rose's handwriting was smudged and tiny, like a hundred spiders had been squished onto the page. Some notes were accompanied by

pressed samples of herbs or flower petals; others were merely illus-
trated with my sister's drawings, which were as difficult to discern as
her penmanship.

I flipped through the pages with mortified deliberation, trying to
make it seem like I was looking for something particular. In truth, I
had no idea where even to begin. I would've had just as much luck if it
had been written in Ionik. Behind me, Derkach was speaking to Sevas
in a hushed tone.

When I dared to glance over my shoulder I saw that he had one
hand gripping the back of Sevas's neck. I recognized the gesture: tenderness and cruelty both. Derkach's voice was low in a way that Papa's
sometimes was, in a way that meant danger. I did not know Derkach
well and I could not make out more than a few words, floating on the
surface like specks of white cream in borscht, but I knew that they
meant danger too.

I heard *theater* and *practice* and *show* and *money*. I heard *ungrateful* and *impudent* and *careless*. I heard *drunk* and *indecent*. I heard my
name.

My head snapped up, but Papa's voice curled its own vise around
my throat. "What are you waiting for? Do you really want to keep me
any longer in this wretched flat?"

Face hot, I returned to the book. On the first page was a table
of contents, which I could mostly read. But just because I knew the
words didn't mean I could understand what they meant all put together. There were two sections, one for *Diseases of the Body* and one
for *Diseases of the Mind*. Under *Diseases of the Body* I found more than
a dozen subheadings: *Diseases of the Skin* and *Diseases of the Liver* and
Diseases of the Gums.

Fedir moaned, his blue-white chest heaving. I flipped to the page
marked *Diseases of the Stomach*.

I had to hold the book up to the meager sunlight cast through
the single dingy window, squinting and squinting. I could scarcely tell
where one letter ended and the other began, but even once I managed

to separate them my prospects did not improve. Everything was written as if it were a riddle; I couldn't fathom why my careful and clever sister did not better organize her book. Perhaps she didn't want anyone else to be able to read it.

I pressed my thumb to the page so hard that my nail tore a small slit in the parchment, taking the time to swallow each word as I went along, turning them over on my tongue like they were sucking candies.

If the Patient is fair of Hair and gray-eyed, use double the Dose and check Appendix I–II.

If it is Sunday and there has been a Bout of Rain, only use Herbs that have been cut twice at the Stem.

If You are angry when You treat the Patient, lick your Thumb before delivering the Dose.

Moisture was gathering at the corners of my eyes and my stomach was as tight as a flower bud. As I scanned down the page, Derkach's voice grew louder and drifted toward me.

". . . after everything that I've done for you, Sevas, at great personal cost, the least you could do in return is not make me look like a damned fool. Am I fool to you? Am I?"

"No," Sevas said. I had never heard him sound so cowed. "I'm sorry."

My heart gave a horrible lurch of hurt, as if I were the one who'd been scolded. Papa stepped closer to me until he was standing on the hem of my dress, the shiny toe of his boot crumpling the pink silk. I could not remember whether Fedir had gray eyes, so I had to hold my breath and lean closer and peel back one of his eyelids to check. His lips were bone-white and cracking like old plaster.

It occurred to me, quite suddenly, that if Fedir had consumed poison, he had vomited enough that it all should have been expelled. If he died of anything now, it would be only terrible thirst.

I turned back to the table of contents and perused the items listed under *Diseases of the Mind*. I remembered Papa saying that Titka

Whiskers's curse had its teeth in his head, too—that it had chewed up all the parts of him that remembered what it felt like to be full.

I flipped to another page of Rose's compendium, then looked up at Niko and asked, "Do you have water here? Good water?"

"Yes, ma'am," he said. "From the bathroom down the hall."

"Go fetch some, please. As much as you can."

Niko nodded and went off, and I stared down at the book in brow-furrowed concentration, trying to close my ears to the sound of Derkach's voice.

When I dared to glance up again, he was gently stroking Sevas's cheek. I felt as sick as Fedir.

In another moment, Niko came back with a pail full of water. I opened the satchel of herbs I'd taken from Rose and sifted through until I found the ones I needed—thyme and motherwort and crushed poppies—all for treating men who needed to be convinced of their own illness, and the potency of its cure. Denial was, after all, a Disease of the Mind.

"Will you help me get him up?"

Niko crouched beside me and pushed Fedir into a sitting position. While he did that, I gently pried apart his lips and laid the herb mixture on his tongue. Then I pinched his nose and covered his mouth with my hand until he choked and coughed and swallowed it. I let my hands drop to my sides. Fedir groaned, head lolling, chin thumping onto his chest.

Seconds dragged past, like garbage caught in a sea net. Out of the corner of my eye, I saw Derkach's lips move against the shell of Sevas's ear, and I looked away, flushing, and then at last Fedir said, "I'm so thirsty."

Relief broke open in me, so warm and sweet that I smiled and even laughed. "Here," I said, as Niko pushed the bucket toward me. I cupped water into my hands and lifted them to his mouth. "Drink."

And he did and he did and he did. He lapped water out of my hands like a puppy and then cried like a child, and I felt my own eyes grow misty when he leaned over the bucket and scooped out water himself, beads of it falling past his lips and down the grooves of his chest, splashing onto the cot and floor. A bit of color returned to Fedir's face, just two faint pink circles like rouge applied with little attention.

I sat there and watched Fedir drink until, above us, Papa cleared his throat.

"You owe me forty rubles for my daughter's work," he said.

Niko's jaw went slack. "But we agreed on thirty—please, sir! That's more than I made these past three weeks and twice as much as I owe in rent to Mr. Papadopoulos. I have work lined up tomorrow at one of the printing shops on Kanatchikov Street, but it will take me some time to come up with the money."

The blood in my veins turned to ice. Niko had made a bad mistake, and now we would all suffer Papa's anger, the rage of the great wizard Zmiy Vashchenko. The words of a spell were already rising in his throat and magic was lifting off him in waves of cold, a frigid mist stealing over the whole small flat. My teeth started to chatter so hard that it hurt, and I bit down on my own tongue and tasted a burst of coppery blood.

Across the room Sevas's lips were bleeding too, the scabs split open and made new. There was a mark of red where Derkach's hand had rested against the back of his neck.

"My daughter doesn't work for free, boy," Papa snarled, "and I don't trust Ionik scum to pay back their debts, especially when they can't make rent! I should call the Grand Inspector; I should have his men come and burn down this whole derelict slum. I'm loath to waste any more spellwork on you, but there must be fitting punishment for your silver-tongued deceit, for all the false tears you shed and all the sympathy you roused in my daughter's simple mind. No—I think I know what I shall do. I think I shall turn you into a yellow-billed magpie. They sing pretty songs too."

"Papa, no!" I cried, and I couldn't believe the vehemence in my voice, my boldness. It was like a little bit of the girl who had danced with Sevas in the tavern had leaked into me. "Isn't it better to have the promise of money in the future than nothing at all? We have no use for a yellow-billed magpie, but a man can work and pay us back over time."

Papa took one step toward Niko and then stopped. When he turned to me his eyes were flashing, like two bright lights were shining out from inside his head.

"This is not only a matter of money," he said. "For your kind and generous heart, you have always been mostly empty-headed, Marlinchen. It isn't your fault, but it's why I have protected you from the world, protected you from the likes of these men, here—inebriates and grifters, little better than the drunkards we saw passed out in the road. They are a mere day's work, or lack thereof, away from being beggars themselves. You see this one and feel pity because you are soft of heart. But more of these men will come and they will descend on this city like a pack of dogs on a dead mule, and so we must hold ourselves fast against the tide of it. Oblya will not miss a single day laborer. If anything, it means more work for the rest."

And then he raised his hand, Niko cowering, and I lurched to my feet, pulling my skirt out from under Papa's boots. He stumbled back, nearly crashing into Sevas and Derkach, but catching himself instead against the wall.

When at last he had righted himself, his face as purple as his beard, Papa only said, "Marlinchen, you've made a bad mistake."

Before I could even flinch, Sevas stepped between us. There was blood smeared on the back of his hand.

"Mr. Vashchenko," he said, sounding more abased than I had ever heard him, and still scarcely looking up from the ground, "there's no need for you to use your magic here. I can pay. I can pay double."

The brilliant violet flush flared at Sevas's interruption, but as Papa considered his words, his face cooled again. In an icy tone, he said, "Eighty, then."

Sevas nodded, and then glanced over at Derkach with a furrowed brow and beseeching eyes. Sighing, Derkach retrieved a sack of coins from his pocket and thrust them all at Papa. Without speaking, Papa snatched the bag from him.

I stared up at Sevas, unable to summon any words myself. There was the cold shadow of Papa's magic, still seeping like damp winter air into my bones. There was my own terror, too, so many awful imaginings turned loose in my mind: What had Sevas offered Derkach, to earn his easy acquiescence?

I had made countless trades like this myself, vows that I would keep like holding a steaming skillet in my bare hands, biting my lip as it burned, debts that would come due only when everyone else had gone and the house was empty and I was lying curled in my bed.

Our gazes met, and Sevas gave me a crooked, trembling smile.

"There," Derkach said, after Papa had counted out all his coins and tucked them away in his tumorous pocket, "now that this has all been settled, we can take our leave. In the future, Ms. Vashchenko, I would prefer not to see you at the ballet theater again. Ever since your visit this week Sevas has been more inattentive than ever. Please, he has enough trouble keeping his mind on his work."

Papa did not speak a word to me as we left Sevas's flat. His fingers were clamped so tightly around my wrist that I could feel the skin breaking under his nails. I did not dare to even whimper.

He dragged me through the streets of Oblya, his footsteps brisk and hard, like stones being dropped from a great height. I was so scared that my mind kept spluttering and stammering around all the possibilities; my fear was a pit too huge to swallow. When at last Papa jerked open the gate and hurled me into the garden, I was panting and sweating profusely, my bodice and corset straining with every breath.

Still he did not speak. Indrik gaped at us over a blackberry bush and the goblin peered out from behind his cloven feet. I could feel my gorge rise, even though I had eaten nothing that day. As Papa pulled me into the house, I had to clap my free hand over my mouth to keep from retching.

My sisters were awake now, and when they heard us they came hurrying out into the foyer, just as the grandfather clock gonged noon. Papa did not say a word to them either. He only hauled me up the stairs, down the long hallway, and into my bedroom, Rose and Undine mewling at our heels.

He let go of my wrist at last, blood welling from the tiny crescents that his nails had dug into my skin. He wrenched open the door of my wardrobe and flung all my dresses onto the floor, clawing through the silk, whalebone snapping in his fists. He dumped out all of my jewelry, whatever hadn't been sold, and pawed at the heap of pearls and gold.

When he found nothing, he stormed past us into Rose's room, gutting her wardrobe and disemboweling her jewelry box and crushing the teeth of the ivory-handled comb that lay on her desk. Mama's comb. I put my wrist into my mouth and licked at the blood there, salt bursting on my tongue. Finally he went to Undine's room.

There, Papa threw her dresses on the floor and scattered her jewelry over the carpet and even smashed her boudoir mirror, glass shards exploding like a dandelion's split seed hull. Tiny sharp bits landed on my dress and in my hair. Beside me, Rose was weeping without making a sound, tears tracking two neat paths down her cheeks. Undine lunged toward Papa and beat her fists against his chest.

"I hate you!" she screamed. "I hate you, I hate you, I hate you!"

Papa thrust her away from him with a mindless, animal twitch, like a bull shaking off a gathering of flies. She lilted to the ground, limp and bodiless as a white linen dress. On her hands and knees, golden hair falling in twin curtains over her face, Undine began to weep too.

"How did you do it?" Papa grasped me by the shoulders and shook me hard enough to make my teeth rattle. "Selfish daughters, thankless daughters, wretched daughters, tell me how you broke my spell!"

Sevas had tried to stop him. As Papa had taken my wrist and

yanked me down the stairs, Sevas had called out my name. I could hear his footsteps following after me until, suddenly, they ceased, and then I heard only Derkach's hushed and livid voice. I thought of Sevas's beautiful face in the moonlight, the white boardwalk stretching out before us like some large creature's spectacular vertebrae.

I thought of the mark that Derkach's hand had left on his neck. I thought of Mama's compact, buried safely under the juniper tree. My secret. My lie.

I did not say a word.

Finally, Papa let me go. He was breathing so loudly and his magic was all heat instead of ice, his rage like oily smoke that made my eyes burn. Undine looked up through the curtains of her hair. Rose wiped at the tears on her cheeks.

"Just get it over with," Undine bit out. "Feed us potions that will rot our lungs like bad fruit. Turn us into hags with chicken feet. It would be just as well. I can't stand another moment being trapped here with you."

But Papa only laughed, and it sounded like wine spilling from the spout of an overfed wineskin. "No, it's not magic I have to visit upon you. That would be a waste of my power. Yet what am I to do with such useless, deceitful daughters living under my roof, daughters whose magic can scarcely bring in enough money to feed me? What would another man do, if his wife had died without using his seed to sprout any sons? There's no spell that can transform inept witch-daughters into capable wizard-sons. But there *is* tonic that Oblya can provide. It is time for my witch-daughters to marry."

CHAPTER EIGHT

When I woke that next morning, I thought at first that it had all been a dream. Niko rattling our gate, Fedir lapping water out of my hands, Sevas cowering under Derkach's stare. Papa tearing through all our gowns and jewelry, crushing Mama's comb. But I lifted my arm from under the covers and held it over my head, a band blocking the pale drench of sunlight, and I saw the small black scabs pitted across it like a scattering of leeches, and I knew that it was real, all of it.

My dresses were still heaped on the floor and when I threw off the quilt and stood, I found my heel gouged with a loose pearl. I peered under my bed, but the monster was gone. It had been killed and eaten.

I pawed through the pile of dresses until I came upon the pink one that I had worn that night with Sevas in the tavern. The silk of the skirt had been shredded, as if with claws. But the pocket was intact and so was the white feather. I clutched it to my chest, inhaling a painful breath.

The feather had magic, but only as a talisman of my hopeless and agonizing and dashed desire. I laid it on my boudoir, where Mama's comb had once been. The comb she had used to brush my hair, weaving stories into my braids. The same story, over and over and over again, like the kneading of dough: Ivan and the swan-princess, Ivan and the winter king, Ivan Ivan Ivan who would not care if I was plain-faced and would come for me anyway.

Had Papa truly meant it, that he wanted to marry us off? He had spent all our lives keeping us safe here. But a change had come over him recently, a greater hunger, a new appetite. I could not predict its ebbs and flows the way I once could. I did not know how to navigate all these new holes in the ground, the changing arrangement of swinging daggers and snagging thorns. Derkach's revelation was terrible, yet something that was *not* my secret had shifted the stones in Papa's stream bed, and done so before today.

It seemed impossible that I could go downstairs and cook my father breakfast like nothing had happened, but truthfully I didn't know what else to do. Everything that had once been familiar felt foreign and strange.

My body remembered what I was meant to do even if my mind was a tumult of dark waves. I put on my housecoat, tied up my hair, and went downstairs.

Sunlight beamed through the half-rounded windows; the stairwell and the foyer were as still as the morning after a snowfall, everything obliterated in white. The grandfather clock's hand ached toward seven.

When I came into the sitting room that was when I first heard it—the sound of metal scraping wood, silverware clinking on china. And when, finally, I got to the kitchen, I saw Papa hunched over the butcher block. His chin and beard were streaked with strawberry kvass, pink and sweet-looking, and in his fist was a hunk of raw dough, what I had set aside for more varenyky.

The plate in front of him held the carcass of a chicken, still half-feathered, sinew draped from the scaffolding of its bones like a corset undone. The chicken's beak and comb were lying on the wood several inches away, and before he noticed that I had come in, I saw Papa put his fingers in his mouth and suck off the gristle and blood. A moan filled the silent room.

And then his gaze snapped toward me. "What are you doing here, Marlinchen?"

"I was going to make you breakfast." The words fell out of my mouth and clattered too loudly on the floor, like marbles dropped.

"I've already eaten," Papa said. He took the chicken's comb and tore off a piece of it with his teeth, then chewed and chewed and chewed. It must have been as tough as salt pork for how long he chewed it. Finally, he swallowed. "Go wake your sisters. Don't think I have forgotten your treachery."

I turned around just as Papa picked up the beak and swallowed it in one gulp; I could see the sickled shape of it as it traveled down his throat. It reminded me of the earliest days of his curse, when his body was still accustoming itself to its new and depthless hunger. When nothing existed outside or between Papa and his appetite.

I trudged back up the stairs and went first to Rose's room. She was still sleeping, curled as tight as a baby bird in its egg, fist closed under her chin. I stood beside her and prodded her shoulder gently.

Rose shot up at once, violet eyes wide as two spills of water, her long black braid lashing.

"What is it?" she asked.

"Papa wants us," I said.

Rose pinched the bridge of her nose. "I'm not going to be angry at you, Marlinchen. Papa has enough anger for twenty. But it was a terribly selfish thing of you to do, and don't you try to tell me otherwise. What's the worst that would've happened, if you hadn't gone? One man turned to a mass of vipers? But if he were an *ugly* man, one with less charm and no seduction in his smile, would you have minded at all?"

"I don't want anyone turned to snakes because of me."

"That's not the point." Rose threw off her covers. "I wish I hadn't helped you on your besotted fool's errand. All this talk of marriage is just a ruse; it must be. Some cunning new way for Papa to punish us, because the old ways weren't working well enough. Go wake Undine. My eyes are weary of looking at you."

I left Rose's room, my mind still roiling with storm clouds, my body working like a cotton mill, unconscious and automated. My sister was clever, but she had not seen the way that Derkach had gripped the back of Sevas's neck. She had not watched Papa devour a chicken whole. Perhaps I would have been clever too, if I did not have so much carnage behind my eyes.

Undine wasn't in her bed. She was standing by the window in one of her ruined gowns, the left sleeve ripped off and the collar torn down the middle, exposing the cleft of her breast and a sliver of pink nipple. I turned around at once, flushing fervently, but before I could get through the door Undine crossed the room and grasped me by my wrist.

She hurled me away from the door, and I stumbled back, catching myself against her unmade bed, and while I was still reeling she slapped me across the face.

The shock of it swallowed a bit of the pain, but when the numbness ebbed, I felt as if I'd pressed my cheek against the lit stovetop. I whimpered at that bristling heat as Undine arched over me, breathing furiously through her nose. I opened my mouth—to protest? To apologize?—and she slapped me again.

This time, I bleated out a shocked little sound, like a rutted sheep.

"Stop being a baby," Undine said as she stepped away from me. "I didn't even hit you very hard."

"It hurt," I said.

"Well, I meant to. Hurt you, I mean. What would be the point in slapping you otherwise? You're such an idiot, Marlinchen."

"I'm sorry."

She heaved a sigh—exasperated rather than exhausted—then pulled up the ragged collar of her dress so that it covered her nipple. "I think you're so stupid you don't even know why I'm calling you stupid. Do you?"

"Because Papa tore up our dresses and jewelry and says he will make us marry and that was because of me."

"It's not *just* that," Undine snapped. She leaned over and plucked up a pair of slippers from the ground, matching the glossy peacock of her spoiled gown. The heels were tattered, like something small had chewed through the silk. "You don't think I wouldn't love to be wed to some man, *any* man, who would take me away from this disgusting place? This shrine to Papa's curse, the instrument of his loathing? But he'll never let that happen. Whatever he has planned for us, it's only more misery."

It was the same thing that Rose had said. Perhaps Undine was just as clever as my middle sister, under all her frothing cruelty.

My cheeks were still prickling with tiny needles of heat. I pulled my housecoat tighter around myself while Undine slipped on her shoes and walked toward the door, turning back to look at me with her hand on the knob.

"You should be angry at me," she said.

"Why?"

She looked at me with disdain. "Because I just *slapped* you. You are insufferable sometimes. You're not doing me, or yourself, any favors by pretending not to mind when you get hurt. I would have slapped you harder if I didn't know the truth—if I didn't know that you would just blush and bat your lashes as someone tied a tourniquet around your thigh and prepared to saw your leg off. Do you know why the worst thing Papa has ever done to me is push me to my knees? Because I wail and scream and beat his chest with my fists whenever he tries to do anything more than bark orders at me from the chaise. You think he wants some mute little china doll to cook his meals and wash his sheets? No. He wants daughters with teeth. The hurting is the point.

I can't believe it's taken you twenty-three years to figure out—if you even understand what I'm saying at all. It's no fun stamping through old dirty snow. People want to ruin things that are clean and new. And you should hear the way *men* talk! Some of our clients, even. A woman's worthless and spoiled once she's been bred. That's why Papa can't stand the idea. He can't stand the idea of anyone spoiling us but him."

And then she pushed through the door and slammed it shut behind her. I stood in the echo of the sound, run over and over again by the wave of my sister's words. By the time I managed to follow her, I felt exhausted and drenched, my throat raw with saltwater.

Maybe it wasn't cruelty Undine had chosen, just the truth, as mean and banal as it was. And maybe I hadn't picked kindness at all. Maybe I'd just shut my eyes and sat as still and silent as one of the women at the cotton looms, face made sallow by the factory lights, waiting for the machine to teach me what to do with my hands.

There was something sick in me, something wrong. Even baby birds knew how to shriek, even kittens knew how to mewl, even puppies knew how to whine. Papa had told me I hadn't even cried when he'd pulled me from between my mother's thighs. I hadn't protested when he dragged me through the streets of Oblya, hadn't protested when Rose had chided me or when Undine had slapped me. My eldest sister was right; I would smile blithely if someone tried to saw off my leg. But no one had ever told me that I was allowed to scream.

I walked down the stairs without hearing my own footsteps.

Papa was in the sitting room, perched on the chaise longue. The front of his shirt was stained with pink juice and I could see the bulge of his stomach under his robe, huge with everything he'd eaten. My own belly growled and I felt terribly embarrassed at the sound, wondering if everyone else could hear it too.

My sisters and I stood in a straight line before him, like saltshakers in dour observance of a feast, waiting for the moment when we would be snatched up and used.

His eyes plucked me up first. "I must thank you, Marlinchen, best and most dutiful of my daughters. If you hadn't taken me to that stinking slum, I never would have landed on the idea that will keep this family from ruin. It is not just the simple thing of marrying off my daughters, my witch-daughters, nor to whom. It is the choosing of your bridegrooms that will save us."

Papa was like this sometimes: speaking words that only he understood, but with the grandiloquence that imagined an audience of rapt thousands. When I dared to glance at Rose and Undine, I saw that their faces were as blank as mine. I turned back to watch Papa's bare feet crush the fibers of the carpet.

"This city is full to bursting with desperate, penniless young men," he went on, rising now and beginning to pace, certainly killing hundreds of dust mites with every step. "Who among them would not leap at the opportunity to wed one of Zmiy Vashchenko's daughters, and to someday inherit his estate?" Papa gestured vaguely at the ceiling with its splitting plaster, at the last of his cat-vases. "As soon as I announce this competition, we will scarcely be able to keep the crowds of men from our door."

"Competition." Rose dropped the word in front of us like a butcher slapping down a cured liver on the counter. "You want these desperate, penniless men to compete for our hands?"

Papa seemed barely to hear her. "I will do as you suggested, Rosenrot. I will go to the printing shop and buy a thousand flyers that all say the same thing: ZMIY VASHCHENKO'S DAUGHTERS TO BE WED—COME TO HIS HOUSE ON RYBAKOV STREET IF YOU WOULD LIKE TO ONE DAY OWN IT. I will post them all around Oblya and by nightfall, daughters, I guarantee it: half the men of this city will be rattling the gate into the garden."

"But how will you choose?" I managed to ask. My face was growing hot. I was thinking of how big a man's hands could be when they were reaching for you.

"I will give each man three nights to spend here in my home," Papa said. "Three nights during which he may speak to each of you, if he chooses, and explore the house as he sees fit. The only rule I demand he observe is not to venture to the third floor; I have already warded the door to the stairwell against any intruders. And, at the end of his three nights, he will tell me how my daughters managed to escape the house without a bowl of black sand. If he does speak the truth, I will give him his pick: golden-haired and sharp-tongued Undine, violet-eyed and clever-minded Rosenrot, plain-faced but kindhearted Marlinchen."

"I don't see how that solves anything," Undine snapped. "Our bellies will be just as empty as before, except with a new host of mouths to feed. Do you intend for these men, our guests, to eat goblin meat or glass apples?"

"I will charge each of them a petty fee," said Papa, scratching at a small red spider bite under his beard. "For three days of lodging and food and of course for the chance to wed one of my daughters. I do not think many of them will refuse. After all, what better prospects do they have in this city?"

I thought of Sevas's flat with its three cots and single grease-smeared window, of Niko's small sack of rubles and how quickly it had emptied. I thought of the smirking men on the stoops and the drunkards and beggars slumped over in alleyways. They were all stretched out and skinny like a length of dirty gray rope, their ends fraying and their eyes dull as knots. If you lifted up the large stone that was Oblya, how many of these ashen-faced men would you find writhing under it? How many had Undine and Rose and I swept by on our way to the ballet theater, our jewelry winking like the points of kitchen knives, our silks hissing like mean whispers?

We did not have much, and sometimes we did not have even enough to feed ourselves, but we always had this: a house with three stories and a sprawling garden and a solid black fence around it, water that ran when we turned the faucets, lamps that flickered when we yanked their pull chains, and of course magic to make everything a little easier, a little brighter. I felt suddenly so guilty and sad that my stomach turned over on itself. The desperation of these men had repulsed me, even terrified me, but really I ought to have pitied them.

Papa stopped his pacing. The grandfather clock on the wall gonged seven. It occurred to me that there was one thing Papa hadn't yet done: punish us. His punishments were usually swift and predictable, a new constraint, a tougher tribulation, something taken away and not replaced. So far I couldn't see what in his plan was supposed to make us freshly miserable. Perhaps my cleverer sisters could, but in truth, I was the one who knew Papa's cruelty better than either of them.

It had taken me so many years to realize this, but there were things I understood that my beautiful sisters never could.

"I don't suppose we have any choice at all," Undine said. Her voice was as frigid as a waft of air from the icebox.

"Why should I let you choose?" Papa's gaze cut to her with scissor-like precision. "Why should you get a say in anything at all? This is my house and you are my daughters and without my seed you would just be a dream in your mother's mind. I have given you everything, even endured the blow of Titka Whiskers's infernal curse, and you have repaid me only with loathing and deceit. It would cause me no grief to see you married off to a man with a face full of boils that spew pus in your marriage bed, or to a man who blackens his wife's eyes for burning dinner. I imagine you will be first chosen, Undine, loveliest and bitterest of my daughters. My black plum, sweet-tasting but poisonous."

"Even the cruelest and ugliest man in Oblya is far better than you," Undine spat, but I could see her face blanch. I thought of what she had said about Papa—that he wanted no one to spoil his daughters but him. I supposed this was one way of doing it. My sisters *would* be spoiled (no man would choose me to take to wife when Rose and Undine were there), but only through his orchestration. If you fed a man a potion that drove him to eat his neighbor's heart, you too would taste a bit of blood in your mouth.

Magic was like that. It always implicated its caster.

Rose stared at me from under her lashes, violet eyes fierce. We both knew the truth of how I had managed to elude Papa's spells, or at least we knew about the black sand. We could save that secret and spend it only on a good man, so that our sister wouldn't suffer with boils or beatings. Still I feared that this was not the worst thing Papa was planning for us. What would he do when he was presented with the truth? How would he fashion it into a sharper blade, a hotter brand? I knew that he meant to make a weapon of it.

My palms were growing damp and I wiped them on my nightgown. Rose looked angrier at me than she ever had before.

Papa didn't berate Undine for her words. Maybe it was true what she'd told me, about him wanting daughters with teeth. He only drew a breath and said, "The very least you all could do is make yourselves look lovely and sweet. Wash your faces and comb your hair, put on your mother's lilac perfume. Wear your finest dresses and shoes. The more men who fall in love, the fatter our feasts will be."

And then he pushed past us out of the sitting room, before Undine could protest or Rose could soberly remind him that he had trashed all of our gowns and jewels. Undine tugged at the torn collar of her dress and Rose fingered the end of her braid. I stared and stared at the flattened carpet, my stomach feeling as empty as a blue porcelain bowl.

"I'll take a bath first," Undine said finally, curtly, "and then Rose can go after. It makes no difference whether Marlinchen bathes or not. We all know that she will not be chosen for a bride."

It was as mean as I expected, but still her words made me flinch. I couldn't precisely blame Undine for her anger now—this was perhaps one occasion where being plain of face advantaged me. Undine stalked up the stairs; in another moment, I heard the bathroom door slam.

In the spell of silence that followed, Rose said, "You would save me, wouldn't you?"

"What?"

"You can only spend your secret once," she said, still fingering her braid. "I don't know how you got that black sand, and I don't think you would tell me even if I asked. That's all right. But say one man comes asking after me and another asking after Undine. You would tell Undine's suitor the truth, and leave mine in the dark, wouldn't you? Of all of us, Undine would survive best being wed to a strange man. You would be too afraid, and I couldn't bear it. I just couldn't. Tell me that you'd spend your secret to save me."

All I could do was gape at her, struck so dumb by her words. Never before had either of my sisters beseeched *my* help. Never before had I held something neither of them could touch. Rose knew as much of the truth as I did, but that didn't matter—she thought I had the secret that could either ruin or deliver her.

It felt like standing at the very top floor of our house and leaning over the railing, dizzy with the possibility of descent. It felt like knowing that you would fall but having to keep on leaning anyway until you did. I didn't want any part of it.

And, despite everything, Sevas was still my secret, my lie. The black sand had come off in *my* bath. It belonged to me and me alone. A new realization sank its dark roots into me: even if I had known where the black sand came from, I would not have told her.

"I told you everything I know," I said slowly. "About the bath and the black sand. You can have that secret and spend it however you wish. I don't know if it's enough for Papa, though."

Rose made a noise in the back of her throat and jerked upright, as if someone had yanked at her braid from above. "I've always been kind to you, Marlinchen. Kinder than Undine. I hope that you change your mind."

And then she was gone too. I stared at the absence of her, the vacant foyer, the grandfather clock's shadow planked across the floor. I didn't know what to do with the time that suddenly bloated up in front of me: hours swelling like dough left to rise, empty of all my usual tasks. Even the perfunctory sounds of the garden—the goblin's wailing and the eyeless ravens beating their wings—had momentarily gone quiet. Dust motes drifted within tracts of sunlight.

Like a trough, the empty space in my mind filled at once with thoughts of Sevas. There was his gray-washed face and the violet bruises under his eyes and his bloody, bitten lip. There was the red mark that Derkach's hand had left on his back and the shell of his ear as Derkach's lips brushed against it. I wondered about the words that he was pouring into Sevas's head, and that wondering held me so tight that suddenly it ached to breathe. It was like someone had twined whalebone around my chest, had made my heart its own strangling ivory corset.

I couldn't bear it, the not-knowing. I put my knuckle in my mouth and bit down on it hard, but the tears came anyway, crowding my eyes until I couldn't see anything through the blur of them. I thought of the grinning boy on the boardwalk and he seemed so very far away, nothing like the Sevas who had lowed himself to Derkach and my father. The tremulous smile he'd given me when he stepped between Papa and me kept playing over and over again in my mind like a bad vision. The bad visions were ones that took weeks to exorcise, that hung on the periphery of my gaze when I was awake and unfolded their black tendrils when I slept. Tears drenched my cheeks and dribbled into my mouth, stinging the newly opened cut on my knuckle. I was very hungry.

If Papa came home and saw me weeping he would punish me. Undine would slap me again and Rose would roll her eyes. I drew in a long breath that seemed to press up against the bones of my rib cage painfully. I dried my face with the sleeve of my housecoat and took my knuckle out of my mouth.

I could have breakfast, but the urge to throw it up afterward would be too strong. I let the possibility of it play out in my mind: I would have to eat the pickled cabbage first, marking the beginning of my feast with its violet color so that when I vomited purple I'd know that I was through. I would have to evade Indrik and bury my sick and wash all the plates and silverware that I dirtied. It was too much, and

Papa had forbade me from it anyway. I would rather go hungry than try to keep all the roiling food down.

I blinked the last teardrops from my lashes and went upstairs instead. Undine was still in her bath; I could hear the water sloshing from the other side of the bathroom door. The door to Rose's bedroom was shut, locked.

At the very end of the hallway was the door to the stairwell that led up to the third floor. The brass knob gleamed like a copper bucket at the bottom of a well. Papa had already warded it against intruders, and I wondered why. None of us had gone up there since Mama had died. The only things left were her empty cage, full of ossified droppings that no one had cleaned, and the white sheet that was draped like a languid ghost over the mirror that never lies. I had sold her charm bracelet and Undine had sold her pearls. There was nothing left of value to be looted.

As if in a trance I walked toward it, eyes trained on that gleaming knob, but before I reached it I turned abruptly, into my room.

Everything was just as I'd left it after waking up: the pawed-through pile of dresses on the ground, in floaty, gossamer pastel colors like beached jellyfish. The monster was still gone, in my father's belly. Sevas's feather was still on my boudoir. I snatched it up again, and the pain tore through me like a gut wound.

I had kept my secret, I had buried my black sand, but none of it had saved me. I couldn't save Sevas, whose throat still bore the tender, merciless wound of Derkach's hand. I couldn't save my sisters from the fate that Papa had planned for us, and I couldn't save myself from the story that had sprouted up around me like weeds, like ivy, like the smothering greenness of a garden left untended. Whatever story I was in, it was not "Ivan and the Swan Princess." My father would let in dozens of men to vie for my hand, but they would all be day laborers and the sons of freed serfs and not bogatyrs at all. They would take one look at my plain face, my carnage-filled eyes, and hurry toward the unspoiled safety of my sisters.

Tears came hotly to my eyes again, and what was the use in stopping them? I sat down in front of my boudoir to catch my breath, and I began to clap my hand over my mouth but then I remembered what Undine had said: *you would just blush and bat your lashes as someone tied a tourniquet around your thigh and prepared to saw your leg off.*

I choked out a sob and it sounded so strange coming from my mouth, like the noise belonged to a creature living in my body that was not me.

I was weeping into the palm of my hand when something gold caught the corner of my eye. It was glinting through the crack in one of my boudoir drawers, bleary but bright, like a coin in a fountain. I opened the drawer and took it out.

It was Mama's charm bracelet.

I would have known it blind, by the sound of it jangling, by the feel of all its charms: the tiny hourglass filled with real pink sand, the miniature bicycle with wheels that actually spun, the thimble-sized whale with a mouth that opened on a hinge, the bell that really rung, the golden box with the paper note folded infinitesimally small, the whistle that sang faintly, the owl with pearls for eyes, the book with mine and my sisters' names in it. I squeezed it in my palm until the chain left little indents on my skin, and closed my eyes, and when I opened them again the bracelet was still there, metal warming to my body.

Impossible. It was impossible. I had watched the broker walk through the door with Mama's bracelet clinking in his pocket. Suddenly, as if the metal had turned too hot in my hand, I dropped it, thrust it away from me and let it skitter to the floor, under my bed. A swell of terror came over me so swiftly and powerfully that it could be nothing but magic. *Bad* magic.

Curled on my chair, knees tucked up under my chin, I replayed the conversation with the broker over and over again. Inside the theater of my mind, I watched him take the bracelet from me and put it in his pocket. Once, twice, three times. I watched him hand Rose the bag of rubles.

If I told my sister, she could not accuse me of imagining it. The gold chain was gleaming at me from beneath the bed like the dead monster's eyes. There was proof I could hold in my hand. I scooped up the bracelet again, even as its dark, eldritch power seemed to singe my flesh, and tucked it into the pocket of my housecoat.

I was a few steps away from Rose's door when I stopped. I remembered how she had implored me to spend my secret on her, and how she had scowled at me with such virulence when I had refused her. It occurred to me for the first time that I could not rely on my sister for answers. I had always thought Rose the clever one, but what had she ever done to truly prove it? She was as trapped here as the rest of us.

I could not rely on my sister to save me. I turned down the hall and went to Papa's room instead.

He always left the door open so I could go inside and clean. Now there were clothes strewn all over the furniture, pants crumpled on the seat of his armchair and shirts spread-eagled on the floor. His bed was unmade, pillows crushed in with the shape of his head and blanket curling around the edge of the mattress like banked snow.

Every time I came in I imagined how my mother's body had looked in the bed, back when she was still a woman and not a bird, all mortal and soft. Her breasts were lumpy from nursing us, nipples masticated by our baby teeth. Papa said it was only the curse that had made him stop loving her, but hearing Undine's words echo I wondered if he thought that she'd been spoiled, too, by the mean banality of motherhood. No longer any good to him as a woman or a wife, better as a bird in its cage.

Out of sheer instinct, I gathered up all of Papa's clothes into my arms. I thought briefly of washing them—that might ebb a bit of his anger; it had worked before. But now I imagined hurling Papa's clothes over the railing; I imagined pulling them into one giant heap and setting them aflame. I imagined beating my fists against his chest and snarling at him like a petulant cat, or like my eldest sister. The possibility bloomed in my stomach and then rose up my throat into my mouth, something I wanted to vomit out.

I had already done the worst thing I thought possible—disobeying my father, sneaking out from under his spell—and I was still breathing thickly and my legs had not turned to chicken feet. What did it all matter now?

Standing there amidst the strewn clothes, charm bracelet burning a hole through my housecoat, I wondered why I had come in here at all. I had turned away from my sister's door because I knew that whatever she said or did would not sate me. Undine had already spoken all the wisdom that she knew, but I was still empty. Yearning.

Suffused with an emotion that I could not recognize or name, I tore through the clothes the way that Papa had torn through our dresses. As if I were a beast with fangs and claws. I had only the strength of a half-trained witch, but I managed to tear the buttons from his shirts and rip the seams on his pants. I used my teeth to work at the leather of his belt until it broke into two pieces. And then, standing in the ruin of it all, I felt my stomach settle, as if I'd eaten a fat meal and had no urge to spit it back up again.

While I was reaching for a pair of pants, something slipped out of the pocket and fluttered to the ground. I knelt down and picked it up. It was a thick square of paper, slightly water-stained, ink blurring the letters so that they looked like wet eyelashes. I could still read them if I squinted and held the card up to the light.

FISHEROVICH & SYMYRENKO 3454 VOROBYEV STREET.

My heart careened in the silence. I knew, I *knew* that I had not taken the man's card, just as much as I knew that I had given him Mama's charm bracelet. I tried to smooth out my memory like a white tablecloth so that I could see any stains or splatters, but everything was ivory and pristine, and not even curling at the edges. The broker had come and gone without leaving anything of his behind.

Possibilities flowered up in my mind: perhaps Papa had chased after him and taken his card. Maybe they had met before, a long time ago, and forgotten each other's faces. But all my imagined reasonings seemed to wilt under scrutiny.

I was filled with icy uncertainty, like the slush that collected on street corners in the winter. Hurriedly, I crammed the card into the pocket of my housecoat alongside the charm bracelet, and clambered down the stairs.

By the time Papa came home the sky was dimming to the color of a bruised peach and he told us that he had posted his signs all over the city. Rose and Undine had used needle and thread and a bit of spell-work to mend their dresses, and they both were so beautiful it would make your eyes well up to look at them. Undine wore her gown of peacock blue and Rose wore one of deep scarlet; they reminded me of little jeweled sucking candies that came inside bronze tins, except Undine's eyes were dangerous and Rose's smile looked mean.

I had chosen my least ruined dress, a pale pink gown that was too snug in the waist and had one of its corset bones snapped. Undine was right; it mattered little how I looked. Papa swept right past me without even a glance. He was standing with his arms drawn over his distended belly, staring out the window.

The charm bracelet was curled in my pocket and the card was folded tightly and tucked between my breasts. I felt as though if I removed either from my person they would vanish, like there was some spell cast over the house that would instantly obliterate anything that Papa might want to keep hidden. But I could feel them both there, the weight of the bracelet and the paper poking into my skin, ink slurring as it mixed with my sweat.

I wanted to pull it out and hold it up to him and demand the truth. I wanted to see him stammer and flush and try to explain it. Courage mounted in me with each passing moment, courage and insatiable hunger. All my fear and good sense once again forgotten—what did I have to lose now? Papa would be furious the moment he walked into his room and saw the ruin I'd made of it. I might as well try to eat the truth out of him too.

It was not just the card or the charm bracelet or the strange filling that had appeared in the icebox the same day Mama had vanished. It was every scream I had swallowed for so many years. If I opened my mouth now, those cries would pour out of me with no way to stop them.

And perhaps the walls around me would begin to show small cracks at last. If there was power in keeping a secret, surely there was power in revealing it too.

But I couldn't quite manage the feat of such a great thing, no matter my heart-pounding bluster. I thought of Sevas and clenched my fist so tightly that my knuckle split open and bled.

All four of us were silent for a very long time, the grandfather clock ticking away the seconds. I opened my mouth and then closed it again, skin chilled with nervous anticipation. And then, before any of us could speak, Papa raised his hand and pointed out the window, toward the gate. "Look."

A trio of men were loping down the road. Their sweat-slicked faces were halved by the angle of the sunset, one side cast in a lucent orange; the other side pale as an egg. The eyes touched by the light gleamed like kopeks in a fountain, bright but bleary, trapped by water.

Day laborers—I could tell by the way hunger and work had whittled down their boyish cheeks. They paused in front of the gate and curled their bony fingers around it, pressing their fists between the bars.

Papa's smile was exuberant.

"And they are only the first of many," he said, looking over at my sisters and me. "Turn up your frowns. Those may very well be your future husbands at the door."

Undine made a derisive, disgusted sound in the back of her throat, and Rose's eyes slid briefly shut. The low, bubbling anger in me surged up and I reached for the paper folded inside my bodice, but as I did, Papa spoke again.

"Well, Marlinchen." He puffed out his chest like a mating dove and grasped me firmly by the shoulders and pivoted me toward the window, all while my mind reeled with mute protestations. "Perhaps I was wrong. A man has come for you after all."

I peered through the glass, over the heads of the day laborers rattling the gate. There was a man who had silver hair and high, narrow shoulders, watching with tepid interest as the suitors squabbled. A noise came out of me, but it was wordless, choked. I felt like someone had thrust my head down into a tub of cold bathwater, everything suddenly muffled and blurred.

When the haze cleared again, I almost laughed at my own stupid brazenness, my own doomed conviction. The girl of a second ago who had believed she had nothing more to lose—she was a fool, and I hated her. My throat closed in slow, aching increments as I watched one of the day laborers get the gate unlatched. He strode into the garden, followed by his companions.

And Dr. Bakay walked nonchalantly after them.

CHAPTER NINE

Here is what I know about Dr. Bakay.

He was educated at a medical college in Askoldir and he was a physician, which meant that he treated only the Diseases of the Body, and only the parts of the body you could feel and see, for surgeons took care of the rest. He carried in his doctor's bag tiny black vials of laudanum and pots of leeches, arsenic in porcelain urns. He wrote out prescriptions on rough slips of paper that curled around your fingers like a cat's tongue, and if you went to a drugstore and they saw Dr. Bakay's signature and looping script the pharmacist would smile and smile as he handed you a tin of cherry-flavored opium tablets. They all liked Dr. Bakay so much that they liked his clients by association.

Dr. Bakay's remedies were not like Rose's—they did not care whether you were a bit melancholy when you dispensed them; they did not work differently depending on where the moon was in its cycle; they did not necessitate a witch's precise, hereditary touch. They worked whether it was high tide or low, whether you were angry or lonely, whether the rabbit whose foot you cut had run clockwise around a birch tree, whether your eyes were gray or green or blue. They were exceptionally good magic, and it was only Rose's charm and beauty that allowed her to compete.

And then there came a new fad, swept in from the West as if by a very strong breeze, or a particularly propitious current. Sailors dredged it out of their nets along with sturgeons and trout. Phrenology, it was called by our wiser Western counterparts, and though its methods were complex and could be practiced only by doctors, its results were simple enough that even Oblya's barely literate day laborers could understand it when they paged open the penny presses. You could buy a diagram of the brain for only a kopek, and it was cleaved into sections like a butcher's drawing, indicating the twenty-seven different Organs of the Mind.

There was an organ for Cautiousness and one for Benevolence, organs for Language and Tune and Time. As it turned out, so many people wanted the topography of their brain mapped by a professional! When Dr. Bakay became the first physician in Oblya to begin practicing this new discipline, even the day laborers saved their kopeks in coffee cans to have him draw up an atlas of their minds.

They could have come to me or Undine for much cheaper.

But that meant meeting with witches. Dr. Bakay was respectable, and would tell them why it was that they were poor, and as it turned out it was not a matter of unfortunate circumstance at all. Maybe your third organ was too small and therefore you did not have enough Attentiveness to stay awake during your shift on the assembly line. Maybe your Approbation organ was far too large and you couldn't bear to work a menial job that did not give you sufficient praise. Either way, there was little you could do but resign yourself to your station in life, or else try to surmount the hopeless augury of your own mind.

Some had a much better prognosis than others. The minds of Ye-

huli men, most phrenologists said, were well adapted to capitalism—
their twentieth and twenty-fourth organs were enormous! That was
why the gradonalchik had to draw up some laws to restrict their ac-
tivities, since they had such an advantage over the rest. For instance,
he banned Yehuli from residing in certain areas of the city, and from
working on Sundays, and from purchasing land. I once saw a sign on a
bathhouse door: NO DOGS OR YEHULI ALLOWED. I did not know if that
was one of the gradonalchik's proclamations, or simply the bathhouse
owner's preference.

Meanwhile, Dr. Bakay chipped away at our clients the way that
land developers stripped layer after layer of steppe soil for their wheat
planting. I was sixteen and Papa was so angry that he spoke only in
short, barbed words, and kicked our poor goblin vengefully.

And then one day Dr. Bakay arrived at our gate, his silver mustache turned upward like a smile. I was afraid that Papa would cast a
spell to turn him into a truffle hog or a horned owl, but before he could
even summon his magic Dr. Bakay lifted up a bag of rubles and shook
it. Dr. Bakay was so clever that he knew without ever meeting him
what held sway with my father.

Papa opened the door, grumbling all the while, and let Dr. Bakay
into our foyer. He smelled clean and nice, like carbolic soap. He took
off his hat and held it in his hands, as decorous and docile as a man a
third of his age, and didn't flinch when Papa bared his teeth at him.

"I don't let any man into my house for free," Papa growled.

"Yes, of course," said Dr. Bakay, and then handed over his sack of
rubles like it was nothing. He was still yet to look at me. "I come both
as a fellow practitioner of medicine, and, quite simply, as a man of
unquenchable curiosity. Some of my clients have spoken of the great
wizard Zmiy Vashchenko and his three very talented daughters.
One man told me that your daughter Rose cured his toothache for
half of what I charge, and only with a fistful of herbs. Another told
me that your daughter Undine foresaw his winning poker hand and
all she asked for was five rubles. I can pay whatever you would like,

Mr. Vashchenko, if you would allow me to indulge my curiosity with one of your daughters."

Papa made some gruff and sputtering sounds as he pretended to consider it, but I knew that he had made up his mind the moment Dr. Bakay had passed him the money. He put the whole bag into the deep pocket of his robe, then glanced around vaguely, like he had forgotten the architecture of his own house. At last, he gave a sigh and said, "My other daughters are busy. But you can speak to Marlinchen."

Undine had a client out by her scrying pool and Rose was in her storeroom, squinting over cut lavender stalks. Dr. Bakay gave a nod, and finally his eyes landed on me. They were warm and brown, the light jumping in them like fish darting through murky water. He looked me up and down, from the toe of my slipper to the frizzy crown of my hair, and said, "It's very nice to meet you, Marlinchen."

I must have stammered out my own greeting, but I cannot say I remember it. In truth, I did not remember so many things that happened during my sessions with Dr. Bakay. There were certain facts that rose to the surface, like dead things awash in the tide: the particular curve of his thumb, the bristly gray hair on the back of his hand, the way one tooth slid over his bottom lip when he smiled. Everything else sank under and was gone.

Papa led us both into the sitting room and settled into his chaise. I went to take a seat on the couch, but Dr. Bakay said, "Wait a moment. Would you mind standing, please?"

"Oh," I said, or something equally doltish and feeble, "all right."

"Your gift is for flesh divinity, is that correct?" Dr. Bakay asked. I nodded. He was standing very close to me, so close that a few loose strands of my hair got caught on his lips and he didn't notice, or else didn't bother to wipe them away. "Of course, as a physician, who studies the Body, I am vitally interested in knowing how a talent like that manifests and reflects in the subject's anatomy. Rather, how does a witch's anatomy differ from those of mortal women? In other words, Marlinchen, I think there must be something unique about *your* body, to make such a gift function as my clients have described."

My cheeks were beginning to pink. Papa was not really listening; I could tell that his attention had gone to the rubles in his pocket and considering what he would do with them and how he might get more of them. His finger rubbed at that swell of fabric as his gaze drifted toward the ceiling. Dr. Bakay pressed the back of his hand to my forehead.

"Hm," he said. "Your body temperature does not appear abnormal."

"I think I'm very ordinary," I said, with a nervous flutter of laughter. "Aside from being a witch."

Dr. Bakay's eyes crinkled when he smiled. "I've met very many ordinary girls. I cannot say you are one of them."

And then, I think, he asked me what I best liked to eat. I told him pork varenyky. He asked me did I like to cook or sew or play dominoes. He asked me if my sisters were kind or mean. He asked me what I thought of the new electric streetlamps, the trams, the art museum on Rybakov Street.

If Papa had been paying attention, Dr. Bakay's questions would have enraged him; he would have chased the doctor from the house and that would have been the end of it all. But he was not paying attention and with each question I felt myself loosening like a knotted bow, undone and smoothed flat as Dr. Bakay spoke.

"Have you ever considered that your witchery is necessarily fixed to your womanhood?"

I must have blinked at him in awful confusion. My sisters were women, certainly, narrow waisted and wide hipped, their bodies growing to look more and more like our mother's with each passing day. But I still felt mostly like a child, like a girl, only just beginning to fill out my dresses. Heat crawled over my cheeks as I replied, "I don't know. I never thought very much of it."

"Well, I would give the theory substantial weight. Phrenology tells us that men and women are of vastly different Minds . . . women's fourteenth and eighteenth organs are much larger than men's, indicating that they have much greater degrees of Veneration and Hope, and their fifteenth organs are positively tiny, suggesting very little propensity for Firmness. And so it must follow that we can map other Organs of the Body using similar methods. Perhaps most fruitful, I think, would be the Organs solely belonging to females."

I hadn't realized he had begun to unlace my corset. I was so shocked and all that came out of me was a little sound, not quite a gasp, just a chirp like a wind-buffeted sparrow. My loosened bodice sagged out in front of me and I quickly threw my arms around myself, covering my breasts. My throat was beginning to feel horribly tight, each breath hot and rough and short. I looked toward Papa.

My father was still reclining on the chaise longue, but his eyes had drifted back toward me. I searched his face for any indication of displeasure, any fledgling protest. His lower lip twitched; a muscle feathered in his jaw. His pocket was huge with Dr. Bakay's rubles. And then he said, "Marlinchen, put your arms down."

That was the moment I came untethered from myself, a horse cut from its hitching post. My body went through its motions, but my mind was jettisoned bulk, left to drift in dark and churning waters. I lowered my arms to my sides, fists curling, as Dr. Bakay moved his hand over my left breast. He squeezed it tenderly, then cupped it, as if judging its heft. With his forefinger and thumb, he pinched my nipple.

"Papa," I said, my gaze clouding with tears.

"Quiet," he said. "Let the doctor do his work. Ordinarily he charges dozens of rubles for these types of evaluations, and here he is paying us for the privilege. Isn't that right?"

"Of course," said Dr. Bakay. "I'm thankful to be able to test the methods of phrenology on a witch for the very first time. I'm sure there are quite a number of medical journals that would be happy to publish the findings." But he had not been making any notes in his logbook or on his thick prescription pad.

From then on he spoke to Papa animatedly, about the particular color and size of my nipples, about the weight and shape of my breasts. He stroked my nipples to hardness and asked me to describe the sensation.

I do not remember what I told him. I was staring at the far wall, eyes fixed on the place where the damask paper was peeling away, exposing the yellowed plaster underneath. Finally, Dr. Bakay drew himself up to full height, narrow shoulders rolling.

"Thank you very much for the opportunity," he said, and then Papa rose too. As I was pulling my corset back up over my breasts, Dr. Bakay shook Papa's hand. He packed up his doctor's bag, his tiny black vials of laudanum and pots of leeches, his arsenic in porcelain urns. Before he went through the door and out into the garden, he gave me a cheerful wave, winking one brown eye.

I stood in the foyer as the grandfather clock made its metered rotation, thinking of nothing but peeling wallpaper. The sun glanced off Dr. Bakay's silver hair as he swung open the gate. I began to think about the bulge of fabric I had seen when I looked down, the swelling beneath the dark buttons of his trousers.

I should have known by the way Papa had fingered his rubles that he would happily welcome Dr. Bakay into our house again, and he did. Several weeks later the doctor was back with his black bag and more theories, a different prognosis, a new set of questions and an arsenal of clever methods.

For the first few times Papa sat in his chaise longue and looked idly on, chattering airily as Dr. Bakay jerked my corset open with surgical precision. Eventually he grew weary of talking and watching, and so Papa left the two of us alone in the sitting room with the door shut.

I memorized the wallpaper's damask pattern, counting each whorl and flower while Dr. Bakay asked me whether there were any men that I had eyes for. I do not remember what I told him, only that it made him smile and thumb a gentle circle over my left nipple, as if it were an amulet to polish.

Once he wanted to see if the nature of organs was affected by Wakefulness, so he gave me a sleeping draught and I laid down on the couch, my vision fuzzing and then going savagely black. When I woke my corset was gone and Dr. Bakay was perched beside me. He was breathing hard; through the fretwork of my lashes I saw the staggered rising and falling of his chest and the dew of sweat on his brow, and at last the rumpled lap of his trousers. His hand moved under the band of his loosened belt with a grasping, jerking motion. I shut my eyes and pretended to be asleep again. Later, when he stood up to leave, he tried only vaguely to conceal the damp patch on his trousers.

The very last time, he wanted to test what was inside my skin. I was seventeen and unmistakably a woman now, my breasts blooming under his hands. Dr. Bakay took a small blade and cut two smiling wounds beneath each of my nipples, blood welling in red pearls. He caught my blood in clear vials; I watched each droplet slide languidly down the glass and puddle at the bottom, half a fingertip high.

He capped off the vials and tucked them neatly in his doctor's bag, right next to the porcelain urn of arsenic. Then he told Papa that he had everything he needed, and handed over his final sack of rubles. Papa's face was as blank and stupid as a boiled ham, but he took the rubles and held them in his fist, the bag rolling and swaying with their weight.

Dr. Bakay tipped his hat to us and went through the door. I watched as he swung open the gate, sunlight clinging to the silver of his hair. I drew my arms over my chest and felt a bite of pain, twin wounds crying out like I was giving suck to a thing with very sharp teeth. In truth I never figured out why Dr. Bakay stopped coming to our house. Perhaps he had exhausted all of his medical curiosity, or perhaps my transforming body had exhausted *him*.

Quickly, though, I found that it mattered little whether he came back or not. My dreams were riotous with his face and hands and the paunch of his trousers. Of Papa with his rubles and the two men shaking hands. Sometimes I woke from the dreams with a dampness between my legs and I had to run down to the kitchen and eat a whole loaf of black bread with butter and strawberry kvass and seventeen pork varenyky. Thinking of Dr. Bakay always made me so hungry.

Papa had been right. By nightfall there were so many men at our gate that they could not all fit in our foyer even if we wanted them to, and our nearest neighbors were so vexed by the noise that they threatened to call the Grand Inspector on us. Papa, in turn, threatened to turn them into shrubs.

Rose proposed a solution before it resorted to handcuffs and sorcery: we handed out numbered slips of parchment to all the men, indicating their place in the queue. Our house could reasonably hold fifteen at once, so we let the first fifteen men spill through the door and into the foyer, grandfather clock gonging their arrival. The rest of the men retreated, shoulders slumped, clutching the slips of parchment in their fists. When three days had gone by, we would let the next cycle of suitors inside.

And so our house was glutted with fifteen men—boys, really, most of them. They had skinny arms with sharp elbows and hair shorn so close that you could see the pits of their scalps underneath it. Hair longer than an inch, they said, was a liability on the factory floor, and they weren't going to wear flowered bonnets like the women.

I had expected them to be mean as hunting dogs, but they were more like lazy wolf pups, draping themselves over our furniture and sprawling flat on their backs in the garden. They spoke deferentially to my sisters and me, their gazes downcast, and quickly left the room whenever our father entered.

The goblin was deeply distressed and hid in the branches of our flowering pear tree. Indrik leered furiously from the wheat grass, breathing white smoke through his nostrils and covering the muscles of his chest with linseed oil so they gleamed in the sunlight. Incredibly, it worked, and most of the men were actually afraid of him, this god from the mountaintops with a thousand years behind his eyes.

Rose was not at all pleased, and locked herself in the storeroom for hours at a time, purple mists wafting out from under the door. Undine was more willing to make peace, or at least happy to bask in all the amorous attention. The men crowded around her scrying pool as she made predictions that were half-true at most, laughing sweetly and plucking up her dress to reveal the smooth white oval of her calf.

They all must have asked her, of course, how we managed to elude

Papa's magic, but if Undine ever answered them, she could only have lied. I worried that she might spin her own stories, just on the off chance that one might be true, not caring what Papa would do to a man who carried her lie up to him like a dog with a mangled bird in its maw. Yet surely even my eldest sister could not be so cruel.

I watched from the foyer, nervously opening the wound on my knuckle, flinching whenever they came too near to the juniper tree. When the men did come to speak to me, they were as polite as men could be, inquiring about hexes and haunted attics. Somehow it had gotten around Oblya that a ghost roamed our halls. I told them Papa had warded against malignant spirits, and they nodded, flushing, but I could tell they did not believe me.

Regardless, it kept them away from the third floor, which pleased Papa. He made nice with the men like I had never seen him do before, asking about their origins if they spoke with accents and offering them cabbage rolls and boiled eggs out of the icebox. He even worried over their skinny arms, the ribs that pushed up against their skin. It was so strange to me that I couldn't even start to make sense of it all, my mind skipping like a broken music box.

His newly peaceable attitude extended even to me. When he saw the mess of his bedroom, I blushed deeply and told him that a monster had broken inside. It was a terrible lie, but Papa pretended to believe it. He said that I looked hungry. He took me downstairs and fed me pork varenyky and black juice. I could hardly taste any of it, and it all sat in my belly afterward with the heft of a stone. I wanted to release it all, but I didn't dare to, after Papa's dire warning.

And what of Dr. Bakay? When he came into our house with those first three suitors, Papa greeted him happily, as if they were two old friends. He scarcely even looked at me. After they'd shaken hands, Dr. Bakay said, "I heard about your competition, Zmiy. I read it on the posters, and then the penny presses picked it up."

Papa scoffed. "The only true story they'll ever print. Don't tell me you're here to compete yourself."

"No, sadly not," Dr. Bakay said. His eyes glimmered merrily behind his spectacles. I did not remember him ever wearing spectacles, but they must have been all the better to see me with. "I hoped you would simply let me observe the goings-on—as a scientific inquiry. Many of these men have been my clients before, and I am quite interested to see how they are faring now. To see if the predictions I made were correct. I can pay you for your hospitality, of course."

And that was that. Papa smiled hugely and took a bag of rubles from Dr. Bakay, who hung up his coat and hat on our rack.

I stood there in the foyer, in the long shadow of the grandfather clock, and the years fell on me like snow. A white deluge compressed the space between the girl I had been at sixteen and the woman I was now; it was as if my own ghost were possessing me. She moved my body toward the stairs, our twin hearts beating crookedly.

Before I could make it there, Dr. Bakay turned.

"Dear Marlinchen," he said. "I almost didn't notice you—quiet as a mouse, just the way I remember, though I could swear you've grown taller."

Then he crushed me into an embrace, fist pressed to the small of my back. The girl that I was squeaked out a greeting, her ghost manipulating my mouth and tongue.

As soon as he let go I slipped out again, up the stairs. Quiet as a mouse.

I did not sleep that night, and barred my door with the chair that usually sat in front of my boudoir. Of all the doors in our house, mine alone had no lock. Dr. Bakay was sleeping in one of the rooms in the disused servants' quarters, on the first floor. I wondered if he was awake, too, his breath curling up toward the ceiling that separated us.

There were fifteen other men downstairs, folded on couches and the chaise longue or splayed out on the floor, using their own balled-up jackets as pillows. And then next door, on either side, were my sisters. I wasn't sure if they could manage to sleep until I heard Undine's soft snores feathering through the wall.

Her words stitched themselves once more through my mind, mean and familiar. *People want to ruin things that are clean and new. It's no fun stamping through old dirty snow.* That part, at least, I could swallow. I wasn't so stupid that I didn't know most people found joy in making beautiful things ugly. I had seen enough belching gray factories rise up out of the steppe grass to understand that.

He can't stand the idea of anyone spoiling us but him. That was the part that rang in me like a wrong note. Undine didn't know what had gone on between Dr. Bakay and me when the sitting-room door was closed; she couldn't see the scars his knife had left. So maybe my cruel sister was mistaken.

But then, I supposed, I *had* only been ruined at Papa's orchestration, only when he had Dr. Bakay's rubles in hand. When the grandfather clock gonged seven, I went downstairs and ate three honey cakes the size of my fist, stomach churning like a river at ice melt.

Then I went into the sitting room. Most of the men were already awake, and when they saw me they sat up straight, smoothing their sleep-mussed hair and stammering out perfunctory *good mornings*. They seemed too sad to be afraid of.

I had become friendly with one man who was not much older than me, with scrubby blond hair like steppe grass and the wide, tired eyes of an old hound. He had an ordinary mortal name, but in my mind I christened him Sobaka, like the sweet, mopey dog he reminded me of.

Sobaka was perched on the very edge of the chaise longue, some crumpled paper in his hand. I peered over his shoulder and asked, "What is that?"

"Just one of the penny presses, ma'am," he said, cheeks pinking. "This one's old news, now."

The front page was crowded with daguerreotypes and exclamatory headlines. The gradonalchik's wife was having an affair with her carriage driver. A restaurant on Kanatchikov Street was found to be using rat meat in their varenyky. My gaze wandered down the page, to a smaller headline, accompanied by a daguerreotype of a solemn-looking man in spectacles. I recognized him as I squinted closer.

It was the broker from Fisherovich & Symyrenko. The one who had bought Mama's charm bracelet. The one whose card I had found in Papa's pocket. The headline said that he'd been missing for three days.

Something very cold slid through my veins. I thought about the charm bracelet in the drawer of my boudoir, burning with its bad magic. I tried to count how many days it had been since we had sold all of our things, since that broker had been at our house. My memory felt like termite-eaten wood, porous with black spaces. Hours were swallowed up by some strange, murky darkness.

I blinked hard, and even squeezed my eyes shut, but I could not will that time back to me. Panic fluttered in my belly—what had happened to make me forget it all? Was there a furtive spell at work?

Once I could make my mouth move again, I said, "Would it be all right if I took that?"

"Of course," Sobaka mumbled, holding the paper out to me.

I took it from him and pressed it against my chest, vision going dim. I did not know what I would do with it, precisely; I only knew that I needed to protect it, like the card and Mama's charm bracelet.

There was a secret here that wasn't mine, something bad and hidden like maggots in an apple, and I had the distinct feeling it was something Papa would want stamped out if he found it.

The men fiddled with the fringes of our cat-lamps; they ran their thumbs along the dusty portraits on the walls. I wondered if there were any among them whom I wouldn't mind marrying. Sobaka would be a kind husband, dutiful and mild. But I was too shy and ugly to imagine that one of them might choose me as their bride.

And, in truth, I would not want them to. The compact was still buried under the juniper tree and that was *my* secret, the only thing that might carry me back to Sevas. I hurried out of the sitting room and into the foyer, blood rushing around my ears.

I was staring determinedly down at the floor, clutching the paper so tightly that it crumpled, and I did not see that there was someone else in the foyer until I ran into their back. I stepped away, apologizing profusely, then lifted my head.

It was Dr. Bakay. All the rest of the words withered on my tongue.

"Marlinchen," he said. Behind his spectacles, his eyes looked tiny, like insect eggs. "Do you always wake so early? The sun has hardly risen."

"I make Papa breakfast." My voice was not much louder than a whisper. *Quiet as a mouse.* I had never once tried to protest when he touched me.

"That's right," he said, as though I had told him before. Perhaps I had. "Your father always says you are the best and most dutiful of his daughters, even if you are plain-faced where your sisters are beautiful. I never did perform a proper phrenologist's reading on you—testing the Organs of your Mind. I am so curious about what I would find, if I did. Maybe I will pay your father again for the pleasure of it."

He reached toward me and took the back of my head into his hand, four fingers cupping my skull while his thumb stroked along my throat.

The dust motes in the room stopped drifting. They hung suspended, like gold veins in marble, like flies trapped under a coat of varnish. Seconds staggered past me. Finally, Dr. Bakay let go.

If he tried to speak again, I didn't hear it. There was floodwater in my ears. I tore away from him and clambered up the steps, tripping over the last one and collapsing on my knees at the top of the second-floor landing. There was a crack—my bone against the hard wood—but I could only feel the distant echoes of pain, pulling back and then rearing up again, like the tide lapping the shoreline.

When I got to my feet again, it was all but gone. I ran into my room, closed the door, and propped the chair against it once more.

I had meant to simply hide the newspaper under my pillow and then go back downstairs to cook Papa's breakfast, but once I was inside the safe bunker of my bedroom I found that I could not make my body move again. I lay flat on my back, sheets hissing against the silk of my dress, staring up at the line of split plaster that fissured across the ceiling like a crack in an eggshell. Where the plaster peeled away was a thin mouth of black space, jagged and sneering.

When I was a child, my mind had tried to constellate that blackness into something safe, and not scary. I had imagined it was home to a family of friendly owls with soft feathers or mice that wore tiny aprons and top hats. I had not let myself imagine what I knew to be the truth of it: that the house itself was riddled with thousands of small wounds, and every day they were wrenched further open, hours pulling at the ruptured skin.

Through the slit of my open window I could hear the eyeless ravens, cawing in languages lost to time. When I turned my head to look out at the garden, I thought I saw the fiery serpent, but it might only have been a black ribbon someone dropped in the grass. One of the men was speaking to Undine by her scrying pool, their faces very close. The wind caught up her golden hair and twisted it like it was wet and needed wringing out. I couldn't see Rose at all.

There was a scrape of wood against wood and my door heaved open. The chair that I had used to jam it shut clattered to the floor, my clumsy defense easily flung aside.

I jerked up, bile rising so quickly in my throat that I nearly retched.

Papa was standing in the threshold, still wearing his robe. His swollen stomach had gone flat again, loose and empty skin flapping as he strode toward me and said, "Why isn't there any food in the sitting room?"

My mind supplied the words *I'm sorry*, but my mouth could not speak them. I only stared at him, heart pounding.

"Well? What is it, Marlinchen? You look as dumb as a struck dog. There is more than enough food in the icebox—I checked last night myself when I went downstairs to have another chicken. The men could not possibly have eaten it all. Could they? Most are docile like lambs. But you can see my belly is empty again, and I'm so hungry I've forgotten the taste of dumplings and kvass. Those rats in my mind are nibbling away at my memory. I need to eat again. I need to *eat*."

I looked up into Papa's brown eyes, the same weak tea color as my own, and upturned slightly at the corners, just like mine were. I looked at the slope of his long nose, as long as mine or longer, and his mouth opening like a black pit, a hole, under the bramble of his beard. Something to fall into.

"I'm hungry too, Papa," I said. "I need to eat."

He made a derisive sound and scowled. "And can you not feed yourself once I've eaten first? You're twenty-three years old, a woman now, certainly capable enough."

"Have I been spoiled?" I asked him. My cheeks were burning hot. "Am I a woman because I was ruined? Was I a girl before? When will I be spoiled enough that you have to turn me into a bird and be rid of me?"

Papa's eyes snapped at me like a fox's jaws. "Why are you talking to me in riddles? Speak plainly, or do not speak at all."

"I'm only speaking the way you taught me to. Girls become women and then women become birds; that's all true. You and your codex both told me so." I rose to my feet, stomach lurching like a drink about to spill. "I don't want any of it anymore. I want to be a girl again, before I knew the taste of my mother's meat."

He laughed then, my father, showing all of his half-rotted teeth. "If I could, I would make you one, Marlinchen. You were better for me when you were small-breasted and silent. But transformations don't work like that; magic doesn't work like that. You cannot make a flower unbloom." Papa took me by the collar of my dress and pulled me toward him, until we were so close that I could count every blue hair of his beard, bristly and sharp. "Get down to the kitchen. And you might as well make Dr. Bakay breakfast too."

Something broke apart inside me and I was filled with the tiny sharp bits of it. Papa hurled me away from him and I fell to the ground, my hair parting in two wild curtains over my face.

I did not look up again until I heard Papa slam through the door and clatter down the stairs, wood groaning under his weight. I stared at my split knuckle again, glistening like a ruby ring. To weep should be easy, but though I tried, the tears would not come.

I stood up, stumbling a bit, my knees humming with nascent bruises. A conversation leaked through the crack in the door, words floating from Dr. Bakay's mouth up the stairs and into my ears. Papa's brisk voice followed. They sounded like two conquering chieftains, arguing over how best to divide their spoils.

I knew, then, without even a quiver of doubt—perhaps it was my witch's instinct rearing—that the next time I heard any footsteps on the stairs, they would be coming for me, a double-headed dragon breathing cold fire. I had thought that Papa had done his worst already. But his anger was insatiable and depthless too. There was always more of me that he could nibble at and gnaw, until he was sucking the marrow right from my bones.

I gathered up my tattered dress in my fists and hurtled out of my bedroom, down the steps, and into the foyer, where the midmorning sunlight made everything gleam like the inside of a snuffbox, gold and hard and close.

Papa and Dr. Bakay were in the sitting room, and when they saw me their eyes narrowed in perfect unison.

They both started toward me, but I was nearer and faster. I burst through the front door and into the garden, cool air stealing into my lungs. An eyeless raven winged past me, scattering black feathers. I waved it off and crashed through the wheat grass, toward the juniper tree.

When I reached it I dropped to my hurting knees and began to claw up the dirt. I was as manic and feral as a mangy dog, soil caulking under my nails. Finally I closed my fingers around Mama's compact, shaking with both terror and relief.

Papa stood in the threshold, one hand shading his eyes against the sun. "What are you doing, Marlinchen? Get back inside."

"What in the world has gotten her so distressed?" Dr. Bakay asked bemusedly, adjusting his spectacles.

I did not hear Papa's answer. I was already running toward the gate. It towered in front of me, so tall that it sliced the sky up into long, thin segments, like wedges of blue-seamed cheese. I fumbled with the lock for a moment before managing to get it open.

"Marlinchen!" Papa shouted.

There was magic in his cry, and it shook white petals down from the flowering pear tree. Even from such a distance, his magic was strong and it chilled in my veins and it made me pause and look back. Papa's hand was outstretched, and his pale, narrow fingers were curling.

But then something happened, and the spell broke. Mama's compact started to sing in my clenched fist, black sand rattling inside, a reminder of the secret I had never given up and the lie that I had stuck to unwaveringly, until the very end. There was power in that, a magic of my own, and it cleaved through Papa's spell like shears through silk.

I pushed through the gate and ran as fast as I could toward Kanatchikov Street.

I paced Oblya's streets aimlessly until evening, sick with unspent adrenaline. Once I would have been petrified to find myself out in the city alone, but no one except slack-jawed beggars even tried to speak to me. The day laborers who had once terrified me were now, I knew, toothless dogs like Sobaka. The brokers and merchants were busy with their work and I looked like just another unlucky drifter, perhaps a factory worker who had injured her hand and could no longer work a machine, or maybe a woman pregnant with the child of a sailor who had left her for more promising waters.

Night robed the city in a gown of opulent black, storefront windows glittering like sequins. That was when the men and women of the upper curia began to trickle in from their beachfront dachas, from their cream-colored townhouses. They trailed down Kanatchikov Street like a spill of good wine, jewel-toned dresses flashing. I pressed myself against the side of a Yehuli grocery, mouth going dry as I watched. Their laughter feathered the air with pale smoke.

All this time I had not considered what I might do. I hadn't allowed myself to sift through my meager prospects, or to think of Papa at all. But as the sky darkened and the air grew pitilessly cold, panic started to turn in my stomach like swallowed poison. I had no money, nowhere to go, and without the heady, blood-warming thrill of my previous outings, my dress felt paper-thin. Already my skin prickled and my breath clouded when I exhaled.

My first instinct was to think of my cleverer sisters, and what they might do. But Rose and Undine would never have found themselves in such a predicament. They would have no wisdom to speak to me. And how could they? They had never been made to bleed from their breasts.

The men and women kept moving past me, smiling their pearl-bright smiles. I did not know my way around the city very well, but I knew Kanatchikov Street like a vein on the back of my hand. They were going toward the ballet theater. Possibility pricked in me.

Without considering it further, I fell into step beside them. Certainly I would be singled out at once, with my mussed hair and my torn dress, and of course I didn't have a ticket. But I followed the busy thoroughfare anyway, until it bore us into the plaza with its great golden fountain, and the theater like a bright, shining bracelet made out of bone.

I stopped then, chest tightening. The stream of men and women continued past me, river water splitting around a rock. I watched them file in, one after the next, women in fox-fur stoles and men with greased mustaches, until all were gone and the double doors were closed behind them. I stood there for so long that my fingers went numb with cold and the wound on my knuckle cracked open again, blood leaking onto the cobblestones. I stood there for so long that certainly the show was almost over, and then with a rush of feckless courage I strode down the half-lit alleyway.

I paused at the door, clenching and unclenching my freezing fingers. Perhaps it would be locked this time. Perhaps there would be an usher waiting to hurl me back out. But what had been my life was in a ruin behind me and Dr. Bakay was perched on the chaise longue in the sitting room, laughing so loudly with Papa that all of their teeth gleamed in their mouths.

I turned the knob and pushed through the door, into the ballet theater.

By the swell of music I could tell at once that the show had reached its climax. The inside of the theater was as bright and gold as a honeycomb, and the violins were pricking with alarm. I crept forward, still hidden in the shadow of the cold white pillar, until I could see the stage.

Flame-men were leaping and twirling. Snow-maidens were simpering and cowering. And in the center of it all was Ivan, bare-chested and wearing his feathered mantle, wooden sword arced over the laughing Dragon-Tsar.

Every time seeing him was like the first time, when I could scarcely breathe for how beautiful he was. But now my gaze searched for pits of dried blood on his lips, for a red mark on the back of his throat. I searched for Sevas's face lurking somewhere behind Ivan's heroic grimace, like a blurry shape under ice.

I hardly realized I was creeping closer and closer to the stage until I felt my eyes water beneath the glare of lights. Sevas plunged his sword into the belly of the Dragon-Tsar (really between his chest and arm; from this angle I could see the perfect falsity of his death), and the cellos warbled and the flame-men wilted and the snow-women rose up like puffs of whipped cream on a pastry, all soft and white. The tsarevna went leaping across the stage, toward Sevas, and I knew it was the moment for their mimed kiss.

But before she reached him, Sevas turned, and somehow his eyes found me. His lips parted, and all of Ivan's false, preening victory drained out of him.

Just as the tsarevna readied herself to vault into his arms, Sevas dropped his dancer's pose and strode forward, to the center of the stage, and then leapt off it, still holding his wooden sword. His face was luminous with awe, jaw taut with determination.

The violins stopped so suddenly it was as if their strings had snapped and the snare drum trailed off like a dwindling heartbeat. Murmurs rose from the crowd, and then shouts of jilted fury, but I scarcely heard them. Sevas paced down the aisle toward me and I moved toward him, as if in a haze, as if in a waking dream.

When we finally met he threw his arms around me, and the audience members lurched to their feet, howling at us like wolves.

CHAPTER TEN

A
s soon as Sevas let go, the crowd rose and nearly swept him
away from me. It took almost a quarter hour for the ush-
ers to press everyone back into their seats, and even then
some had already stormed up to the ticket booth, demand-
ing refunds. The curtains drew quickly shut over the stage, erasing the
befuddled snow-maidens and the gaping, blank-faced Dragon-Tsar.
I locked eyes briefly with the tsarevna before she vanished, and my
breath caught with how balefully she stared at me.

As the chandeliers winked back on, I could better see all of the
outraged expressions from the audience members, the hard, sharp
gazes that cut me down like scythes. I shrunk back against Sevas's
chest, still naked and gold-daubed and heaving. A man in a velvet suit
dashed out onto the stage and began to make wheedling reassurances,
summoning invented excuses with the showmanship of a street-corner
magician.

It was Aleksei, not Derkach, who finally shouldered his way through the throng and grabbed Sevas, yanking him backstage, and me along with them.

He dragged Sevas and me into a room with mirrors on all four walls, our reflections doubled and then doubled again, as if we were standing inside a kaleidoscope. I looked wild-haired and ugly; Sevas looked pale-faced and beautiful; Aleksei looked furious. He began to strip off his red jacket, embroidered with its pretending flames, and said, "What were you *thinking*? Have both of you gone mad?"

I could not summon a reply. Sevas ran a hand through his hair and simply said, "Maybe so."

Aleksei let out a long breath. "Why do you always make things worse for yourself, Sevas? You can never manage to just keep your head down and your mouth shut. Derkach was already livid; I can't imagine what he's going to do now."

"It doesn't matter what I do," Sevas said, but his eyes were darting to the mirror, following his own reflection. The line of his own bent elbow. "Derkach is always angry."

"Well, that's quite a juvenile attitude, isn't it? And it reflects poorly on the rest of us too. The rest of the company . . . they're going to cut our salaries to pay for the ticket refunds, you know."

"I know," Sevas said miserably. He looked at me and bit his lip. "Marlinchen, you have to go."

I thought of Derkach's fingers curled around the back of his neck and Dr. Bakay in the foyer, speaking cheerfully with my father. "I don't have anywhere else to go."

Silence fell over the mirrored room, irregular and unpleasant, like a music box suddenly halting its song.

Sevas gave a brief nod, as if he had expected little else, and Aleksei sighed with the weariness of a harried mother. "I'm sorry," he said, though it wasn't clear if he was speaking to me or to Sevas. "I can't protect you from your own foolishness."

"You've done a commendable job of it up until now, Lyosha." Sevas's smile was crooked and strenuous; I could see the great effort that it took to quirk his lips. "I don't blame you for growing exhausted of it."

Aleksei's mouth went pale and tight, but then he clapped a hand over Sevas's shoulder. He held it there for a moment, saying nothing, while Sevas stared at him from under his thick, dark lashes, some mute communication happening between them that I could not understand. Aleksei's gaze flickered briefly to me, then back to Sevas again.

I wondered if he thought it was all my fault. Most likely it was. I hadn't considered what might happen if I'd let Sevas see me; I hadn't even considered that Derkach had warned me and my sisters away from the ballet theater. I'd only been cold and stupid and desperate.

Aleksei's lips parted, but before he could speak the door clattered open behind him.

It was Derkach of course, and with him the man in the velvet suit who had tried to calm the riled crowd. He had an extravagant mustache, once waxed but now drooping at the corners, and his brow was beaded all over with sweat. He took a handkerchief to his forehead and began to mop it while Derkach said, "Aleksei, out."

His words struck the air like two loosed arrows. Aleksei let his hand drop from Sevas's shoulder and then he slouched toward the door, vanishing through the threshold with only one last helpless glance over his shoulder.

In his absence Sevas straightened, chest swelling. "You can be cross with me later," he said.

Derkach's eyes misted. He traversed the room in two long, brisk strides, pausing with no more than an inch between Sevas's face and his own. "I'll be cross with you now, and later, and whenever I damn well please."

"Now, now, Ihor," said the man in the velvet suit, folding up his handkerchief into a small triangle and placing it back in his breast pocket. "Anger won't get us anywhere; there are already half a hundred angry audience members ready to beat down my door. They'll be wanting refunds, of course, but we may be able to—"

"Excuse me, Mr. Kovalchyk," Derkach cut in coldly, "but Sevas is *my* charge. You may be the manager of the company, but it's my prerogative to care for Sevas, and punish him as I see fit."

Mr. Kovalchyk stared at him with his mouth as wide as a hooked trout. "Well, Sevastyan is my charge insofar as it relates to his dancing, and it's *my* theater's coffers that empty to pay both of your salaries. Certainly there must be appropriate consequences for his behavior; we are happily in agreement there. But I've seen many a principal dancer collapse inward on himself because his superiors demanded the impossible. We must both also agree that Sevas is too valuable to lose."

Sevas said nothing. His gaze dropped to the floor while Derkach and Mr. Kovalchyk squabbled like two speculators over the same spit of land, caring nothing for it except that they might be able to till it and till it until the soil had exhausted itself. An awful feeling rose in me, and I wanted nothing more than to take his hand, the way he had taken mine and pulled me up into the carriage with him, to carry him off away from this place. But guilt unmoored me from that wishful fantasy.

"It's my fault," I said in a rush, stomach clenching painfully. "I made him lose his focus; I shouldn't have come at all . . ."

I trailed off, wilting under Derkach's vicious stare. But Mr. Kovalchyk only blinked at me, his face sweaty and stupid. "And who are you exactly?"

"One of Zmiy Vashchenko's daughters," Derkach said, through the clench of his jaw. "The wizard who lives up on Rybakov Street. I warned her and her sisters to stay away from the theater, as it was apparent that Sevas found her presence to be a distraction."

Mr. Kovalchyk frowned, mustache quivering, and looked me up and down with bemused scrutiny. He must have been pondering how I could have been a distraction to Sevas, with my homely looks, my unremarkable ugliness. Even I could scarcely believe it myself. But I remembered with fervent clarity the feeling of his arms braced around my waist, every ridge and groove of his bare chest pressing against me through my dress. I flushed deeply even thinking of it.

At last Mr. Kovalchyk said, "It's no matter if she's a witch or a girl or a particularly alluring pigeon. If her presence is a detriment to Sevas, we must have her gone."

Fear gripped me for the briefest moment, like a corset made of cold steel. I was preparing to stammer out a reply, but before I could Sevas looked up from the ground and said, "No."

Derkach raised one pale brow. "What was that, Sevas?"

"No," said Sevas, at last meeting Derkach's gaze. "She isn't going anywhere. I want her to stay. You're the one who should leave."

A low chuckle rumbled out of Derkach's throat, and his eyes grew bright with amusement. "Sevas, please. So many years have gone by and you still behave like the child you were when we first met, twelve and petulant, protesting every small rule just for the sake of it. It's disappointing how little you've learned. You've always had a penchant for the impossible. Come home with me and we can put this misbehavior behind us. Far better than the filthy flat in the slums that you paid too many rubles for."

So that was the promise Sevas had made to ebb my father's wrath—he'd gone to live with Derkach again. There were so many hideous things drifting through my mind, the same thoughts that I visited upon myself every night before I fell asleep: those small, imagined violences. I imagined Derkach clipping off Sevas's nipples with a pair of gardening shears, two neat cuts so they fell like flower petals, bloodless and pink. I imagined him pulling back the white band of flesh around Sevas's nail, peeling it in spirals like potato skin, until his whole hand was gloved in red. My stomach churned. I remembered how I had seen Derkach's face float up when Sevas had taken my hand, that deeply submerged thought leaching into me like dark water. A stammered noise of protest escaped my lips, but no one was paying me enough mind to hear it.

"I liked that flat," Sevas said. "And my flatmates, and living in the slums. That's where you found me, anyway—the ghettos of Askoldir. I'd rather that a thousand times than living under your bell jar like a taxidermied dove."

Derkach only shook his head, laughing again. "Oh, Sevas. Sevastyan. These little rebellions have gone on long enough. You can fool yourself into thinking that you would have enjoyed that kind of life—a life of derelict misery, sharing a one-room flat among three men and swallowing more vodka than bread—but the truth is you couldn't have survived it. You're too delicate, too precious, too wanting. And you could hardly have hoped for better back in the slums of Askoldir, if I hadn't found you. What do Yehuli boys from Yehuli ghettos have to look forward to? Street-sweeping jobs and rocks tossed through their windows? I absolved you of that ugly fate and furnished you with the most enviable position of any dancer in the whole Rodinyan Empire—principal dancer of Oblya's ballet company." He sniffed. "I won't ask for slavish gratitude, but I will ask for obedience. Come with me now, Sevas."

I had seen Sevas wear Ivan's face before, his warrior's grave frown and then his saint's resplendent smile, and I had seen him pin up that infallible smirk, the one that made it seem like nothing could touch him, the one that made you wonder if your knees would ever stop quaking. Now he wore a guise of beautiful rage, his eyes like two chips of smoldering sea glass, and it terrified me to think that this had been living in him all along, fettered under his lying bogatyr's clothes.

Sevas tore the feathered mantle off his back, white down floating up like kicked snow. He lifted Ivan's sword and hurled it against the far wall; it hit the mirror and shattered it, hard, shiny bits constellating the still air.

Before any of us could speak he leapt forward, chasing after Ivan's sword, and plucked it up again and beat the hilt of it against the mirror, over and over and over. All the glass split further, with a sound like a pearl necklace snapped and scattering across a wooden floor.

"Sevas, stop it!" Mr. Kovalchyk cried. There was broken glass gleaming in his mustache.

Derkach lurched toward him, grasping Sevas by the shoulders. I could see his skin turn red in ten places where Derkach's fingers pressed in. Derkach's eyes were glazed with his fury and there was a streak of blood across his cheek, just kissing the corner of his mouth. I hadn't realized that I was bleeding too until I put my hand up against my own cheek and my palm came away smeared.

"What are you going to do to me?" Sevas demanded, and his lips curled into a savage smile, the wicked cousin of the smirk that always left me weak in the knees. "No one will pay to see an Ivan with a blackened eye or a limp. Strike me if you like, Mr. Derkach, but be sure not to leave a mark."

For a moment I truly thought that he would. I even gasped out, "No!" but all Derkach did was dig his fingernails further into Sevas's bare shoulders and give him a brisk, vicious shake.

Sevas dropped Ivan's sword, chest heaving. Derkach let go, leaving a small welling of blood in the crescent-shaped cuts he'd made. His chest was rising and falling, too, with each arduous inhale, and then he spat into the broken glass at Sevas's feet.

"It would bring me no greater pleasure," Derkach rasped, "to see you try and survive a week, a day, even an hour without me. You've been coddled and cosseted and you know nothing of a world beyond the theater, where dancing well is enough to make everyone worship you. The rest of the world is not so kind to Yehuli boys, no matter how pretty their faces or coy their smiles. I have done little more in these past nine years than try and protect you from it, and all you've given me in return is your spite and loathing. So I welcome you to try and live this grand life you've imagined for yourself outside the theater, freed from my oppressive care—just remember, Sevas, I always loved you."

With that, he leaned forward and took Sevas's face into his hands and kissed him, right on the mouth. I could scarcely breathe for the awful, searing pain that the sight loosed in me. Derkach released Sevas and turned toward the door. Mr. Kovalchyk's eyes darted between them, and then over to me, looking as if he'd just been blown back by an exceptionally strong wind. His jaw unlatched like a wooden doll's.

After several moments passed, he cleared his throat and said, "Sevastyan, I will leave you to your own devices for now. I hope that in the morning we can come to an agreement that is tolerable to all parties."

It seemed such an absurd thing to say, hysterically reasonable, as if there were any sense to make out of the shattered mirrors and Derkach's kiss—still burning on Sevas's face like a live ember. I put my arms around myself, skin suddenly prickling with an unexplainable cold, and watched as Mr. Kovalchyk slunk through the yawning threshold. He walked carefully backward with his hands up, like he was trying to evade an angry bear, like he was trying to keep from riling it further.

The door clattered shut behind him, leaving Sevas and me alone in the extraordinarily loud silence.

I stayed quiet for as long as I could stand it, staring at Sevas as he stared, in turn, at the closed door. Then guilt boiled up in me and I couldn't bear it.

"I'm sorry," I mewled. "I never should have come here."

At last Sevas turned, his blue eyes shining darkly. I looked for evidence of Derkach's kiss, a mark left by that cruel tenderness, and found only Sevas's tremulous smile. The great effort of that smile snatched me up and closed over my heart like a clenched fist.

I wanted to wipe away everything that made his smile so difficult to erect. I wanted to do an impossible transformation—I wanted all the hurt to unbloom, all the glass to unshatter, all wounds to close and the skin made new. I wanted to weep, and this time the tears came easily, pearling hot at the corners of my eyes.

"Oh no," Sevas said, striding toward me. "I can't bear to watch a woman cry on my account. Unless I've moved her to new heights of ecstasy."

But his jest lilted slowly to the ground in front of me, like a shed white feather. I scarcely even flushed. Sevas came close enough that I could see the places where gold paint was peeling off his chest, the beginnings of his black tattoos leaching out from underneath. I noticed after a moment that his slippers were pricked all over with bits of glass, red marks blossoming on the pale satin like the tenderest, newest poppy buds. I had the feverish urge to kneel down and take off his slippers and pick out the glass and lick the blood from his skin until it was clean.

"Your feet," I managed to say, hoping that my lewd imaginings hadn't somehow scrawled their way across my face. "This is my fault, all of it."

"You didn't force me to leap down from the stage. You didn't force me to shatter the mirrors." Sevas moved closer still, until I felt the whisper of his breath across my cheek. "And you didn't force Derkach to be his ordinary, awful self. He hardly needs any prodding to turn mean and monstrous."

"He kissed you." Even the words sounded bald and ugly, laid out like a dead sow on a butcher's block.

"He's been known to do that." A muscle twitched in Sevas's jaw, smile waning. "That and more, but not since I was a child. I think it makes him angrier than anything to know that I don't desire him, that he repulses me. Dancers are supposed to love no one more than their handlers, and forswear all other bonds as idle distraction. Derkach is meant to be my father and my master and my lover and I'm not meant to want for anyone else."

I thought of my bird-mother in her golden cage. I remembered how I had fed her from my palm and whispered my secrets through her bars and hummed to myself while I cleaned her droppings. I remembered how desperately and happily I had administered to her and wondered if I had more than a bit of Papa's badness in me after all. I had loved my mother most when she was shuttered and safe, when mine was the only hand that tended her.

It was with a rush of rising acid that I said, "I don't think that's right. And even if it is, Derkach is too late. Oblya is already in love with you."

Sevas exhaled a humorless laugh. "And how long will its affection last? Not much longer than it takes to recover from a night of drinking, I'd expect, or to dissolve a bar of lavender soap. By the time I'm thirty, the ballet will be done with me. I'll be washed up and ugly and there will be a new boy to whet their appetites. I might as well die before then, when my face is still pretty and my smiles are still coy."

"You could never be ugly," I said, heat coiling in my belly. "And besides, it isn't so bad."

"What isn't?"

"Being ugly. I used to think it was a curse, that my sisters were beautiful and I wasn't, but not anymore. Now I think that there are some advantages to being plain of face."

Sevas frowned so deeply it carved trenches into his cheeks. "And who says you're plain of face?"

I almost laughed, because where would I even begin with naming them all? "Undine of course, and Papa, and Mama before she was a bird, and sometimes Rose when she's in her foulest moods, half our clients—even if they don't say it with their mouths, they say it with their eyes, and Dr. Bakay . . ."

"Oh," Sevas said. "Dr. Bakay told me that the sixth Organ of my Mind was twice the size of a normal man's, and that the sixth Organ of the Mind is what measures Destructiveness." He glanced around at the matting of broken glass on the floor and the mirrors veined with cracks. "What a resounding endorsement of phrenology I've just given. I didn't realize his services also included evaluating the plainness or beauty of women's faces."

My chest ached. Part of me wanted to say no more of Dr. Bakay, ever, until his face rinsed from my mind like dirty water down the drain. But there was another part of me that wanted to scream his name through empty hallways so I could hear the way it echoed. I wanted to whisper it into the ear of every person I ever met; I wanted to burn it onto me like a brand. I wanted, most of all, for someone to steal the wretched, awful burden of it away from me, and to explain precisely how wretched and awful it was. I wanted someone to write it down like a story in Papa's codex so I could know what lesson there was to be learned.

"He told me I was as quiet as a mouse," I said, at last. "And he liked that about me. He never measured the Organs of my Mind but he evaluated all the things that made me a woman, back when I was only a girl, and said it was because he wanted to understand witches." And there it was, the neat dissection of my life: girl, woman, witch. Three small things that were easy to swallow. "Dr. Bakay was not a wizard, but he worked good magic all the same. You should have seen the way I became a woman under his hands."

Sevas tensed. I could see the cord of muscle straining in his throat, the blades of his shoulders pressing high and close. He said, "That's not right, and that's not magic. Magic is the first sip of good wine that makes the edges of your vision blur. Magic is the cool breeze of the boardwalk at night and organ music in the air. Magic is landing a grand jeté and nearly going deaf with the crowd's applause. Magic is the low flicker of tavern lights and the girl you're courting leaning close so you can kiss."

As he spoke I felt an unnamable feeling bubble up in me, something even crueler than grief. His words were so lovely but strange; he might as well have been speaking in his Yehuli tongue. I didn't want to weep again after hearing how much it had distressed him, yet I felt tears gather along the line of my lashes, and Sevas's face swam before my eyes.

"I've never tasted wine," I said, around the hot thing in my throat. "I've only once been to the boardwalk at night and heard the organ music; the one time I've ever gone inside a tavern was that night with you. And I've never been kissed. I only know the old magic of what this place was before the tsar ever planted his flag here. Before there were electric streetlamps on every road and rotary presses ticking away in basement copy shops. If the tsar had never come, I would be better for it. I could've run away to the hut of a forest hag—they give shelter to young girls with cruel families and all they ask for in return is for you to separate grains of rotten corn from the sound, and poppy seeds from soil. I never would have needed to come here and ruin everything for you. Sevas, what am I going to do?"

"You haven't ruined anything that's worth replacing," he said sharply. "I could have stayed up onstage and finished my performance like a good boy, like Derkach's docile little puppet, like Kovalchyk's perfect Ivan. But I'm so tired, Marlinchen. I've been playing Ivan since I was twelve years old. How many more times can I kill the Dragon-Tsar? Maybe one night I will let him kill me instead. Just for the thrill of something new."

And then the most astonishing thing happened: Sevas put his hands over his eyes and began to cry. His shoulders trembled with his sobs and all I could do was stare and stare as he dropped to the ground, pulling his knees to his chest.

I had never seen a man cry before. I felt as if I might die myself, just from watching it. I didn't think I could stand to live in a world that could make him weep like this, as plaintively as a child. Even with my mind spasming around the thought, I found myself kneeling beside him.

"Please, Sevas," I whispered. "I don't want to see you die."

He gave a muffled whimper and his arms lifted to circle my waist. I scarcely even thought of what I was doing as I lifted my own arms and gathered up his head to my chest. His cheek was flush against the bare skin of my breast, right above where the tattered line of my corset ended. I held him there with the ferocious tightness of a bear-mother cradling her cub, of a merchant clutching his most precious ware.

In several moments his sobs ebbed, shoulders stilling. My heart

was beating so rapidly and crookedly I wondered if it might wear itself
to the bone like an old racing hound. Sevas turned his head and, very
briefly, pressed his lips to the cleft of my breasts.

I nearly fell over. My hands dropped to Sevas's shoulders and he
lifted his gaze, staring up at me from beneath dark lashes. The whites
of his eyes were shot through with red, but still he was so beautiful
that I could hardly bear to look back at him.

"You told me you've never been kissed," he said. "It's good magic,
you know. Maybe the best."

"I couldn't say one way or the other." My skin was so warm and I
could see a flush of bright pink spreading from my forehead past my
collarbone in mirror after mirror.

Sevas smirked, with the reckless charm of the man I had strolled
with along the boardwalk that one impossible night. "Let me show
you," he said.

And then he wrapped one arm around my waist and brought the
other hand to the back of my head, snarling a fistful of my wild hair.
He pulled me down toward him and kissed me so thoroughly, so relentlessly, that I thought I would faint before he was through. His
tongue parted my lips with gentle insistence.

My own hands went to his face, his throat, his chest, touching all
the places that had featured in my feverish nighttime fantasies, and
still I felt almost surprised that there was no noose to jerk me back
into the gray-washed waking world. Behind my eyelids, everything
was blooming hot and red.

When at last he pulled away, I said breathlessly, "If that were true
magic, I would have turned into something else by now."

"Perhaps I didn't try hard enough," he said, and then bore me
down beneath him. My hair spilled across the floor, mingling with
bits of broken glass. He kissed me resolutely on the mouth, and then
trailed his lips doggedly down my chin, along the line of my jaw, over
my throat. All the while I could do nothing but gasp and pant, my
arms locking around his neck to pull him closer and closer and closer.

"I do feel different now," I said faintly, the next time he gave me leave to speak. "Maybe it's good magic after all."

Sevas smiled, and it was so lovely that my heart broke a little bit, the way a hundred other girls' hearts had certainly broken when he looked at them like this. "What are you now, do you think?"

It occurred to me then that perhaps this was *my* magic: that the secret I'd held in my belly without spitting it back up and the lie I'd told over and over again to keep the secret safe were now made manifest.

"A just-kissed girl," I said. "A woman, maybe."

I could feel the press of something hard and stiff against my thigh, and my dress had gotten rucked up over my knee. I ran my hand along Sevas's chest, along all the coils of muscle and the planes of bone, his skin pulled tautly over them. Everything was twined and hard and strong.

When I reached the slope of his abdomen and the knob of his hipbone, Sevas shivered, and through his parted lips there came a soft moan.

"Do you mean to torment me?" he asked.

I was as light as dust motes drifting through a tract of sunlight, as light as air. I took Sevas's hand in mine and guided it to the small of my back, where the laces of my corset began.

"Take it off," I said, and then remembering my long-gone governess's etiquette lessons, added, "Please."

Sevas's fingers scrabbled at the laces, but he did not find much purchase. He exhaled through his nose, lips puckering with a little scowl, and at last I rolled over onto my belly, propping myself up on my elbows. Sevas's breath caught a bit at my boldness and I felt so glad to hear it, glad that for once *I* was the one who had flustered *him*.

I looked over my shoulder, through the loose strands of my irreparably mussed hair, and saw the shape of his hardness through his tights. That thrilled me even further, so much that I didn't even mind the way he tore my corset laces like a savage animal, peeling off my sleeves and taking down my skirts, nor even the way the wooden floor chilled my breasts and made my nipples knot with cold.

He kissed his way across my shoulders, down the length of my back, over my bottom, and sucked at the sweet place between my thighs. I whimpered and then he turned me over, sliding between my legs. As he held himself there above me, he said, "Marlinchen . . ."

"Don't," I said. "Don't stop, or you'll be a liar, a cheat—"

He laughed. "Who says so?"

"I do."

Transformations were a fickle, dangerous magic, and every spell came with a high and terrible cost. Once you turned into one thing, you could no longer be what you once were. A cat turned into a cat-vase lost its whiskers and darting pink tongue. A carriage turned into a gourd lost its wheels and glass windows. And once you became a woman, you gave up all the trappings of girlhood, all its precious bounties.

I knew once I was through with this I could no longer hope to be rescued from a tower or kissed awake from my cursed slumber. Princes didn't come for women; they only came for girls with intact and immaculate maidenheads, opening them up like flowers waiting to be plucked. I was excising myself from half the stories in Papa's codex, and perhaps it ought to have terrified me. But I only felt a pull of want in the bottom of my belly, and between my legs I was almost embarrassingly slick.

Sevas stripped off his tights and then he was kneeling there above me, naked. I drank in the sight of him like it was sweetest kvass: the gold paint still smudged on his cheeks and throat, the tattoos scrawled over his shoulders and the back of his hand, the rippling muscles of his chest, the straining hardness standing taut against his stomach.

He kissed me again with a tender desperation, stroking two fingers inside me. I quivered and bit down on his lip, hard enough to taste the salt of blood. Sevas drew his mouth down my throat and over my breasts, gently circling my nipple with his tongue. His touch was so soft, so sweet, that I could almost forget Dr. Bakay's knife had ever been there at all.

Finally he entered me, and a fiery braid of pain and pleasure laced from my broken maidenhead up my spine. It hurt, and then it didn't, and then it hurt again, and sometimes it felt so good that I wished he would never stop. When the ache returned I couldn't help it; I sobbed quietly, muffling the sound against his shoulder.

Sevas paused at once, blinking at me in alarm, and said, "I told you I can't bear to make a woman weep."

I felt sorry that I had upset him, and I didn't want him to stop. Sevas brought up a hand to cup my cheek, thumb brushing over my lips, and once it was there I felt the urge to taste him, so I took two of his fingers into my mouth.

He let out a long trembling breath and started to move again, slowly at first and then lengthening his thrusts until I could feel how hard his heart was beating through our adjacent chests. With each bolt of pain I bit down on his fingers, hands fisted against his back.

"Do you know what I would do to everyone who ever called you plain-faced?" Sevas panted, lips brushing the shell of my ear. "I would kill them."

I laughed, and it did something strange to the place where our bodies were connected, jostling us both. I took his fingers out of my mouth. "With your wooden sword?"

"I think you're making fun of me."

It was not long before he finished with a groan, spilling himself inside me. Sevas collapsed like a card house, breathing hard into my hair, against my throat. I shut my eyes and felt the seconds drag past as he went soft within me, and when at last he pulled out I opened my eyes and turned my head to look at our reflections.

There was my naked body and my soft, heavy breasts, cut into jagged pieces by the cracked mirror. There were Sevas's eyes, damp and blue and shining, and chest rising and falling hugely, like something very large was trying to press out from under his skin. The fingers that had been in my mouth were pricked with small wounds, in the shape of my sharp little incisors, just like the gash on my knuckle.

I kissed his cut fingers, as if in apology. Sevas wiped away the mess of blood on my thighs, staining his palms the color of sour-cherry kvass. Already I felt so horribly empty without him inside me. I wished I could catch him there, keep him there, swallow him whole.

CHAPTER ELEVEN

There were no windows in the mirrored room and so I only
woke when I felt the wooden floor pressing hard against my
hipbone, and something prickling at my scalp. I sat up and
shook glass shards from my hair. Sevas rolled over onto his
back, flinging one hand over his eyes even though it was as dark as it
had always been. His lips were wonderfully swollen and it made me
flush just to look at him, still unclothed, our bare legs tangled like an
extraordinary nexus of tree roots.

I could have stared at him this way forever, and perhaps stayed
curled there with him, if not for the pain in my side and the throb of
something torn open between my thighs. I gave him a soft nudge in
the shoulder and Sevas groaned, lashes fluttering.

The moment he'd sunk himself inside of me a vision had burst
across the insides of my eyelids, painting everything in lurid color.
I saw Derkach's hands, huge and hairy, and the flash of a silver belt

buckle. It was so awful that I'd bitten down on Sevas's lip and hoped that as he bled the memory drained out of us both.

And then I'd wanted only to pour myself into the space that the memory had left in him, like sugar in black tea, thinning it and making it sweet. I kissed him back as hard as he kissed me, and with every moment that he thrusted into me, Derkach's face faded from both of our minds. Now I saw the stain of my blood on his palms, darkened with the hours to a color that was nearly black. I almost thought to lick it off, to see what my broken maidenhead tasted like—it had to be as heady and good as honey wine to make Papa want to guard it like a panting dog—but I figured that would perturb him. Instead I jostled Sevas again, with greater force this time, and heaving a weary sigh he opened his eyes at last.

"Marlinchen," he said. His gaze traveled slowly over me, over the hair that lay in coils covering my breasts. Last night I had not felt ashamed of them, their softness and heaviness, but now I did, and I was glad that they were hidden. "I'm sorry for making you bleed."

I wasn't sorry at all, but I didn't tell him so. Instead I reached for my gown, torn nearly beyond repair, all the snapped corset laces strewn about the broken glass. As I tried to smooth the pleats of the skirt I felt like a ghost returning to its body, only I was both the body and the ghost. The ghost's words bubbled up in me. "I have to go home."

Sevas propped himself up on his elbows, swollen mouth twisting. "What?"

When I'd run last night, tucking the compact into the cleft of my breasts, when I'd turned away from Papa's outstretched hands, the magic of my long-kept secret breaking this spell, I hadn't thought of returning. I'd only thought of fleeing from the dragons at the door.

But now I knew I would have to return. I knew it in my marrow and blood. I belonged to that house like one of Undine's china dolls or the grandfather clock or Papa's last cat-vase. It had birthed me in all of my ugly, feral strangeness, and so it would have to take me back. Only—

My breath caught in my chest, like a pin in the hem of a dress. A film came over my eyes, fear turning my vision milky as marbled glass.

Sevas sat up with a jolt of alarm, pushing himself onto his knees beside me, all the while I was panting and gasping and trying not to cry. Whatever impossible magic had existed in this mirrored room last night was gone, dried up, burned down. Sevas's hand hovered above my shoulder, like he was afraid to touch me, and the absurdity of it almost made me laugh; his palm was still matted with my blood. It was only then that I managed to say, "My father will have my liver, for what I've done."

"Your liver?" Sevas's brow furrowed with hard, deep lines. "Marlinchen, please, you'll have to explain the workings of his wizard's mind."

So I told him about Papa's potion, that vile-tasting black draught that he tipped down our throats every week or whenever he thought that he could smell a lie on us. I told him about how he guarded our maidenheads like a jealous lord guarded his most fertile lands, so that only he could plant there.

By the time I was done, my teeth were chattering as if I'd been gripped by a sudden bout of cold, and Sevas gripped my arms, smearing my own blood into the crook of my elbow.

"Why wouldn't you tell me?" he asked, voice tipping up on the last syllable, high and thin with despair. "I wouldn't have done it if I had known."

I inhaled sharply. "Maybe you ought to have considered what an awful mess it would make, to couple with a plain-faced witch."

It was the only time I had ever seen Sevas flush. He let go of my arms and said, "I don't choose my conquests like a woman shopping for hats, imagining how each will make me look when I preen in front of my friends. Is it so preposterous to think that I was only a foolish man, like so many others, who desired a woman that perhaps he shouldn't? It's the oldest story there is, men wanting things that will kill them."

"I wouldn't kill you," I said, but the words felt both heavy and empty. "It's only Papa that would try."

"I'd sooner let him try than play Ivan one more time," said Sevas, and even as he attempted a smile I could see the muddled misery in his eyes. "A Dragon-Tsar or a wizard in his manor: what's the difference, really?"

The difference was that Papa didn't breathe paper flames. His magic was as real as my bird-mother's white feathers or the black snakes in the garden, as real as the terror coiling in the bottom of my belly. I rested my palm flat against the wooden floor to steady myself, then began to put on my dress.

Sevas watched me in silence, eyes tracing the slope of my breasts, the curves of my calves and thighs, looking enraptured. I had seen the proof of his desire; I had felt it stiff inside me, and yet it was still almost impossible for me to believe that he had wanted me just as desperately as I had wanted him. Sevas put on his tights again and swept up his feathered mantle, shaking out the bits of broken glass.

Mama's compact was lying on the ground, in a bed of glittering shards. I closed my fingers around it and drew it to my breast, the metal cool against my feverish skin. Last night when Sevas had torn off my corset, the compact had clattered to the floor, spilling out some of its black sand. I had waited for him to ask me about it, and his gaze had gone to it briefly, curiously, but then he'd only turned back and kissed me again, with the desperation of a man near to dying. I held that memory in the black space of my mind and licked my lips, tasting the saltiness of him.

"I don't know what to do," I said. Tears were gathering again at the corners of my eyes. "Papa will have my liver and I cannot stop him. There are fifteen strange men at my house, and that's not counting Dr. Bakay. He is laughing with Papa on the chaise. Both of my sisters hate me for keeping my secret, for telling my lie. And I've ruined myself from ever being in a good story again."

My heart was thrashing like an open window in the rain. Sevas came to me and cupped my face in his hands, very firmly, and said, "I know about the men. Your father's posters were everywhere and then the penny presses printed them on the front page. You said he wants to protect your virtues, but now he wants you married to any one of Oblya's desperate bachelors who can solve his wizard's riddle."

"My sisters," I said softly, looking at him through wet lashes. "The man who figures out the truth can have his pick, and no man of sound mind would choose me when he could wed Rose or Undine."

Sevas pursed his lips. "Of all the things Dr. Bakay said about me, he never suggested that I was not of sound mind."

"Speak frankly." My stomach swooped like a gull. "What need do you have of a plain-faced witch-wife? You must know that witches have a tendency to become wickeder when they become wives. I could grow a second set of teeth. I could eat my husband."

"You must stop calling yourself plain-faced," Sevas said sternly. "I do not think of plain-faced women the way I think of you. And you are sharp-toothed already." He showed me his fingers, nicked all over with my bite marks. "If I took you to wife, I would not mind being nipped in our marriage bed."

My face was torridly hot. "You can't really mean to say that you want to be in Papa's competition."

"And you don't think I could survive it?" He lifted a brow. "What is his wizard's riddle, anyway? Dr. Bakay said that my Organ for Cleverness was exceptionally large."

"It's not a riddle that cleverness can solve." But something was turning in my mind. "He wants to know how I managed to escape from under his spell. To come to the theater."

"Your secret," Sevas said. "You never told me how."

I opened the compact, my fingers shaking. The black sand was still there, smelling faintly of brine and sea air, as impossible as it had always been but now imbued with the strange new magic I hadn't known I'd possessed. "This came off me in the bath. Papa's spell was that none of us could leave the house without black sand from Oblya's beaches."

"It came off in the bath?" Sevas frowned. "But you told me you never visited the beach until that first night with me. How could it have gotten there?"

I had put the thought out of my mind for so long that returning to it now made my stomach lurch. I could only explain it the way that Papa always had, when there was a question that was like a steep drop off the edge of a cliff, when there was nothing but a black chasm instead of an answer.

"Magic," I said. The word seemed somehow feebler in my mouth than it ever had in Papa's.

"Whose magic? Yours?"

That, in truth, I still did not know. If my wanting could be transmuted into real power, surely I'd have been able to alter the course of my life far sooner. Maybe I'd been told to want nothing more than Papa's happiness, and that had stifled any magic of my own. Or perhaps I had never wanted anything so badly as I had wanted Sevas. I only blushed and did not reply.

Something else had slipped out with the compact. A square of paper, folded once. I leaned down to where it had lilted to the ground and picked it up. A few shards of glass were stuck in the paper and they pricked the pad of my thumb as I opened it.

The ink was blurred with water, but I could still make out that it said FISHEROVICH & SYMYRENKO 3454 VOROBYEV STREET.

With a bolt of knowledge, perhaps even cleverness, I snapped the compact shut and held the paper out to Sevas wordlessly.

He frowned, brow furrowing as he tried to read it. "What is this, Marlinchen?"

So I told him about how we had sold all our things, Mama's pearls and charm bracelet, and how this broker had come to try to buy some magic off us. He had wanted things like bottled spirits and haunted amulets and dolls that stood up and moved of their own accord. I supposed that was the capitalist view of magic, that it was something that could be neatly packaged and sold. That was what these developers and brokers had wanted to do to Oblya, after all: they wanted to wrap up the city in muslin and twine like a bar of lavender soap. They wanted to lock it up inside a pearl-enameled snuffbox for the tsar to fondle as he pleased. Well, we did not have any bottled spirits or haunted amulets, and Rose's herbs turned ordinary in the hands of mortal men.

"But Mama's charm bracelet came back to me," I said in a rush. "Perhaps—perhaps my wanting has magic after all. The broker paid a lot for it."

"A lot," Sevas repeated slowly. "How much?"

"I don't know exactly. But it was more rubles than I could get from my clients in a month. Perhaps enough to rent a flat in the slums." My cheeks were pinking as the words came out. Even so far away from Papa's house, speaking it felt treasonous. "And there's still something that hasn't yet been sold. A mirror; my mother had a mirror."

"A mirror?"

"A magic mirror, one that never lies. If you look into it, it will tell you the truth, no matter whether it pleases you or not. If not this broker, I know there would be one or the other who would buy it off us."

"But the mirror is not here." Sevas's lips thinned. "Nor is the bracelet."

No. They were not. I took the card back from Sevas, feeling that bolt of cunning dissipate. If I had truly thought of escape, I would have brought something with me when I left—the bracelet, stolen rubles, even just a coat for when the day turned to night—but I had only been reckless and desperate.

"You should not have bothered with me," I said. "The only thing I've brought here to you is blood and ruin and a lot of broken glass. If Papa's potion kills me, it will only be because of my own foolishness, and no fault of yours. Sevas, you should let me leave here alone, and excise all thoughts of me from your mind."

Sevas drew a breath, stepping away from me. His eyes turned incandescent and for a moment I wondered if he might pick up Ivan's sword again. But he only clenched his fists, still dark with my blood, and said, "Marlinchen, don't you understand? I would rather die than play Ivan again. I would rather hurl myself off the docks and into the sea than put on that gold paint. I would rather go vodka-blind than twirl for Kovalchyk one more time. And I would rather set myself aflame than return to Derkach."

His voice trailed off by the end of it, low and tremulous, and his gaze dropped to the ground. I stared at him with a tightness in my chest, watching a spectacular and awful metamorphosis. I had seen Sevas don Ivan's feathered cloak and bogatyr's resplendent smile; I had seen him smirk like a man who knew the way it made women swoon, who knew in that moment he was untouchable. I had felt him kiss me with the fervent yearning of an ascetic before the altar.

Now I saw only this: a boy who was terrified of being alone.

I went to speak but he caught up my face in his hands again, bitten fingers brushing over my lips. Still I went weak-kneed at the way he looked at me, like he wanted never to look at anything else.

"If I kiss you again," he said, mouth so close to mine, "will you turn into a girl who believes me?"

"You aren't being fair," I protested. "Do you plan to kiss your way out of any predicament?"

"Only the ones with women involved." He paused. "I am not afraid of your father's anger. I am afraid of his gentleness."

"What?"

Sevas looked down. "Even Derkach was capable of kindness. You heard him say that he loves me. Any predator can choose to smile without teeth. I'm afraid your father will choose to treat you tenderly if you return and then I will never be able to get his teeth out of you."

My heart plummeted. He was right. Papa could be tender. For all the fear his magic laid on me, my bed at home was still the softest place I had ever known. Although Papa's moments of kindness were so rare, so meager, they ballooned so hugely in my mind that sometimes they obliterated everything else.

"I wish," Sevas said quietly, as though he could see inside my mind, "that I could give you a softer place to fall. But you're right; I only have a wooden sword and handful of rubles and a face that gets older and uglier and less useful with each passing moment."

As much as he wished for a soft place for me, I wished the same for him. I remembered the vision that he'd spilled into me and now I wanted again to kiss it out of him, to make the space between him and Derkach vast and long. I wanted to give him the gift of hours, to gather them up in my apron like fresh apples and empty them into his lap. I wanted to feed him hours that were free of Derkach's black, curdling rot.

I did not know if kisses could do such a thing, but Sevas was right—they were very good magic indeed. So with a quiver of boldness I pressed my lips squarely to his, fingers circling his wrists. Sevas held my face and sucked my tongue into his mouth and didn't let go until both of us needed desperately to breathe.

"I'll harden myself against Papa's gentleness," I whispered, "if you can solve the riddle that's not a riddle and steal the mirror from under his nose."

"I promise," he said, "I will be the canniest glass-thief you've ever seen. Besides," he added, "I'm good with mirrors."

I gave a small smile, even as his promise tugged me along like a wooden toy on a string, to Sevas's dressing room where he put on his clothes and I looked at myself in the mirror of his boudoir, trying to track my own metamorphosis. There was a bruise on my throat in the shape of Sevas's mouth, and my hair was mussed with the movement of his hands. Would Papa notice it all when he looked at me, proof of the blood spilled between my thighs? The old fear surfaced like a shipwreck dredged up out of the sea. If he suspected my misdeed and forced the potion down my throat, there was nothing Sevas or I could do about it. And if Sevas's very presence stirred him to a vengeful fury, what power did I have to keep Papa from turning him to a spewing of black snakes at my feet?

I watched Sevas put on his coat and could only feel myself fill with dread. He had worried over Papa's kindness, but Papa's anger was a churning, roiling thing, always changing its shape. It could coil around me like a serpent or snap me up in its jaws like a wolf.

I would have to be clever enough to evade his anger, and cruel enough to turn away from his kindness. My problem was that I had spent my whole life being told I was neither, only a plain-faced third daughter whose magic was just for seeing, not doing or changing or making.

Was I being clever now, with my plan, or was it just Papa's magic working on me from afar, slowly pulling me back to the garden, to the house, to the sitting room where he and Dr. Bakay were chatting like old friends?

Sevas took my hand. He led me through the labyrinth of dressing rooms, looking determinedly ahead. I was glad that his grip did not give me a choice in the matter, because otherwise I would have stayed there, frozen, the mirror holding me in place.

Voices rippled the velvet curtain, only whispers at first, too low to make out, and then rising to a chorus of shouts. Sevas halted abruptly. "It's Kovalchyk."

"Is there another way out?"

"No. We'll have to go past."

There was more shouting, and then a sound like a great number of boulders tumbling down the side of a mountain. Metal screeched against metal, and Sevas drew a breath. In another moment he parted the curtain with the flat of his hand and pulled me through it after him.

Mr. Kovalchyk was standing center stage in a rime of spotlight, dabbing at his forehead with the same damp handkerchief as last night. There were four men gathered around him, day laborers by the look of their lean faces, and a spate of dancers lingering back. I searched and searched, but Aleksei was not among them, and I did not see Derkach either. When Mr. Kovalchyk noticed Sevas and me standing there, he turned quite lithely on his heel, half like a dancer himself, eyes growing huge.

"Sevastyan—" he started.

"You can take the money from the mirrors from what was my salary," Sevas cut in. "I quit."

Mr. Kovalchyk only gaped at him, mouth opening and closing and opening again, like a windup toy stuck on its stupid loop. "I will pretend I did not just hear those words leave your lips, Sevas. You can speak with Mr. Derkach about that when he gets here. For now I have more urgent problems to attend."

He did not appear to even notice me, despite all the grief he'd given Sevas about my presence last night. The dancers began to whisper, voices as soft and low as wind through willow fronds, and one of them pointed up. I drew my gaze toward the ceiling, and Sevas did too. The rafters were dark and I had to squint through whorls of dust, but then I saw it: crammed up among the metal beams, limbs splayed out like a four-pointed star, was the corpse of a man whose eyes had been ripped from his skull.

In one hot rush, all the breath went out of me.

And then my eyes were missing, some haze falling across my vision that removed me from the room in small, agonizing increments, like a slow and throbbing exorcism. I watched through the film as the day laborers got the body down with an elaborate rope-and-pulley system, dancers looking on and tittering in their tights. A hard swallow ticked in Sevas's throat. The body crashed onto the stage like a big dead bird, and the smell that billowed up from it nearly made me retch.

"He must have been dead for near a week, perhaps longer," one of the day laborers said, pinching his nose shut. "Look how rotted it is."

A week. What had I been doing a week ago? My days blurred together, rote and near-identical. I had been pouring Papa tea or grinding meat into filling while someone, something, picked off the men of Oblya like a hawk snatching up its quarry. While this man's flesh was curdling off his bones.

The memory of Papa's voice struck me suddenly: *Oblya will not miss a single day laborer. If anything, it means more work for the rest.*

"How could we have gone so long without noticing it?" Mr. Koval-chyk demanded, covering his own nose with his handkerchief.

The day laborer shrugged. "Too high up to smell. Too bright when all the lights are on."

Where the man's eyes had been there were only two small pits, opening to an oily darkness. His chest had been flayed open almost precisely, rib cage and sternum split down their centers like the bodice of a dress torn in a moment of great ecstasy, and under it there was the pink of flesh and muscle. But inside his sternum there was nothing, no red withering heart, and his rib cage was absent of gristle and blood, looking as white as taxidermy tusks mounted above some conqueror's mantel. The liver was absent, the slick garland of intestines gone, and even the stomach had been slit open and emptied. Everything was scraped as clean as a white porcelain bowl.

It reminded me of how I had flayed the monster, carving out its entrails. It had come to me so easily, as if such butchery were as natural as breathing. I squeezed my eyes shut and held my breath until I was dizzy, until when I opened them again my vision was blinkering with false stars.

Two neat wounds grinned above the dead man's knees, as if some-one had used a knife to hobble him so he could not get away. At least, that was what the Grand Inspector said when he arrived, with six of his black-clad men in tow.

"A week or more," he proclaimed, nudging the body with the toe of his boot. "It's hard to tell at this stage, before we can get it to our mortician. Sir, I am going to need a list of everyone who has been in-side this theater in the past two weeks—dancers, workers, managers. And I'm going to need to see the log of ticket purchases."

"But who *was* he?" I pressed, even though a part of me already knew. Papa's voice returned to me again. *If anything, it means more work for the rest.* He was any man. He was a man no one would miss.

"Oh," Mr. Kovalchyk said, blinking from under his sweaty brow. "Some day laborer or another. We hire them at market rate to mop the floors."

The Grand Inspector nodded grimly and asked if the man had any family, but I could not hear Mr. Kovalchyk's response over the rushing of blood in my ears. I only heard him laugh, and what an absurd question it was. Men like Niko and Fedir and even Sevas had no family but one another. The Grand Inspector took down some notes on his pad. I watched him through that ghostly haze as Sevas's hand pressed against the small of my back, thinking of everything Papa had told me about the man before me and his black-clad enforcers.

Since he was Oblyan, and not Yehuli or Ionik or Merzani, Papa could not properly say that he had horns hidden in his hair or silverfish crawling over his suit jacket, but still he said that the Grand Inspector was a demon of a man, and as dangerous as a serpent coiled under a rock. He looked more like a raven to me, in his long dark coat, very tall and with a nose that jutted magnificently over his mustache. When he spoke, his mouth made a snapping sort of motion, as if his lips were veined with a taut elastic band.

He had his men wrap the body in a sheet and roll it up into a large sack, which all six of them together hefted toward the door. As they heaved the body onto their shoulders, two small things tumbled out of the sheet.

I watched them clatter to the floor, dark and grooved and each the size of a marble: plum stones.

"I want the theater shuttered for now," the Grand Inspector said. "No one in or out. My men will need to conduct an investigation, and it will take days."

Mr. Kovalchyk's jaw went slack. He daubed at his forehead. "Do you think . . . sir, is it possible . . . I read a story in the penny presses . . . was it a monster?"

All at once the Grand Inspector's bird face went pale with anger. "Do not speak another word to me of penny presses or monsters. It is hard enough to investigate the death of a man without everyone in Oblya frothing at the mouth for me to execute an imaginary villain. Say no more of this matter, Mr. Kovalchyk, and do not let slip to anyone the state in which the body was found. I will not tolerate another mob at my door."

I still had the broker's card, and the hard edges of the paper pressed cruelly into my breasts. My secret, or Papa's secret, a suspicion I could not even bring myself to speak aloud. Mr. Kovalchyk shut his mouth and turned away, blushing furiously. The dancers pressed in together, whispers darting around in their tight little circle, and I was sure that, no matter what the Grand Inspector decreed, the penny presses would hear about this by tonight.

The day laborers went away, and Sevas guided me off the stage, down the long hallway, and through the door. Sunlight poured on us like hot melted butter. At last he turned to me and said, "Marlinchen."

"Please," I said. "I don't want to talk about the dead man." I was thinking of plum stones. I was thinking of missing hearts and the small, ground-up pieces of meat that made the filling of varenyky. All of a sudden I wanted to crumple up the card and cast it into the wind, and not let its bad magic seep into me further. I wanted to uproot the ideas that it had planted in my mind.

Sevas nodded, hand slipping off my back. And then we went down Kanatchikov Street together, the ground rolling out slowly under our feet, toward my father's house.

The garden was soft and damp, the way it was after a rainstorm, but I didn't think it had rained at all. There were no dirty puddles gathered on the cobblestones. It was as if one fat, dark cloud had gathered around our house and our house alone.

I pushed open the gate with my breath burning in my throat, and when I stepped through, my shoe sunk into the wet soil. I took another step, the mud still sucking at my slipper, and then beckoned Sevas after me. He was squinting in the sunlight and then a gust of wind went through his hair and I was so afraid and filled with tremulous affection that I wished that I could scoop him up and tuck him into my bodice and keep him safe and warm there between my breasts like a she-wolf nursing her cub.

He stepped through the gate and did not turn into a spewing of black snakes. That was my first relief.

My second relief was that no profound transformation had taken place in my absence; the garden did not look very different from how I had left it, except that most of the white petals were gone from the flowering pear tree. They stuck on the ground like shed feathers. The goblin was digging a little hole in the dirt to sit in. The eyeless ravens were stretching their wings and cawing out vowel sounds that no mortal knew how to make.

From behind a marvelous begonia plant, Indrik emerged, his chest slick with oil and his goat's tail lashing. He saw Sevas and huffed loudly through his nostrils.

Sevas made a startled noise and darted behind my back. "Marlinchen, what is that?"

Indrik drew himself up to his full height, shoulders rolling, and narrowed his man's eyes. "Well, mortal man, when you hear thunder from the mountaintop or see clouds gather overhead, when winter melts into spring and wheat flowers up out of the ground to make into your morning kasha—"

"That's Indrik," I said.

"My dear supplicant, is this man imperiling you?" Indrik asked, huffing again with even greater indignation. "Would you like me to strike him down with a precisely aimed bolt of lightning?"

"No, thank you," I said as Sevas blanched. "Indrik, where are my sisters?"

I had been afraid that Papa would punish them in my stead, but I'd tucked that fear away like an earring in the bottom of a jewelry box, and only now did it shake loose again, shining. What if I had ruined them already? I began to feel the plan I'd made was foolish and doomed, and how would I manage to get up to the third floor and take

Mama's mirror at all, and even if I did could I find a broker to sell it, and what if Papa found me out before then?

There was a crunching sound as Rose stomped out from behind the black plum tree. Her hair was loose and knotted with briars and her hands and wrists were filthy all the way up to the elbow and she looked just the way I remembered her.

I had thought she would be angry. But to my great surprise there were tears rolling down her cheeks, and she came toward me and wrapped me up and kissed my temple and smoothed back the frizzing curls from my forehead. She smelled like soil and sour-cherry kvass. When she finally let me go she wiped her tears from her violet eyes and I felt like an imp, a scoundrel, for making my sweet sister cry.

"Marlinchen," she said breathlessly. "I was so afraid you wouldn't come back."

My throat constricted. "I had to."

Her gaze darted over my shoulder, to where Sevas stood. Her eyes narrowed. I saw Sevas run a hand through his hair, mussing it to intentional dishevelment, and begin to pin up his coy and beguiling smile. I wanted to tell him not to bother, that it would be like trying to draw blood from a stone. I had never met anyone more resistant to being charmed than Rose, and she looked at most men with beetle-browed disdain, as if they were nothing better than the squirrels and other pests that menaced her garden.

He was undeterred. "My name is Sevastyan," he said, smiling brilliantly, and held out his hand. "Sevastyan Rezkin."

Rose gave him a dour stare. "This one won't last long here."

Sevas's smile waned, just a little bit. "I'm less fragile than I look."

I dug a nail into the cut on my knuckle. "What has Papa done? In the meantime? And all the men . . ."

"Well, he was furious, of course." I heard the edge of blame in her voice, and I felt like I had caught myself against the side of the counter, one brisk, hard blow to the belly. "So he raged for several hours, and turned one of the men's leather boots into a yapping black dog and killed it. Dr. Bakay tried to soothe him, but Papa is resistant to being soothed."

Sevas was no longer smiling. A powerful wind came through the garden, shaking big pink petals loose from the begonia plant, and nearly blowing up my skirt along with it. Hurriedly I pulled it down again, wondering if Rose had seen the dried blood there on my thighs, or if she had noticed the bruise on my throat in the shape of Sevas's mouth, or if she had noticed that my corset was gone, abandoned to that broken-glass room. Was her magic good enough to sense the way I had changed?

"It was foolish to bring this man back here," Rose said sharply. "Don't you think Papa will remember how you swooned for him that first time? Don't you remember his promise to turn him to a mass of black snakes at the door?"

Nearly all my certainty and bravado curdled under my clever sister's stare. With difficulty, I said, "Papa's spells were dismantled, to let the day laborers through."

But Rose's expression did not shift. "Do you really think you can trick him, Marlinchen? One night away has not made you into a powerful witch. If anything, you are less clever now than when you left. This dancer has just infected you with his foolhardiness."

I shrunk back, but before I could reply, Sevas said, "Perhaps you've infected her with your gloom and pessimism." I'd never heard anyone speak to Rose that way. "I'm not as daft as I look, either."

I'd never heard his voice so cold before, either. I felt a bit like I had when I'd watched him kill the Dragon-Tsar for the first time, full of a strange bloodlust.

"Go on then, both of you," Rose bit out. "Papa's waiting. And he's hungry. It's all he's been able to speak of since you left. How his stomach is eating itself in your absence."

Another hard blow to the belly. I was swept through the garden as if by a very strong wind, trampling ferns and dandelion fluff that was sticking to the wet soil like a scattering of dirty snow. Rose was leading the way, her steps swift and sure, her gaze forward and know-ing. Sevas gripped my hand and squeezed it.

But as soon as my sister pushed open the door and I stepped in-side, I felt the fog of Papa's magic lay upon me the way I had never felt it before. There was the grandfather clock, its shadow planking the wooden floor. There was the staircase that wound up to the second floor like a fat red dragon's tongue. There was the hallway that led down into the kitchen, and the sitting room on our right, and all the men with their sad hound faces draped over our furniture.

There was Dr. Bakay, feeling one man's skull, yellow measuring tape cutting the man's head into halves. There was the waft of warm, stinking air from the kitchen. There was Undine on the stairs, looking beautiful and mean.

And then there was Papa, standing in the mouth of the corridor, tall and narrow and pale, his white shirt and face bright as bone. He did not appear even to see Sevas, or Rose. His gaze was like a cocked pistol and it was aimed only at me.

The grandfather clock gonged three. Papa spoke a word that sounded like a spell, though I couldn't be sure. It was neither kind nor cruel. It was simply a wheel going into its groove. All I knew then was that I was falling through time, years opening up into a black abyss that swallowed me whole. When they spit me out I was sixteen again, Dr. Bakay's hands on my budding breasts; I was thirteen, eating my bird-mother for supper; I was eleven and Papa was dragging me down the stairs and into the foyer so I could tell fortunes for men with lust in their eyes. I was nine and lying awake at night as Papa's footsteps made the wood ache and groan.

It was such incredible magic that it moved my body for me, and I crossed the foyer toward Papa. If I had allowed Sevas's foolhardiness to infect me, it had left behind holes for Papa's hunger to seep into me too. My stomach growled so loudly that everyone must have heard it, Sevas and Dr. Bakay and the day laborers and my beautiful sisters, who looked at me with loathing.

I knelt at Papa's feet and bent down until my nose was brushing the floor. I pressed my lips to the toe of his boot. I wondered what he had done with the black dog, and then knew that he had eaten it, and then wondered if there would be any left for me.

Against the leather of his shoe, I whispered, "I'm sorry, I'm sorry, I'm sorry. I'll never leave you again."

CHAPTER TWELVE

H ere is what happened when I returned.

Papa welcomed Sevas into the house without even so much as a scowl; it was as if the scene at his flat had all been forgotten. He even took Sevas's coat and hung it. I stood up, flushing and shaking with the ebbing of Papa's magic, letting it bleed out of me as the world shuddered back. The day laborers in the sitting room mumbled like crows.

Dr. Bakay took Sevas's hand and shook it, remarking upon the firmness of his grip and how that related to his overlarge fifteenth Organ, the Organ for Firmness, which he had previously measured. Sevas held Dr. Bakay's hand so hard it was like he meant to hurt him. When at last he let go, Sevas's knuckles were white.

Undine traipsed down the stairs, conspicuously tugging the neckline of her dress lower. She shouldered past me and smiled at Sevas and asked if he would like a tour of the house. Sevas smiled back at her, and how could I blame him?

But he declined her offer, and I felt a perverse nip of satisfaction to see the way her face crumpled like last week's grocery list. Her mouth puckered and she went away, into the garden. Rose stood there in the shadow of the grandfather clock and rolled her eyes with a sigh.

Papa said, "Well, Marlinchen? I'm hungry."

I could see the bags under his eyes, blue and fat, and the dramatic hollows of his cheekbones, like someone had taken a scalpel to him. It filled me with a terrible pity and guilt, so perfunctory it was as if I'd been made for it, a machine for dispensing grief.

In that moment I forgot all about my own gnawing hunger, and plum stones, and missing hearts and livers. I almost forgot about the card tucked between my breasts and the compact in Sevas's pocket and the charm bracelet upstairs and the mirror that never lies on the third floor. There was some powerful amnesiac magic running through the whole house, a quiet current that swept me along, through the sitting room, and into the kitchen.

Dirty dishes were stacked precariously in the sink and the butcher block was soaked through with blood. Knife blades were marbled with grease and forks were clotted with fat and gristle. Who had made such a mess in my absence? Could it have been the day laborers? None of them seemed bold enough.

It must have been Papa, though I could scarcely imagine him pinning the squealing black dog down on the butcher block and slicing open its belly. Papa wasn't made for such quotidian violences. I was his blade against the banal and grotesque. I butchered monsters and rubbed my knuckles raw scrubbing up their blood. Not him.

I turned on the faucet and let the hot water run over everything, steam clouding up in front of my face.

I did not realize Sevas had followed me into the kitchen until I heard something clatter to the ground. I spun around and saw him bend to pick up a dropped spoon and lay it on the bloody butcher block, then smile beatifically as if nothing had happened at all.

"You shouldn't be here," I said. "Papa will be suspicious."

Sevas laid one hand on the counter, his voice low. "Tell me it was all a clever ruse, a false promise. Kneeling in front of your father."

"Of course." My cheeks warmed. "I was trying to be convincing."

Sevas nodded. He believed me, I could tell, or at least he *wanted* to. I wanted desperately to believe myself. It was better than the alternative: that the ghost of the girl I was still haunted these halls, and she would possess me whenever my body ached like a wound that would let her slip inside. Perhaps she would never let me go.

For a moment, there had been no ruse at all, only Papa's magic and the grandfather clock ticking as it always had. I had to remember the plan, the mirror, or else I would be lost to the house again.

"And cooking for your father will further convince him?" Sevas asked.

"I have to pretend that everything is as it should be," I said, "or else he'll know. But first I have to wash up."

"I can help," said Sevas, and without waiting for my reply he began to gather up an armful of dirty plates.

Watching Sevas clean my kitchen felt absurd, more intimate and intrusive even than him thrusting hard inside of me. I felt as if he could see my whole life laid out in the arrangement of dishes, the used teacups, the heap of leftover chicken bones.

He took a wet rag and wiped down the counter with surprising tenderness, the same way he had fondled my nipple with his tongue. I was entranced by watching him work, and even aroused, so much that I hardly noticed the sink filling and filling before me, filthy water lapping at the brim, very near to spilling over and onto the floor.

Hurriedly I turned off the faucet, then looked back at Sevas and said, "You don't have to do this woman's work."

He arched a brow. "What if it pleases me?"

"Why would it please you?"

"Because there's something useful I can do besides dancing," he said. "Even if it's scrubbing dishes. Perhaps I'll find restaurant work once we leave here. It can't be worse than the theater."

I looked down and bit my lip. "There is a story in Papa's codex," I said. "It is about a king and a queen . . ."

"Is this Ivan and the tsarevna?"

"No," I said. "Although the queen dies in this one too. But before she dies, she makes her husband promise that he will only wed someone who is equal in beauty as she. He promises such. But the only person equal in beauty is the princess herself. So the king sets out to marry his daughter."

"I don't think I like this story," Sevas said. On the bloody butcher block, our hands were close.

I continued anyway. "In order to make herself ugly, the princess cuts off her arm and her breast. Her father wants nothing to do with her after that." I remembered how I had butchered that poor monster. I remembered how its blood had soaked into my skirts. I had killed it to keep my secret. Perhaps that was the magic of it all. Would Sevas think I was something worthy of saving if he knew that I had given the monster such a slow, bad death and cooked it up and served it to my father?

I wondered if he would treat me so tenderly if he knew how I had licked the spoon I'd used to serve up the monster's meat, and even eaten a little piece of it myself before bringing Papa his plate. That bite had landed softly in my stomach, lonely as a baby bird fallen off its branch.

"If a severed arm is what it takes to free you—" Sevas paused, bringing a hand to his mouth. I could see where my bite marks still circled his fingers. "You would not be ugly, not to me."

Before I could reply, the sink gurgled. I realized then that the water was not draining. Rolling up my sleeve, I stuck my hand into that oily water and into the drain until my fingers closed around something big and hard. It took me several tries to yank it free, and when at last I did I stumbled back a few paces, dizzy with exertion.

Sevas came over to me and we both looked down at the thing in my hand. It was a long rib bone, curving like a whittled conch shell, still thick with sinew and far, far too large to have once belonged to a chicken.

"Marlinchen—" Sevas started as I held the bone so tightly in my fist that I thought I might crush it to dust.

"Oh," I said. "Papa must have killed a pig."

Neither of us spoke. The water circled down the drain. At last, Sevas said, in a quiet voice, "We must take the mirror tonight."

"No," I said hurriedly. "Papa has warded the third floor with spells. I have to speak to him. I have to know what the magic is and how to break it."

Sevas nodded once, slowly. "But you must be wary, Marlinchen. Wary of his claws and his toothless smiles."

"I know," I said. "But now we need to eat." I was very hungry.

I cooked varenyky with leftover filling, enough for Papa and all the men and my sisters, and made two jars of plum preserves. The plums in our garden were ripe as bruises, pulsing with the risk of rot. I wondered about the stones inside of them.

There was no kvass, so we drank water, all of us sitting around the big ebony table. I couldn't remember the last time we had eaten here. Or eaten together, let alone with guests. Watching Sevas eat the food I had prepared filled me with an unspeakable feeling, somewhere between yearning and grief. I wanted to kiss the streak of sour cream from his mouth and the grimace from his face.

I ate, too, ravenously, even knowing that I could not throw it up later. But when everything was finished the food sat in my belly without roiling guiltily. More, I now had even more reason to keep it down: I knew Sevas would not like it if he found out that I had been making myself sick in the garden. Already he was glancing between Dr. Bakay and me around every bite, gaze sweeping down the long table like a scythe.

Papa ate double portions, and when he was done his stomach was bulging over the band of his trousers. I could not bring myself to look at him; I was afraid of what the glare of his magic might do. Perhaps it would jerk me up on the table and make me prostrate myself in front of him, limbs splayed like a belly-slit chicken. Sometimes before I went to sleep at night I imagined myself laid out on this very table, naked, while my clients all cut small, neat bites from me with forks and knives. Sometimes I imagined that Papa plucked out my eyes and ate them.

Now I could only think of the curved bone I'd found, the rib of some large creature. Too large for even a pig, though I could not let that thought settle in me like yeast at the bottom of a kvass jar. Instead I rose and gathered the plates, counting the sound of each one as they clinked against the others. Three for my sisters and me, one for Sevas, one for Papa, one for Dr. Bakay, one each from the fifteen men—

It should have tallied to twenty-one, but when I got back to the kitchen I realized that I had carried back only twenty. I peered around the corner, back into the dining room, narrowing my eyes as I tried to focus on each of the day laborers' faces. Guiltily I realized that they all had blurred together to me, that I had not spoken to any of them, save for just one.

Sobaka. He was nowhere to be seen.

I nearly opened my mouth to ask, but already the knowledge was calcifying in me, the seed of a secret that I could not speak until it bloomed. I went back to the sink wordlessly. I washed the grease of strangers from our cups and bowls and plates.

I was afraid of how Papa had said little during the meal, and even smiled at the men and Sevas, his yellow teeth wolfish. I was afraid of how Dr. Bakay had his papers strewn out all over the little bedroom in the disused servants' quarters. He was keeping a log of the men's skull shapes and sizes, and divining their futures accordingly. I wondered if he would ask to measure Sevas's head again, and the thought made me want to wrap my own fingers around my throat and press down hard until there were stars behind my eyelids.

At last, dusk washed over the sky like a tide slick with spilled oil, starless and complete. I left Sevas in the sitting room with the other men, after more assurances that I would be fine, after more promises that had the taste of warm tap water. I went upstairs to my room.

All of it was how I had left it, the dresses strewn all over the floor, my bed an unmade wreck. The white feather on my boudoir. The charm bracelet glinting under the bed. I dropped to my knees and fished it out, blowing dust off the little owl with pearls for eyes.

I had the bracelet and I had the card and I had the strange, large bone from the sink and I was trying to piece them all together, to turn them into something that I could wield like a blade or barter with like ceramic beads, but before I could make sense of it, I heard the floorboards creak behind me.

Papa pushed the door open just a crack and wriggled through it like he was a knife trying to saw a bit of gristle off a chicken bone. His stomach was still distended, and I thought, I did that. I made him full. Who said my magic was only for showing?

His power was crackling in the air like distant gunshots, but I didn't yet feel the urge to grovel or kneel. We only stood there in perfect silence for several moments until I said, "Papa, we are short one day laborer."

He raised a brow. "And what makes you so sure of that?"

"I counted the plates at dinner. There were twenty when there should have been twenty-one."

My father only made a gruff sound. "Oh, I sent one of the boys on his way after he tried to sneak up to the third floor."

My heart lurched in two directions, like frogs leaping off the same lily pad. I could have accused him of lying. I could have flashed the card and Mama's bracelet at him; I could have spit up the secret half-bloomed. Or I could take the opportunity to ask, "What spell did you cast over the door to the third floor?"

"That's nothing for you to worry over," Papa said. "Sit down, Marlinchen."

Another leap of my heart, this one jagged and painful. "Are you going to punish me, Papa?"

I had never asked him such a thing so bluntly before. I had only tried quietly to evade the traps he had laid in the floor, not to squirm against the daggers he pressed to my back. Yet this boldness was not Rose's or Undine's; it was mine. It was the boldness of the girl who had danced in a tavern and let a dancer rut between her thighs. Her ghost inhabited me for a moment, and I felt my chest swell.

For a long while Papa did not answer. At last, he said, "I knew you would return to me."

"Well," I said, still with too much boldness, "you are a wizard."

"Not because of that. A father knows his daughter the way a tree knows all its branches, the way a serpent has memorized the pattern of scales on its belly. That is its own sort of magic, the hereditary kind, the kind that can't be learned or taught."

But you don't know me, Papa, I thought. *You know the girl who cooks you dinner in dutiful silence. You don't know the girl who bled out her maidenhead in a room full of mirrors and who felt only a dark, bitter pleasure in remembering your prohibitions against it.* I did not have quite the boldness to say it.

There was another stretch of silence.

"Do you know what I thought when you were born?" Papa asked, eyes snapping to me in the dark. "I despaired, in truth, because I had divined that you would not be lovely like your sisters. I didn't know then what use a plain-faced daughter could be to me. Now I understand. This competition has made it more apparent than ever before. If you eat black plums, Marlinchen, I will never let you taste the poison. If you bathe naked in streams, it will be without ever drawing a hunter's wanton eye. I will make certain that all the bears you meet are friendly and pliant, and never men in disguise. I will never let you fall prey to the banality of the world. I will never let you fall in love."

You have failed in that, Papa, I thought, but the words were stuck in my throat.

With one hand, he reached up and cupped my skull, drawing his thumb along the back of my neck, as if he were doing a phrenologist's reading. I realized that there was something in his other hand, a glass filled to the brim with murky liquid. It was not kvass; we were out of kvass.

"What about Dr. Bakay?" I asked, my heart still racing, the brave girl's ghost still possessing me. I could take out the card at any moment. I could hurl the charm bracelet at him so hard that it hit his face and hurt.

"What about him? He is a wizard in his own way. I know you are a bit simple-minded, Marlinchen, but can't you see? That was my spell to keep you safe. In the old days of Oblya, before it was Oblya and it was just a steppe that ran into the sea with nothing to stop it, we had a chieftain who made his own laws. He punished criminals harshly, but he never killed them. If they thieved, he took their hands. If they raped, he had them gelded. For smaller offenses you might only have to part with an ear or an eye or a little finger. None of these men ever broke a law again—it was like teaching your dog the sting of the whip. But best of all, no one would hire these men anymore, and their wives wouldn't touch them, and their children cringed away when they saw them. They could not walk to buy bread without everyone knowing that they had been spoiled, that they were rotted to their core like bad plums. They could not stand the stares and the slurs, so they stayed in their houses, hidden away from the cruelty of the world."

His words fell into my belly like sleet on snow, washing away the dinner I'd kept down. I grew cold, too cold for the brave girl's ghost to inhabit me, and she fled, leaving me alone with myself. Now I felt so hungry, so terribly hungry, as if I hadn't eaten since my cradle days.

All this time I had blamed the rubles and only the rubles. I had let Papa's greed absolve him. But he'd wanted more than money after all. Papa had let Dr. Bakay saw off my leg so I could only ever hobble around this house, from the kitchen to the sitting room to my bedroom, like a lame dog. He had tied the tourniquet himself.

A whimper fell out of my mouth. I was seventeen again, and I knew how the doctor's blade felt against my breast.

And then a fantastic transformation began to take place before me. Where Papa's face had been, there was now only a skull, flesh and muscle stripped away. In the pits of his eyes were two plum stones. His jaw was fitted with some large creature's rib bone. In his teeth he held the broker's card and his hair had turned to white tail feathers. I choked back a scream, and abruptly the terrifying metamorphosis reverted. I was once again looking at a man, a wizard, my father.

It's not true, I told myself. *Papa loves you and he loved Mama and he didn't mean to turn her into a bird or eat her. He only wanted to keep us safe from the world.*

Papa regarded me queerly, as if he could see the tumult in my mind. "Are you thirsty, Marlinchen?"

All of a sudden my throat was parched.

"Yes," I said. "I'm so thirsty, Papa."

"Here," he said, holding up the glass to me. The dark liquid bubbled like a cauldron. "Drink."

For a moment I thought, with a sluice of panic, that it was the potion he would use to test our purity, but I quickly saw it was not. It was the same black juice I had seen before, left out for me in the kitchen, offered to me by Papa as I limped around him in the sitting room. It had not tasted bitter like the potion; it had tasted sweet.

No moonlight spilled through my window. I was not thinking of Sevas, of the mirror, of the card, of the bracelet, of Sobaka or the missing broker or the man who had been found dead at the theater. I was only thinking of how to slake the terrible thirst. I put the juice to my lips and swallowed.

I woke the next morning with a spectacular headache, the sun laying ribbons of light across my eyes. I blinked dust from my lashes and sat up, which made everything in my stomach jostle like an overstuffed jewelry box.

My conversation with Papa seemed as hazy and half-remembered as a dream. Perhaps that was all it had been. I was lying here in bed, the softest place I had ever lain, and my body remembered the comfort and curled into the memory like a crab into its conch.

But then the grandfather clock gonged six, and my wheel fell into its groove. I stood and drew on my housecoat and went downstairs. Everything was still and silent. The men were asleep in the sitting room, draped over furniture, as if someone had strewn out a basket of laundry. Sevas was lying near the chaise longue, head resting on his own bent arms. He looked beautiful and peaceful.

I did not want to risk waking them as I made my way into the kitchen, so instead I opened the front door and stepped into the garden. It was pleasantly cool, autumn just starting to light up the foliage like a brushfire, greens making their transformations into yellow and orange and maroon. The sky was the tender, throbbing blue of a frost-bitten finger. My head badly hurt.

Something made me want to pick down the rest of the plums before they rotted. Perhaps I could make kvass out of them. Perhaps it would please Papa. The garden was oddly silent, the eyeless ravens still dozing on their branches, the goblin nowhere to be found.

Out of the corner of my eye I saw something black gleam in the wheat grass. At first I thought it was a dropped ribbon, but when the clouds rinsed away and the sun beamed through the trees at a perfect angle, it looked like a tongue of flame. The fiery serpent. I blinked again, and it was gone.

The plum tree was behind the shed, past Rose's herb plantings, and half-ensconced in a ring of vividly blue sage flowers that grew nearly waist-high. When the sunlight glanced off them they were as bright as live wires. I trampled through them, gathering burrs in my nightgown, but stopped only when I heard a strange panting sound.

Short, sharp breaths that cut the air like thousands of little thrown darts. I thought for a moment that it must be a trick, that it was only the wind trapped in some small space, and with each gust trying to escape. But then I heard a labored grunting noise, and followed it around the back of the shed, as if in a trance.

Undine was on her knees in the dirt, blue dress rucked up over her bottom, her hair spilling over the ground like a slow pour of honey wine. She was gasping and gasping, her cheeks splendidly pink, and one of her breasts loosed from her corset so that it swung with the heaviness of a pendulum. Her nipple brushed the ground. Indrik was crouched behind her, his hands braced on her hips, rutting. His goat's fur was all mussed and his tail was flapping with every thrust.

It was not even the mere fact of it that shocked me, but the violence—he ground himself into my sister with determined fervor, but absolutely no warmth. There was none of the aching gentleness I had felt when Sevas moved inside of me. It felt like hours that I stood there, watching, but it could not have been longer than a few moments before Undine saw me and screamed and Indrik pulled out of her and stumbled back, still hard and glistening.

"You idiot!" Undine screeched, rising to her feet. Her skirts tumbled back over her bottom but her breast was still hanging over the top of her corset, and it flopped with her every movement. "What are you doing out here?"

"I wanted to pick the plums." My voice sounded so obscure and distant, it was as if it belonged to someone else. My sister was staring at me with such venom in her eyes that I went on in a rush, "Undine, I swear, I won't tell Papa—"

She laughed, a high and keen sound that startled the eyeless ravens from their perch. "Tell Papa if you wish, or don't. It matters little to me. He's a fool. It's been seven years since his daughter has been coupling with a monster in his own garden and he never lifted his head from his plate long enough to notice."

My mouth was hanging open like a dead carp's. Her words landed on me, but they left no mark; I couldn't understand.

Indrik huffed with indignation, but I was surprised that he did not contest Undine's description of him as a monster. Whatever Indrik liked to boast, the gods in Papa's codex did not couple like this with mortal women; they did not even couple like this with witches. They turned to swans and left their flushing consorts with three eggs in a wicker basket; they transformed into showers of golden light and spilled themselves onto maidens trapped in towers. It was never anything so brute, so rough, so mundanely human.

The ache in my head sharpened to a blinding white pain behind my eyes, and only when it cleared again was I able to say, "But Papa's potions . . ."

Undine made a hacking noise in the back of her throat, and then spat in the dirt in front of me. "You are so much more simple-minded than I ever imagined, Marlinchen. Do you really think that Papa's potions have any real magic at all? He's not even an herbalist! You must not even know that Rose takes her clients to the garden shed or the storeroom and does the same with them, all those women that come to her with desperation in their eyes. But of course Papa's stupidest magic worked on you anyway—he convinced you that it was real. Did you fall asleep at night worrying that one of us might cough up our livers?"

She laughed again, loudly and terribly. "Of course, you would never worry such a thing about yourself! Plain-faced, kindhearted Marlinchen would never dream of defying dear Papa, nor would she ever catch a man or woman's lustful eye."

It was no crueler than anything I had heard from her before, but now her words smoldered in my belly like the black end of a match. All these years Rose and Undine had both known that Papa's potions didn't work, but they had let me go on believing that they were real. They'd enjoyed their furtive rebellions while I was butchering chickens and worse for Papa, while I was folding his laundry and scrubbing the floors and walls until the whole house gleamed as if it were an amulet. They could have told me the truth, but why would they—I cooked all their meals too.

My head was still throbbing and my mouth was dry, but I remembered the way that Undine had shouldered past me to bat her lashes at Sevas, and a bit of my own cruelty flowered up.

"You don't know everything," I told her, each word trembling like a plucked string. "You don't know that when I ran away I went to the ballet theater, and when he saw me there Sevas stopped dancing and leaped off the stage and took me into his arms. Then he coupled with me right there in the theater, in a room full of shattered mirrors, and afterward he said that he would come back to Papa's house and compete for my hand."

I said it all in a rush, and hearing it aloud it sounded better than my favorite story in Papa's codex, better than the swan-tsarevna and Ivan. It sounded better than any dream I might've conjured in my own mind, where I was a blushing mortal girl rescued by a valiant bogatyr. Best of all it was my secret that had made it so, the magic of my own little rebellion.

It scarcely even occurred to me that Undine's face was darkening, turning the shade of a plum near to rot. But then she lurched forward, one breast swaying, and caught me by the throat. Her hands pressed down hard until tears gathered at the corners of my eyes and my breath could only come in short, hot gasps.

"You don't *deserve* it," she hissed in my ear. "You're the ugliest and stupidest of us all—I've never seen a plainer face or a duller mind than yours. And worst of all, you're like a dog that loves its lashings. You bow to Papa's every word and smile as he works his knife into your breast. What right do you have to be rescued? The dancer was a fool to come at all. You would rather sit meekly at Papa's feet and lick his boots than run away with a beautiful man. You're too much of a coward. You won't leave with him anyway."

My vision was starting to narrow and my throat burned with pressure. I reached up and clawed at Undine's face, drawing three lines of blood across her cheek.

She let me go and stumbled away, shoulders heaving like a pair of wings was ready to unfold from between the blades of her back. Then she snarled, "Maybe I'll tell Papa the truth before you get the chance. You're better off dead to him than defiled."

Before she could reach for me again I turned around and hurled myself through the sage flowers and the wheat grass, nearly tripping as I clambered up the stairs to the house. My heart was pounding so loudly and furiously that I could count each crooked beat, and my head was aching like an egg about to hatch.

I shoved my way inside and collapsed to my knees in the foyer, just as the grandfather clock gonged seven. I could hear the drowsy voices of the day laborers from the sitting room, yawning like old cats. I worried over the sound of footsteps from the second-floor landing, wondering if Papa had already woken. He would be angry. He would want his breakfast.

But as I rose, trembling, to my feet, it was only Sevas that I saw in front of me, his blue eyes fierce and bright with concern. In the wash of early morning sunlight, he looked too beautiful to touch. Grief and horror made my own eyes water.

"Marlinchen," he said, taking my face into his hands. "What happened? Is it your father?"

At first I wanted to tell him what had just happened, but I couldn't bring myself to speak. After several moments passed I realized the futility of saying anything at all. My words were too gruesome and ugly for his ears. Worse still, this house was too horrible to keep him cached in its belly; it didn't deserve such a sweet meal.

"No," I managed. "I didn't get anything from him last night; I'm sorry. And just now I only fell down in the garden."

"That's all right," Sevas said softly. "We have time to try again."

A tiny furrow emerged suddenly between his brows. He let go of my face, but his gaze did not leave mine. It bore into me, tender and wanting, as if his lovely stare alone could dredge more words from my throat. After another beat I saw him wince, gaze lowering to the ground.

"What's wrong?" I asked. I might have laughed at such a quick and neat reversal if my head wasn't still ringing with Undine's threat.

"It's nothing," Sevas said, trying a pained smile. At least the humor of it wasn't lost on him either. "It's just my feet. Usually after a show I have someone treat them, but this last time I was a shade preoccupied."

"Oh," I said. It was so perfectly mundane that it washed away all my deep, churning horror. "Let me see."

I drew him into the dining room and pulled out one of the chairs so that he could sit, while I knelt in front of him. He did, and then began to slide off his boots, sucking his lower lip into his mouth. When at last he was free of them I looked down, alarmed at the sight of his bare feet before me.

They must have been the only ugly thing about him, his toes mangled and knobby like the small pieces of birch branches that we cut for casting lots, his heels rough and callused, and half his nails blackened with the welling of old blood. I was not a healer, and I could not even think of where to start. A single filthy bandage was peeling off his left ankle.

Sevas leaned over, huffing a laugh, and said, "I wouldn't blame you for falling out of love. If the audience could see their Ivan's feet, they would retch."

My face went magnificently hot. "It's a good thing that I'm a witch, then, and not a blushing mortal girl. I can wrap your cuts and bring you one of Rose's elixirs for the pain."

Sevas's lips turned up faintly at the corners. "You know, this is the first time in years that I've gone a single day without dancing. If I stay out of the theater long enough, I wonder if my feet will begin to look like a normal man's."

"You told me once that when you dance, you have to beat your body until it obeys you," I said. My finger brushed over the tendon of his ankle, pushing outward through his skin, and he shivered. "Perhaps you should treat it kindly instead."

Sevas lowered his head so that our eyes were nearly level. "You will have to show me how."

I felt a fast and desperate rush of affection, so complete that I could forget about the throbbing pain behind my temple or the soreness in my throat from my sister's fingers. I bent over and kissed his ankle, then all the way up his calf, until my chin came to rest on his knee. Sevas gave a soft moan and it made me go slick between my legs just to hear it. He cupped my face for a brief moment and then trailed his hand down my throat, across my collarbone, and over my breast.

This time I shivered, and as his thumb brushed my nipple through my dress I thought abruptly of Undine and Indrik and the look of her breast jostling with each of his thrusts.

I pulled away from Sevas and said, "Would you have me on my knees in the dirt? Would you take me without any tenderness? It would be all that I deserved, being a plain-faced witch with a dull mind—"

Sevas drew a quick sharp breath. "How could you ask that? If I have you it will be as a man has a woman, a husband his wife. Do you dream of Bogatyr Ivan when you kiss me? Do you wish I entered you while holding a wooden sword? I would not like any story to lie between us like a third body in our marriage bed. When I touch your breast I am touching the breast of Marlinchen Vashchenko, not a witch, not a swan-girl, not a flesh diviner, not a third daughter. Even I am not near lusty enough to satisfy five women at once."

His words left me flushing even more deeply. "I will pull the secret out of Papa, I swear it. I will figure out how to break his spell and then we will sell Mama's mirror and you will never have to dance again."

"I would like that, Marlinchen," he said, and leaned down to kiss me.

I pushed myself up to meet his lips, but as I did an astonishing bolt of pain went through my skull. My vision daggered with tiny needles of white light. For a moment I could see nothing, hear nothing, feel nothing except Sevas's hands on my shoulders as he slid off the chair and knelt beside me. My head rolled back and when it snapped forward again, I saw his blue eyes blown wide with panicked desperation.

"My head," I managed. There was spittle gathered on my tongue that hurt too much to swallow, and a bit of it dribbled past my lips. "I think I need to lie down."

It occurred to me, suddenly and terribly, that I hadn't told him about Undine's threat. But when I tried to speak again there was another stroke of dizzying white pain.

Sevas helped me to my feet and all but carried me into the foyer, up the stairs. His lips were moving and I knew that he was talking, that perhaps he was even asking me questions, but it felt as if my ears were packed with cotton. He brought me to my room and I collapsed on my bed, everything sharp and bright and stinging.

The cotton dissolved just long enough to hear him say that he was going to fetch my sister, that he was going to find Rose. I tried to mumble something back, but I could not tell whether or not my mouth managed to form the words.

I thought of Undine in the garden, her hair spilled in the dirt, her hand curling around my throat. I thought about how I had laid my secret on her tongue like a sweet red berry, the way I had given her a knife with which to cut both Sevas and me.

I reached for Sevas's arm as he fled the room, but then the white light drowned me, and I saw nothing more.

There was only darkness and a thin blade of moonlight when I woke. I could not tell how many hours had passed, but the blinding headache had vanished just as inexplicably as it had come, and when I lifted my arm up there was dirt caulked under my nails. Everything smelled of soil and damp.

As I sat up, a cold girdle of fear gripped my heart. I hadn't gotten the chance to warn Sevas about Undine's threat. That fear propelled me out of my room and down the stairs, but the foyer and the sitting room were both empty. The grandfather clock was casting its usual shadow, lengthened by the day's late hour. Its small hand was brushing eight and the windows into the garden were painted the deep blue of Papa's beard.

On the other side of the door, I heard a commotion. I took the knob in my hand and opened it, cool air blowing right through my nightgown. When I glanced down I saw that the hem was ragged, as if it had been torn, and a thousand loose threads were feathering against my ankles. Had it happened when I was running through the garden earlier, and I simply hadn't noticed?

Fireflies lit up the blue-washed garden; the one-eyed goblin pattered through the wheat grass, not weeping for once. But there was sound, at the line of the fence, where all fourteen of the day laborers were gathered, along with Papa and Sevas. They were clamoring loudly, and pressed so tightly I couldn't see past them to what was beyond the gate, so I walked forward barefooted, feeling as cold as if I'd been doused by frigid seawater.

When I got to Sevas's side, he was so surprised to see me that he gave a little jump. "Marlinchen," he said. "Where have you been?"

I frowned at him. "I was sleeping soundly, wasn't I? Where you left me."

Sevas opened his mouth to reply, but before he could the flutter of voices called our attention to the gate. Papa was standing on one side, hands steepled over his full belly (we all had feasted well on varenyky since my return), looking perfectly sedate. In fact he had the look of a feudal lord again, and all the day laborers clustered around him the serfs who broke their backs tilling his land.

On the other side of the gate was Derkach. My heart dropped like a stone.

"You must return him to me," Derkach was saying. His hands

gripped the fence, fingers so pale and thin they looked halfway dead. "Sevas is my charge, and you cannot keep him here."

"Do you think I hold this man, or any of these men, here against their will?" Papa laughed, and it sounded like someone shaking coins in a jar. "These men came to my house of their own accord, to regale themselves in my generosity, to compete for one of my daughters' hands. If you'd like to enter the competition yourself, you may pay the fee and come agreeably inside."

"You're a crook," Derkach said, jabbing his finger through the bars. "I ought to bring the Grand Inspector to your door."

The thought chilled me, and so did a sudden gust of frosty air. I pressed closer to Sevas, but he was staring and staring at Derkach, as if he had forgotten I was there.

Papa's voice grew quieter, and his shoulders went up around his ears like a piqued alley cat. On the other side of the fence, Derkach reached into his pocket.

I wanted to say something, say anything, to stop Derkach from offering up rubles and Papa from taking them, but when my lips parted with a protest, there was a sudden rustling noise behind us.

Rose crashed through a briar patch, trampling her own herb beds, scattering lavender buds like blown dust. I had never seen my sister run like this, with such frenetic purpose, nor had I ever seen her eyes so wheeling and wild. I put my knuckle in my mouth and tasted an explosion of blood.

"Papa," she panted. "Marlinchen. You have to come. You . . ."

The absence of her voice as she trailed off was louder than any ringing church bells, than any shattering plates. Papa frowned deeply and I half expected him to protest, but his brows were raised with a bit of his own alarm—certainly he had never seen Rose so undone either.

Wordlessly we followed her, leaving Derkach where he stood, the whole crowd of us, Papa and Sevas and the day laborers and me, through the garden. The eyeless ravens were not singing.

Rose stopped just past a bushel of lamb's ear, and at first I was too far behind the crowd of men to see. I shoved my way through, all the day laborers and Papa standing as still as dead oaks, and when I made it to the front of the throng I froze, too, all the way down to my marrow.

I saw a spill of golden hair in the dirt, and my beautiful sister's body mangled and blood-spoiled at the base of the juniper tree.

CHAPTER THIRTEEN

A loud and terrible sound rent the air, the way an animal squeals before it dies. I didn't realize it was coming from me until Papa's hands closed over my shoulders and he shook me roughly enough to rattle my teeth. I could scarcely see his face, his spittle-flecked beard. My sister's body was painted on the insides of my eyelids like a fresco on a cathedral ceiling, so lurid and bright.

All I could see was the ruby collar of blood ringing her throat, the mangle of her breast, the sinew that unfolded from her wound like the cut strings of a cotton loom. It felt perverse, profane, as if I were looking right between a woman's spread legs.

I stopped screaming, and Papa let go of me. Then I doubled over, clutching my stomach, and vomited into a clump of sage grass. The sick splattered my bare feet and the ragged hem of my nightgown and it was the color of spilled ink, of crushed elderberries, viscous and black. Dark juice.

Sevas held back my hair and I couldn't even thank him for the kindness or warn him that Papa and the others might see. But no one was looking at us. All the day laborers were staring at Undine's body without blinking, their gazes running across her like sweet-cherry sauce poured over mlyntsi, making her death even more obscene.

Even now they were hungry for her, moved to arousal by the vulgarity of it. Their ravenous eyes ate her up. I felt as if I might retch again, but my stomach was empty now, clean as a porcelain bowl. I couldn't think whether Papa would be angry at me.

Rose had collapsed to her knees before Undine's body, sobbing. I had never seen her weep like this, so loudly, her shoulders shaking as if she were undergoing a violent exorcism. I stared at my dead sister, her blue eyes flung wide open, the precise color of the sky in the earliest hour of dawn. The three shallow wounds my fingernails had left were still vivid on her cheek. I stared down at my nails now, at the dark stuff under them that I had thought was dirt.

Dr. Bakay pushed through the throng and crouched next to her body. He lifted the curtain of her hair and examined her face as if it were some fascinating thing he'd found under a large flat rock. He peeled open the bodice of her dress, already falling away like two shed flower petals, and stared at the wound between her breasts with a furrowed brow. His scientist's eyes autopsied her like a crow picking over carrion, seizing on the lustiest bits, lingering on the sweet buds of her nipples.

At last he said, "It seems entirely apparent to me that no man killed her. Nothing mortal could have made these wounds."

"Enough of this madness," Derkach said, striding forward. I had not even seen him follow us through the gate. "There is no monster in Oblya, only a very sick and twisted man. In fact, the Grand Inspector has offered a reward—three hundred rubles!—for any information leading to his capture and arrest. He and his men will come for the corpse soon, I expect; as soon as word gets out. But none of this is any concern of mine. Sevas, I hope this has extinguished the charm of your little rebellion. Come with me."

Sevas's hands slipped from my hair. He turned toward Derkach and said, "No."

Derkach barked a laugh. "Why must you always make things so terribly difficult for yourself? There is nothing this world can offer you that is better than what I have already provided, and there is nothing you can offer this world aside from your lovely face and your skillful dancing. You're not a boy anymore, and it's too late to dream of being a sailor or a doctor or a street-corner magician. You are Ivan, nothing else. Would you rather live under the thumb of some madcap wizard than preen before an audience that adores you?"

"It's Ivan they adore. And I'd rather live anywhere that isn't with you." Sevas's words drifted icily through the air; I could almost feel the cold of them from where I stood beside him. "There's nothing you can offer that would ever make me return, Mr. Derkach."

Derkach's expression did not shift. He merely turned to Papa and said, "How many rubles would it take for you to throw this boy out of your home and into the street?"

I gave a choked noise of protest, imagining the exorbitant sum Papa would demand in exchange for his acquiescence. But Derkach's words had hit him wrong; I could tell that right away. Papa stiffened like a hunting dog that had caught a downwind scent.

His eyes narrowed and he replied, "These men are here because they clamored for it, and because I lifted my enchantments to allow them inside. No one enters this garden unless I permit it—no beggars, no brokers, no Grand Inspector or his men. I am not some capitalist wretch who is jerked around by the yoke of gold. Leave these grounds now, sir, or I will turn you into a jabbering crow."

"I leave of my own accord, wizard, just as I entered," Derkach said, though he began pacing backward through the sage grass. "But if it's the Grand Inspector that you fear, I will bring him and his men right to your door, and he will put a stop to this whole sham of a competition. Hear me, Zmiy Vashchenko. Never again will you welcome one of Oblya's men into your garden. Never again will you bait them with the empty promise of your daughter's hand. It's only justice that she was slain now, before you could use her further for your greedy ends."

The callousness of his words struck me like a blade to the belly, and I was nearly sick with the pain, sick with the fear that Papa would do something terrible. Now he drew himself up to his full height, sucking in a breath that felt like danger.

He laughed a hacking, humorless laugh. "Your words are nothing to me, mortal. Not even the curse of a true witch could fell me. I will cast a spell that clips your vocal cords before you can so much as whisper to your Grand Inspector."

But Derkach had already turned his back; it was as if Papa's words, too, were clumsy arrows that did not strike him. I had never seen my father so casually and summarily unheeded, and for a moment I could envision him the way Derkach did: as a mad old man in a crumbling house, raving about obscure indignities. For a moment, it was as if Papa had no power at all.

When I blinked, though, it all returned to me: the magic crackling in the air, the rage on his face, the flush of his cheeks that lingered from when Derkach had said the words *Grand Inspector*.

As Dr. Bakay rose to his feet again Undine's body rolled over, landing facedown in the dirt and weeds. Derkach vanished back through the gate and it flapped open after him, swinging and swinging, as if it were a dress on a clothesline.

Instantly I felt Sevas relax, his shoulders slumping, though the wind picked up and I could smell the salt tang of Undine's blood on the air. Rose was still kneeling beside her, though her sobs had ebbed to little whimpers, another sound I had never heard my middle sister make.

Before Papa could even say another word, before he could even look upon his dead daughter and weep, one of the day laborers poked up his head and said, "I need to go."

Papa's gaze landed on him like a hawk seizing its quarry. "What was that, boy?"

"It's only—well, the monster, the murderer . . . he's targeted your estate." It was a freckle-faced man who spoke, one who was not Sobaka. "And now that your daughter is, ah, dead, well—that's half the reason I was here, isn't it? To compete for her hand. I mean no offense, sir, of course, but your middle daughter is vicious as a wounded bear and your youngest daughter, well . . ."

He did not have to finish his phrase for everyone to know what he meant, and Papa himself had called me plain-faced so many times before. This time, though, storm clouds gathered on Papa's brow and he said, "My daughter's hand comes with more than just a beautiful woman to share your bed. It is my estate you will inherit someday, in all its sprawling glory."

But the men had been here for nearly three days, and they had seen the cracking plaster, the weeds and thorns running over the garden, the ivy growing on the walls like an old man's beard, the taps that worked only half the time and the floorboards that were rotting under our feet. Our house was no great prize. It was a racing dog years past its prime, gray-muzzled and limping, moments away from a mercy killing.

The man did not say as much, but it was clear in his eyes, in the way his gaze dropped to the ground and he began to back up slowly, toward the open gate. In another moment, the rest of the men followed.

I stood there in the grass, watching my sister's body go pale and stiff. Papa marched after the men with more vigor than I had ever witnessed before, shoving through the throng until he was blocking their way through the gate.

"Aw, come on, sir," the freckle-faced man said. "There are fifteen of us, and only one of you."

Not fifteen, I thought. *Fourteen. One less than had entered.*

But the man had made more than just a mistake in his arithmetic. Papa threw his shoulders back, and then his magic loosed like a thousand poisoned darts. It spread like a front of cold blown off the frigid

Half-Sea. And then, as the men started to press past him, the bars of the fence turned into hissing, spitting black vipers.

The men all leapt back, scrabbling over one another as the snakes lunged and snapped at them. When they had all fallen down fleeing, or cowered behind the flowering pear tree, Papa closed his magic back up in his fist and the snakes ceased their hissing.

They went still and taut, but his transformations only worked in a singular direction. Our fence would never be a fence again. From now on it would be a latticework of black snakes, standing at fixed attention and suspended in the air, but spitting and lunging at anyone who drew too close.

One of the men started crying. Papa gave a loud and exuberant laugh.

"Fifteen of you, yes," he said. "But there is just one wizard Zmiy Vashchenko. I am the only wizard left in Oblya, and I have the strength and power of all the dozens that I ate before their downfall. If you break your vow to me, I will eat you too."

And then he was gone, brushing past Undine's cold body, but his magic lingered in the air like choking black smoke.

We buried Undine right there at the base of the juniper tree, and all I could think of was how I had swept up Mama's tiny bird bones and put them out with the trash. Rose cried while she dug, watering the earth where we planted our sister's body, and Sevas and I mostly watched as the wind bristled through our hair, his jacket, the ripped-up hem of my nightgown.

Indrik watched from behind the huge begonia plant, and I thought he might come and eulogize her, or promise vengeance by his divine magic, but he only cried, too, like a man and not a goat. I did not know if goats could weep. The goblin certainly could, but he was nowhere to be found, and still the eyeless ravens were silent.

I had never thought much about how my sisters and I would die, and so it had never occurred to me that Undine, the most beautiful of us three, would have such a poorly attended funeral. Even the day laborers who had slavered over her, both alive and in death, now cached themselves in the shed or under the plum tree; some of them tried to bait the snakes and got bitten for it.

Now that the lurid obscenity of her death had receded, now that her blood had dried to the color of rust and her body had begun the slow and humiliatingly mortal process of decomposition, they were not interested in watching. Witches died just like regular women, or at least they *could*. That was something I learned by watching my sister's lips drain of their color.

When it was done, Rose stood up. Her hands were caked in dirt. She came to me, without speaking, to embrace of course, but for some reason I anticipated being struck and flinched away from her. Hurt flashed in her violet eyes.

"It's not my fault," I whispered. "I didn't mean to."

"What are you talking about?"

My mouth opened, and all the swallowed poison spilled out. I told her and Sevas everything: how I had revealed my secret to Undine in a fit of spite, how she had threatened to turn it over to Papa, how Sevas had only come back because of Derkach, how we had planned to come and steal Mama's mirror. Sevas took Mama's compact, still gritty with the black sand, out of his pocket and showed it to her. It seemed like such a stupid trinket now, this thing I had guarded so jealously for so long, the thing I had imbued with wishful, powerful magic.

I wanted to tell her about the rib bone too. About Sobaka. About the man in the theater with his missing heart and liver, but my voice curdled up in my throat like something at risk of rot.

"Marlinchen, you could not have done this," Rose said when I was finished, when I was trembling and gasping with the strain of all I had confessed. "Your magic doesn't work like that. You can't make a spell out of just a mean thought. If you could, don't you think we would all have been able to turn Papa into a roach or a toad by now? You being angry at Undine didn't make her die. Your magic is just for showing; it's not for doing or changing or making."

But wasn't it? I had wished for Ivan, one who would not care that I was plain of face, and he had come. I had buried my secret, spilled blood to keep it, and it had hatched like an egg, full of hope and promise. I looked at the dried blood under my nails, at the worried wound on my knuckle. Words rose in me, but I did not want to upset my sister further, so I let them drift back down again.

"What is it that killed her, then?" I asked instead. "A real monster?"

"Of course not," said Rose. Her voice was sharp and quick and left no room for argument. "It must have been one of the men; perhaps she refused their advances. I will make a truth elixir tonight and sneak it into their soup and the culprit will reveal himself. But Marlinchen, is there any other tonic or elixir you need from me?"

"What sort of tonic do you mean?"

"Well," she said, eyes darting between Sevas and me, "you do know how it works, that when you couple with a man there's risk of something taking root in your womb? If you want to tear out the root, I have elixirs for that."

A furious blush came over my face. I could not bring myself to look up at Sevas. Papa had always said that the seed of mortal men did not grow easily in witches' wombs, but I did not know if that had been just as much a fraud as his potions were. If witches could die just like mortal women, couldn't we breed like them too? I didn't want to offend Sevas by sounding so eager to rid myself of his imagined child, but he spoke first anyway, saving me from replying at all.

"As much as I enjoy inquests into my virility—" he started, but Rose held up a hand.

"I wasn't asking *you*," she said sourly. "Marlinchen, come to my storeroom later and I will make certain that this man's seed never comes to bloom."

I was still too mortified to answer, so I only nodded. And then I remembered what Undine had said, about how Rose knew Papa's potions weren't real and she had coupled with women in the store-room or the garden shed. Something turned hard in my belly, like a plum stone. For so long I had wondered what it was my middle sister wanted, what she dreamed of, and now I knew that she'd had it this whole time, and I was the only one bereft. She and Undine had con-spired to keep this secret from me, and I could only guess that it was because they thought it might make me too reckless, too willful, that it might imperil their own little rebellions in the process.

It hurt badly, to even linger on the thought. I was glad when my middle sister took her leave. I was afraid that my anger might kill her, the way it had Undine. I had considered such a thing before: that if there was magic in keeping a secret, surely there was magic in spend-ing one too. My magic might only have been for showing, but it *was* magic.

When Rose was gone, I turned finally to Sevas, hoping that the flush had faded from my cheeks. I drew a breath and a long silence stretched between us, broken only by the sibilant noises of the vi-pers and the men baiting them. At last, he said, "Marlinchen, I'm so sorry."

"Why? You didn't kill her."

"Yes, but she's your sister, and she's dead. And if one of the men here is a murderer, it means that he might strike again. Why does your father want so desperately to keep them here? Not that I don't feel relieved he didn't hand me over to Derkach like a spoil of war, but why has the great wizard Zmiy Vashchenko begun tending to the day laborers that he claims to despise?"

In the dark, with only the pale drench of moonlight and the fire-flies glittering like a fistful of tossed coins, for a moment I thought that I could pretend. I could go on acting as if I believed we were menaced only by a sick and twisted mortal man, an enemy that could easily be killed. But it would be like Sevas dancing Ivan, or me smiling and batting my lashes while someone tied a tourniquet around my thigh.

"Sevas," I said. "Do you remember the dead man from the theater?"

"You said you didn't want to speak of it."

"But now I do." I chewed my lip. I barely resisted putting my knuckle in my mouth. "If the murderer is a mortal man, he could not have managed to get the body up into the rafters. It took five day laborers and a rope-and-pulley system just to get him down. And his heart and liver were gone, just like the two men they found on the boardwalk."

"Those were dogs, I thought."

"And dogs carried that man to the theater?"

Sevas frowned. "And what sort of creature do you think could have gotten that man into the rafters?"

"Something with wings," I said, my voice trembling.

"Speak frankly, Marlinchen." He took my face in his hands; even now I was thrilled a little by his proximity, by the way his bitten fingers were inches from my mouth. "I want to hear what's inside your mind."

He could not want that, not really. How could I explain the things that ran through my head whenever I closed my eyes, whenever I heard a door slam too loudly, whenever I caught my own reflection in the back of a teaspoon? He could not want to know how I imagined clipping off my nipples with Rose's gardening shears, two neat cuts so they fell like flower petals, bloodless and pink. He could not want to know how I imagined pulling back the white band of flesh around my nail, peeling it in spirals like potato skin, until my whole hand was gloved in red. He said that he loved me as plainly as any man loved any woman, but he did not know how much of Papa's poison had seeped inside of me. And, in truth, neither did I.

"I think my father is the monster," I whispered. "I think he killed those men and ate them."

Sevas did not wince or blink, and for that, I loved him so deeply and completely that I could barely stand it. He did not let go of my face. He only said, "And your sister?"

"I don't know." The memory of Undine's naked, blood-ruined breast flashed against the insides of my eyelids. "Her heart and her liver were still in her body. But Dr. Bakay said it could not be the work of a mortal man."

Sevas inhaled sharply. "The doctor has been wrong before."

I loved him for saying that, perhaps even more. Tears pricked at the corners of my eyes, for the first time since I'd seen my sister's corpse. "Before I left there were fifteen men in Papa's sitting room. Now there are fourteen, plus you. I think he wants the men here so he can eat them too."

Still, he did not flinch, and I could have laughed for how grateful I was. I had expected the words to sound like lunacy when I spoke them aloud, but Sevas's steady look made them seem more solid and real, the way egg whites stiffened up when you whipped them, taking on some strange new shape.

It was terrifying how quick and facile the transformation was. The ground did not roll out from under my feet; the sky did not crumble and come raining down in deep blue shards on my head. It was only this: one moment ago Papa had only been my father, the great wizard Zmiy Vashchenko, and now he was a monster with men's livers lining his belly.

"He'll want to eat *you* now," I went on in a rush, before Sevas could speak. "That was his reason for this competition, and the reason he welcomed you so warmly into our home."

"There must be some way to stop him," said Sevas, but I was already shaking my head. "Some spell, some enchantment—a potion of your sister's, perhaps? I know your magic is good, Marlinchen."

But there was no way for whatever little power I had to match Papa's, and he would turn Sevas into a fish or a frog if I even threatened to try. The stories in Papa's codex that spoke of great wizards always assured they had weaknesses of some kind. Their soul hidden inside the head of a needle, or their heart guarded in the nest of a firebird. There were wizards who could be burned or frozen; wizards who could be slain by errant knights. Even the Dragon-Tsar fell to Ivan's blade.

But if Papa had any weakness, it was not the stuff of fairy tales.

"He's afraid of the Grand Inspector," I said. "He's warned us about him and his men ever since we were children, told my sisters and me how he could ruin us. I swear he even shuddered when Derkach spoke his name. If Derkach does intend to bring the Grand Inspector here, perhaps it will be enough. But how will they get past the snakes? And what will we do after?"

"Snakes can be killed," Sevas said. "They are mortal, aren't they? And once your father is in chains, we can take the mirror and sell it."

My mind blinkered suddenly, as if someone had shined at me a beam of bright white light. I could not fathom Papa in chains. It was impossible as any dream I'd had as a child, the dream that I might toss my long braid from my bedroom window and a handsome prince might clamber up it, the dream that a man named Ivan would love me so much he would let me eat him. My empty stomach turned over on itself, and very abruptly I thought I might retch again.

"I have to speak with him first," I managed. "I have to ask him—I need to hear him speak the truth himself."

"Marlinchen, he is a monster. He'll kill you."

I shook my head, blood rushing in a furious torrent around my ears. "He won't. I'm of greater use to him alive. The worst he will do is hobble me further."

"I don't want you *hobbled* at all." Sevas's voice tipped up at the end; I did not think I had ever heard him sound quite so frayed, quite so close to snapping like a worn thread. He had seen Derkach today, after all, and I had just told him that he was living in the house of a man who wanted to eat him. "What happens when you hold up a mirror to a monster? In my experience, nothing enrages them more than the truth."

But I had made up my mind. "Papa wouldn't kill me. Who would fix his meals and clean his clothes and sweep his sitting room, if I were gone? Who would ease the burden of his curse?"

"You blame his curse for too much."

A heat rose in my cheeks. "Who says so?"

"I do," Sevas replied. "And if you say you must go, I cannot stop you. But please, Marlinchen—come back. Come back to me."

"I will," I said. I kissed him there in the garden, the sky bottomlessly dark. I closed my eyes, and when I did I imagined myself a snow-maiden, a swan, something out of a story, something that was so unreal it could not be harmed. "I promise."

I floated up to Papa's room as if I had wings. I knocked on the door.

Papa's voice sounded from the other side, thick with arrested sleep. How had he slept after slaying his daughter? Strange men were one thing, but Undine was his own blood. It made my skin chill to think, my brow dewing with sweat as I pushed open the door and stepped through the threshold.

Papa was swaddled up to his chin in blankets, the swell of his stomach visible beneath them. His magic suffused the air, thick as the smoke that blew from the Merzani coffeehouses on the boardwalk, and my eyes burned with it.

My legs quivered under me, but somehow I resisted the urge to drop to my knees. If I lowed myself to him now, he could kill me just with gentleness.

"I'm tired, Marlinchen," Papa said. "I've just seen my daughter buried. Why must you disturb my rest?"

The empty space in the bed beside him was where I always imagined Mama's ghost, if she were real, the sheets rumpling with the shape of her though she was otherwise invisible to the eye. I thought of how soberly Papa had served up the varenyky that night when I was thirteen, when I was freshly mourning my bird-mother. How could I have not known sooner? How had I cut that memory at the root so it couldn't grow its long black tendrils in my mind?

"Please, Papa," I whispered. "Speak frankly. Do you know how Undine died?"

Papa pushed himself up with a grunt and threw the covers off. When he spoke it was with no timidity, no hesitation, but as a king delivering a proclamation, as a lord announcing the new tithe to the serfs who work his land. "The doctor said she was killed by a monster. Rose believes it was a man. But what does it matter to me? My daughter is gone. It is a spell that cannot be undone, and certainly not by your cringing and weeping."

My stomach dipped, and I nearly bent to his magic then, to the thunderous power of his words and the spells that hovered around my head.

"Two men dead by the boardwalk," I said, choosing my words carefully, so that each one would land with a shuddering heaviness. "Another in the ballet theater. A broker from one of the big firms; I read it in the paper. I found his card in your laundry. And you know that one of our own men has gone missing. You thought Oblya wouldn't miss just another dull-eyed day laborer. But there is something bad in Oblya and you know it. It is an Old World badness, nothing that was brought here on merchant ships or freight trains."

"What are you saying to me, Marlinchen?"

The unflappable power in his voice had me reeling, and the question knotted up my tongue like the sash of a dress. Sevas had been right; there was nothing to gain from this, only a thousand new pits to avoid and a dozen more daggers at my back. Only the same risk there had always been: that Papa might find a new way to chain me to this house. To him.

But my tired mind tried anyway: through the haze of his spells, I squinted and squinted at my father. I tried to constellate his face like a cluster of random stars; I tried to find love in his eyes, like some dark water seething under ice. I tried to call him *Papa*, but my lips would not form the word. All I could see was a flurry of white feathers, and then Dr. Bakay smiling back at me from within the swirling murk of my father's face.

In the end the force of the vision was what toppled me to my knees, not obeisance. When I did manage to speak again, it was in a desperate and tremulous whisper. "I don't want it to be true. Please, make it not true. Take it all back. Say you take it all back. Say that none of it was you."

And then, astonishingly, Papa knelt beside me. He cupped his hands around my cheeks. He looked at me with something I could believe was love, if I didn't know the curse had stripped that from him like so many steppes had been stripped for new roads and factories.

"Marlinchen," he said, so gently. "If you want me to tell you a story, then I will. You need only ask. I will tell you a beginning and a middle and an end. I will tell you that your mother flew off to live on a lovely green island in the middle of the sea, where there is always rose nectar to sip. I will tell you that it was some hideous creature that killed your sister, be it monster or man. That little I can do for you."

"No." I shook my head, even as he held my cheeks fast. "I don't want a story. I—I don't understand."

Papa sighed, with exasperation and a bit of affection, whatever the curse still afforded him. "I think you *do* want a tale, Marlinchen. Especially because in this story, you loved your sister. You would never do her harm. And you love your father too. You would swallow any poison so that he didn't have to."

"Stop it," I whispered. We were so close that my breath touched his lips. "Please."

"You wanted a story, didn't you? I am simply telling it. I do not think you would prefer the truth—it is ugly and mundane, and stories are safe and sweet."

I tore myself away from him, a sob wrenching out of my throat.

Could you ever escape the story of your own life? Sevas would battle the Dragon-Tsar and kiss the tsarevna, and I would walk the same path from my father's chamber to the kitchen to my bedroom, like the gears turning behind the face of a grandfather clock, both of us following our fated rotations. And what was a story except a berry you ate over and over again, until your lips and tongue were red and every word you spoke was poison?

I got to my feet and lurched toward the door, but Papa didn't give chase. I had almost wanted him to. I had almost wanted to see him grasp for my nightgown, tear through the silk with his claws, give me cause to fear him further and believe that what I had told Sevas was true.

I made it halfway down the hall before something began to drag like a sodden dress, slowing me down. Papa's words were heavy, so unbearably heavy, that I knew I could not bear the weight of them for long. At the top of the second-floor landing, I looked over the foyer, the open door to the sitting room, the cat-lamps and cat-vases and the water-stained portraits of long-dead wizards named Vashchenko. There was nothing in this house that was not part of Papa's story, that he hadn't written to please himself. Nothing that I could rely on to speak the truth. Except—

The bolt of knowledge propelled me down the stairs, heart guttering, and sent me racing down the hallway through the disused servants' quarters, so that I did not risk running into Sevas. I was too buoyant with adrenaline to fear even Dr. Bakay.

I shoved open the door to the garden, gulping cold night air. The moonlight washed pale all of our briars and overgrown weeds, the ivy that crawled up the side of the house with a desperate perseverance. The lavender thistle grass looked white. My eyes searched for something dark weaving through its blanched stalks, something that I shouldn't be able to see.

So of course I saw it then, so utterly black that it looked like the absence of a thing, just an empty gash in the world. Our fiery serpent.

I crept up to it, silk nightgown swishing around my bare legs, as if I might startle it away.

But it didn't flee, only lifted its head and cocked it toward me. I knelt before it, sinking a bit into the wet soil, and said, "I want—"

It spoke in a human voice, without moving its mouth, and the voice seemed to enter my head as if my own mind were conjuring the words. *Be careful what you say aloud, third daughter. Whatever you ask for I am bound to provide, and you are bound to pay for it.*

"I know," I said. I had heard Papa's stories, but it was not silken handkerchiefs or ceramic beads that I desired. "I want the truth."

You know the truth, Ms. Vashchenko. What you want is the courage to believe it.

My head started to pound again, that ice-white ache teeming up behind my eyelids. "Then give me that. I will pay whatever price."

The serpent's black tongue flicked out of its mouth. *I've been so hungry for so long. If you feed me, I can give you the thing your heart desires.*

Without hesitation I stripped off my housecoat and pulled my nightgown over my head. There were two slashes cut into the back of it, right where the blades of my shoulders were; I had not noticed them before.

My nipples knotted with cold. I knelt there in the dark garden, naked and shivering, and the serpent began to slither up my thigh. The scales on its belly were smooth as river stones. It circled my breast the way I imagined it would curl itself around a mouse it meant to eat. And then it latched itself onto my nipple.

The bite of pain was sharp and brief, like the prick of a needle. I could feel the leak of blood, too, as if some faucet in me had been turned, and that was worse than the pain itself, the sensation of un-bidden release.

A whimper came out of my mouth, and then the fiery serpent's voice once again crowded my mind. *Go to the third floor, young maiden. The door will open for you.*

I rose to my feet a bit unsteadily, the serpent still curled around my breast, and walked back toward the house with the bone-deep purpose of a dog following a scent.

I scarcely had to touch the door to the third-floor stairwell before it swung open, old wood groaning. If Papa really had put some sort of enchantment over it, I passed through it easily, like it was no more than a veil of cobwebs.

The stairwell was dark, but I felt along the wall with one hand, and the serpent's voice in my mind was a better guide than any candlestick might have been. *Two more steps to the top. There's a loose floorboard here; be careful not to trip. You're so close, Marlinchen.*

I paused to catch my breath, and farther down the hall there was a square of white light gridded across the floor, cut in two pieces by the shadow of an open door. The serpent did not need to tell me to go toward it.

The last time I had been to the third floor, my mother was a bird in her cage. The ten years that had passed in between then and now piled on me like snow; I felt both ancient as a crone and young as a child, before my breasts had budded. I felt both like the girl who had tended so fastidiously to her bird-mother and also like the girl who had eaten her. I felt both like a witch of indeterminate power and like a mortal woman who danced in taverns and bled between her legs.

I stopped in the threshold and stared at my naked silhouette in the moonlight. Right there before me was my mother's cage, golden door flung open, and the mirror that never lies, with the white sheet laid over it. The fiery serpent let go of my nipple and slithered up to my shoulder, where it curled around my neck like a string of pearls. A few beads of blood gathered in the small wounds that its teeth had left.

I had not heard anyone come up behind me until Sevas's voice drifted into my ear. He was standing beside me in the threshold, our breath mingling in white clouds. "Marlinchen, what are you doing here?"

"How did you find me?"

"I followed you. The door was open." He did not mention the snake, but his gaze went up and down my naked body with some amalgam of desperate yearning and bewildered fear. "What did your father do?"

I was already crossing the room, past my mother's empty cage, standing before the white sheet and what was hidden beneath it. "This is the mirror that never lies. The only thing in this house that will tell the truth instead of a tale, even if you don't like what it is that you see." I paused, the snake's head coming to rest in the hollow of my throat. "Stand here with me and look."

Sevas shook his head, smiling thinly. "I'm afraid."

"Afraid of what?"

"Afraid that I'll be ugly," he said, no longer smiling at all.

My own heart filled up with tender affection. "That's impossible."

He sighed, then crossed the room to join me. His shoulders were tensed the way they were when he played Ivan, when he prepared to slay the Dragon-Tsar. They were tensed as if he still wore his feathered mantle. I wondered if that was what he was truly afraid of: seeing Ivan staring back at him.

Exhaling a breath of my own, I took his hand and twined our fingers. Then, with my other hand, I reached for the white sheet that covered the mirror.

I was scared, too, as scared as a little girl who saw horned silhouettes painted against her bedroom wall at night, as scared as a young woman who heard men asking after her while she cowered under her covers. But some transformation had happened inside of me, where no one could see.

I yanked the sheet off with a flourish, letting it puddle to the ground, as bodiless as a dress flung off the clothesline. Sevas's grip on my hand tightened, and I heard him stammer out my name.

In the mirror, I watched my own shuddering metamorphosis as my reflection warped and cringed and bloomed, all in the span of seconds. I watched black scales pattern my naked belly and cover my bitten breasts. I watched my lips part, redder than red, my forked tongue lashing over rows of blade-sharp teeth. I watched the truth unfold before me, just like the wings that spread from my back.

CHAPTER FOURTEEN

I had prepared myself for Sevas to let go of my hand. For him to stumble away, for him to scream. In his mirror, his reflection was unchanged, except that his clothes were gone. Pale bands of scar tissue wrapped around his arms and legs like white ribbons, and there were raised gashes all over his chest, as if every single one of the Dragon-Tsar's blows had landed. Even his face bore the evidence of old wounds, but he was still so beautiful it made my breath catch to look at him.

I let my fingers go slack, anticipating the moment when he would wrench away from my grasp. But he only held me tighter and faster, like I was a lifeline tossed to him in churning waters. I turned to look into his eyes; in the mirror, my monstrous head turned, too.

"Go," I told him. "Run."

"No," he replied.

"I'll eat you," I warned, my voice a whisper.

"You have already tried." He drew his bitten fingers to my mouth, showing the small cuts I had left. "I welcome you to try again."

I choked in disbelief. "You would be a fool to stay. The two men on the boardwalk, the one in the theater, the broker who came to our house . . . my very own sister. All of them killed by me and eaten by my father. I slit them open at the belly and tore out their hearts and livers to serve up on Papa's plate. I could tear out your heart. I could even eat it myself. Do you ache for your own gruesome death so badly?"

"I have died a thousand times already," Sevas said. "Cruelly, at the hands of the Dragon-Tsar. Gently, in Derkach's bed. If this is what I am in truth, a man made up of nothing but wounds, why should I fear such a thing now? There is no more perfect mate for me than the one who wears my own mortality around her throat like a jewel."

As he spoke, he lifted his hand and brushed the hollow of my collarbone, right where the serpent's head rested, like an amulet of precious onyx.

"I don't believe you," I said. "What sort of man cares so little for the blood of innocents spilled? What sort of man weds a woman with such terribly sharp teeth?"

"I do," Sevas said. His blue eyes were so bright, pooling with moonlight. "I could spend the rest of my days proving it to you. I have the patience and fortitude of seven thousand Ivans."

His reflection in the mirror reached up to touch the end of my wing, and I felt a phantom shiver go through me, some disembodied sensation that was so faint I thought I must have imagined it.

Was I a woman inside the body of a monster, or was I a monster inside the body of a woman? I had wondered the same thing of my bird-mother, when she had first been transformed. Did she still have a woman's heart and a woman's mind within all those delicate bones and beneath all those white feathers? Papa's potions had cut out a black space in my mind where the memories of my murders ought to have been, but that was not enough to absolve me. Those men and that broker and my sister were all still dead by my hand, even if it had been guided by Papa's magic.

Tears came springing to my eyes, and when they fell, the fiery serpent opened its mouth and lapped them up off my cheeks.

"No," I whispered. "I won't let you take their deaths from me. Your love cannot make me less of a monster."

Sevas let out a breath. "I wouldn't presume my love could do such a thing. I would have you as you are, nothing less."

Again, I said, "I don't believe you."

"Does the mirror tell the truth?"

"Yes," I said, barely a whisper.

"Then look."

A great tremor went through him, and his chest swelled. He drew himself up to his full height, assuming Ivan's glorious bogatyr's posture, shoulders raised high.

And then he took a rough fist to my hair, wrapping the wild, loose curls around his whitened knuckles, and jerked my face to his and kissed me. He kissed me so hard that it almost hurt, and I whimpered into his mouth, but he did not let go. I braced my arms around his neck and he gripped me at my waist and the serpent moved between us and in the mirror I saw a terribly scarred, terribly beautiful man embracing a monster.

His hand moved down my belly and I parted my thighs for him, moaning against his lips. I unfastened the button of his trousers so quickly that I nearly tore them. He lifted my hips and held me up against the mirror, the serpent slithering from my throat to his, and then he thrust into me without hesitation, without contrition.

Over my shoulder I could see my monster's head falling back, mouth open with distraught pleasure, scaled breasts swaying. My wings were crumpled against the glass. The corners of Sevas's eyes were pulled down by snaking lines of scar tissue, but the rest of his face was buried in my hair. At last he spent inside of me with a groan, and my legs slid back onto the floor, both of us panting and heaving.

Sevas stepped away, breathing hard. The serpent had wound itself around his throat instead, gleaming like a black jeweled collar. The mirror was fogged with the heat of our bodies, both of our reflections obscured. I could only see him standing there in the limpid moonlight, inches from my mother's flung-open cage.

Something broke apart inside of me, like a glass sliding off the table and shattering. I reached out for Sevas again as my hair tumbled down over my bitten breast.

"Don't you see?" he asked, his voice ragged and low. "You can take my heart and liver; slit open my belly and eat what's inside. I would sooner bear it than lose you to those who call you plain-faced, who make you kneel and kiss their feet. Do not leave me alone. Do not leave me to lick my wounds like a dog before it's put down. Do not look at the truth of me and then look away. Please, Marlinchen."

I almost laughed. "You would rather me eat your heart than look away in disgust?"

"Of course," he breathed. "Every time."

So I stepped toward him and took his face into my hands, drawing my thumb across his lips. He shivered under my touch, lashes painting a feathered shadow on his high, slim cheekbone. I tried for as long as I could not to blink, to stare him down to his marrow, to the truth of him. The serpent wound its way up his throat, tightening its body around him like a vise. When I saw his pulse throbbing between the coils of muscle, I pried the serpent off him and let it wind around my wrist instead.

"Perhaps," I said, "this story can have a happy end."

The corner of his lip pulled up into a beautiful, crooked smile. "Who says so?"

"I do."

In the dead of night, I plucked up a candlestick and went to Rose's storeroom. I had half expected to see the men back in the sitting room,

lolling on our couches like tired hounds, but they were still outside in
the garden, dozing under the flowering pear or prodding at the snake
fence. Papa was still in his room with the door shut, and it seemed
so funny to me now, that he could sleep peacefully as I prowled the
house. His daughter was a monster, but he did not fear her. She only
became deadly through his orchestration. A dog that bites its master
is not long for this world.

I slowly pushed open the storeroom door, letting in a little knife
of light. There were just the cobwebbed shelves and vials of chopped
motherwort, the dusty chopping block where the dried-out lavender
stalks decayed in the darkness. The herbalist's compendium was laid
flat on the desk, open to a page on "Diseases of the Mouth." I set down
my candlestick and began to try to decipher my sister's handwriting in
the puddled yellow glow.

I had scarcely managed a single word when I heard the patter of
footsteps behind me, and I snatched up the candlestick and whirled
around. Rose stood silhouetted in the doorway in her nightgown, still
smelling of soil and of Undine's blood, the tang of it cutting through
all the musty herb scent in the air. Beneath the curtain of her tousled
hair, her face was pinched and small.

"What are you doing, Marlinchen?"

I looked my beautiful sister up and down, and for the first time I
saw her the way the men had: like a velvet carpet laid over a hole in the
ground, something that could fall out from under your feet. She was a
good witch, and a clever woman, and she was a liar.

Papa isn't even an herbalist, Undine had said. Every time I had
drunk that black juice it had tasted of nothing. It had left behind no
sign of being poison. Only an herbalist could have made a thing like
that.

"You helped him," I said. "Papa asked you for a potion that would
turn me into a monster, and you went into this storeroom and crafted
it for him."

My words pinned her to the wall like a volley of arrows. Her mouth slackened; her face went pale. After a moment, my not-so-clever sister said, "It must have been Undine who told you."

"Is it so unbelievable that I could have figured it out myself? Kind-hearted but plain-faced Marlinchen, who knows nothing of the world, who fixes Papa's dinner with dull eyes while her shrewder sisters have their little rebellions right under her nose." My heart was pounding. "I know Papa could not have made a potion like that on his own. That black juice. It was good magic, Rose. It made me forget that I'd ever had scales on my belly and blood under my nails."

Rose put a hand to her lips. Silence stretched between us, an impassable gulf. Once I had swallowed whatever my sister had given me too; once I had wept into her hair and let her comfort me the way I imagined a mother would. Now I let my fury pour into that chasm until it teemed like a black tide and then spilled over.

"You were as cruel to me as Undine," I said. "You let me eat up all of Papa's anger so it wouldn't poison you. You didn't mind that he ruined me as long as you were unspoiled and safe. If you ever loved me, it was only because I was a soft thing you threw down into the bottom of a pit to break your fall."

"Marlinchen, please." There were tears in her eyes. "We were all of us trapped like kvass in a jar, frothing and bubbling so hard we cracked the glass. I'm sorry Papa held you tighter and closer. But I never relished your pain. Please don't say such terrible things to me."

"They are not terrible. They are just the truth. And you're still picking your way around the rotted heart of it. I've killed four men now for Papa, and Undine too. Because of you."

Rose's hand curled into a fist. Her knuckle slid into her mouth, tears slipping out. "He said he would punish me if I didn't help."

"But you didn't mind all this time, the way he punished me for nothing at all?" My voice was shaking. "Did I kill that sweet day laborer, too, Rose? We let fifteen men into our house and now only fourteen are asleep in the garden. Did I serve him up for Papa's supper?"

"No," Rose said with vehemence. "Not him—that was the night

you left. Papa was furious, and he was so hungry. He slit the man's throat himself, and then . . ." She trailed off, meek as a wood mouse. "That's why he brought the men here at all. But I suppose you know that now too."

I nodded. I let my memory stretch back, as far back as it would go, like a spool of thread nearly to the point of snapping. There were the two men on the boardwalk, and that was how the black sand had gotten into my hair. There was the broker who had bought Mama's charm bracelet and that's how it had ended up back in my drawer. There was poor, sweet Sobaka, whose death had not been my fault at all. And then there was the man at the ballet theater, strung up like a turkey that had been trussed.

"But why *those* men?" I asked around the lump in my throat. "I could have killed any man who walked down Rybakov Street; it would have been easier. But I went all the way to the boardwalk instead, I chased down the broker, and I flew up into the rafters of the ballet theater."

Rose looked at me with her damp violet eyes. "Think of a potion like a sprinkling of rainwater: it can sprout a seed, but it cannot coax up a plant from a tract of barren land."

Her words were terrible, but they were true. My monstrous form had still thrummed with all my human desires. I'd gone to the boardwalk because I wanted to see the ocean. I'd killed the broker because I wanted Mama's charm bracelet back. I'd gone to the ballet theater because I wanted to see Sevas again.

And I'd killed Undine because she had nearly imperiled the one thing I wanted most in the world.

The mirror that never lies had already told me as much: the seed of Papa's monster had been living inside me, at risk of blooming, long before he had even begun feeding me the black juice. Perhaps it had been born with me, a fetal twin. Perhaps so many of Papa's furious words had made it calcify in me like a pearl. Perhaps eating my mother's meat had made it swell like a growth of rot. Perhaps it had blossomed under Dr. Bakay's hands the way a skilled wizard could raise the dead from their graves.

Whatever the cause, I could only try to guard that small, ruined piece of myself, administer to it carefully without encouraging it to grow, until it could be lulled to a gentle death. I would not allow it to be fed any longer.

"Show me how you did it," I said at last. "Show me how you made that black juice."

Rose stared at me for a long time, and I stared back. In the gauzy nightgown that showed the shape of her breasts, her violet eyes watery and clouded, she looked so much like Mama that it broke my heart, just a little bit. I had to believe there was a small, tender morsel of love still at the core of her, like a plum stone.

Without a word, Rose turned and vanished through the doorway. I followed close at her heels. Our footsteps were matched to the ticking of the grandfather clock as we walked out into the garden, abruptly bathed in bone-pale moonlight.

I crossed the threshold and walked into the cold soil, and it sucked at my feet as if it were water. We passed the sleeping bodies of the day laborers, mounded in our garden like knuckles of rock, so still I could imagine moss growing over them and vines flowering up to lash them to the ground.

At last Rose stopped walking, and I skidded to a halt behind her. The whole garden was quiet as midnight, and even the snakes had stopped hissing. The twisting branches cut the blue sky into jagged, uneven shapes, like pieces of a shattered vase. There was the canopy overhead, lush with its scraggly foliage, and below us, folded safely under the dirt, was our dead sister. Rose stepped right to the base of the tree, hiding herself from the moonlight. When she turned back to look at me, her eyes were pearling with tears.

For all the stories Papa told us, he had never spoken a word about this. He had only ever warned us away from it, without giving a reason why. Stories weren't meant to be questioned; they were answers in and of themselves. They were meant to preempt any question you might ever have, to steal the words right from your mouth. If you were a third daughter, your fate was written out before you even drew your first breath. If you thought to ask why certain plums were suffused with poison, well, you might as well be a loathsome scientist. If you began to wonder how a wizard came to own his tower, you were a capitalist, with viperous schemes behind your eyes. Who else would ever dream of asking why?

"Come on, Marlinchen," Rose said, and I stepped forward to join her, both of us embraced by the slender branches of the juniper tree.

Together we reached up and began to pick down the berries, working in mirrored silence, until the whole tree had been stripped bare.

The grandfather clock gonged seven, and I was leaning over the stove. Oily smoke rose from the pan of varenyky, and hot droplets of grease leapt up at my hands and face. I shut off the burner and spooned the varenyky onto two plates.

Just as I had knelt down and began to open the oven door, I heard Papa's footsteps on the stairs. A thrill of fear raced along my spine, and I finished my plating hurriedly, not caring that the sleeve of my nightgown trailed a bit through a heap of sour cream. I cut six fat slices of black bread and smeared them with butter, then licked and licked the knife until it was clean. I poured two glasses of tepid water, watching dust motes drift across the surface like dead fruit flies.

In the garden, the eyeless ravens were singing long-forgotten lullabies. The goblin was tracing a short path in the herb plantings, pacing with its hand on its chin, looking contemplative. Indrik was accosting one of the day laborers, who perhaps had not shown him proper deference. The man in question stared up at the pale blue sky, as though he could imagine hurling himself right over the fence made of snakes. Early morning sunlight turned everything the sweet pink-and-white color of an eyelid flipped inside out.

I took both plates into the sitting room and laid them out on the cloven-footed coffee table just as Papa settled himself onto the chaise longue. It was as if we had not spoken in his room last night, and as if his first daughter were not dead.

"Thank you, Marlinchen," he said, looking down at what I had served. "But who is the other plate for?"

"Dr. Bakay," I replied. I wiped my damp palms on my nightgown and brushed back the curls from my sweat-dewed forehead. "Shall I go fetch him?"

"He will come," Papa said, grasping his fork and knife. He ate one varenyky whole, dipping it first in the sour cream, chewing and swallowing. I watched the shape of it travel down his throat, blue beard rippling like rings on water. "What is this here?"

He was pointing to the pile of cooked meat I had laid so carefully on his plate. "Chicken," I said.

Papa raised one brow but did not question me further. In another few moments, Dr. Bakay strode into the sitting room, appearing well rested. Papa remarked cheerfully upon it, and the two lapsed into genial conversation. I could not very well hear their words, as I could focus only on the way their mouths moved as they chewed, teeth gnashing and tongues flicking and lips smacking. A bit of pickled cabbage got caught in Papa's beard. There was a smear of sour cream across Dr. Bakay's chin.

Another thrill went up my spine, but this time it was a thrill of fearlessness, adrenaline, and terrific power.

"You stoked the embers of your own funeral pyre, Papa," I said softly.

His gaze snapped up from the food. "What did you say?"

"When you sent me down to the boardwalk to kill those men," I went on, my voice perfectly even, "I brought you back their hearts and livers, but I brought back something else too." I reached down the collar of my nightgown and pulled out Mama's compact from where I had tucked it between my breasts. I flipped it open and let the black sand pour out onto the carpet. "I saw this slough off me in the bathtub, and

I thought you would punish me for it. I couldn't explain how the sand had gotten there. But I swept it up into Mama's compact and used it to escape this house—there is the answer to your preposterous wizard's riddle, incidentally. By rights, I should be able to wed myself now, and inherit this crumbling, hideous house."

"Zmiy," Dr. Bakay said, eyes widening in alarm, "what is she talking about?"

Papa held the knife blade-up, and under his beard I saw his face grow pale. "Have I not taught you better to hold your tongue? You are worse than simple-minded; you are insidiously stupid. Your mouth will damn us both."

My heart was beating very fast. "Maybe. I know your own mouth is damning you," I said, looking at his empty plate.

"What?"

"When that old chieftain, who ruled Oblya before it was Oblya, had a man arrested for murder, did he also detain the sword that was used to kill? Magic always implicates its caster. You were the one who taught me that."

"You think you are nothing more than a blade in my hand?" Papa laughed, flinging his mouth open so wide I could see the bits of food stuck between his teeth, and all the way back into the dark abyss of his throat. "I might have clothed you in scales and claws, but I did not order you to kill your sister. That was all your own cruelty and violence. You will sleep with that cold body beside you for the rest of your life."

"Perhaps," I replied, fisting the silk of my nightgown. "That will be my own seed to nurture or to kill as I see fit. But you have let a whole tree sprout up inside of you, and its branches are dripping with fat black berries."

At that moment, Dr. Bakay was seized by a vicious fit of coughing. He bent at the waist, hand clapped over his mouth, hacking and retching. Papa leaned away, lip curling with revulsion, and the coughing went on and on for so long that the small hand of the grandfather clock tipped past eight.

Finally, he spat something out onto the carpet: a juniper berry, fat and black.

Papa stood up and lurched toward me, grasping me by the shoulders before I could stumble through the door. "You foolish, ugly girl," he snarled, saliva frothing. "What have you done?"

"I did nothing. It was your own hunger that made you eat."

He shook me hard enough to make my teeth rattle, and my vision blurred at the corners, but I did not go limp in his arms. I wrenched myself away from him instead, even as his fingernails tore long gashes in the silk of my nightgown and left six neat lines of blood behind on my skin. I took a step backward, then another, as Papa breathed hot and loud through his nose like a bull stamping the earth.

Before he could, there was a commotion in the garden. Papa's head jerked toward the window.

Rose was pacing the line of the fence, flinging the contents of a small vial at the snakes as they spat and hissed. When the potion splattered on them, their black scales began to pale and turn gray, and their long, writhing bodies went limp. As soon as they did, Sevas came, hefting her gardening shears, and cut them down one by one until the whole fence collapsed like a row of dominoes on the gambling table.

Roused from their despondent slumber, the day laborers hurtled out of the garden and fled toward Kanatchikov Street, holding their hats so they wouldn't fly off as they ran.

Papa turned to me again, and the whites of his eyes were cracked through with red. "You and your sister have both made a bad mistake, Marlinchen," he said. "And that Yehuli boy has made one even worse. I will turn the three of you into black rabbits and skin you slowly, relishing every squeal and whimper."

"Zmiy," Dr. Bakay said weakly. He was still slumped in the chaise longue. "I think I've eaten something rotten."

"Didn't your varenyky taste sweeter than usual, Papa?" I asked, my back pressed against the far wall. "I cooked the filling with juniper berries from the tree in our garden, the same juniper berries you had

Rose use to make the black juice. You always said that there was a poison in them that we could not be inured to. Now it is inside of you."

Dr. Bakay fell out of the chaise and onto his knees, retching. Papa lunged for me again, but I rolled away just in time, and he slammed against the wall instead, shaking down the portraits of many dead Vashchenkos.

He let out a growl of frustration, hands clenched into tight pink fists. Magic was steaming off him like mist down a mountainside, rolling in great waves of white. When it feathered onto my skin I felt myself chill, blood turning cold and feet rooting to the ground as if I were myself a great stolid oak.

My chest compressed with fear. But before Papa could move toward me, or utter the words of a spell, there was a loud knock from the foyer.

A voice carried through the front door. "Open up right now, Mr. Vashchenko. This is the Grand Inspector."

My head turned slowly toward the window. Standing outside was indeed the Grand Inspector, with his fastidiously waxed mustache, and five men with him all clad in black, wearing the signet of the gradonalchik pinned to their chests and sleek silver pistols sheathed at their hips. Rose and Sevas were standing a bit farther away, under the shadow of the flowering pear tree. When I managed to peer over the men's top hats I saw Derkach there, too, his face angry and red, and looking right at Sevas with a buzzard's snapping eyes.

Papa was as still as a marble bust, arm raised halfway over his head.

The Grand Inspector's voice had momentarily broken Papa's spell, and I rushed to the door and flung it open. I stood there panting in the threshold, so many bewildered gazes taking in my wild hair and my nightgown, and Papa frozen in the sitting room, and Dr. Bakay retching on the floor. The Grand Inspector blinked furiously and said, "Are you Ms. Vashchenko?"

"Marlinchen," I said. "Please, come in."

And so they did. They walked neatly into our foyer like a line of marching ants, and Derkach followed after, grumbling some half-intelligible curses.

In the sitting room, Papa had unfrozen and lowered his hand, but there was an odd sheen to his face, like he'd been gripped quite suddenly by a very bad fever. Even his lips had turned white and chapped.

"I have heard rumors, Mr. Vashchenko," the Grand Inspector said, "and I've seen the flyers myself. You have been keeping fifteen of the city's day laborers here, against their will, under the guise of some wizard's competition. Well, you may be a wizard, but you are not exempt from the gradonalchik's laws against kidnapping and extortion. You must let the men go free at once, and—"

"I don't give a damn about a dozen hapless day laborers!" Derkach snarled, wheeling on the Grand Inspector. "He's been keeping my charge here as well, Sevastyan Rezkin. You must make him return Sevas to me."

Sevas edged into the threshold of the front door as he spoke, Rose at his back. His cheeks were flushed and he said, "No one is keeping me here against my will, Mr. Derkach. I am twenty-one years old and have no need of being tended to. Leave here now. I will not come with you."

"I've no interest in mediating a lovers' quarrel," the Grand Inspector said, quite coldly, turning back to Papa. "But if there is truth to the rumor that you have kidnapped these men, then you must face the gradonalchik's justice. And I should tell you, it is not a propitious time to be a criminal in Oblya, not when I have three mutilated men and a missing stockbroker on my hands. Half the city is convinced there is a monster afoot, and they will seize on any evidence they can of such a thing."

"You foolish vulture of a man." Papa's voice was a seething whisper; there was a bit of spittle gathering at the corners of his mouth. "The men are gone, all of them. My snake-fence has been destroyed, and they have fled, the way that the steppe foxes fled when your predecessors tore up the grass for your dachas and factories. If you are looking for something to satisfy Oblya's stupid masses, look elsewhere. I am a great wizard, and I will not be fixed like a hog for the slaughter."

It was a good speech, and Papa's magic made it even better, spreading its cool mist through the sitting room and the foyer. The Grand Inspector's mustache twitched. It might even have worked, if Dr. Bakay hadn't suddenly given a roar of anguish, of rage, breaking the hold that Papa's spell had cast over us all.

The Grand Inspector pushed past Papa and me and ran toward Dr. Bakay in the sitting room. The doctor's shoulders were heaving, the veins in his throat pressed up blue and fat against his skin. The Grand Inspector crouched beside him and asked, "Are you all right, sir?"

Dr. Bakay gurgled a reply. And then his shirt tore open and a pair of enormous black wings unfolded from his back.

The Grand Inspector uttered a scream that I didn't think possible of a grown man, something that more befit a little girl, and trailed off at last into a whimper. He stumbled away as Dr. Bakay staggered to his feet, his gurgles turning to growls as a stunning metamorphosis took place right there in our sitting room.

Obsidian scales crawled over his chest and hands and face, glittering iridescent in the slant of sunlight that beamed in from the open window. His teeth lengthened and jutted out over his lip, sharp as icicles on eaves. The flesh of his hands peeled back and shining silver claws burst from the gashed skin; the whites of his eyes were dyed black, as if with ink. A forked tongue spilled from his mouth, curling and uncurling, viperous and luridly red.

The Grand Inspector tripped as he tried to flee back into the foyer and scrabbled along the floor as his men drew their pistols, and I had the sudden, unbidden urge to laugh. For so many years I had shaken in terror when Dr. Bakay touched me, had let his face constellate the darkness of my bedroom at night, and now even the Grand Inspector was quaking before him.

The bitterest satisfaction welled up in my throat. I had done this; I had made him a monster that ordinary men knew how to fear.

The monster that was Dr. Bakay lurched forward, unsteady on its new feet. It beat its wings, filling the air with dust and the smell of ash. Sevas grasped my arm and hauled me back into the foyer, pressing toward the door where Rose was standing, blank-faced and horrified. But as we all turned and began to clamber away, even the Grand Inspector's men, we found ourselves running into another monster, black-scaled and black-winged and black-eyed.

I thought at first that someone had erected a large mirror, and that we were seeing only the reflection of Dr. Bakay. But then I saw Papa's robe hanging in tatters from its long spiny tail and my breath caught so painfully in my throat that I doubled over, Sevas's hand still on my back. The Grand Inspector screamed, and his men fired off their pistols, but the bullets only made small holes in Papa's wings and he kept staggering toward us while Dr. Bakay advanced from behind.

"Reload and fire!" the Grand Inspector cried. "We must strike these unholy creatures from the Earth!"

I felt another thrill of satisfaction at watching all these men tremble as they raised their pistols again, raised them at the monsters I had made. I was no great wizard, just a simple flesh diviner, a witch without the defunct Council's blessing, but I had performed the most spectacular transformation of them all. I had outdone even Papa. And perhaps my magic was only for showing, not for doing or changing or making, but I had shown everyone the truth.

I imagined what the penny presses would say. I imagined how many Oblyans would thumb them open and put their hands to their mouths, horrified. I imagined each one giving my arm a gentle squeeze, telling me that I had been brave, so brave and strong, to have lived in the same house as these monsters all my life.

More bullets burst through the air, and one of them lodged itself in Papa's shoulder. He gave a mindless, animal twitch, black eyes narrowing. I didn't look back until I heard an arrested scream: Dr. Bakay had lashed his claws at one of the Grand Inspector's men and now there were three long, bloody wounds scored down the front of the man's jacket. His pistol tumbled out of his hand and skidded across the floor.

Derkach surprised me by leaping toward it and grabbing it. When he rose, his carefully gelled blond hair was rumpled like an unmade bed, and he was panting.

"What do you even carry these pistols for, you useless buffoons?" he spat. "I will teach you how to fire a killing shot."

He raised the pistol at Papa and cocked it, but just as his finger brushed over the trigger, Papa reached out and snatched him up, claws piercing his chest and his soft belly.

A scream boiled somewhere deep in my throat, though it never made it past my lips. The pistol slipped from Derkach's grasp. He looked around wildly as Papa lifted his body into the air, breathing in shallow gasps, blood flowering on his white shirt.

"Sevas, help me!" he wailed. "Please—"

But Papa had already taken his other hand and ripped out Derkach's throat. The sound of it was awful, like silk being cut with a great pair of shears. The wound on his neck was so wide, so open that it resembled a second mouth, red with still-throbbing muscles and sinew that trembled like gusli strings.

One of the Grand Inspector's men bent at the waist, retching. I turned to Sevas, but he had frozen stiff at my side, pupils grown so vast and black. It took me a moment to recognize the look on his face as arousal, the same way he had looked at me while I lay naked beneath him, the same way I had looked at him when he struck down the Dragon-Tsar.

Papa dropped Derkach's limp body to the ground, the obscene wound of his throat spasming once more before going utterly still.

The Grand Inspector was weeping plainly now, tears turning his mustache damp. He grasped me firmly by the shoulders and said, "You—you are a witch, are you not? You must know of some way to kill these hideous creatures!"

I had thought that bullets and guns would kill them; I had never imagined that even the power of the Grand Inspector and his men might not be enough. Perhaps even the shiniest and sharpest ax could not fell an oak that had grown a hundred years strong.

I looked helplessly between Sevas and Rose as Papa crouched over Derkach's body and began to tear into his chest with long, sharp teeth. Blood spurted in thick ropes across the floor, falling in the shadow of the grandfather clock.

And then Rose surged forward, uncapping the vial in her hands. There was a finger of silvery liquid left, and as Dr. Bakay advanced, she hurled the vial at him. Droplets of the potion landed on him like rainwater, and he gave an anguished howl. At once his black scales began to pale and turn gray, and his terrible, monstrous body went limp.

As his shoulders slumped and his chest bowed, five pistols cocked and fired. There was an extraordinary blossoming of gun smoke as nearly half a dozen bullets struck his heart. Steel and shrapnel fissured outward like a nexus of black veins, and Dr. Bakay folded to the ground.

I felt as though I had just seen a great stone pillar shatter; I felt as though I were staring at the colossal wreckage of something too huge to comprehend, like watching an enormous warship be taken under by a storm and sinking irretrievably under the waves. Tears squeezed out of my eyes. The wings on Dr. Bakay's back shrank like withered tulips. When the scales faded back into skin I could see his naked, hairy chest, the buds of his nipples, and the blood that welled up between them, the color of an overripe plum.

A sob tore from my throat and Sevas fitted his arm snugly around my waist, pulling me against him as I wept the most bewildering tears.

The Grand Inspector gave a manic, warbling laugh as his men nudged at Dr. Bakay's body with the toes of their boots. "You brilliant woman," he said. "You wonderful witch."

Rose was breathing hard, hands on her knees. "I don't have any more of the potion."

Even the Grand Inspector's mustache seemed to droop as we listened to Papa masticating Derkach's flesh. "Can't you make more?"

"It requires the feathers of a bird that has made its nest in the branches of a willow tree and must be aged with elderberry juice for seven and a quarter hours. Unless you can hold off the monster for that long, I think we must find another weapon."

Papa was now devouring Derkach's liver, the bones of his rib cage nearly stripped of all their meat and gristle and gleaming like the antlers of some dead stag. A red hunk of muscle hung from his jaws, and with an awful slurping sound he sucked it into his mouth and swallowed it whole. I watched the shape of it as it traveled down his throat, and then Papa pushed off the floor with his clawed hands, black wings beating.

"No!" the Grand Inspector cried as Papa lumbered toward the open door. "Don't let it escape into the city!"

One of the men bolted forward and slammed the door shut right before Papa managed to slip through. The monster that was my father hissed, forked tongue lashing. Quick as a breath, he snatched up the man and then lifted them both into the air, sailing up toward the second-floor landing.

He perched there on the railing, and the Grand Inspector's man screamed and screamed until Papa silenced him by tearing out his heart. He ate it as if it were a piece of very sweet fruit, blood staining his lips and teeth like juice.

A few more useless bullets flew, piercing Papa's chest but leaving behind only wisps of purple smoke, as if the metal turned to mist when it touched his skin. He dropped the man's limp body over the railing and it thudded to the ground before us, his chest a gaping cavity, an abyss that held only the absence of his organs.

I knew at once what we were doing wrong, because I knew how all the stories in his codex ended. Though I had made him a monster, underneath those scales and wings he was still a wizard, with Old World power seething in his blood. It was the same power that had protected him from the banality of the world for so long, the hereditary magic that insulated us all from the wrath of cotton looms and day laborers, from tobacco smoke and lecherous sailors. I thought the Grand Inspector would have enough power to overcome it, but I was wrong.

If Papa was going to die, it would not be by men and their guns. He would have to die a wizard's death.

Our house was suffused with Old World magic, but we did not have any weapons. Papa was a wizard, after all, not a bogatyr or even a king. But as Papa hissed and beat his wings, I was overcome suddenly with a fierce and unthinking determination.

I tore away from Sevas and ran through the sitting room and into the kitchen, where I collapsed against the butcher block, breathing hard. I grasped the longest, largest knife we owned, the one that I had used to kill and carve the spiny-tailed monster.

Sevas was there with me in the kitchen before I could race back into the foyer, and he planted himself in the threshold, blocking my way.

"You have the look on your face of someone who's about to do something very brave and very stupid," he said.

"Please, Sevas," I said, looking at his beautiful face and feeling my chest swell with terrible and aching affection. "I made my father into a monster. I must be the one to kill him."

Sevas grasped my wrists in his hands and held them tightly, so tightly that the knife nearly slipped from my fingers. "He'll eat you."

"He won't. If his heart can still beat and his mind can still think, he won't. He loves me." It was a wretched love, and nothing like what I felt when Sevas had wept into my breast, but I knew it was love because it was powerful. It had turned me into a monster, too, transfigured me through its cunning magic. What else, then, could it be?

"Marlinchen." Sevas's voice had the sound of someone tearing apart a dress at the seams. "I couldn't bear to wage war with this awful world alone."

I almost faltered when I saw his blue eyes turn bright with water, but I drew a breath and gently wrenched myself free from his grasp instead. Without letting him see the tears prickling at my own eyes, I pushed past him and fled into the foyer, just as Papa winged down from the railing and closed his clawed fist around one of the men's throats.

The Grand Inspector had thrown himself behind Rose, weeping. The whole house stank of blood and gun smoke, and when I inhaled I could taste the coppery tang of these men's deaths, all through my own orchestration.

I had become a very powerful witch indeed.

"Papa!" I cried, holding the kitchen knife behind my back. "You must let him go!"

My father's monstrous head turned on an impossible angle, and he dropped the Grand Inspector's man. Just like I had hoped, he lurched toward me instead, and as he drew closer I tried to discern something of Papa in those depthless black eyes; I searched for a flicker of mundane humanity. With my last desperate, mangled bit of hope, I searched for love. I searched for the love that I had believed in for so long, the love that had made Papa's black juice so easy to swallow.

He had the front of my nightgown snarled in his claw before I could find it.

We were so close now that our noses almost touched, the noses that had been nearly identical when Papa was still human. I could have been staring right into the mirror that never lies, observing my own monstrous reflection. Magic always implicates its caster; that was the simplest axiom and the most honest. Here, gazing baldly at the truth of it all, I was my father's daughter.

The thought filled me with such an awful, wrenching grief that I did go limp in Papa's arms, my knife clattering to the ground, as he wound his clawed fingers around my throat. My breathing slowed under the mounting pressure of his grasp, and my vision rippled darkly at the edges.

And then, through the haze of my near-death, I saw a blade flash. My dropped knife looked as long and lusty as a sword in Sevas's hand, and when he plunged it into Papa's scaled belly, for a moment, I thought that I had receded from the waking world and was merely watching the memory of Ivan and the Dragon-Tsar play on the insides of my eyelids. Sevas twisted the knife cruelly and then jerked it out again, and my father gave such a plaintive, miserable cry that I knew what I had seen was true.

His grip on my throat slackened and I fell to the ground among the ruined silk of my nightgown. Papa collapsed before me, his scales fading to gray and vanishing, his wings shrinking and then flaking away like the husks of dead insects.

Sevas stood above him, holding a knife slicked with blood. I watched his own transformation occur then, withering and blooming and withering again in the span of seconds, Sevas and then Ivan and then the scarred man, all the moments between them compressed into one flat circle.

When I blinked again, though, he was Sevas, just Sevas, and I began to weep for how utterly and helplessly I loved him.

He let the knife slip to the floor, his whole hand gloved in my father's blood. The Grand Inspector peered out from behind Rose's back and blinked furiously. Papa lay in the shadow of the grandfather clock, fetal and naked, curling around himself like a snake whose large flat rock had just been turned up.

Rose started weeping then, too, but there was a smile burning under the rheum of her tears. The surviving men picked up their pistols and winced at their wounds. I looked down and very gently took Sevas's blood-spoiled hand.

The grandfather clock gonged, but I did not hear the hour. I was resting my head against Sevas's shoulder, and he was kissing it with plain and familiar tenderness, and the moment stretched on and on, as if time itself held no more power here.

CHAPTER FIFTEEN

A nd so, in the end, here is what happened to us all.

The Grand Inspector dusted himself off and wiped the sick from his chin. He said in a gruff and reluctant voice that perhaps there had been a monster after all. Two, in fact. He would have liked to take daguerreotypes of them while they were still alive to prove it, but all that was left now was a great amount of blood and pale coils of shed skin scattered around our foyer like blown wheat chaff.

I showed him the rib bone that I had found in the sink, and Rose led him to the place in the garden where my father had buried what remained of poor Sobaka. I showed him the broker's card that I had kept hidden in my bodice, and when he and his men went upstairs to the third floor, they found the broker's desiccated corpse tucked into one of the closets, maggot-ridden and glutted with black flies. His heart and liver were, of course, gone.

The Grand Inspector retched again, and one of his men offered him a handkerchief for his chin.

He gave me the reward for leading him to the monster, three hundred rubles, and I split it three ways, between myself and Rose and Sevas. In my hands, the coins felt as light as white feathers.

The Grand Inspector brought back more men to bundle up all the bodies, and when they were gone, I got on my hands and knees and scrubbed the blood from the floor, from the grandfather clock, from long kitchen knife. The shadows were vast and black when I was done, and the windows were grids of blue light.

The next day, all of the penny presses printed some variation of the same story: there were two monsters in the house of Zmiy Vashchenko, and one of them was him. It said nothing of juniper berries or black juice or suspicious varenyky. It mentioned his witch-daughters, who had lived with him all this time and finally helped to put an end to his murderous ways—so brave and so strong, those versions of Rose and me were!

It did not mention that those two daughters had once been three, and I had a small thrill of pleasure—then a long bout of guilt—knowing how much Undine would have hated being ignored, even in death.

Oblyans began leaving bouquets of chrysanthemums and blushing protea flowers at our door, along with bars of pressed lavender soap, enameled snuffboxes, ostrich eggs hollowed out and painted blue. Rose took the flowers to her storeroom and cut them to bits. Sevas washed himself with the lavender soap. I put my new rubles in the snuffboxes, and we all had great fun tossing the ostrich eggs from the second-floor landing onto the ground below, seeing whose broke the most spectacularly.

At last there came the brokers and the petty buyers, the land surveyors and the real estate agents, all of them with capitalist schemes behind their eyes. We showed them around the house and let them fondle whatever they liked: the portraits of dead Vashchenkos on the walls and the last of Papa's cat-lamps and the mirror that never lies.

We got a lot of good money for that, and the brokers from Fisherov-ich & Symyrenko did not seem to mind that one of their affiliates had been decaying in the third-floor closet not more than a week prior.

Indrik sulked tremendously as they carried off the mirror and the lamp and three more vases, but we assuaged him with praise and scratches behind the ear. The goblin cried and cried until I picked it up and rocked it against my chest, and then it fell asleep in my arms.

I was surprised that we came to have many eager and competitive offers on the house, and Rose mediated the auction with a seabird's watchful weather eye. In the end, it sold to a Yehuli man from a large surveying company, who wanted it only for the land underneath. He was going to have the whole house leveled so he could build up new apartments or maybe a hospital.

At first the prospect filled me with terror; I was imagining a skeleton of magic that had been laid out under the house like a network of tree roots, and once it was uncovered it would turn all the workers and the Yehuli buyer into lizards or toads. It did not seem unlike Papa, to do such a thing.

In fact, the moment we signed away our claim to the house and the garden, I expected some spectacular transformation to take place; at the very least, I expected a great wind to come along or the sky to darken overhead or the ground to tremble beneath our feet. But I saw only the Yehuli man blinking at me through his spectacles, and the pen's ink bleeding onto my thumb.

As soon as the deed had been signed, the eyeless ravens took flight from our flowering pear tree and never returned. I had not seen the fiery serpent since I had given it suck that night in the garden, and I would never see it again; if it had fled, I did not notice it leaving.

I worried over Indrik's fate, but not for long: a traveling circus hired him right away and gave him his own silk-and-velvet tent, where he entertained both admirers and skeptics for ten rubles apiece. I saw a daguerreotype of him in a newspaper many years later, his chest gleaming with linseed oil, his pockets heavy with gold.

I worried more over the goblin. It did not have the fortitude for circus life and hid in my skirts whenever the buyers and managers came loping around like scavenging dogs. So I plucked it up and held it and did not put it down as we walked out of the garden for the last time.

Behind us, a great many day laborers had already descended, shouting in at least two foreign tongues, axes swinging with shuddering force against the trunk of the juniper tree.

We had so much gold that Oblya seemed to open up in front of us like a rare and beautiful orchid. I saw my sister only one other time after we left the house with our rubles weighing down our pockets. She took an apartment above a coffeehouse and planted herbs in the window boxes. She smelled like a different sort of perfume, and there were a stranger's slippers tucked under the bed, a coat that wasn't hers hung on the back of the door.

She ate Merzani jelly candies and told me that her elixirs and herb mixes sold as well as they ever had, perhaps even better now that she was not buffeted this way and that by the tempestuous business models of our father. She had done a great deal to convince her clients that her potions worked because of science, not whimsy and magic, and for the most part they believed her.

When I was at the door, saying my farewell, Rose gripped my hand hard. "I sleep with the windows open every night so that I can feel the cold and imagine what it must have been like for you, forced to become a cold-blooded killing thing. Will you forgive me, Marlinchen? Please?"

I removed her grip and did not answer. I did not want the last thing my sister heard from me to be a lie.

And what of Sevas and me? We took an apartment together near the boardwalk, with two large, bright windows that overlooked the harbor and the stretching sea. I woke when the sun gently caressed my eyelids, and not because of the gonging of a grandfather clock. I taught Sevas the proper way to fold dough for varenyky and how to tell when the kvass in the jar had finished fermenting.

We smoked narghiles in Merzani coffeehouses and played dominoes in gambling dens. I was very bad at both, and at the end of the night I was always coughing and bereft of rubles. We admired the dachas along the shoreline and took mud baths at the sanatorium. We drank kumys on the boardwalk and sipped vodka in taverns. We danced half-soberly in the street, beneath the puddled lamplight, Sevas tucking his feet under mine so he could teach me the steps to a waltz.

I bought dresses with fashionable bustles and got my hair cut at a salon. The goblin lived with us, in a bed made out of moss and white gull feathers that we kept under the kitchen table. Sevas fed it scraps from his hand and I chained the icebox to keep it from ravaging our vegetables. I turned twenty-four and Sevas took me to a restaurant on Kanatchikov Street that served an Ionik custard drizzled with syrup; I dreamed about the taste and smell of it for weeks afterward.

But there was still some vestigial magic at work inside of us, thousands of tiny transformations always happening under our skin and inside of our minds. Some nights I woke up drenched in a frigid sweat, monstrous faces scored onto the insides of my eyelids, the shadows on our walls resembling the silhouettes of claws and teeth. On those nights Sevas held me in our bed, until the warm press of his body against mine lulled me into a tenuous slumber.

Other nights I woke panting with the memory of strange hands on my breasts and I could not bear to be touched, so Sevas took his pillow up off the bed and laid down on the floor beside me, filling the moonlit room with his soft breaths and aimless chatter. I fell asleep to the sound of him babbling about the high price of courgettes.

And then there were the nights when Sevas was the one who woke wild-eyed and weeping, and I held him and stroked his hair until his shoulders quit their shuddering. Other nights he, too, could not stand to feel another warm body beside him, and so I curled up on the floor with our goblin and recited Oblyan nursery rhymes, stopping only when I heard Sevas begin to snore.

There were, of course, the nights where I needed to feel him brace his arms around me and he recoiled at even the brush of my fingers, but still, somewhere in the black space of those conflicting desires, we found each other.

Autumn froze over into winter, and winter cracked open into spring.

Neither of us returned to the ballet theater; nor did we ever venture too far down Rybakov Street. Sometimes I heard whispers in the coffeehouses: that Rodinya's most famous principal dancer had quit at the peak of his career and now the theater was broke and scrambling; that the wizard on Rybakov Street had died and now his manor home and garden were being turned into an orphanage or an infirmary. Sometimes they even whispered about his witch-daughter—how brave and strong she was! I clenched my fist around the edge of the table and the wound on my knuckle was so old now that it didn't bleed.

Sevas met Aleksei for tea and they laughed at their shared memories of Kovalchyk, of Taisia, even of Derkach, on good days. On bad days his face shuttered at the very mention of the ballet theater, or when he spied a head of meticulously gelled blond hair. The mangle of calluses on his heels turned soft, and his feet began to resemble those of a normal man.

When he entered me, I did not think of Ivan. As he spent, Sevas whispered *Marlinchen, Marlinchen, Marlinchen* into my hair.

The most banal thing of all was this: my father lived.

When Sevas had stabbed him that day in the foyer, the knife had propitiously missed every single one of his major Organs and arteries. Luck, the doctor who was not Dr. Bakay said. To myself, I said: perhaps a bit of lingering magic.

If this had been Old World Oblya, when it was ruled by chieftains and the steppe fell into the sea with nothing to stop it, he would have perhaps been executed for his monstrous crimes, or at least been relieved of a hand or an eye. But since this was gridiron Oblya, municipally planed Oblya, and the tsar and the gradonalchik were both seething to prove that we were as progressive and metropolitan as the cities in the West, no longer did they summarily hang criminals.

There was a trial that stretched out for weeks and then months, as spring was swallowed up by summer. I took the stand and so did Sevas, and so did the Grand Inspector, and so did Rose, though I was careful to never meet her eyes. All the while Papa sat there in chains, pressed between his two Yehuli lawyers.

On the day of his sentencing, there was a terrific thunderstorm that broke the sky like it was an overlarge ostrich egg, rainwater spilling out of it like a yolk. It rinsed all the garbage into the sewers and washed the cobblestones clean. Carriage horses flicked droplets of water from their ears. Couples ran to take cover under grocery-store awnings. Brokers from the stock exchange waited out the storm miserably from beneath their enormous black umbrellas. I watched the courtroom window turn marbled with rainwater, as if it were a puddle of oil catching the light.

In the end, they sentenced Papa to prison for the remainder of his life. Already the trial had taken its toll on my father; when I went to visit his holding cell beneath the courthouse, his skin was mottled and gray like cream gone bad and his beard was grown as long as the untamed ivy that had once crawled over our house. There were flecks of silver in it, where time had begun to eat away the Wizards' Council's enchanted blue.

His eyes did not snap like a hawk's but wavered dully, like a dog in its kennel. He looked skinnier than I had seen him since the earliest days of his curse.

When I came over and leaned up against the bars of his cell, he did not rise from his seat. There was a tray of untouched food on the small table beside him.

"Papa," I said. "Won't you eat?"

"Do you think I care to taste even a bite of this slop? They are feeding me the same kasha that they feed the other prisoners, kasha with no butter. They give us only water and not kvass. And we get beef stew and borscht instead of pork varenyky. Why should I eat?"

"So that you do not die," I said.

He scoffed. "I would think you wished me dead, sweet Marlinchen. You fed me poisoned berries, and your Yehuli lover stabbed me in the belly."

"You fed me those same berries. And your doctor friend took from my breast like a serpent." I curled my fingers around the bars, knuckles whitening, that old wound stinging. "Do you really think you are innocent of it all? That there was no blood spilled through your orchestration?"

My question was a hole in the floor, Papa hovering above the spiked pit below. His teeth came together with a sound like coins rattling in a can.

"What do I care for these city laws, made by mortal men?" he said at last. "Whether I am guilty or innocent by their determination, it does not matter to me. I am the great wizard Zmiy Vashchenko. Even the laws of sorcery bend to me. You were always so small-minded, Marlinchen. Can you not imagine a world beyond this city?"

"I can," I said. "I do."

Papa scoffed again. "How is it that the ugliest and most simple of my daughters orchestrated my demise? I would loathe this cage less if it had been your clever or beautiful sisters who had put me in it."

"You made a bad mistake, Papa," I replied, sighing. "You put too much of yourself in me. Those little bits whispered the truth. My bones hummed with it and my blood sang with it. If we had been less the same, I might never have known. But now we both remember the taste of hearts and livers."

Those were the worst nights: when I woke from dreams of dying men and frantically checked my belly and breasts for the spreading of black scales. Sevas held me then, and kissed my fingers, reassuring me of their blunted ends.

"They taste better than anything," Papa whispered, at last rising from his seat. He came up so close to me that our noses nearly touched through the bars and I could smell the acid and bile of nothing eaten for days on his breath. "Better than sour-cherry kvass and pork vare-nyky, better than a whole raw chicken and its crunching little bones. Better than the meat of your bird-mother. They were the only things that came close to sating the hunger, the hearts and livers of men. Would you deny me this one small relief? Would you let the curse swallow me whole?"

"It has already," I told him, very gently, and then took my leave. There was no use telling him of my awful dreams, or about how some-times the rage in my belly reached its boiling point and I could release it only through my mouth, and I pressed my face into my pillow and screamed and screamed, even though it made the goblin weep. Papa's magic was good, as good as Titka Whiskers's had been, and it would outlast our proximity. Perhaps it would outlast even his death. As I went toward the door, Papa rattled the bars of his cell, spittle flying.

"They will not keep me here!" he shouted. "I will turn these bars into a spewing of black snakes and they will poison every single one of the guards and barristers, and then I will eat their hearts and livers with sweet wine. I will curse every single one of the day laborers who worked to tear down my house, so that they wake up with chicken feet or yellow bills, like magpies. I will transform you and your sister into hags."

His words grasped at the strands of my newly trimmed hair, but I was up the stairs and out of the building before my heart could flut-ter with the urge to turn back. After the thunderstorm, the sun was exceptionally bright. I had to put up my hand to shield my eyes as I walked along Kanatchikov Street; all around me the rainwater drip-ping off awnings had turned golden, like honey.

I could have hired a carriage, but I decided to go on foot, nod-ding bracingly at the women as they bemoaned their ruined gowns and ruined hair, stepping aside to let the tardy stockbrokers hustle past. There were day laborers playing cards in an alley, their laughter carrying down to the road. Carriage horses shook out their damp manes and clopped cheerfully on. In the distance, the sea was just a stripe of glistening color, like a knife of light.

Sevas was waiting for me at the boardwalk, leaning against the railing and looking out at the endless spreading water. I could easily imagine him as a ship's captain then, bold and dashing and weather-eyed, as he smiled his beautiful, crooked smile.

"I hope," he said, "that the sky has exhausted all its rain for a very, very long time."

Our trunks were propped up on the ground around him, and the goblin was sitting on the largest one, rubbing miserably at its one big eye. I knelt down beside it and said, "There are still marshes and lovely bogs for you to live in, but they are far away from here."

The goblin sniffled. I stood up again and Sevas said, "Anyway, the weather will be different in Askoldir."

"How different?"

He arched a brow. "You will have to learn to love the snow. Even most in Askoldir do not. But they have great fun grousing about it, the way aunts and grandmothers love to commiserate over the same hated relative."

"What if your mother hates me?"

"She won't," Sevas said. "She only hates my third great-aunt, and parsnips, and her landlord, and the woman down the hall who sings to her cat, and . . ."

He trailed off, and I laughed, and the sound warmed me all over, as if I'd dipped into one of the heated baths at the sanatorium.

There was a clock mounted on the wall of the nearby bank and it said that we were nearly at risk of missing our train. So I leaned down and scooped up the goblin, swaddled it in a blanket, and held it to my breast. If one of the ticket attendants saw me, they would think I was only a mother with her child.

Sevas grasped our trunks, one in each hand, and started to walk toward the train station. Two gulls on the boardwalk pecked at someone's spilled kumys. A cargo ship released itself from the dock, horn sounding out deafeningly across the blue-white ocean. The sailors on-board clambered to their posts, and I imagined that they were all as thrilled and terrified as I was, to be going somewhere new.

I paused suddenly, the goblin holding in its small fist a loose clump of my hair.

Sevas stopped, too, and turned around. "Are you all right?"

"Yes," I said, righting myself and pulling my hair free of the goblin's grasp. "I'm thinking of what Askoldir will look like, all covered in snow."

"Very beautiful," he said. "Like you. Come on now, Marlinchen."

I followed him into the train station, which arced over us like the rib cage and vertebrae of some extraordinarily large creature soldered from iron. I imagined that with every train that left, the creature was amputating one of its finger bones, a little piece it wouldn't miss until the train came back again. I quite liked the thought of that, and re-solved to tell Sevas about it as soon as we were in our seats, my head resting on his shoulder and the goblin scurrying at our feet, both of us watching the steppe unfold on either side of the train, the yellow summer grasses resembling parchment that hasn't yet been spoiled with ink.

ACKNOWLEDGMENTS

Thank you first and foremost to my agent, Sarah Landis, who believed in this book even when I didn't, and who coaxed me back from the ledge all the many, many times I felt like giving up. This book would not exist if not for you.

Thank you to my editors, David Pomerico and Sam Bradbury, for all their support and insight. Thank you to Mireya Chiriboga, Kelly Shi, Lisa McAuliffe, Rachel Kennedy, Róisín O'Shea, and everyone at Harper Voyager and Del Rey for helping to bring this book into the world.

Thank you to Allison Saft and Rachel Morris, for giving me a soft place to lie while I dredged this story out of me.

Thank you, always, to Manning Sparrow, for ten years of companionship and unflagging love.

Thank you to Sophie Cohen and Courtney Gould, for giving me another reason to write this story.

Thank you to James Macksoud, for whom words are never enough. Everything good in my life is because of you.

And thank you, of course, to Dorit Margalit. You gave me the language to write this book, and the courage to survive it.

ABOUT THE AUTHOR

Ava Reid was born in Manhattan and raised right across the Hudson River in Hoboken, but currently lives in Palo Alto. She has a degree in political science from Barnard College, focusing on religion and ethnonationalism.